A MAN WITH ONE OF THOSE FACES

Book 1 of The Dublin Trilogy

CAIMH MCDONNELL

McFori Ink

Caimh McDonnell

Visit my website at www.WhiteHairedirishman.com

First Printing: September 2016 Reprinted January 2021

ISBN: 978-0-9955075-0-0 (paperback) 978-1-912897-29-2 (hardback)

CHAPTER ONE

"You remember Gearóid, your father's first cousin from Clare?"

"Do I?"

"Ye do! Two dogs and only one eye, never married – he came around the house when you were young a couple of times."

"Oh yeah."

"Dead! Died of a heart attack, God rest his soul. I saw it in the paper last week."

Paul had never realised before how cold an old person's hand was. As her frail fingers patted his, as if reassuring herself that he was really there, he couldn't help but notice. To be honest, he was having a hard time thinking about anything else.

"Heart attack in the bath," she continued. "I think it's all these new bath salts they have. Sure you wouldn't know what they're putting in them."

Paul nodded, giving the bare modicum of assent she needed to ramble off down whatever mental path she was on.

Aren't corpses supposed to be freezing? When they were kids Barry Dodds had told him that when he'd knocked his granda's body over at the wake, it was like being buried under a dozen frozen turkeys. Mind you, he had also told Paul that groping a woman's breast felt like squeezing a roast chicken. Come to think of it, that kid had a weird obsession with poultry.

"Such a young man. He could only have been..."

Margaret trailed off, staring at the ceiling, trying to do a sum that she didn't have all the figures for.

Are babies really warm? Do you start life as a tiny boiling inferno of energy, and you just get colder and colder until you eventually reach corpse temperature? He was only speculating on the baby thing. Despite being twenty-eight years of age, Paul had never held one.

Not for the first time, the needle on the record in Margaret's mind skipped. "I was talking to a woman from Dunboyne on the other ward. She said the Triads are running Dublin now."

"Did she?"

"It was in *The Herald*," she confided. "Apparently you can't move for Chinese lads these days. I don't know what's happening at all. You'd be afraid to go out at night."

"I hear a lot of them carry swords."

"Really??"

"Oh yeah," he said. "They're big into the beheading and all that—"

He was halfway through miming it when he was interrupted by a throat being pointedly cleared behind him. Bloody typical – 45 minutes of nodding and 'ah hum'ing along, and Nurse Brigit comes back just in time for the beheading. There she was, arms folded, leaning against the doorframe – giving him that condescending look.

"How're you two getting on?" she said, moving into the room.

"Grand," he said. "Chatting up a storm."

"This is my Gareth," said Margaret, pointing at Paul.

"Oh I know, Margaret. Sure, didn't I meet him on the way in?"

Her crinkly little face lit up with pride. "He's a lawyer," she beamed. "Flies all over Europe. He was in Brussels just last week."

"Imagine that!"

Margaret leaned forward automatically to let Brigit fluff her pillows.

"Isn't it great of him to find the time to come in and see his granny," said Brigit.

"Mother," Paul corrected.

"Yes he's my..."

For a moment the old woman stared quizzically at Paul through the fog of age and fading memory. Paul felt that sickening creak, like the ice he was standing on was about to crack.

Brigit finished the pillows and clapped her hands. The sound drew Margaret's attention and the smile returned to her lips. Paul relaxed.

"Next time," said Brigit, "he should visit during the day and the two of you might be able to go for a walk outside, if your physio is going well."

She looked at Paul expectantly, being that heavy-handed with the hint that he was tempted to let it pass without taking the bait.

"Yeah, that'd be nice," he said.

He smiled up at Brigit from his seat beside the bed, her ample bosom framing her pissed-off expression perfectly. She was not a bad looking woman, truth be told; a couple of years older than himself, short brown bobbed hair, decent figure – she wouldn't be launching a thousand ships any time soon but she'd undoubtedly create a fair bit of interest in a chip shop queue.

She had one of those country accents. Like most Dubliners he'd never bothered to learn how to distinguish them from each other. She had that 'farm strong' look about her too, not fat or muscly, just that kind of firmness that implied she could wrestle a cow if she had to.

"It's fierce wet these days though," said Margaret.

He looked across to see Margaret beaming at him once more.

"Yes Ma." He raised his voice to make sure she was listening. "It is very important you keep doing your physio, so we can get you back on your feet. That way we can go out nightclubbing."

"Oh, Gareth, you're terrible," she grinned. "You'd want to keep your eye on this one, nurse."

"Yes, I'll have to."

Paul said his goodbyes and gave Margaret a light peck on the forehead. Again, cold, clammy. The memory of sniffing ham to see if it was fresh came back to him unbidden. He'd be sticking with cheese on toast for the next few days.

Out in the hall, he was reaching for his mobile as he got cuffed on the back of the head with a rolled-up *Woman's Weekly*. Not hard enough to hurt but hard enough not to be entirely playful either.

"What was that for?" he said.

"Take a wild stab in the dark."

"Relax. The old dears love a bit of scandal."

"That's easy for you to say. You're not the one who has to calm them down when they're convinced the Chinese lady who collects the medical waste is dealing drugs."

"Are you sure she isn't?"

"Oh believe me, I've asked."

"Well," said Paul, looking at the time on his phone, "I make that three hours and seven minutes, so if you could just sign my note…"

Brigit shifted nervously. "I need you to do another one."

"Three hours and seven minutes," repeated Paul, looking at Brigit like she was slightly hard of hearing, "plus the two hours and fifty eight minutes of visits I did on Monday makes six hours and five minutes. That's five minutes you've already got for free there."

Brigit gave him a confused look. Paul could see the question she wanted to ask and the favour she needed briefly tussling for control. The favour won out. She softened her tone a bit. He could tell asking nicely didn't come naturally to her.

"Please, it's just a quick one. There's an old man up there in a private room."

"I'd love to help," he lied, "but I've got to catch a bus."

Which was true. Great-Aunt Fidelma's Ford Cortina that'd outlasted the Berlin Wall, Concorde and Nelson Mandela had gasped its last in the fast lane of the M50 four weeks ago and he hadn't got the money to get it back on the road. In fact, it'd taken up all of last month's disposable income and half the emergency fund just to get it off the bit of road it'd broken down on.

"Do you still live up off the North Circular?" Brigit asked.

"Yeah."

She stopped to think, clearly weighing things up in her mind.

"Do this for me and I'll drop you home after. My shift finishes in an hour. Deal?"

It did beat freezing his knackers off at a bus stop, plus that was another €3.30 towards replenishing the emergency fund.

"Alright," he said, "but no funny stuff, I know what you nurses are like."

She rolled her eyes. "I'll try and restrain myself."

He held up his cigs – she pulled another of her seemingly endless supply of disapproving faces before inclining her head for him to follow her.

Brigit opened the fire exit with a flourish and Paul stepped out past her into the sharp November air. It was cold enough for him to want the coat he'd left back in the staff room, but not cold enough for him to actually go and get it. He was surprised when she followed him out and stood beside him, hugging her arms to herself and shuffling her feet to keep warm.

"Fuck's sake," she said.

"Isn't it weird to think that not that long ago, you used to be allowed to smoke inside a hospital?"

"Yeah," she sighed. "Those were the good old days, back when people just died."

As he pulled out his second-to-last cigarette, he noticed her eyes linger on the packet. He held it out.

"It's your last one."

"Don't worry about it, I've got loads of them." This was technically true. He had acquired 25 packs of 20 off posh Padraig for €80 six months ago and had disciplined himself to smoke only one a day. He had considered giving up entirely but then *she* would have won. He was not prepared to let that happen. Still the €3.30 he saved on bus fare minus the 16 cents for Nurse Conroy's cigarette, still left him €3.14 up on the transaction.

"Ta," said Brigit as she cupped her hands around his lighter, puffing the cigarette into life.

They both took a drag and looked at their shadows stretching out across the manicured lawns, half-illuminated by the antiseptic lights from the hospice.

"Can I ask a question?" she said, and he felt himself sag. He knew what was coming.

"Why do people say that?" he said. "A – you just have, and B – nobody has ever accepted no as an answer."

"Alright, no need to get all arsey. I was just making conversation."

She flicked her ash towards the drain and hugged herself a little tighter. They both took another drag, in silent agreement that he was an arsehole.

Through the cast-iron railings, Paul could see a fox on the pavement across the road, darting in and out of the pools of yellow streetlight.

He broke the silence. "I have one of those faces."

"Excuse me?" she said.

"That's what you were going to ask wasn't it – how do I do what I do?"

"Well yeah, but—"

"And now," he interrupted, "you're going to say – but there has to be more to it than that..."

"You're a mind reader as well?"

He looked at her. "OK – so what were you going to say?"

"Oh no, Sherlock, you're dead right. I was going to say exactly that. You can't just have 'one of those faces' – everybody's got a face. Yours is nothing special. No offence."

"You do realise that just saying 'no offence' does not magically make whatever you say inoffensive?"

She was right, of course. There was nothing special about his face – just the opposite in fact – it was entirely ordinary, as was the rest of him. Five foot nine, blue eyes, brown hair. His sheer ordinariness was the whole point. He was a medium everything; his features were the most common in every category. He had nothing that came close to qualifying as a distinguishing anything. His every facial attribute was a masterpiece of bloody-minded unoriginality, an aesthetic tribute to the forgettably average. Collectively they formed an orchestra designed to produce the facial muzak of the Gods.

"But," she said, "Margaret thought you were her grandson—"

"Son," corrected Paul.

"Right," continued Brigit, "whereas old Donal down the hall thinks you're his neighbour's young fella. Mrs Jameson thinks you're..."

"I'm not sure," said Paul. "Butler would be my best guess."

"To be fair, she talks to everyone like they're staff. She asked me last week if the contents of her bedpan are put in with everyone else's. The woman literally thinks her shit doesn't stink."

Paul smiled; she did have that way about her.

"My point is," said Brigit, "why do you pretend to be all these people you're not?"

Paul shrugged. "It's just easier." And it was. That wasn't the whole truth, not by a long shot, but it was truth nonetheless. "The patients the hospital asks me to visit are old and confused. You've seen people coming in, visiting their relatives with dementia or whatever else, what's it like?"

"Not easy," Brigit conceded. "They're often faced with a loved one who doesn't know who they are. It's heartbreaking. Gradually those patients get fewer and fewer visitors because it's upsetting for everybody."

"Exactly. The patient knows enough to get that they should know who this person is. So when I walk in and say hello—"

"You just pretend to be anybody?"

"No. I just agree with whoever they think I am."

"But you're not that person."

"I know but it isn't exactly hard. How's so'n'so? Fine. Did whats-her-face's Lumbago clear up? It did. Most of the time, they just like nattering on about whatever, happy to be chatting. If you want the honest-to-God truth, most people have a lot they want to say and not that much they want to hear."

The hospital administrators didn't officially approve of this approach of course but they turned a blind eye. The sad truth was, feeling like they still had one foot in their past life made patients happier and, in his more cynical moments Paul thought, easier to manage too. His services came free, which made him a lot cheaper than drugs.

Paul took another drag on his cigarette and savoured the counterfeit taste. As he exhaled and looked across the lawn, he could see the fox watching them while it dragged a half-eaten sandwich out of the bin in front of the newsagents. It didn't have the look of a fearful animal readying itself to bolt. This was a Dublin fox. Its look said, 'I'm having this, what're you going to do about it?'

"So," said Brigit, "how did you become the granny whisperer then?"

Over the last few years, he'd heard a couple of nicknames for what he did. This was undoubtedly the nicest.

"A few years ago, a woman who... used to take care of me," there was no need to go into exact details, "was ill over at St Katherine's. She was in one of those wards that... well, there's only one way out."

Brigit nodded.

"I went to see her a fair bit. While I was there, another lady on the ward – late stages of Alzheimer's amongst other things – mistook me for her brother. They knew he wasn't coming back from America and she had some things she needed to say so—"

"You did your trick," she finished.

"Not a trick!"

She flinched at the edge of annoyance in his voice before putting her hands out in a placating gesture. "Sorry."

"I was asked to help, so I did."

"And then your fame spread throughout the land..."

"Something like that."

Actually, it was almost nothing like that but he didn't want to go into those particular details right then. He'd needed to do his six hours of charity work a week and the matron on the ward had made some calls. Visiting patients was, after all, indoors work that involved no heavy lifting.

Paul glanced at Brigit. Her eyes were turned towards the overcast sky, mentally working her way down a list of questions. She was always going to be the 'further questions' type.

"So what's the deal with the slips then?" asked Brigit. "Are you on parole or doing community service or something?"

"No," he said, cringing slightly at the defensive edge in his own voice. "I've never even been arrested." Now that was a lie. "I'm just the charitable sort."

"But since when do the charitable sort have to get someone to sign a form to verify that they've done six hours of visits a week?"

In lieu of an answer, Paul tossed the butt of his cigarette into the drain and pulled his phone out of his back pocket.

"We'd better get a move on if you want me to do this visit."

"Right, yeah," said Brigit. She dropped her own cigarette and crushed it under her foot, while simultaneously pushing her hair back behind her ear, embarrassed at having over-stepped the mark.

Paul glanced across the road. The fox was now sniffing at the sandwich it had retrieved. Rather than eating it, it elected to urinate on it instead. As reviews went, it was pretty damning.

CHAPTER TWO

"Have you been listening to me?"

"Of course I've been listening to you."

He hadn't been listening to her.

To be fair, Paul had started out listening to her, as she'd explained the exact nature of the favour she was asking for, but then, he'd started thinking about disinfectant. Why did hospitals smell quite so strongly of it? They reeked of the stuff. He passed so many teary-eyed people in the halls, it was hard to know if gramps had popped his clogs or the fumes were just making their eyeballs burn.

Brigit stopped outside one of the private rooms, so abruptly her plastic soles gave a tiny screech on the tiled floor.

"So." Paul pointed casually at the door. "This is her?"

"Him!" she said. "This is *him*."

"I knew that. I meant 'her' as in the room. Rooms are feminine, everybody knows that."

"My arse."

"Also feminine, and may I say—"

"Shut up," she said. "So, to recap, for those who have been paying absolutely no attention: this gentleman came in three weeks ago but he's not had any visitors."

"Who is he expecting? Family? Friends?"

"No idea, but he asks three or four times a day."

"Right," he said. "And refresh my memory. His name is?"

She rolled her eyes. "Martin Brown. He's doped up quite a lot of the time and when he isn't, he's not exactly sunshine and lollipops. He made one of the trainees cry yesterday."

"Oh excellent," he said. "He sounds like a blast."

Brigit placed her hand on his arm and lowered her voice.

"Look, he's a miserable pain-in-the-hole for sure, but he's not going to be here long. He's riddled with cancer. From what I know, he ignored all advice and treatment options for three years, and now he's come home from America to die. He's all alone – trying to come to terms with the inevitable. So just – y'know…"

Paul took a deep breath, tasting antiseptic at the back of his throat, and sighed it out. "OK. Let's do this."

She knocked on the door and opened it quickly. As he stood outside, Paul could hear an inhalation of artificial air, followed by a low, rasping voice.

"Fuck's sake, call that…" A gasp. "Knocking? What if I'd been—"

"I'd have hit it with a spoon. They teach us that in training."

"Fucking… c…" Paul could hear a couple more agitated inhales.

"Now now, Mr Brown," she said. "Let's not have you wasting your breath proving chivalry is dead. You've a visitor."

Paul slowly stepped inside the room. It was all he'd come to expect of the modern hospital room – clean, neat, soulless. There was a TV, stuck up in the top corner opposite the bed, soundlessly showing a repeat of a sitcom that nobody liked the first time. The only attempt at decoration was a picture of the Virgin Mary hanging on the wall facing the door – her lips pursed, head tilted – like she was listening with the most sincere concern. Jesus may've died for your sins, but his ma was the one who was willing to listen to your excuses.

The lighting was dim but Paul didn't need to be a doctor to see that the frail figure sitting up in the bed wasn't long for this world. He looked like a big man that someone had let the air out of. His flesh hung, pale and loose. It looked as though his skeleton was wearing a suit of skin that was now several sizes too big for it. Various wires and tubes led to surrounding machines, to ease the pain or prolong the suffering. It was hard to tell how old the man was. He'd reached the place where time isn't measured in birthdays, but days, maybe hours, until the end. His gaunt hand held an oxygen mask up to his face. He glared at Paul as he inhaled a shallow breath of air. There wasn't enough antiseptic in the world to get the stench of death out of this room.

Brigit took away the tray with the untouched meal that was sitting on the table in front of him.

"Get out." Brown spoke in a coarse whisper.

Paul was all set to turn on his heels when he realised that last comment wasn't directed at him.

Brigit looked between the two of them. "Right – I'll leave you boys to it. I'm sure you've a lot of catching up to do." She folded the table down and stowed it at the side of the bed, before carrying the tray towards the door. As she left, she shot Paul a look that said 'have fun'.

Paul watched the door close. Suddenly, a rainy bus stop didn't seem so bad. This man made his flesh itch beneath the skin. He'd met many people who were near the end but it hadn't felt like this. This was different. He didn't know how, but he knew it was.

They stared at each other for a long moment. Paul was trying to leave Brown time to decide, to decide for the both of them, who Paul was. He wondered if the man was ever going to speak. Maybe he was dead? Was it possible for someone to die without moving – eyes still open, peering out from his glowering death mask? Was life that binary? Could someone just silently flick the switch to off?

Brown sucked in a ragged breath and held the oxygen mask up to his face again. He wasn't dead yet.

Paul cracked first. "So, how're you feel—"

"I knew you'd come," he interrupted. He said it with a simple air of finality, like Paul was the unavoidable tax bill in the post.

"I just wanted to see how you're getting on."

"Oh fucking peachy." He waved his free hand at the chair beside the bed. It was tough to discern Brown's accent amidst the wheezes and growls but there was definitely a hint of inner-city Dublin in there somewhere, mixed with the twangs of someone who'd spent time on the other side of the Atlantic.

Paul walked over and sat down. He didn't attempt to touch Brown; he got the definite impression that he wasn't the handholding sort.

"So, how's the food?" Paul ventured.

"Do you believe in heaven?"

Ah OK – it was going to be one of these chats. Not one of Paul's favourites, but he at least felt like he knew where he was again. He glanced up at Mary on the wall, her calm head-tilt asking, 'Well, do you?'

He settled into his one-size-fits-all script, designed to work for God-botherers and atheists alike. "I personally think there is an afterlife where we see our old friends again and—"

Brown's eyes bored into his. "Don't threaten me."

"No, I..." The brief moment where Paul had felt like he'd a handle on the conversation slipped away.

"If there's a heaven, there's a hell and..." A gasp. "I know where I'm headed. Six feet under the rock..."

A juddering fit passed through Brown's body. He convulsed slightly and wheezed into his mask. Paul considered calling for a nurse until a slight change in Brown's facial expression stopped the words in his throat. The crazy old bastard was laughing, although it descended fairly quickly into a coughing fit. With his right hand, Brown pulled the oxygen mask slightly further away from his lips, while with his left, he dabbed at his mouth with a handkerchief. As he moved it away, Paul noticed a spot of blood on it. He quickly averted his gaze and stared into those big brown eyes of the Virgin Mary. How do they know they were brown? Every hospital room he sat in had a picture of her on the wall and she had those big, brown, puppy-dog eyes in every one. Were they mentioned in the Bible? Right after the bit where they explained that, surprisingly for a man born in the Middle East, Jesus was a white dude.

The reason Paul was so ardently maintaining eye contact with

Our Lady of the Unimpeachable Fu-Fu was that he was not good with blood, people's in general and his own in particular. This normally wasn't a problem. It was surprising how long you could go around a modern medical facility without actually seeing blood. It was like the oil in a state-of-the-art car: you only saw it when something was really going wrong.

Brown dabbed the handkerchief on his lips and then waved it across his face, as if swatting away an imaginary fly, before shooting an annoyed look at Paul. He waved the hankie again with a tad more urgency. With a jolt of embarrassment, Paul realised he was trying to indicate the glass of water on the bedside cabinet. He reached across and brought it over to him.

When the storm had passed, Brown took his lips from the straw and Paul carefully placed the water back on the bedside cabinet. As he turned back, Brown had angled his head slightly and was giving him an appraising look.

"You really are the spit of him. There's a fair bit of your uncle in there too..."

Paul didn't know what to say, not least because the way Brown said it, it didn't sound like it was meant to be a compliment.

Brown looked up at the ceiling with a thousand-yard stare, as a long silence stretched out between them. Paul was taken aback to see a solitary tear navigate its way down the creases of the man's careworn face. "I swear to God, I didn't know... what he... I never knew."

Then two seconds later, Brown's tone changed to almost chatty. "Last time I saw you, you were only a wee baby." He looked away and down, his already weak voice sinking further. "I've not seen my girl in thirty years..."

Brown stared at the TV in the corner, not following it but just for somewhere else to look.

"Would you like to?" Paul ventured.

The look Brown shot him left Paul in no doubt that he'd said the wrong thing.

"She wants nothing to do with me... I mean... She knows nothing..." He drew a breath from his mask again. "Leave her be."

As he sucked in more of the precious air, he gave Paul a look he couldn't read. Sadness, defiance, anger – there was too much going on that Paul didn't understand for him to have any hope of keeping up.

"Y'know, when you get to the end, it's not the..." Brown paused, "surprises that get ye, it's the sheer fucking predictability. You're Gerry's son. You're going to do your damnedest to be him, whether you realise it or not. So when I tell you I've said nothing, you're not going to believe me. You're going to use her... because that's what we do." He looked at Paul again, his voice falling to a whisper. "You... do look a lot like your uncle."

This had gone far enough. Whoever this guy thought Paul was, it clearly wasn't somebody he wanted to see.

"Look, I think there's been some mistake, I'll let you..."

As Paul got up to leave, Brown's hand shot out with surprising speed and grabbed Paul's wrist.

"No, don't... please." There was a whimper in his voice now. "For an old friend of your father."

Paul looked towards the door, floundering. Maybe the best thing for this man's tortured soul would be a sedative to give him rest from whatever was tormenting him? At some point, he clearly must've been a nasty individual, but that was long ago. Now he was a sad and empty husk, being crushed under the weight of his own conscience.

Brown started coughing again. He brought his left hand with the handkerchief back to his lips. His eyes turned pleading towards the glass of water. Paul reached over to get it and sat on the edge of the bed.

As Paul held the water out, Brown lowered his left hand back and slipped it under the bedding.

"Thanks."

He took the straw into his lips and started slowly drinking from it. Paul could see him fidgeting around under the sheets out of the corner of his eye, but he was keen to avoid another sight of the bloodied handkerchief. That was why he kept his eyes firmly locked on Brown's. As he looked into them, he instantly realised something was wrong, very wrong.

Brown's right hand clamped onto Paul's throat. Paul dropped the glass, which bounced on the bed before shattering on the floor below. His hands instinctively latched onto Brown's arm, trying to pull it away. Brown's eyes were wild and he seemed freakishly, desperately strong. Focused as he was, Paul barely registered Brown's left hand, swinging up at the edge of his field of vision. Through some primeval survival instinct Paul turned his body at the last moment, causing the swinging hand to miss his head and instead make contact with his right shoulder. He felt a stabbing pain, followed by an inexplicable wetness, expanding on his arm.

In the rush of confusion and fury, Paul couldn't really register what had happened. He tried to stand and heave himself bodily away from his assailant but his left foot slipped on the wet floor, sending him tumbling to the ground. Brown lost his grip on Paul's throat, but grabbed at the collar of his shirt. Paul's momentum dragged Brown down to the floor on top of him. Various machines clattered to the ground in his wake, coming off worse in a clash with gravity and a mad man's fury.

The blessed respite from Brown's vice-like grip around Paul's throat was short-lived. Brown may have been not much more than skin and bone but he was more than enough to knock the air painfully out of Paul's lungs as he landed on top of him.

There was a moment of peculiar calm as both men searched for breath. They gasped like two landed fish left to suffer on the deck. Paul could hear an unpleasant rattle in his own throat, a clicking sensation accompanying every struggling breath.

Brown recovered first. He worked his body around, like in some demented game of Twister, bringing his face to within inches of Paul's. Brown's blood-stained mouth gaped under wildly leering eyes. His breath was putrid, as if whatever was rotting his insides away was bubbling up, coming to consume them both. Paul lay transfixed – like his mind had decided this was all too much and it was just going to shut down and wait for reality to come to its senses.

"You... took... everything... from... me!" The breath that carried the words blew like a foul wind across Paul's face.

Then Brown reared back.

Paul's arms were pinned. He struggled to free them as Brown raised his left hand above his head. Paul registered a flash of something there. He flinched as Brown's hand descended.

Halfway through its arc, Brown's arm spasmed, and whatever he'd held in his hand flew from his grasp, skittering across the floor. Enraged, Brown turned to see the IV cable that was restraining him. He howled in animalistic frustration as he heaved at it. The effort sent him crashing headfirst back onto Paul, leaving them lying face-to-face once again.

Brown croaked a harsh laugh of madness, which quickly transformed into a retching cough. Something hot and wet landed on Paul's face. All he could see now was the snarling mouth above him, blood dribbling down between the uneven, yellowed, tombstone teeth.

Then there was the sound of the door crashing open, a scream and motion.

The hands of unseen angels grabbed at Brown, dragging him away. Paul's last sight of him was his death-mask face leering back. Paul turned his head away, which was when he noticed the blood beginning to dye the shirt around his shoulder red and then...

Then he blacked out.

He was not good with blood, people's in general and his own in particular.

CHAPTER THREE

"You are, in fact, extremely lucky!"

He beamed at Paul with the kind of warm, disarming smile that'd be highly likeable in most situations. Right then, Paul was having a hard time not punching him squarely in the face.

"Really?" Paul asked, "because I thought I'd been stabbed in the shoulder. Have I not been stabbed in the shoulder?" He decided to go with sarcasm. He'd already been in one violent encounter that night, and he didn't think he had another one in him. Besides, the doctor seemed genuine, if a tad weird. He would've expected to see a lot of unusual stuff in casualty in the wee small hours, but enthusiasm from a medical professional was still unnerving. It was especially unnerving coming from one who had just explained to him how he now had seven stitches in his right shoulder. It was heavily bandaged and the attached arm was in a sling to keep the pressure off.

From what Paul could gather, he'd been transferred by ambulance from St Kilda's Hospice to the A&E unit at St Katherine's. He'd been pretty out of it. He guessed that, somewhere along the line, he'd been given something for the pain.

Dr Sinha was 27 and from India. He had a full licence to practise medicine over there, having qualified third in his class. Then he'd passed the Irish clinical exams first time and with flying colours. He decided to come to Ireland as he'd heard how friendly the people were. He was educated in an international school, which explained him having considerably better English than anyone else in the building.

The reason Paul knew all this was that he'd listened to Dr Sinha patiently explain it three times to the drunken husband of the woman with a broken leg on the far side of the ward.

Hubby was a lawyer and had spent a considerable amount of time trying to negotiate his way out of the shattered limb on his wife's behalf. Apparently they had a skiing holiday booked, and this 'did not mesh' with her having a broken leg. With the patience of whatever Hindus had in lieu of saints, Dr Sinha had understood entirely when Hubby had insisted on a second opinion. He was now sitting beside his wife's bed, waiting for the 'proper doctor' to show up. Hopefully somebody he'd gone to school with, so they could do some secret handshake and get the whole thing downgraded to light bruising.

Having watched Dr Sinha handle the husband from hell with such good grace, Paul had been naturally inclined to like him. However, the good doctor's assessment of his situation was beginning to sway him from that point of view.

"Yes, lucky," Dr Sinha repeated. "You see the back of the shoulder is actually a pretty great place to get stabbed. Once the knife avoids the rotator tendon, which I'm pleased to say it did in your case, there is little chance of permanent damage."

"Oh... good."

"Very much so. Don't get shot there though, that would be most unfortunate. There's a large artery and important nerves controlling the arm in that area, not to mention a joint no surgeon in the world can reconstruct. That would be nothing but bad news."

"Good tip," said Paul. "Just so I know, where is a good place to get shot?" He'd not yet realised that Dr Sinha was not at home to sarcasm.

"Gluteus maximus – most definitely. Gunshot, stab wound – if you get the option, go ass every time."

Clearly, the doctor had been around some very polite gunfights.

"Now, when I say ass, obviously I mean the cheeks and not the—"

"Super," Paul interrupted. "I think I've got it."

Sinha's cheery demeanour changed and Paul instantly felt guilty – like he'd just dropkicked an excited puppy.

"Sorry," Dr Sinha said. "I have a tendency to become overexcited about medical issues, leading to an inappropriate bedside manner."

"I wouldn't say that."

"Well somebody did," said Dr Sinha. "I was quoting from the report I got at the end of my probationary period," before adding in a hurt tone, "apparently, I enjoy my work too much."

Paul glanced over at Hubby again. "Give it time. I'm sure it'll wear off."

"Actually, I wanted to ask you about something else." Dr Sinha unclipped Paul's chart from the bottom of the bed. "I'm a bit confused. It says here that your assailant..." He paused to read from the chart, "coughed blood onto your face?"

"Yes... erm." Paul's stomach turned at the memory of Brown's demented death mask leering down at him.

"Was he wounded?"

"No!" Paul was rather offended by the question. "I didn't..." he stammered, "I was purely defending myself."

"Right, I see." Dr Sinha's expression made it very clear that he didn't see at all.

"I believe he is in the late stages of terminal lung cancer," offered Paul.

"And he stabbed you in the shoulder?"

"Yes."

"Why did he...?"

Dr Sinha was beginning to really irritate Paul now. "You'll have to ask him that."

"Oh... OK," he said. "It is just, it says here, that he is... dead."

"Oh..."

"Massive heart attack it says here."

Paul didn't know how to feel about that. Right then, he didn't want to feel anything about that. He hadn't spent nearly enough time feeling sorry for himself, and now he was expected to move onto dealing with that piece of information.

Dr Sinha gave him a peculiar doe-eyed look. Paul could see he viewed this as a bedside manner training opportunity. He tilted his head to the side, unknowingly giving it the full Virgin Mary.

"He must've died after..."

"Yes, because he was definitely alive before and during."

"Did you know him well?"

"No," Paul responded. "I'd just met him."

Dr Sinha's face brightened. "Oh – well that's not so bad then, is it?"

"Isn't it?"

"I mean, I'd much rather a stranger tried to kill me than somebody I knew well."

"I guess." That was certainly one way of looking at it.

"The good news is, St Kilda's have sent over a copy of Mr Brown's most recent blood work and, as far as we can see, he had nothing contagious. No AIDS, Hepatitis, Ebola—"

"Fantastic."

"So, you're perfectly fine—"

"Other than the stab wound."

"Ah yes, ha ha. Sorry." He actually said 'ha ha' in a way that Paul found irritating. "Still though, you and I have dealt with some difficult information and now look – we are making jokes! This has gone very well." He resumed beaming at Paul. "Which brings me to the next issue we must address. There appears to have been an issue with the emergency contact details the nurse took from you when you were admitted."

"Oh?"

"It happens all the time. People are rushing about—"

"I'd been stabbed."

"You'd been stabbed. We rang the number you gave us and, apparently, it is a Chinese takeaway called the Oriental Palace."

"It's not just a takeaway. They've recently expanded to include an in-dining area with ambiance."

Mrs Wu would've been proud. She had been answering the phone 'Hello Oriental Palace, now including an in-dining area with ambiance' for nearly three months. She clearly didn't know what ambiance meant, but somebody must've told her the place had it, and she was damn sure going to sell it.

"I see," said Dr Sinha. "And do you have a relative working at the Oriental Palace?"

"No, not as such." Or at all. "Ask for Mickey."

"OK. Mickey who?"

Paul had been dreading that question. Who really knew the second name of their regular delivery guy? Sure, Mickey had come in and nabbed the occasional smoke or life-threateningly cheap Eastern European beer on a slow Tuesday. He'd even stayed to watch half of *Roxanne* on DVD once, but a second name seemed like a very personal question. Mickey had told him he was not from China, and how annoyed he got when people assumed he was. Unfortunately, Paul had forgotten where Mickey was from, so that was another no-go area.

"Just Mickey."

"So, no relatives you'd like us to call?"

"Nope. None."

Dr Sinha was clearly uncomfortable at this. "Well, as someone from a very large family, may I say, I envy you. I spend half of my salary on birthday cards alone."

"That must be tough."

"It is!" Dr Sinha started warming to his subject. "Seven siblings and twenty six nephews and nieces the last time I counted. Bang – another baby. Bang bang – twins. It does not stop."

"Wow."

"So, I'll just put down here 'patient has no family'?"

"Yep."

"What about a partner?"

"No."

"OK, great. So you are totally alone," said Dr Sinha. "I mean, other than this Mickey?"

"Yes."

"Super."

"You're certainly making it feel that way."

Dr Sinha flipped over the pages on the clipboard. "Well, I think that's everything, unless you have any questions for me?"

"Nope," said Paul.

A loud attention-demanding cough from Hubby echoed around the ward. His second opinion still hadn't shown up.

"Absolutely any questions at all?" asked Dr Sinha, a hint of pleading in his eyes.

Paul felt obliged. "When can I get out of here?" Once he'd thought of it, Paul realised that he really did want to know the answer to that one. He was starting to develop a strong dislike of hospitals.

"We will check everything again tomorrow and, assuming it is all OK, you could leave in a couple of days." He hesitated. "But... you wish to speak to the Gardai." He actually pronounced it 'Gar-dee' in the overly careful way of someone trying to use another language's word.

"Not really," said Paul. He didn't – what would be the point? Yes, he'd been stabbed, but the person who'd done it wasn't anywhere the police could reach, at least not without a Ouija board.

Dr Sinha looked embarrassed. "Sorry, I may've got that wrong. This is my second language. The Gardai wish to speak to you."

Paul got a sickly feeling in his stomach. The whole getting stabbed thing had rather distracted him from the bigger picture. He'd gone into a room and five minutes later, a guy had died – after a physical confrontation with him, during which the aforementioned had felt moved to stab him. Paul could see how that would look bad. In fact, the more he thought about it, the more difficult he found it to make it look anywhere close to good. He couldn't get in trouble with the police; it violated the second commandment. *She* had been very clear on that.

He glanced around the ward and noticed the flash of a high-vis jacket through the swing doors at the end.

"Is there a guard outside?" he asked.

"Yes," said Dr Sinha. "And between you and I, myself and the rest of the staff are very pleased by his presence. Earlier on, he was kind enough to assist us in calming down a man who had taken a little too much methamphetamine."

Paul ran his fingers through his hair and rubbed the back of his neck, as he was want to do when stressed.

"Oh God, oh God, oh God," said Paul, "this is bad."

Dr Sinha patted him reassuringly on the hand. "Relax Mr Mulchrone, I'm sure it will all be fine."

"Yeah," said Paul, "because that's the kind of night I'm having."

CHAPTER FOUR

Paul knew exactly where he wasn't.

He wasn't in the offices of Greevy and Co Solicitors, even though Shane Greevy was sitting across the desk from him, reading from a large leather-bound book. Greevy was his usual self – forties, balding, thin and wearing a perpetual smile despite never looking happy. The man grinned like minimum wage workers wore seasonal fancy dress; as if he were being forced to comply with a memo from head office. Actually, come to think of it, this really wasn't the offices of Greevy and Co Solicitors. Paul noted that his subconscious had somehow upgraded the decor to be all mahogany and padded leather, even adding an imposing grandfather clock in the corner. In reality, their offices were a couple of dingy rooms in Phibsboro, located above a sofa shop that had recently, after a three-year-long closing-down sale, unexpectedly closed down.

This dream was one of only two Paul could ever remember having, although both recurred with great frequency. This was the one he normally preferred. Apparently it was unusual to be aware that you were dreaming while it was actually happening. Knowing he was didn't mean he could wake himself up though. He seemed to have no choice but to sit there most every night while the whole thing repeated over and over again.

Greevy looked up from the leather-bound book and coughed pointedly, clearly unhappy with not being paid full attention to. That was another thing, the book. Fidelma's actual Will had just been a few pieces of mundane A4.

Greevy continued reading: "...my property of any nature and description and wherever situated, including my house in Richmond Gardens, my savings accounts and share portfolios, I leave to Donegal Donkey Sanctuary."

At this point, the donkey situated behind Greevy's right shoulder made its usual ominous growling noise. Paul was pretty sure real donkeys didn't growl but he'd be damned if he was going to fact-check his own nightmares.

"However, prior to that endowment, I leave the following provision to my great-nephew Paul Mulchrone."

Paul looked up at his great-aunt Fidelma, sitting astride the donkey's back as always. No matter what he said or did, she never spoke. She just wore that same 'what's that smell?' look of disapproval on her face. She had not spoken directly to him on either of the occasions they'd met in real life. The first time, he had been a 6-year-old boy fidgeting behind his mother. He had been utterly focused on his assigned job of minding the big blue suitcase. Fidelma and his Ma had argued before she had slammed the door in their faces. Paul hadn't understood. He'd complained and cried about the cold, until his mother's tears had stopped his own. The next, and last, time he'd met Fidelma was the week after he had turned twelve years old. His birthday had been the day before his ma's funeral, so nobody had remembered. The room they'd brought him to had featured a big tree painted on the wall. Paul had stared at it as Fidelma had once again ignored him and delivered a sermon on the wanton behaviour of 'the young' to a pair of confused and increasingly angry social workers. Then she had stormed out. The man from social services had opened the door to scream a rude word after her and then Paul hadn't seen him again.

"He is to be given use of my house in Richmond Gardens and a stipend of €500 a month to live off. This is only a temporary measure while he endeavours to find proper employment, a challenge given his poor start in life."

And there they were, the five words that had come to define him: 'his poor start in life.' It had been those five words that had so enraged him that he'd decide to game her system. Instead of looking for a job, he would live forever off €500 a month. Fuck her. Fuck the donkeys.

"Allowing for the following provisos. One: he is to receive no other assistance of any kind from the state, charities or any other source. Two: this provision will end should he get in trouble of any kind with the police."

At this point, the other occupant of the dream hooted and jumped up and down in the seat behind Greevy's right shoulder. It was Martin Brown. Still in his hospital gown, blood dripping from his open howling mouth. He was hammering away on an old typewriter as if taking notes, for reasons beyond Paul's understanding. His presence was a new and unwelcome addition. Paul kept trying to lock eyes with the donkey; even in his dream the sight of all that blood turned his stomach. Unhappy at being ignored, Brown leapt from his chair and ran around the desk, his gait stooped like a chimp. He disappeared from Paul's field of vision but his bony hands clasped around Paul's neck. Paul tried to prise them off but they were freakishly strong. Greevy continued reading.

"Three: to improve his moral fibre, he shall be required to complete six hours of charity work a week, to be verified by Mr Greevy."

Paul screamed as he felt Brown's teeth sinking into his right shoulder. As he struggled to get free, Greevy's voice droned on. Brown's hands started to drag him back off the chair. Paul looked up into Fidelma's ever-disapproving face.

Then he felt a hand gently shake his left shoulder and another voice, softer and further away.

"Paul? Paul? Are you OK?"

He turned to see Brigit Conroy looking down at him, her face a picture of concern. This was new too.

And then the grip of the skeletal hands around his neck grew tighter and he screamed.

Paul awoke with a start, gasping for breath, looking into the concerned face of Brigit.

Strip lighting and antiseptic air. Starched sheets against his skin, tucked in too tight, restraining his body. He knew where he was. The hospital. He lowered his head back onto the pillow as the pounding rhythm of his own heartbeat receded in his ears. Now that the 'where' of his situation had returned to him, the 'who', 'when' and particularly 'why' followed close behind. He took a couple of deep breaths.

"How're you feeling?" she asked.

His senses recovered, Paul was able to establish his position vis-à-vis Brigit, namely – being angry.

"Oh super, thanks for asking," he said.

"I'm sorry about..." she trailed off.

"Sorry about what? Getting me stabbed? Oh don't give it another thought. I'd nothing else planned for the evening, and they've given me a shed-load of free drugs, so I'm making out like a bandit here."

She made to speak but he wasn't anywhere near done. He'd played this conversation through in his head several times, and he had plenty more script loaded up in his internal teleprompter that was raring to go.

"Or – are you sorry that they've to do tests, to make sure the blood coughed into my face wasn't filled with anything too contagious? Or that I'm now a suspect in a murder investigation?" His voice started to rise along with his anger. "Exactly which of those things are you sorry for?"

"OK, well... all of..." Her voice faltered and her eyes began to well up.

"Oh no!" he said and pointed at her accusingly.

"What?"

"Don't you dare – don't you bloody well dare!"

"What?" A hint of annoyance crept into her voice as she pushed a knuckle into the corner of her eye.

"You know what," he said. "Don't you dare cry! I have every right to be angry. Don't you take that away from me."

She nodded her agreement.

"And don't agree with me. You don't get to be reasonable," he said. "Thanks to you, I could be dead! So you stand there, not crying – and take the damn good tongue lashing you've got coming."

He'd never used that phrase before in his life and, even as it came out of his mouth, the little internal editor in the back of his brain looked up from his newspaper and sneered. Where the hell had that come from?

As Brigit dabbed a tear away from her left eye with the corner of a tissue, her right eyebrow rose ever so slightly, in the tiniest acknowledgement of his peculiar choice of words. For some reason that made him even angrier.

"And don't you... don't you DARE find my choice of words funny."

She shook her head furiously but even as she did so, a nervous smile played across her lips.

"Stop – stop it right this minute!" His tone was becoming pleading now. He could feel the conversation slipping further off the course he'd planned out.

A giggle escaped her lips. She immediately clamped her left hand over her mouth and extended her right in a gesture of placating apology.

"Stop being so immature!"

She nodded now, her eyes clenched tightly shut as tears of another kind started to trickle from their corners.

She drew a long deep breath in through her nose and removed her hand from over her mouth.

"Sorry, I'm... sorry," she said. "It's been a long night and... OK, I'm fine. Keep going."

She breathed out, rolled her head around her neck and jiggled her arms, as if she was loosening herself up for a run at the long jump.

"OK... right," he said. "Where was I?"

"Giving me a tongue lashing."

She collapsed into the chair behind her, burying her head in the mattress near his feet, as spasms of body-shakingingly uncontrollable laughter overcame her.

"Do not..."

Damn her! Despite himself, Paul started laughing too. She looked up at him and, when their eyes met, the laughter redoubled. All the tension of the situation released itself into a wave of hysterics that would make no sense to anyone who wasn't caught in its undertow. Brigit was so far gone, she was clutching at her chest, unable to breathe.

The curtain at the bottom of the bed was pulled back and the head of Dr Sinha popped in. He was wearing that unsure smile of people everywhere when joining the hilarity of others, too late to understand where it came from.

"Is everything OK, Mr Mulchrone?" he asked.

"Yes, thank you, doctor." Paul spoke through his laughter. "This is Nurse Conroy... She's the one responsible for getting me stabbed."

Brigit, unable to speak, waved cheerfully at him from her seat.

The doctor looked between the two, bewildered by the collective frenzy.

"OK... well. I'm glad you are feeling better about things," he said. "But if you could keep it down please. You're disturbing the other patients."

Paul tried to raise his hands in apology. The stab of pain from his right shoulder helped slow the tide of laughter to a trickle.

Brigit, for her part, was now pushing the heels of her hands into her eyes – the laughter having subsided to giddy jumping breaths.

"Great, thank you," Dr Sinha said and, with a slight shake of the head, he departed, pulling the curtain closed behind him.

Paul's eyes met Brigit's across the calm air that now stretched between them.

"I really am sorry," she said.

"For which bit?"

"All of it." She hesitated. "Especially the stabbing bit."

"Excellent. Well, I fully intend to come up with several different ways for you to make it up to me. You can start by delivering on that lift home you promised."

CHAPTER FIVE

Paul clenched his eyes shut and prayed. He'd never been a religious man but circumstance can make believers of us all.

He was dimly aware that Brigit was talking him through what'd happened at the hospice, between his less-than-fond farewell with Mr Brown and her rocking up at his bedside. Apparently, a patient having a coronary in the midst of an attempted homicide results in a real paperwork tsunami. Paul couldn't concentrate on that though, as he was too focused on his own life. Specifically, how Brigit's driving abilities were all but certain to bring it to an untimely end.

"And then Dobson, the old battleaxe..." she said.

A car horn squealed in protest behind them.

"Feck's sake!" she exclaimed. "Drivers in Dublin are always honking."

He couldn't contain himself any longer. "No, they're not," he said. "Not unless you're driving like a maniac!"

She turned and gave him a look of outrage. "He came out of nowhere!"

"He'd the right of way!" Paul pointed furiously with his left hand, the one not trapped in a sling. "You see the lights, right? The ones that are green and red, especially the red ones: they're important. You do have them where you come from?"

"It was orange!" she protested, whilst glaring at him. "And FYI – I learned to drive in Dublin, smartarse."

Another horn blared.

"That wasn't even meant for me."

"Course not," he said, "but let's just stay on the left-hand side of the road anyway."

All he'd done was throw fuel on the fires of outrage that Nurse Conroy seemed to have permanently simmering away. "This – is the typical male chauvinistic attitude about women drivers. That's so typical—"

"No it isn't!" he interrupted. "There are many many fine women drivers in the world but none of them… are in this car."

It was the kind of dull dreary Friday morning that Dublin did so well. The sky was the colour of wet newspaper, and it seemed to be bleeding into the day, making everything look like a bad photocopy of itself. Every passing face had that stoic commuter's grimace; marching ever forward, towards the promised land of the weekend. It was raining, the kind of fine misty rain that meant even if you had an umbrella, you'd reach your destination to discover you were still inexplicably wet. That was assuming, of course, you didn't get mown down on the way there.

"And by the way," said Paul, "there's also supposed to be a police car behind us – so y'know."

Brigit hadn't been happy about Paul's insistence on signing himself out of the hospital, but nowhere near as unhappy as the fresh faced Garda Danaher, who'd been tasked with 'protecting him'. He'd got flustered when asked who he was 'protecting' Paul from, seeing as the only person who'd shown any serious intent to harm him was already dead. Admittedly, if he'd known what Brigit's driving was like at that point, Paul would have re-evaluated that assessment. Somebody once said you know you're getting old when the policemen start looking young, but Paul was pretty sure Garda Danaher would've looked young to anyone. He gave off the air of a young fella who'd borrowed his daddy's uniform and was playing dress-up. There was a distinct aroma of Clearasil and terror about him. Paul guessed Danaher was the sort who had secretly longed his whole life to be blessed with a commanding presence, and was now gutted to find out it didn't come with the uniform.

There'd been a brief discussion of whether or not Paul was under arrest for anything, Brigit going into a spiel about Miranda Rights. Paul was pretty sure a lot of it had been gleaned from American cop shows. Officer Danaher appeared to be more intimidated by being spoken to by a member of the public in possession of breasts than he was her in-depth legal knowledge. The poor lad hadn't known where to look but he kept looking there anyway. Paul ended up feeling bad for him, and so he gave him his address. He told him he was more than welcome to follow them and 'protect' him there if he liked. Officer Danaher nodded gratefully and went off to call his mummy to ask if it was OK.

Brigit turned around fully in her seat to look behind them, presumably engaging in her head the autopilot her car definitely did not have. "I can't see any police car."

Paul decided Officer Danaher must have stopped to deal with one of the three car crashes Brigit had definitely caused since they had left the hospital. Dr Sinha hadn't been too put out by Paul's departure, once he'd signed his *Against Medical Advice* form. Brigit had brought Paul's coat with her from St Kilda's staff room but he was still down a shirt and jacket due to the excessive bleeding he'd done earlier. Dr Sinha had supplied a T-shirt from the hospital's lost and did-not-want-to-be-found box. It was left over from a fun run apparently. Despite looking very hard, Paul had been unable to locate even the slightest glimmer of sarcasm in the doctor's eyes as he had held out the yellow t-shirt proudly emblazoned with the slogan 'I Beat Cancer'.

Brigit threw the car around a corner whilst still in third gear, and a pedestrian narrowly avoided becoming a statistic. After a few more honks, a couple of hand gestures and an outright rejection of the concept of a one-way system – they finally made it to Richmond Gardens, where Paul lived.

About five years ago Richmond Gardens and its surroundings had been one of those up-and-coming areas, but it had never quite made it all the way up. Instead, it had splattered hard against the wall between working-class ghetto and middle-class paradise, and slid back down to earth. The delicatessen had gone back to being a chip shop and the 'wine boutique' was now an offy advertised by a drunken five-euro note.

The street itself was a cul-de-sac of one-bedroom terraced houses, backing onto the Royal Canal on Paul's side. From the outside, they looked like they must be horribly cramped – mainly because they were. And towering over it all was Croke Park. The national stadium dominated the skyline like a futuristic spaceship that had landed amidst rows of terraced houses built at the beginning of the twentieth century.

Brigit undid her seatbelt and reached behind her into the back seat to locate her handbag.

"See? No problem. You worry over n..."

She paused as she noticed the houses behind Paul slowly moving. Then she remembered the handbrake. Paul said nothing, in a way that left nothing unsaid.

Brigit came around to the passenger side of the car because the door was a bit 'tricky' – by which she meant difficult to open due to traumatic bodywork damage. With a pained yowl of unhappy metal, it opened, and she helped Paul out. He was worried the noise would garner unwanted attention though. Mrs Corrie wasn't a massive fan of having his crappy car permanently parked outside her house, and she wasn't shy about sharing the sentiment. Thankfully there was no sign of the tell-tale curtain twitch. Maybe she'd finally gone off to complain to the council, as she'd repeatedly threatened to do.

Paul had once considered getting a dog but the only 'garden' the houses had was an 8-foot by 6-foot paved area at the front, and he didn't believe a dog should be kept in a smaller space than a convicted murderer. The rear of the house backed directly onto the canal, which, if nothing else, acted as a moat against the larcenous tendencies of the local urchins. So, no dog for Paul and instead his front garden was dominated by a great big bush. It was green and had leaves. He wasn't exactly a keen horticulturalist. Every year or so, Paul had a fight with it when it poked him in the eye. He'd hack a couple of branches off with a carving knife and they'd scowl at each other for the following fortnight. This year's barney was overdue. The bush was dominating the garden again, obscuring the view. That was why they got all the way to the gate before...

"Now aren't you two sweet?" Paul knew the voice without having to see its source. Sitting there on his front step, beaming up at him: Bunny McGarry.

CHAPTER SIX

Paul's heart sank when he heard that mocking Cork lilt float up from behind the garden wall. Not that it was a surprise. Bunny was always coming. He'd just hoped for a few hours' kip before having to deal with him.

Bunny McGarry sat on the front step, his large frame stretched out as he happily worked his way through a bag of croissants. He had a plastic knife and a couple of tiny tubs of spreadable butter. Brown flakes of pastry were liberally scattered down the front of his crumpled suit, his black sheepskin overcoat bunched around him to protect him from the morning chill. The hurling stick he brought everywhere with him stood propped up against the garden wall.

"Well young Paulie, as I live and breathe." His voice always carried a lilting edge of joyous mockery to it, like there was a joke in the offing but you weren't being let in on it. His face was a shade of red you only generally found on a baboon's arse – Paul could never tell if it was from a liking for the booze or the bubbling anger that lived just below the surface of the man, or both.

Bunny had beady jet-black eyes that never looked in the same direction, thanks to the left one being lazy. It gave the disconcerting impression that one of them was keeping lookout while the other went about its nefarious business. He used it to his full advantage. Paul had heard people claim that they'd stared Bunny McGarry down but he'd never believed one of them. Bunny's age was impossible to tell, he'd looked exactly the same for all the years Paul had known him. Logically, he must be hovering around fifty by now but that was in human years. They didn't really apply to Bunny. He was like one of those Easter Island statues, if they were able to sneer.

"Hello, Bunny." Paul could feel what little energy he had flowing out of him. "I see you've got a nice little picnic on the go for yourself."

"Ahh, the best part of the morning, Paulie – fresh croissants straight from the bakery…"

He held one up to his nose and breathed in its scent theatrically. "Fecking glorious." He dropped the croissant back into the paper bag and started to stand. "The French may be a shower of goat-bothering cheese-sniffers, but they can do bread."

"I didn't think you got up this early in the morning," Paul said.

"Ohhh, Paulie," he laughed. "I never sleep. You of all people should know that."

Once on his feet, Bunny moved forward to stand in his normal position. He had the unnerving habit of standing slightly too close to people when he talked. He lived in other people's personal space. Six foot two, he carried weight, but in a powerful way. You could never be sure what the fat to muscle ratio was, but you'd be a fool to find out. Not least because Bunny not only fought dirty but he took a gleeful delight in doing so.

Paul could still remember the incident from his youth when Gary Kearney, the ex-boxer, had confronted Bunny outside Phelan's pub. Paul had been one of a group of young fellas who'd been playing ball nearby at the time. Alan Murphy had been in Paul's class. Kearney had recently shacked up with Alan's ma. A few months after Kearney moved in, Alan had started falling down stairs quite a lot, only they lived in a ground floor flat. Bunny had dropped over and had a long talk with Alan's ma about the situation, which Kearney had not appreciated. When Bunny had offered to settle it like gentlemen, Kearney couldn't believe his luck. He'd gotten half way through taking his coat off, when Bunny pounced. Kearney never even got a punch off. When it was done, Bunny handed a roll of tightly wrapped coins he'd been holding in his hands to Alan, and told him to take the rest of the lads down to the shops for sweets. After that, Kearney moved out and Alan never fell down the stairs again. Kearney also spoke with a stammer for the rest of his life.

Bunny noticed that the front of his suit was covered in flakes of croissant and turned his eyes to heaven. "Would you look at the state of me? I must apologise, I wasn't expecting company of the female persuasion."

He patted himself down, popped one of the bigger flakes into his mouth and bowed courteously, extending his hand towards Brigit palm up. "M'lady!"

Bunny left it a beat and then shot Paul a warning glance. "Now, Paulie boy — don't be rude. Introduce me to the young lady."

Paul always felt tempted with Bunny to push back but, if experience had shown him anything, it was that the path of least resistance was always the way to go.

"Bunny, this is Brigit Conroy."

He could feel Brigit looking back and forth between them, trying to figure out whether Bunny was friend or foe. She hesitated then extended her hand sheepishly. Bunny grasped it and shook it furiously: "Bunny McGarry at your service."

Brigit pulled it away before Bunny could go in for the creepy hand kiss. Bunny turned his movement into standing up, so smoothly the casual observer might not have noticed.

"Nice to meet you," said Brigit.

"Well now, country girl – Sligo is it?"

"Leitrim actually."

"Feck – Leitrim, God forsaken shithole that it is. Hasn't produced a decent hurler in a decade. I'm not surprised you left, love. If all the men from there have the same aim as the hurling team, you'd have been ear-fucked to death by now."

Brigit's mouth opened and closed a few times in the breeze. Bunny had that effect on people.

"You can head off if you want now, sweetheart," Bunny said. "Paulie and I have a lot of catching up to do."

"No, thank you," she said firmly. "I think I'll stay."

Bunny glanced at her briefly. "Ha, you can always tell a Leitrim girl, but you can't tell her much. So how've you been, Paulie?"

"Super, Bunny. How's that hurling team of yours doing? I hear you got relegated again."

Stupid. He'd known it was as soon as he'd said it, but Bunny was getting under his skin more than usual.

Bunny raised his eyebrows, as if acknowledging that it had been noted and it would be returned to at a later date.

"You've had an eventful couple of days, I hear. Killed a man."

"No, he didn't," Brigit chimed in, "and what business is it of yours anyway?"

"I'm a very dear old friend of..."

Just then, a Garda car rounded the corner and screeched to a halt.

Bunny glanced briefly in its direction. "Oh dear, Paulie, I do hope you're not in any trouble with the law?"

Officer Danaher stumbled out of the car. He looked visibly relieved to see Paul. Clearly he had been dreading explaining how a crippled suspect had wandered away from right under his nose.

"Good morning, Officer Danaher," Paul said. "We did wonder where you'd got to."

"Yeah, sorry, I..." He stopped as he took in the body language of the group, picking up on the tension. "Is everything OK?"

"Oh, peachy," said Bunny. "We're just some old friends catching up."

"Actually," said Brigit, a misplaced tone of victory in her voice. "This gentleman is making a nuisance of himself."

"Oh deary me, am I now?" asked Bunny, all mock innocence. "I do apologise."

Officer Danaher started to move forward.

"Excuse me, sir..."

"It's not sir to you, sonny, it's Detective Sergeant McGarry."

Danaher stopped, like he'd just ran into an invisible wall. His mouth must have been racing ahead of his brain, because even he sounded surprised when he said, "Do you have any ID?"

Bunny snapped. "My ID will be my boot up your fecking arse in a minute, son. Are you out of Glasnevin?"

Danaher, shell-shocked, nodded dumbly.

"Then go tell Sergeant O'Brien that Bunny McGarry said he needs to keep his wee babies in their place."

Danaher took a step back, then one forward, then hovered – like a rabbit in the headlights.

"Piss off," said Bunny softly. "There's a good lad."

Red-faced, Danaher turned and headed back towards his car.

"I thought everybody knew you, Bunny?" Paul said.

"What can I tell you? Ye just can't get the staff these days." He looked at his fingernails, as if dismissing the whole thing. "But enough about me – murder, that's a bit of a step up for you, isn't it Paulie?"

"It wasn't murder," said Brigit.

"Oh really, Missy?" He spoke to her but never took his eyes off Paul.

"Maybe you should head off now, Brigit," said Paul. It was like trying to hold back the tide.

"It was self-defence," she continued.

"Was it?" said Bunny. "How I heard it was he walks into a room – five minutes later a terminally ill patient is trying to fend him off."

"It wasn't like that," said Brigit.

"And how would you know, love?"

"Well 'love'," she said, "the reason I know…"

The world slowed down with a sickening judder. Paul could see the oncoming train heading straight for him, with an inevitable momentum.

"Is that I was there." Brigit finished with a flourish of unmistakable defiance. Paul couldn't see her face, but he imagined her look of righteous fury must've stalled somewhat when she saw Bunny's face light up.

"You were there?" he repeated.

"Yes," she said, trying to sound more confident than she was. "I'm a nurse at St Kilda's."

"And you let him into the victim's room..."

"Yes. No. It wasn't like that."

Bunny finally took his eyes off Paul and looked directly at Brigit.

"Paulie's little girlfriend. Well this explains a lot."

"No, I..." she stammered. "I'm not and... you've got it all wrong."

"Have I now?" said Bunny. "Are you one of these angel of death types? Is that it? Was he helping you hold down the pillow?"

"No, it..." Brigit actually stamped her foot in frustration. "You're just being..."

"Anyway," Paul said, "you've had your fun, Bunny. I'm tired."

Bunny smiled. "Course you are. I'd imagine she keeps you on your toes. It was good to catch up, Paulie. I'll be seeing you very soon."

He picked up his hurl and moved forward, looking Paul up and down. "Lovely t-shirt by the way." Bunny shoved the brown paper bag with the remaining croissant into Paul's sling and saluted. He winked at Brigit and walked off down the pavement, swinging his hurl jauntily by his side as he went. As he passed the mortified-looking Officer Danaher in his squad car, he banged on the bonnet twice and waved.

"How dare he? He can't..." Brigit started.

"He can do whatever he likes." Paul failed to keep the anger out of his voice.

"That's police harassment," she said.

"That's Bunny McGarry," he snapped. "You don't understand anything but it sure as hell doesn't stop you talking, does it?"

Brigit took an indignant step back.

"What's that supposed to mean?"

Paul tossed the brown bag onto the ground, and dug his good hand into his overcoat pocket, looking for his front door key.

"Never mind. Thanks for the lift."

"Now hang on…"

But he didn't. He was in the door in one fluid motion and slamming it quickly behind him. Without looking up at the portrait above the mantelpiece, he could sense Great-Aunt Fidelma's judgemental eyes following him across the room.

After a moment, he heard the gate slam.

CHAPTER SEVEN

"How come there isn't a mirror?" asked Brigit.

Detective Inspector Jimmy Stewart was 59 years, 11 months, 3 weeks and 2 days old. It was old enough that, when he had started on the force, having the same name as a movie star from Hollywood's golden age had been considered highly amusing. Old fellas had made jokes – not good ones, but they'd killed a bit of time and given people something to do around the station. They'd also done impressions, badly – but the name and the odd voice were usually enough for people to realise who it was supposed to be. He'd not really minded. All those old men were up on the big wooden plaque down the hall now, the one his name was going on in five days whether he liked it or not. Well, there was one way of avoiding it; he could get shot by next Monday. Then he'd end up on the marble one in the lobby instead.

"Do you need a mirror, Nurse Conroy?" asked Detective Wilson. "Ehm... you look fine."

Stewart shook his head but didn't look up. Wilson was an idiot of the worst kind: a highly educated one. Babysitting him was just one of the indignities he'd been lumbered with over the last six months as his role had been 'wound down'. Almost every Garda does their 30, takes the pension and runs. Stewart was an exception; he'd clung on to the bitter end. They'd not known what to do with him. What was worse than being unwanted was that he'd have stayed longer if they'd let him. This was all he knew. He was institutionalised. Anyone who stayed on for the max was typically senior management. Stewart's ascent, not fast-paced to begin with, had stalled at DI. Nobody ever said it of course, but his broad Finglas drawl had stood against him. Senior officers weren't supposed to possess the same Dublin accent as the boys they were locking up. Stewart didn't care. He knew where he came from and so would anyone with ears. Besides, he was a thief-taker at heart. If he'd gone any further up the food chain, he'd be spending his days in strategy meetings thinking outside the box. Screw that. He loved the job, even if it wasn't reciprocated. And now his time was coming to an end. His only chance of being involved in a decent murder investigation from here on out was if he snapped and beat Wilson to death with the bottle of champagne they'd given him as an early retirement present. It didn't speak well of the detective skills of his colleagues. Jimmy Stewart had only ever drunk once in his life. He'd not liked it.

"To be clear," said Wilson, "when I said you looked fine I didn't mean that in any form of sexual context."

Stewart was re-reading his notes, making absolutely sure, for the second time, that he'd covered everything. He let the tension that Wilson had just created hang in the air until he reached the bottom of the page.

"She means a two-way mirror, like you see in the cop shows on the telly." Stewart looked up and smiled at Nurse Conroy. "We don't have them I'm afraid."

"Oh." She looked disappointed.

"So," continued Stewart, "if you fancy throwing a headbutt into Detective Wilson, I'm not paying attention and nobody else can see you."

He turned the page and continued reading.

Stewart was annoyed.

There was the general background hum of annoyance at the fact he was retiring. He had no hobbies. Fishing bored him to tears, DIY brought him out in hives and golf would've been a good walk ruined, if he'd actually been a fan of walking in the first place. The only sport he liked was American football, thanks to a stint working nights as a desk sergeant back in the nineties when there was nothing else on. That was Sunday nights sorted for five months of the year. Even on a good week, that left him with six and a half days of fuck all to look forward to.

Then there was the specific annoyance he felt every time he saw Wilson's big shiny ginger-headed face, or heard his whiny voice or, worse still, listened to him casually crowbar into conversation his degree in Criminology from Trinity fecking College. Stewart was supposed to be showing him the ropes but he was more concerned with the strings, like the ones that'd been pulled to get the wet-behind-the-ears grandson of a former Minister for Finance a detective's badge. He'd been lumbered with Wilson for nearly three weeks now. During that time Stewart had quoted Danny Glover from Lethal Weapon exactly nine times, none of which the younger fella had spotted. Stewart really was getting too old for this shit.

All of that was just responsible for his day-to-day level of annoyance, but not today's excessively high dosage. No, the cause of that was Brigit.

During 36 years of marriage, the long-suffering Mrs Stewart had convinced her workaholic husband to go abroad on holiday exactly twice. DI Jimmy Stewart didn't like abroad. He didn't like the sea, the sun or foreigners. Not in a racist way, they just insisted on having their own languages and he had a copper's pathological dislike of things he didn't understand. The second time they went abroad, they'd gone to Crete. He'd not liked it but he'd kept that largely to himself. The woman had given birth to and raised four kids, all of whom he loved and three of whom he liked. Once he'd given in, he'd decided it was only fair to let her enjoy the holiday and not be a moany prick about it. He'd known on the second night that he was going to get food poisoning. The meal had tasted fine as they'd eaten it and he hadn't felt ill after, yet he still quietly went to reception and acquired extra bog roll. Then he'd waited patiently, and been decent enough never to say 'I told you so' over the next few days. Not even on the rare occasions on which neither of them were in the bathroom. Nowadays, she went off on bus tours of Europe with the bridge club. The dog ate the frozen dinners the long-suffering Mrs Stewart had lovingly prepared for her husband while he scoffed takeaways he wasn't allowed to have. Marriage, thought Stewart, was all about compromise. Compromise and lying. The right kind of lying. The point was, DI Jimmy Stewart had an uncanny sense for when unpleasant shit was coming. One look at Nurse Conroy's beaming face and he wanted to go get extra bog roll.

She'd turned up voluntarily to give her statement about the events that had taken place the night before at St Kilda's Hospice. It'd been a mess but then death was messy. That didn't bother him. He'd been at the scene first thing this morning and her version of events tallied with the evidence. By all accounts, this poor sod Brown had been hanging on to both life and sanity by a thread, and he'd not been able to keep a firm grip on either. He'd stabbed some do-gooder visitor in the shoulder, before his heart had given out in the melee. Thankfully all the patients had their valuables locked away on admittance, so there was no possible robbery angle. How Brown had come to be in possession of a flick knife was a rather awkward question that somebody somewhere was going to have to answer. To be fair, who thinks to frisk a dying man for weapons?

Nurse Conroy had been very clear; Mulchrone had only gone in to see Brown as a favour to her. People did favours for people all the time. Favours for favours, it was the Irish way. The only reason Stewart found himself sitting beside the waste of space that was Detective Wilson was that somebody somewhere had done a favour for an old drinking buddy, and bumped his grandson up the tree. That Stewart was in that interview room in the first place was the result of another favour. This non-murder murder wasn't something the National Bureau of Criminal Investigation would normally deal with but Chief Inspector Drake had asked. The Chief was, no doubt, doing somebody else a favour in turn. A discreet phone call had been made. Patients attacking random idiots could be embarrassing for the hospice etcetera etcetera, could it be handled 'sensitively', especially as the patient in question, although Irish, apparently held an American passport. In other words, Please Jimmy could you hold Wilson's hand so he doesn't royally fuck it up, and for the love of Christ keep it out of the papers. Favours for favours.

What was annoying Stewart specifically about Nurse Conroy was this: most people giving a statement were either nervous or angry or just pissed off for being there. Conroy was neither of these things. She was delighted. Not in a 'psycho getting off on death' way, at least not unless Stewart's detective senses had completely left him. No, she just had the kind of enthusiasm you normally only found in witnesses who'd found God, not a dead body. She appeared genuinely excited to be helping the police with their enquiries, and that, in Stewart's experience, was unusual. DI Jimmy Stewart disliked unusual. Before you knew it, unusual became awkward, and then it was just a hop, skip and a dodgy chain of evidence to awkward becoming complicated. More than anything, Jimmy Stewart hated complicated. This was all instinct and he was fully aware it didn't make sense, which was why he wasn't sharing it with the criminology kid. That didn't mean it wasn't real. In the meantime, he was dotting the 'I's and crossing the 'T's, waiting for the S and the H to show up.

Brigit, for her part, was fighting off a rather heavy dose of the anti-climaxes. All those Scottish crime novels, containing more dead bodies than Scotland actually had living people, had left her with high expectations of the criminal justice system. She felt bad that Brown was dead of course, but that had only really been the rescheduling of an event that was already on the cards. She also felt terrible about Paul getting stabbed, although less so after he'd slammed a door in her face. Still, though, she'd been an almost witness to a death while in the process of attempting murder – that was exciting stuff, wasn't it? Apparently not. An old fella had laboriously taken notes for an hour, while his ginger partner attempted to make small talk, giving the whole affair the feel of a terrible blind date. A thought occurred to her.

"Shouldn't you be recording this?" she asked.

"I am. I'm writing it down."

"But..."

Stewart looked at her again. Unhelpfully, he realised that she reminded him of his youngest daughter. He put his pen down.

"We record most interviews but, as this is just taking a straightforward statement, we don't need to," he said.

"What's the difference?" she asked.

"You're a witness, not a suspect," Stewart said. "Unless you'd like to make a shocking confession?"

"No thanks."

"Can't blame a guy for asking." Stewart went back to his notes. "And besides, the only interview room currently available with a working tape recorder is number three, and the heating is bust in there. I'm too old to go lugging the heater down from upstairs."

Brigit looked pointedly at the younger Wilson.

Stewart glanced up and gave a short mirthless bark of laughter. "He's got an 'ology'. He doesn't do heavy lifting."

Wilson pulled a face.

"Fair enough," said Brigit. "I just, well... I was expecting a bit more of a grilling. Like you'd do good cop, bad cop or something."

"Those are very out-dated techniques," said the 2:2 in Criminology.

"Yes," said Stewart. "Good cop and bad cop have left for the day, I'm a different kind of cop."

Brigit's eyes lit up. "Did you just...?"

"What?"

"Did you just quote Vic Mackey?"

Stewart suppressed a grin. "I might have done."

"Who?" said Wilson.

"The guy from *The Shield*," said Brigit.

"Oh – I've never seen it," said Wilson.

"He's a big fan of those Scandinavian crime dramas," said Stewart.

"They are excellent," added Wilson.

"Yeah," said Brigit, "as long as you don't mind people staring wistfully at fjords for an hour when they're supposed to be solving a crime."

Stewart grinned. He was really starting to like her despite himself.

There was a brisk knock at the door, followed by it opening and Desk Sergeant Moira Clarke putting her head around.

"Can I've a word please, DI Stewart?"

Stewart stood and made his way to the door. "I'll be right back," he said to Nurse Conroy, before nodding in Wilson's direction. "If he tries anything of a 'sexual context', scream."

"What about if I try something?" Brigit said.

"Ah," said Stewart, "trying to establish an insanity defence early doors, are you? Clever!"

Wilson blushed as Brigit tried to hide her smile behind a nervous cough.

Stewart joined Clarke in the hall, closing the door of the interview room behind him. "You will not believe what Wilson..."

The words died in his throat as he saw the expression on Moira's face.

"About your corpse..."

A few minutes later, Stewart returned to his seat in interview room two, picked up his pen and looked across at Brigit.

"Miss Conroy, have you ever heard of a gentleman called Jackie 'Grinner' McNair?"

Stewart's heart sank as her face lit up.

"The guy from the Rapunzel case? Known associate of the

infamous Fallons and..." She noticed DI Stewart's facial expression and stopped talking.

Stewart put his pen down, closed his eyes and rubbed the bridge of his nose between the thumb and forefinger of his left hand.

Complicated.

He spoke without looking up.

"Wilson, be a good lad and go and get the heater."

CHAPTER EIGHT

Fidelma O'Brien 1935-2010
God's humble angel has been returned unto Him.

Paul looked down at the grave. It was always so annoyingly well maintained. He wondered if she'd paid someone to look after it. He preferred that to the idea that the sour-faced old biddy had friends. A wreath of purple flowers, only slightly withered around the edges, sat at the base of the headstone. Maybe there was a florist somewhere that was getting paid a monthly stipend just like he was? He hoped so. Anything that took money away from those bloody donkeys was alright by him.

As tired as he'd been when he'd arrived home from the hospital, he'd not been able to sleep. He had to stick to schedule. Today was Friday. Getting stabbed by a demented corpse-in-waiting didn't change that. If anything, it made sticking to schedule all the more important.

Every Friday, without fail, he visited the offices of Greevy and Co Solicitors to deliver his slips, calling at the graveyard on the way, not that it was actually on the way. Although he refused to discuss it, Paul got the definite impression that Mr Greevy was due a percentage when Fidelma's estate was finally liquidated. Certainly, Paul's gaming of the system seemed to wind him up no end. Greevy had even hired a private investigator to make sure Paul wasn't doing anything to violate the terms of the will. Darren had followed him for a fortnight and they'd got on. Paul had brought him out the odd cup of tea and Darren had given him a lift to the shops that time. It'd been a shame when that investigation was over; Paul missed the company.

Over the last seven years, four months and two weeks, Greevy's speeches had gone from encouraging, to exasperated to openly hostile, before finally arriving at their current state of virtual non-existence. 'This stipend was meant to be a temporary measure Mr Mulchrone, your Great-Aunt Fidelma never meant for you to live off it permanently.' Which of course was exactly the point. What was it they said? Living is the best revenge. It certainly was for Paul. He was aware that he'd got himself into a staring match with a dead woman and he was unwilling to blink first.

Paul looked around him. The only living souls in sight were an old man at the far side of the graveyard and the incongruous poodle yapping at his heels. Even from a distance, they didn't fit. Paul wondered briefly if the dog had been the beloved pet of a dearly departed wife? Regardless, the dog was an inappropriate bundle of energy amongst the dead; perhaps it was just excited about being in the presence of all these bones?

Paul turned back to the gravestone.

"Humble angel?" he read. "You picked that inscription yourself ye daft old... You know as much about irony as you do about compassion."

There had been a time when Paul had wondered why he did this. Why he called to Fidelma's grave every week. Not any more. Now he knew. It was to refill the anger. It was the thing that kept him going when he was wearing three jumpers indoors to save on the heating, or eating 'whoops sticker' potluck most every night, or spending six hours a week visiting the near dead to prove a point to one long-dead old battleaxe. John Lydon had it right, anger is an energy. He didn't need approval. He didn't need people. All he needed was the anger.

He recited his own special weekly prayer:

"You could've helped Ma, but you didn't. You could've helped me but you didn't. And then you think you can run my life from the grave? Fuck you."

On a couple of occasions previously he'd spit after he said it, but he didn't do that anymore. It felt like it was only confirming exactly what Fidelma had thought of him. 'The bastard son of a wanton hussy' – that was what she had called him on the second and last time they had met. He'd discussed it with that psychiatrist they'd sent him to. He'd had a Mohawk that made him look like a white, skinny Mr T and he'd told Paul that he was suffering from acute abandonment anxiety. Then the Health Service had transferred the shrink to Limerick. Unlike his great-aunt, Paul was intimately familiar with irony.

Paul turned on his heels and started walking away into the cold November wind. He got two plots down before he turned back.

"Oops sorry, nearly forgot." Paul put his hand into his jeans pocket and pulled out the two slips. "There you go ye mad old bitch, six hours and five minutes of charity work, consider my moral fibre duly improved. See you next week."

He shoved the slips back into his pocket, before reaching down, snatching up the wreath and walking away.

Janet Mulchrone 1968-1998

Paul stared at the blank space under the name. He'd scrimped and saved for two years to get her a proper headstone and when it had come down to it, he'd not known what inscription to have. It'd felt too big, too complicated, too overwhelming. How did you sum up a life in a few words?

The graves down this end were noticeably not as well-maintained. Her pristine bed was conspicuous amongst the others, which were all over-run with weeds to various degrees. Last summer, he'd spent a day cleaning up the entire row. She'd have liked that. Perhaps it was time to do it again, when his shoulder was better.

"Hiya Ma, I'm fine. Don't mind the sling, it's just a... Well, it's hard to explain. I kind of got caught up in something. I'll sort it out. It'll be grand. I did a favour for that nurse I mentioned a couple of weeks ago. It all got a bit stabby. I'm alright though, better than the other fella anyway."

He struggled over what to say next. He realised how stupid it was to not want to worry a dead woman. Still, he couldn't bring himself to go into details. The memory of his mother's smiling face flashed before him again. At least, he thought it was her. He didn't have any photos. He tried hard to hold onto her memory but he was worried that other faces, other smiles, other eyes, were leaking in and polluting it. He'd attempted to learn how to draw when he was a teenager but he'd never come close to capturing it. He'd stopped when he noticed that the memory was starting to resemble the drawings, rather than vice versa. Every week he stood here and tried to refresh an ever-fading picture in his mind.

He didn't cry any more but not in the good way. It didn't feel like healing. It felt like dying. The second of the two recurring dreams he had, was the stuff of pure nightmares. He'd wake in his bed and everything would appear normal until he pulled the sheets back. His toes would be a shade of granite grey. Try as he might, he couldn't move them. And then he'd blink and his feet would be the same. He'd reach down to touch them and they'd be as smooth as marble and as cold as ice. As he pulled his fingers away, he'd notice they were stone now too. And so it would spread up his body. The dream always ended the same way. He'd be desperate to scream but unable to draw breath. And then he'd wake, covered in sweat.

He bent down and carefully placed the purple wreath at the foot of the gravestone.

"I'll see ye next week Ma."

CHAPTER NINE

"Is this a wind-up?"

DI Jimmy Stewart and his now thoroughly foul mood had gone up to the sacred rooftop to enjoy some much-needed peace and quiet. Well that, and a cigarette he'd bummed off Desk Sergeant Clarke. The rooftop was dubbed sacred by the smokers on the National Bureau of Criminal Investigation as it allowed for an unobserved cheeky fag, while also giving a view of both the car park of Garda Headquarters and a couple of enclosures of Dublin Zoo next door. Admittedly, the view hadn't been the same since they'd moved the giraffes, but it still beat the official smoking area hands-down. Between its location being downwind of the bins and within sight of the window of the Commissioner's offices, the official enclosure was only inhabited by the slow-witted or fatally unambitious.

There was a bite in the air that felt like snow might be coming. In a move that showed he either didn't understand gravity or the extent of DI Stewart's heartfelt dislike for him, Wilson had followed him up to the roof. The only thing cheering Stewart up was the image of assisting Wilson in taking a headfirst dive into the nice parking spaces below. He'd do it too – the long-suffering Mrs Stewart had informed him over breakfast that she'd signed them both up for a pottery class.

"You've seriously never heard of Rapunzel?" continued DI Stewart.

"The fairy tale?"

"Not the f…" Stewart could feel his eyelid starting to twitch. "The case! One of the most famous cases in Irish criminal history."

Wilson gave him a blank look that reminded Stewart of what it was like to have teenaged children.

Stewart sighed before rolling out his most deliberately patronising tone. "The year was 1985 – Bono was into Jesus, Bob Geldof was into Africa and statues of the Virgin Mary were moving about so much you were doing well to catch one standing still. In the middle of all that, the shitstorm that was Rapunzel hit."

"To be fair, I wasn't even born."

"You weren't around for World War II either, but I assume the name Hitler rings a bell? What were you doing on that Criminology degree, just sitting around watching *Silence of the Lambs* over and over again?"

"I've never even seen that film."

"What the… how've you… it's an absolute classic! Were you hatched out of an egg six weeks ago or something?"

They descended into a frosty silence as neither man looked at the other. A pigeon landed on the ledge between them, took a quick gander about and quickly decided that being anywhere else was a wise move.

Stewart tossed the remains of his fag over the ledge and immediately regretted it. There was half a drag left in it and he didn't have another one. He couldn't buy a pack. If the long-suffering Mrs Stewart found out he was smoking again, cancer would be way down the list of things likely to kill him.

"So are you going to fill me in?" asked Wilson warily.

Stewart considered it. The reality was, they were right in the middle of this thing now whether he liked it or not – and Wilson needed to at least know enough to know when he should shut the hell up, which was pretty much always as far as Stewart was concerned.

"Alright kiddies, gather round for story time." He pulled his overcoat closer around him and noticed Wilson hadn't brought his. If he dragged this out long enough, the wintry conditions could do law enforcement a massive favour.

"The biggest thing to remember about criminals is they're mostly not that smart. In the 1970s – the IRA needed money to fund their blah blah blah, so they ripped off banks and post offices. The ordinary decent criminals saw this and they copied it, so the next thing you knew every gobshite who could cut two holes in a tea cosy thought he was John Dillinger."

"Who?"

Stewart rolled his eyes and ignored the question. "So many banks were getting ripped off, they were having to open a separate queue for withdrawals at gunpoint. Gradually security got better, we got armed response units and surveillance. Some gurriers got gunned down and the whole bank robbing thing went the way of prog rock."

Stewart could see Wilson consider the prog rock question and reject it. Maybe there was hope for him yet.

"Around rolled the eighties – shoulder pads, synth pop and the IRA had a new game, kidnapping. You weren't anybody back in them days until the Provos had tried to kidnap you. And what the Provos did...?"

"The others followed."

"Exactly. Soon every wannabe gangster was stocking up on rope and masking tape, and every off-duty guard was coining it in protecting the rich and the famous. Actually, mainly the rich – you'd be an idiot to go after the famous. People would notice if Chris de Burgh went missing. There'd be parties in the street."

"Who?"

"Now on that one, you're not missing much," said Stewart. "So anyway, there's plenty of high profile kidnappings; some we foil, some get screwed up, some go horribly wrong, but a lot just get paid off.

Then along comes Sarah-Jane Kruger née Cranston, the new blushing bride of one Daniel Kruger. She is the only daughter and apple in the eye of daddy Cranston, Duke of Berkshire or some such – cousin and hunting buddy of HRH Lizzy Windsor herself. Daniel is heir to the Kruger fortune, a family with no shortage of money thanks to owning an honest-to-God goldmine in South Africa, but they're low on kudos for the same reason. This being back when auld Nelson Mandela, God rest him, was still taking on all comers in the prison chess championships."

Wilson nodded his understanding – so at least he'd seen *some* movies.

"Rumour has it the Cranston-Kruger nuptials weren't the most romantically inspiring of affairs. The Cranstons were flat broke and needed the Kruger dirty money to keep living like the royalty they almost were. In exchange, Danny-boy Kruger gets to be Lord of whatever when the old fella eventually pops off to the big members-only golf club in the sky."

"Nice."

"He also gets a genuine Disney Princess for a bride to boot, and she is not exactly hard on the eye."

"Very nice." Wilson threw in an attempt at a blokey eyebrow waggle that Stewart entirely ignored.

"Yes, especially as he's like... what ye call it..." Stewart held his hand over the left side of his face.

"Blind?"

"No, not... like thingy – Andrew Lloyd Webber." Stewart clicked his fingers in frustration at the words that wouldn't come.

Wilson face scrunched up in confusion. "He's Andrew Lloyd Webber?"

"No I mean... like the musical, the famous one... and if you say *Cats*, I will boot you off this roof."

"*Phantom of the Opera*?"

"Yes!" Stewart threw his hands up in relief. "Thank you. He's like the fella in that, you know – his face all messed up on one side."

"How'd that happen?"

Stewart considered the question. "D'ye know, I can't remember. I think it was something in his childhood, accident or something."

"That's the rich for you," said Wilson. "They think up more ways to mess up their kids by breakfast than the rest of us could come up with in a lifetime."

"What did your da do again?"

It was Wilson's turn to ignore a question. "So this bloke's virgin bride gets swiped?"

"Yeah," said Stewart, "from their massive country estate down South somewhere, while hubby and his mates are out shooting half the local wildlife."

"So what happens?"

"All hell breaks loose is what. They get a demand for three million in uncut diamonds."

Wilson whistled.

"They've done their homework, Kruger can get that – given time. An exchange is set up and..."

"And what?"

"Nothing. The kidnappers never show. No further communication either. Everybody blames everybody else. There's rumours big Lizzy herself gets on the phone to make her displeasure known."

"Holy shit."

"Oh, you've no idea. Keep in mind, a woman who is all but royalty has disappeared, and this is about the time of the Anglo-Irish agreement so everybody is trying to play nice. This shitstorm is a national embarrassment. All police holidays cancelled, overtime up the wazoo as the biggest manhunt in the history of the state is launched – aka Operation Rapunzel."

"Any leads?"

"Oh yes, thousands. Crackpots are coming out of the woodwork and that's before the half a mill reward is announced. People are taking their kids out of school to go play find the princess."

"I bet."

"After about a week, somebody finally notices that one Gerry Fallon, a young up-and-comer in the Dublin underworld is looking a little lonely because his brother Fiachra and his best mate Jackie 'Grinner' McNair have disappeared."

"Have they now?"

"Yeah, according to Gerry the boys are on holidays, backpacking across Europe."

"Nicely untraceable."

"Indeed, although there's no record of them leaving the country. They've been low-key up until this point but serious. McNair is mainly muscle; everybody knows Gerry is the brains of the outfit. Younger brother Fiachra, on the other hand, is the baby-faced beauty of the bunch, quite the hit with the ladies. The three of them were previously as tight as tight can be. Their mother raised the brothers McNair alone, their father having disappeared. There's even a legend that says a 12-year-old Gerry killed daddy with a wrought iron poker for putting his hands on their ma."

"Holy shit," exclaimed Wilson. "Did he?"

"Ah, who knows? Maybe he hopped a ferry. He wouldn't be the first. Anyway," said Stewart, "the days drag on and nothing more concrete comes up. The two boys stay disappeared, as does poor old Sarah-Jane Cranston-Kruger. Fiachra is known to have lived in Scotland for a while but all investigations over there lead nowhere too. In the absence of any real news, all kinds of rumours start to circulate: she was never kidnapped, something fishy happened at the exchange and the diamonds are now with some dodgy South Africans or..."

Some dodgy Gardai, was the other rumour that even now, Stewart didn't want to mention within an arse's roar of this building. Some careers sank without trace on this one.

"Then another story emerges. Ms. Cranston was seen getting on a boat off the Kerry coast in the middle of the night in the company of the dashing young Fiachra Fallon, and she doesn't look like any kind of prisoner."

"Noooo!"

"Yeah. Young love's fresh bloom and all that."

"And people buy that?"

"Well, it's looked into but so is every theory. There's all kinds of pressure to get a result remember. Six months later, out comes the infamous *Hostage to Love* book— "

"Awful title..."

"You're not wrong, but people lap it up. Tells the tale of a miserable princess sold into marital slavery and rescued by the handsome pauper, who kidnaps her and then steals her heart."

"A modern day fairy tale."

"Yeah," said Stewart. "Every few years there's talk of a Hollywood film. Colin Farrell is supposed to be interested."

"Jesus."

"Kruger sues of course, which just makes the book an even bigger seller. He becomes a laughing stock and nobody has seen him since. The book makes us peelers look like the Keystone Cops too. In its version of events, Gerry Fallon risks all to get his beloved baby brother and his hostage cum love-of-his-life out of the country while evading the entire Irish police force."

"Ahh, pass the tissues."

"This is *the* Gerry Fallon, mind you, the coldest of cold bastards. The one gangster above all others we've never got our hooks into. The guy that outran the Criminal Assets Bureau. Fuck it, scratch that – he lapped the fecking thing. They had to issue an apology when his name ended up in the paper. It was a joke. Everyone assumes these days that Gerry is free and clear on legit street. Making him untouchable by us poor simple Johnny Law types."

Stewart leaned back and looked up into the darkening winter sky.

"Here's the kicker though; in the book, Grinner McNair dies after he turns on Fiachra and decides he doesn't want to give up a million quid so his buddy can get his end away. As of two hours ago we know that's bollocks. He didn't take a dive off a trawler in the North Atlantic. He was right there – in St Kilda's for the last three weeks – Grinner bloody McNair! The man who knew what happened to

Sarah-Jane Cranston. Not to mention being the one bloke who could very probably put Gerry Fallon behind bars."

"Shit."

Stewart looked down and watched as a large Merc with a motorbike escort pull up to the front gates.

"And now all we've got left is the poor sod who killed him."

CHAPTER TEN

She took a long, deep breath.

"Mr Mulhare, I want you to know that I am a competent, confident and committed lawyer. Rest assured that here at Greevy and Co Solicitors our number one priority is you, the client. You are more than just a customer to us. To us, you're family."

"Great," said Paul. "My second name is actually Mulchrone."

"I knew that..." she responded quickly. "Just a little lawyer joke there, trying to lighten the mood and – oh my God, will you stop kicking me in the vagina!"

The last part of the statement was not directed at Paul. It was directed at her own immense belly because Nora Stokes was pregnant. Heavily pregnant. She'd not actually said so but Paul had picked up on the signs. The laboured breathing, the obvious discomfort, the fact she was currently occupying what felt like more than half of the available space in the unpleasantly clammy office. Paul had had very limited experience of pregnant women but he was discovering that he found them incredibly intimidating. The whole conversation felt like a game of verbal Buckaroo. As if him saying the wrong thing at the wrong time might result in her giving birth right there and then, just to spite him.

"Sorry," said Nora, "that remark wasn't meant for you," as she repositioned herself in her chair and winced slightly. "The little fella has incredible aim. Every time he... never mind. You're here, you've got a problem – you don't want to hear about my v..." She put out her hand as if to physically stop herself talking. "Sorry, sorry, you were saying?"

Paul looked at her across the desk. She was perspiring, her blonde hair was matted to the side of her face and, he didn't want to say anything but, her left breast appeared to be leaking. There was a small patch on her pale blue maternity dress that was getting steadily larger. He was unsure of the etiquette in this situation.

Nora Stokes appeared to be the entirety of the Co in Greevy and Co Solicitors. They had never spoken before. Paul had always dealt with her boss. It wasn't as if he actually liked Shane Greevy, the lawyer tasked with administering his great-aunt's will, quite the opposite in fact. Their relationship was built on mutual loathing, but there was an odd kind of comfort in it. Paul knew Greevy was going to try and use his current predicament, vis-à-vis being a potential murder suspect, to say Paul had broken the terms of the will. He had a carefully constructed argument lined up in his head to try and stop Greevy in his tracks before he started. He couldn't argue his case if his opponent had, for the first time in seven years, declined to show up. Greevy was reliable and ever-present; as far as Paul was concerned, it was his only redeeming feature.

"Just to recap," said Paul. "Mr Greevy is definitely 100% unavailable?"

"Correct," said Nora.

"Is there any way we can..."

"Not going to happen."

"But..."

"No way, no how."

"It's just..."

"Alright, look, Mr..." She gave him an impatient look, indicating he should fill in the blank for her.

"Mulchrone."

"Mulchrone," she repeated. "Here's the situation. Shane Greevy is not here. He is in Italy with his wife, trying to save the empty shell that is their marriage."

"I see," said Paul.

"It's pointless, but whatever."

"Could we..."

"He doesn't love her!" said Nora. "He's just scared to leave her."

"You see," said Paul, "he's been my lawyer for seven years now and he's fully briefed on..."

"It's the money." She interrupted. "He can't stand the idea of how much she'd get in a divorce. He's a cheap bastard, always has been. That's why a heavily pregnant woman is here, holding down the fort, on her own, while he is off in Milan wining and dining that sour-faced bitch."

"Right," said Paul.

"Now," said Nora, "before I ran to the toilet you mentioned you thought you were about to be arrested. Can I ask what for?"

"Murder," said Paul.

"Oh for fuck's sake!"

"Was that the baby again?" asked Paul.

"No," said Nora. "No. That was all you."

Nora picked up her handbag.

"It is all a big misunderstanding," said Paul.

"Of course," said Nora, "I believe you."

"In which case, would you mind taking your hand off the can of Mace you're currently holding in your bag?"

She stared across the table at him. "Excellent. Good. Those powers of observation will serve us well in mounting a vigorous defence of your innocence."

"Yeah," said Paul, "you're still holding it."

"I'm going to be honest with you Mr..."

"Mulchrone," said Paul.

Mulchrone," she repeated, "because I think we need to build a relationship based on trust. I'd like to put the Mace down, I really would, but I'm not in charge of my own body right now. I'm being swept along by a tidal wave of raging hormones and, apparently, they want me to hold onto the Mace. OK? "

"OK," said Paul.

"Don't be offended," said Nora, "I'm not in control. Yesterday – peed myself in the supermarket. The baby head-butted me right in the bladder. Did you know they could do that? Oh yeah – they keep that one quiet."

"Oh," said Paul, because he felt something was expected.

"My point is…"

Nora looked around for a point she'd long since misplaced. The moment of silence stretched out. Weirdly, it didn't feel awkward. Nora gave Paul a sad little smile that managed to be both strong and brittle at the same time. "OK, look," she said. "We're both in a tricky spot right now but, if we work together, I think we can get through this. Alright?"

"Alright."

"Good," said Nora. She smiled at him again. "I'm not supposed to ask this but – did you do it?"

"Absolutely not," said Paul.

"Good. I believe you."

"Phew!" said Paul, "Now if we could just convince everyone else of that."

Nora felt suddenly compelled to straighten some of the paperwork on the desk.

"Seeing as we're being honest," said Nora. "This… is Greevy's baby."

"Oh," said Paul, because he felt something was expected.

CHAPTER ELEVEN

Tyrion 4.12.AX4 – Secure server software
Initialising private peer-to-peer communication
Please wait............. Initialised.

RoyTheBoy07: We have two jobs that require your services.
CerburusAX: OK. when?
RoyTheBoy07: ASAP.
CerburusAX: U give details, I will check out and come back to u with schedule.
RoyTheBoy07: We have a schedule. You've got until 2PM today.
CerburusAX: Not possible.
RoyTheBoy07: Double your normal fee.
CerburusAX: U can triple, not matter. We not work like that.
RoyTheBoy07: It is an emergency.
CerburusAX: Ur emergency, not ours.
RoyTheBoy07: It must be done.
CerburusAX: We r surgeons, for this u need butcher.
RoyTheBoy07: My employer wants you.
CerburusAX: No.
RoyTheBoy07: Time is running out.

CerburusAX: I recommend people.

RoyTheBoy07: He wants you.

CerburusAX: No. Final word. U r wasting u time.

RoyTheBoy07: As you wish. Your name is Draco Dangash.

CerburusAX: LOL. No.

RoyTheBoy07: Your partner is your brother Gregor.

CerburusAX: This bullshit. Goodbye.

RoyTheBoy07: Your niece…

RoyTheBoy07: Draco?

CerburusAX: Yes?

RoyTheBoy07: She will be returned safely to you, once the job is completed. You have our word.

CerburusAX: Funny man. I have no niece.

RoyTheBoy07: Theresa. 13. She has not come home from school yet. Feel free to check.

CerburusAX: She is fine, is right here.

RoyTheBoy07: Don't bluff Draco. Time is running out.

CerburusAX: U hurt her, we fucking come for u!!!

RoyTheBoy07: We don't want to. Do not force our hand. Do the job – easy targets I assure you. She is safe, you will get quadruple the normal fee.

CerburusAX: Send details.

RoyTheBoy07: Sending…

CHAPTER TWELVE

Paul slumped into his armchair, causing a stinging pain to run from his wounded shoulder down his arm. He'd have to be a little more careful with his slumping for a while. He was in a thoroughly bad mood. Today, if anything, was turning out worse than yesterday, and seeing as it had ended with him being stabbed by a homicidal octogenarian that was really saying something. He should probably try and get some sleep but he was too annoyed right now. Instead, he sat in his careworn and ragged throne and surveyed his kingdom.

When the bloke had come around last year to install the water meter, he'd asked Paul if he was one of those survivalist nutjobs. He had to admit, it was an understandable mistake to make. In one corner of his sitting room stood a tower of toilet rolls, in the other, a tower of tinned goods. It wasn't just that Paul loved a bargain, the paltry amount the monthly stipend provided meant that he relied on bargains for survival. He had become an expert forager in the urban jungle. The tinned goods were from one of the cut-price German supermarkets. He checked the three within walking distance every Wednesday. He still had 98 cans of peas that he'd managed to get for 5 cents a throw thanks to a printing error on the label. They were absolutely fine once you got by the 'pees' thing. The loo roll was a batch from an office building that was closing down; five euros for literally as much as he could carry. Sure, he'd got some funny looks walking back through town but it had been worth it. He hit Moore Street markets every Saturday and Tuesday afternoon just as the stalls were closing up, looking for any fruit and veg that was taking a turn for the cheap. The stallholders called him 'The Dumpster', not entirely out of affection. Last month, one of them had taken the hump with his haggling so much that she'd elected to use the browning bananas he was negotiating over as projectiles instead. She got really annoyed when Paul had calmly picked them up off the cobbled street and put them in his bag. God, he missed the horse meat scandal. That had been a blessed few months. He had eaten like a king!

Paul shivered. He'd removed his coat and jumper as soon as he got home and he was starting to feel the cold now. He was training himself to get used to not having the heating on. The electricity company had raised the rates yet again. He'd taken the jumper off so he could hold it in reserve for later on when the temperatures really took a tumble. He was still wearing the 'I Beat Cancer' T-shirt that Dr Sinha had given him. Normally, he was delighted with any freebies but this one didn't have many happy memories associated with it.

Paul's mobile vibrated on the counter again. He pointedly ignored it. He had come out of the meeting with Nora Stokes to find six missed calls from Paschal Clarke, a manager at Mountainview, the hospital he visited on Mondays.

"Hi, eh, Mr Mulchrone... Paul. This is Paschal Clarke here. Just wanted to say that there's no need for you to come and visit next Monday or... no need really. We appreciate you popping by but, we've changed the visiting rules to be relatives only because of... overcrowding and... We hope you're OK and... probably, probably best not to mention Mountainview in any... y'know because.... Y'know... and... yeah, so..." BEEP.

Overcrowding? That was a laugh. Last time he'd been there the oldies had been so desperate for conversation, a queue had formed.

He'd not returned the call. There didn't seem any point in

pleading his case. Inexpertly though it was delivered, the message was all too clear. It seemed getting stabbed by a lunatic was going to be very bad, if not fatal, for the granny whispering business. He'd have to find some other charity work. Work he could do with a banjaxed shoulder. Fingers-crossed some old dear had died and one of the charity shops might have an opening.

On the upside, today was Friday, which meant it was treat night, i.e. dinner and a movie. The dinner would consist of a takeaway from The Oriental Palace, the second cheapest takeaway in all of Dublin. Paul wondered if there was any way he could find out Mickey's second name in casual conversation.

The movie would be a DVD. Paul didn't own a TV licence for obvious reasons. On the floor surrounding the TV were piles and piles of DVDs, 427 at the last count. They'd all been bought for a euro or less. That was the rule; any movie was a bargain for under a quid. While he found the occasional cinematic classic in a charity shop, he proudly considered himself a connoisseur of the arse-end of Hollywood. He took a perverse delight in watching dreadful straight-to-DVD, bargain bin stuffers. Last Sunday had been entirely filled up with a Steven Seagal marathon. Watched in chronological order, the man's career was a damning indictment of punching as a cardiovascular exercise to aid weight loss.

In addition to dinner and a movie, he had a six pack of truly awful unpronounceable Eastern European beer that had been on a very special offer. After tasting one, Paul had understood why. Still, after two, you couldn't taste anything so he could comfortably get pissed on it. If the government ever did pass that minimum unit price for alcohol, it'd be a toss-up between giving up booze or having to take cold showers.

The front room was light on traditional decoration. Above the mantelpiece hung the picture of great-aunt Fidelma that had been there when he'd moved in. What kind of warped individual had a portrait of themselves hanging above their own fireplace? Paul left it there to warm the cockles of his hatred on the coldest nights. Three framed photographs that did belong to him sat on the mantelpiece.

The one on the left contained a family photo; a dark-haired father with his slightly-too-hot-for-him wife, and their three blonde haired, blue-eyed kids, frolicking around in the park. Their Yorkshire terrier leapt about, orgasmically delighted just to be involved in the whole thing. The picture had come with the frame, which he'd found in EuroWorld. He'd often wondered if those people really were a family, or just models hired for a job. He hoped it was the former. It'd be nice to know such things existed. When drunk on sour-tasting beer, he'd occasionally considered going on a quest to track them down and see if he could join. Even if they weren't a real family, maybe he could convince them all they should be. It could work.

The picture in the right-hand frame had also come with it. It was of a boat. He'd no strong feelings either way about boats.

The large central frame contained a team photo of the St Jude's under-12s hurling team that he'd been a part of. Paul stood up and moved closer to it. He looked at the faces, lingering on his own. There he was, sitting just left of centre on the front row of a squad of 27 young fellas, all grinning back at the lens, full of hope and devilment. He remembered being happy at the time, proud to belong. It bothered him that, looking at it now, his smile looked forced. Like, even then, he'd lived with a perpetual wince, always waiting for the other shoe to drop. At the end of the line stood their coach, one eye on the camera, the other looking for any little bowsers daring to try and sneak a cheeky V sign into his picture. Bunny McGarry, the mad-eyed missionary, bringing hurling to the soccer-loving heathens of inner-city Dublin, whether they liked it or not.

He was disturbed from his reverie by his phone vibrating yet again. Right, that was it! Paschal Clarke was about to get both bloody barrels. Paul walked across and snatched his mobile up from the counter. Unknown number.

"Hello."

"Paulie?"

"Yeah."

"Run!"

Paul had been mentally gearing himself up to give a middle

management busybody a piece of his mind, and now he was having trouble resetting himself.

"Who is..."

"There's no time. If you want to live, RUN!"

"But? What?"

The phone went dead.

"Hello? Hel..."

Two thoughts occurred to Paul in quick succession. Firstly, he realised with a jolt who the voice was. On reflex, he looked back to the team picture on the mantelpiece. There he was, a lanky bundle of ill-fitting limbs, gurning in the back row, 16 years and a world away. It'd taken a while to process as it had been a few years since they'd spoken. In the brief gap between thoughts, several complicated emotions welled up, before being washed away when the second thought hit.

That wasn't complicated at all.

He had to run.

CHAPTER THIRTEEN

"Who else knows about this?"

DI Jimmy Stewart stared calmly across the table at Veronica Doyle and didn't answer her question. She held some unspecified position at the Ministry for Justice. Early 30s, black hair tied up in a bun, long neck, pert little nose. In general, Stewart was a sucker for a woman with a cute nose. The long-suffering Mrs Stewart had a beauty. Every night before he went to sleep, regardless of what time he got in, she'd wake to ask how he was. He'd always say 'fine', and then kiss her on the forehead, the lips and then on that cute little button nose. It was the kind of tiny private ritual that made up a 36-year marriage. The thought gave him a little smile in an otherwise crappy day.

He didn't like Veronica Doyle's nose so much, however, mainly because she was trying to stick it into his business.

"Do I need to repeat the question?" she asked.

"I'd certainly like you to take a run at asking it more politely," Stewart responded. Beside him, he could feel Wilson shifting in his seat, as if trying to distance himself. The young fella might not have been the brightest, but even he'd been smart enough to keep his mouth shut in this meeting.

"Alright, enough of this bullshit, Jimmy." The interjection came from the man sitting to Veronica Doyle's right, irritation now etched across his face. A notable face it was too – Assistant Commissioner in Charge of Operations – Fintan O'Rourke no less. Beloved of the guard on the street and everyone's sure-fire certainty for the big job one day, especially as herself had been having a rough time of it since taking it on 18 months ago. O'Rourke was maybe seven years younger than Stewart but the gap looked more like twenty. He'd been a long distance runner back in the day. He might not be knocking out the marathons like he used to anymore, but he'd certainly kept himself in trim. There was an almost suspicious lack of grey anywhere on the man's well-groomed head of dark-brown hair.

They'd crossed paths a few times over the years. Stewart had in fact given O'Rourke a tour of the station on his first day up in Clondalkin as a newly-minted detective officer. Up from the country, a wet-behind-the-ears Waterford lad, possessed of that mix of nervousness and arrogance that all young bucks have when they first get that detective's badge. Stewart had found him amusing. When he'd met him again a couple of years later, the difference had been stark. He may've been thrown in at the deep end, but O'Rourke had learned to swim with the ease of a newborn shark. His subsequent rise up the ranks had been fairly close to meteoric. His belief in intelligence-led policing had taken down some big game along the way, and made him a hero to the rank-and-file. He was maybe better at politics than detective work, but that was a skillset that had its uses too.

"Why don't you just spit it out, Jimmy?" said O'Rourke. "What's on your mind?"

"Well, Assistant Commissioner O'Rourke, sir, what's on my mind is this: as you well know, in any murder investigation the first 24 hours is crucial and, for the last three, myself and my colleague have been told to sit on our hands and do nothing while we wait for your good self to get here, from officiating at a passing out ceremony in Templemore I believe. Then, we get dragged into a meeting – sorry 'unofficial un-minuted chat' – where I've been spoken to like an idiot by someone who, unless I'm very much mistaken, isn't even a member of the Garda Síochána." Doyle glared daggers at him. "Furthermore, I'd guess that said person is about to question the integrity of some of my fellow officers. That is mainly what is on my mind, sir."

"I resent those remarks," said Doyle.

"Good," responded Stewart. "If you didn't, it'd mean you had not understood them correctly."

"Alright, enough," said Assistant Commissioner O'Rourke. "Jimmy, you've made your point — as always — with the barest minimum of tact, but you've made it."

O'Rourke looked down at the peaked cap of his dress uniform, sitting on the polished table of the meeting room attached to his office, and sighed. Then he glanced around, as if to confirm for the third or fourth time that the blinds were closed and nobody was watching.

"First off, Jimmy, from what you've said, it sounds like the cause of death was a combination of natural causes and self-inflicted stress, so this is hardly a murder investigation."

"It is one until it isn't." Stewart said it with more force than he'd meant. O'Rourke shot him a warning glance. Stewart could feel Wilson shifting slightly further away from him in his seat. By this point, thought Stewart, he must have nearly a whole arsecheek dangling in mid-air.

"Fair enough," continued O'Rourke. "But you know what this is Jimmy. Like it or not, this thing is a PR disaster in the offing and we want to manage that side of things as best we can for the sake of all concerned."

Stewart resisted the urge to roll his eyes. He knew what O'Rourke was saying was true. He more resented that they felt he needed to be told.

"Perhaps DI Stewart would like to step aside if he..." O'Rourke raised his hand to cut Doyle off, while simultaneously stopping Stewart's response dead.

"That is not your call, Veronica, and I would appreciate you remembering that." O'Rourke kept his eyes fixed on Stewart, so he didn't see Doyle's face snap around to look at him like she'd just been slapped in it. "DI Stewart is a superb officer and I have every confidence in his abilities."

Doyle's mouth flapped open and shut wordlessly.

Clever boy, thought Stewart. Old Rigger O'Rourke, always knew how to get somebody back onside when he needed to.

"Now, Jimmy, if we're done with the pissing contest. Who knows about Mr Brown's real identity?"

"As far as I know, Samantha from the coroner's office, Gerry from tech who ran the fingerprints and DS Moira Clarke who handled the results."

"And are they...?"

"I had a word as soon as. Everybody knows to keep shtum."

"Good."

"I checked the records and, as far as we can tell, Grinner McNair has one surviving relative, a daughter. We think we've located her living out in Tallaght. I asked for a patrol from the local station to do a knock and confirm. They've no idea why they're doing it. I told them it was just to update a record."

"Alright," said O'Rourke.

"And as I mentioned, we also had Nurse Brigit Conroy in earlier, giving a voluntary statement. She was made aware of Mr Brown's true identity, in order for us to ascertain whether she or Mr Mulchrone had had any idea who Mr Brown really was at the time of the incident."

"Where is she now?"

"Gone home I'd imagine." Doyle threw her hands up in the air theatrically. Stewart didn't fail to notice the irritated sideways look this elicited from O'Rourke. Doyle didn't know it yet, but she'd just lost the support of the most important person in the room. "I told Nurse Conroy that, as part of our ongoing investigation, we required her not to share the information with anyone at this time. She agreed not to."

"Oh great," said Doyle, not trying to hide her sarcasm.

Stewart turned calmly to her. "What would you have had me do? In this country, we don't lock up people who we believe have committed no crime."

Doyle folded her arms huffily.

"Jimmy?" said O'Rourke.

"Look, she's solid enough. You know as well as I do, Fintan, this thing is getting out at some point regardless."

O'Rourke sighed. "I know, Jimmy, I know. Lord knows how many senior coppers heard about it before it got to me. Somebody somewhere will see a chance to get in a journo's good books. Herself is shitting a brick on this."

Stewart raised his eyebrows. 'Herself' here meant the commissioner, Jane Horsham.

"I thought she was in Brazil?" It'd been on the news, global conference on something or other. She was co-chair. The Irish public loved to see anything about one of them being in charge of anything on the international stage. The Six O'Clock News would cover an international symposium on tortoise haemorrhoids if you could show an Irish person banging a gavel in a big conference hall.

"Oh she's in Brazil all right, but she still had to be informed. This chat was her idea in fact," said O'Rourke, shifting uncomfortably. "Look you know as well as I do, we've had a disastrous couple of years in terms of PR. First there was that thing down in Limerick and then that gobshite in Galway thinking he was Eliot Ness and making us all look bad." Stewart was aware of the force's current perception issue, he'd heard the jokes just like everybody else. "The last thing we need is this old mess being dredged back up again. So we need to make sure it's a one-day thing and not..."

There was a knock on the door. O'Rourke's eyes flashed annoyance.

"Come in."

His secretary, a serious looking woman in her forties, entered.

"I said not to be disturbed, Janet."

"I know, Assistant Commissioner, but I have a Sergeant Moira

Clarke outside, sir. She says it is urgent." O'Rourke and Stewart shared a look.

"Show her in."

Janet waved Moira Clarke into the room and then departed, closing the door behind her.

"Sorry, sir, but…"

"Alright, Moira, what is it?"

Moira looked at Doyle nervously. O'Rourke followed her eyes.

"You can speak freely."

"Right, sir. The patrol from Tallaght went to knock on Pauline McNair, the daughter of Jackie McNair. No answer but they heard water running. They checked the back and then booted the door in on suspicion of a member of the public being in harm's way." Clarke drew in a breath and looked nervous. "She was dead in her hallway, sir."

"Christ!" said Stewart.

"With her baby in the front room fast asleep."

"Does this…" Doyle's words were left hanging in the air, silenced by a look from O'Rourke.

Stewart asked the question that nobody wanted an answer to. "Out with it, Moira. Cause of death?"

"She had taken two shots in the chest and one in the head."

Nobody spoke… everybody moved.

CHAPTER FOURTEEN

Paul stared into the cold calm eyes of a killer...

Seventeen minutes ago, he'd put the phone down on the call telling him to run. Within 30 seconds, he'd had his hand on the front door and he was prepared to do just that. Then he realised that he didn't know what he was running from and how far he might have to go. He'd need a few things.

He'd spent the next 15 minutes packing and unpacking everything he owned into a battered old suitcase he'd inherited from great-aunt Fidelma.

Two minutes ago, the doorbell had rung. The doorbell never rang. He'd run through the possibilities. Mickey always did the 'shave-and-a-haircut' knock, plus even the best restaurants didn't deliver food you hadn't ordered yet. There wasn't an election for another couple of years. Was a door-to-door salesman still even a thing? The Jehovah's Witnesses didn't knock on doors anymore. They'd started hanging around on street corners instead. He'd read an article – apparently conversion rates were up by 400%.

Paul had crouched at the top of the stairs and peeked out. Through the warped glass around the front door, he could see a bulky figure in a leather jacket. It was either the world's keenest politician, the last door-to-door salesman on earth, or a Jehovah's Witness who'd not got the memo. He'd known deep down it wasn't any of those things. It was the thing he was supposed to run from.

One minute ago, he'd removed two framed pictures, a vinyl album and two packs of itchy underpants from the suitcase and placed them in a plastic shopping bag. The itchy pants had been a disastrous bargain purchase. Three packs of three for five euros, it turned out, really was too good to be true. They had an asbestos-like itchy quality that seemed to be heightened by the presence of any form of perspiration. Paul's future seemed unlikely to be sweat-free. He took a pack of them anyway, for the same reason he'd been unable to throw them out. It was like a low-level form of self-harm.

Then he'd closed the suitcase and opened the angled window that led onto the roof. It was less of a house and more of a two-room bungalow with an attic conversion. Standing on the suitcase had given him just enough height to drag himself awkwardly out the window with his one good arm, while his slinged hand hung onto the plastic bag.

Which brought him to now.

Seventeen minutes after the phone had rung, when a voice from his past had given him a warning. In short, 'run'. And he hadn't, at least not fast enough.

Now Paul found himself just about balanced on the three-inch-wide line of concrete between where the slate tiles of the roof stopped and the plastic leaf-filled guttering started. The cold wind whipped at the bright yellow t-shirt he still wore with the slogan 'I Beat Cancer' emblazoned across it. The smell of the Royal Canal drifted up from beneath him. Its scent was a heady mixture of stagnant vegetation and whatever cocktail of figurative and literal crap a waterway picks up as it meanders its way through a modern city, one where it had long since outlasted its usefulness. A couple of miles away the canal was gentrified, for people to stroll alongside in the fading light of happy days with significant others and thoroughbred dogs, but not here. Next stop from here was the Irish Sea. This was the flushing point.

Paul couldn't head to his right towards the top of the street. His house was three from the top, which meant it wouldn't put him far enough away from whoever was ringing his doorbell. Also, there was no possible way down at that end, bar a two-storey drop to the pavement. No, going right was out.

Then left...

That way lay the cold calm eyes of a killer.

She'd sauntered down the roof in front of him, a mouse lying casually dead in her mouth. Chairman Meow had dropped her most recent victim and then stretched out about six feet in front of him, like she was considering a mid-afternoon snooze. She was the cat belonging to Old Man Maguire over the road and she was, even by feline standards, an absolute bastard. Every time Paul had seen her over the last three years, she had been carrying some poor dead creature in her jaws.

She looked at Paul, then pointedly down at the Royal Canal below.

A couple of summers ago, Derek Carr, the previously dull civil engineer from two doors down, had cranked up The Doors' greatest hits and tried LSD for the first time. Amidst all the psychedelic furniture dancing around him, and the deep and meaningful conversation he'd been having with his own feet, he'd decided he'd love a swim. He'd opened his bedroom window, climbed out onto the roof, and dived into the canal. Lucky for Derek, there'd been a lot of flooding that summer. The water had been at about the five-foot deep level. Despite the thirty-foot drop, he'd only broken both legs.

In the one glance directly down at the waterway that Paul had allowed himself, he'd seen a shopping trolley buried in the mud at the deepest point. Its handles were sticking a foot out of the water. He reckoned it was maybe three feet deep at best – just enough water for Paul to kill himself or to wish he had.

Paul took a deep breath and tried to gather himself. He couldn't go right, he couldn't go down and, assuming that Death had really rung his doorbell, he definitely couldn't go back either. No, his only choice was going left, a 50-feet precarious walk along a three-inch wide strip of concrete to the other end of the row of terraced houses. It would have been a doable escape but for the psychotic feline that was currently blocking his path.

You learn a lot about yourself in a crisis. Paul learned he could definitely bring himself to kick a cat. He tried to build himself up to do just that, but then he played it through in his head. He could see his swinging foot failing to connect, followed quickly by the inevitable stumble to his watery doom. The last thing he'd see would be The Chairman's little white face peering down at him.

He could just step over the cat. Then, of course, she'd want to rub against his legs, playfully – just enough to trip him up and...

"Shoo!"

Paul hadn't expected it to work. He'd been right.

"Piss off — Please go away? — Din-dins!"

The Chairman showed a level of stillness that a moving statue would have found admirable.

Paul wafted his bag forward, in a motion too gentle to be threatening. The cat yawned.

"BOO!"

It hadn't surprised the cat at all but it had been enough to knock Paul's balance slightly. He felt himself tip alarmingly towards the water. He threw his arms out, awkwardly trying to right himself. He got a stab of pain from his injured shoulder for his trouble, but after a briefly sickening moment of wobble, he'd regained himself. Chairman Meow licked her lips.

Paul felt the mobile phone in his back pocket vibrate. He considered not answering it, then it occurred to him that maybe it was the voice from the past – giving him an update on the whole 'run' situation. Or... he had the unnerving image that perhaps whoever had been at the front door, was looking at him right now, possibly through a sniper rifle's sights. He looked around nervously but he couldn't see anybody. He fished it out. Unrecognised mobile phone number. For want of any clue what else to do, he answered the phone.

"Hello?"

Chairman Meow gave him an annoyed look, the kind you'd give your steak if it had stopped to take a call.

"Paul, it's Brigit."

"Oh ehm... Brigit?"

"You know, the nurse who drove you home and then you slammed a door in her face. I got your number off your hospital admittance files."

"To be honest, now isn't a great time."

"Charming! I've been trying to ring you for nearly two hours."

"Yeah I've been..."

"Whatever. Look, there's been a development. That Brown fella – not really called Brown. He's..."

A thought struck Paul and he interrupted her. "Do you know anything about cats?"

"Oh yeah, because obviously any single woman in her thirties has a dozen cats!"

Paul wasn't certain what, but he knew he'd said the wrong thing.

"I wasn't implying..." Paul stopped, as he realised he wasn't entirely sure what he was not implying.

"Listen, will ye?" said Brigit. "This is serious – you might be in trouble!"

"I definitely am in trouble. Do you know how to get rid of a cat?"

"Are you high?"

Paul looked around him.

"In a manner of speaking. Look, I'm sorry about before but please – I think somebody is trying to kill me. I'm trapped and – I've no time to explain but seriously, it's life and death. Now, for the love of God, please tell me how you can really annoy a cat!"

There was a moment's silence.

"Well, my cat hates when I whistle."

"Right. I can't whistle."

"What kind of a person can't whistle?"

"Me. That's who."

Chairman Meow stretched her legs and casually started walking towards Paul. She seemed annoyed to have lost her prey's undivided attention and had decided to retake the initiative.

"Can you please whistle?" Paul tried to keep the panic from his voice as he watched the cat's casual advance.

"Are you taking the piss?"

"Please – I'm begging you – whistle!"

There was an achingly long moment of hesitation before the sound of whistling started emanating from Paul's phone.

He held it out in front of him. Chairman Meow stopped moving forward. She tilted her head and gave him a quizzical look.

Paul began inching forward, until the whistling stopped.

"Keep going!" he shouted at the phone.

"Any requests?"

"Louder!"

The whistling resumed, this time to the tune of The Cure song 'Love cats.'

Paul continued to shuffle slowly forward, Chairman Meow remained motionless – participants in the world's slowest game of chicken. Their eyes locked – they were all of a foot away from each other now. Paul pointed the phone directly at her, like a crucifix to fend off evil. Brigit had now reached the middle eight of the song. She redoubled her efforts in a subconscious attempt to cover for not knowing that bit.

There! Just the slightest twitch of a feline ear. Chairman Meow didn't like it.

Paul continued his painfully slow shuffle of feet.

Then, as if she'd suddenly remembered a previous engagement, the cat darted off up the roof tiles and disappeared out of view.

Paul realised he'd been holding his breath and let it out in a relieved sigh. He glanced back at the four feet he'd managed to move along the ledge. The hardest won territory since the battle of the Somme. (He'd found a series of World War I documentary DVDs in a three for a euro bin).

He started moving more quickly, placing one foot in front of the other as fast as he dared, tightrope walking his way up the narrow strip. Paul put the phone back to his ear. "You can stop now."

"You're weird."

"Fair point."

"Seriously," said Brigit, "we need to talk. I found out some shocking stuff. Brown wasn't really Brown, he was there under a false name."

Paul found the walking easier when he was distracted by the call. Like his body was a lot better at coping with stuff once his mind got the hell out of the way.

"That might explain why somebody is trying to kill me," he continued.

"With a cat?"

"No..."

Paul thought about it but couldn't think of a way to offer any further explanation of what had just happened.

"Look, can we..." Paul paused to think. "Can you meet me in St Stephen's Green in about 30 minutes?"

"The park or the shopping centre?"

"The park."

"Alright."

"Thanks."

He'd reached the end of the walkway.

"But, do you not think you should go to the police?" Brigit asked.

"No way. Hang on a sec."

He looked down at the graffiti-covered 8-foot tall wall that divided a couple of empty parking spaces beside the row of terraced houses from the canal. At the other end of the wall, lay the pedestrian bridge over the canal and freedom.

With difficulty, Paul managed to slowly lower himself down to a sitting position on the roof, getting a soggy left arse cheek for his trouble, as it dipped into the black plastic guttering.

"Hang on."

Paul slipped the phone into the pocket of his jeans, then awkwardly turned himself around. He braced himself with his left arm and started slowly lowering himself down – his feet scrabbling around, trying to find purchase on the wall below.

He looked up to see Chairman Meow looking down at him. She'd gone from nowhere-to-be-seen to right in front of him, with no perceptible movement having taken place. She looked down at him, her smug satisfaction all too evident.

The cat threw a clawed left hook at his defenceless face and, by instinct, Paul pulled away. His fast reactions saved him from the Chairman's claws but only to throw him into the unwelcoming arms of gravity. He lost his grip on the roof and fell backwards. His feet fell on either side of the wall, leaving his body to land on top of it, testicles first. He hung there, captured in a perfect moment of exquisite slapstick agony. After a couple of pain-filled seconds, Madam Fate decided she hadn't had nearly enough fun with him yet, and tipped him right – away from the canal – to tumble off the wall and land on his back on the pavement 8 feet below.

The air left Paul's lungs in one percussive heave.

"Paul? Paul? What are you doing now – Paul?"

With one hand he massaged his meat and recently mashed potatoes, while with the other he slowly withdrew the phone from his pocket.

"Paul? Stop dicking about! Paul?"

"I..."

"Yes?"

His voice sounded like it was coming from a long way away. "...really hate cats."

CHAPTER FIFTEEN

DI Jimmy Stewart was in a thoroughly rotten mood.

He slammed on the brakes as an over-sized black 4X4, that cost more than twice Wilson's annual salary, pulled into the bus lane in front of them. Wilson was concentrating on keeping his face a mask of determined resolve, in an attempt to hide the fact that this was bloody brilliant. He'd been initially gutted when his offer to drive had been rebuffed, but he was glad it had been now. Stewart was livid about something and Wilson preferred his anger was directed at other road users rather than at him.

"Wilson, have you got your gun?"

"Yes, sir."

"Excellent. Then be a good lad and shoot this idiot."

This was Wilson's first trip through Dublin in an unmarked car with the siren on. If it proved anything, it was that the only way to get through the rush hour traffic quickly enough to prevent a murder was to commit several yourself.

An excited school kid in the back seat of the 4X4 was making finger guns out the window at them. At least he'd noticed they were police. His daddy seemed utterly oblivious. In fact, he looked positively outraged that the police felt they had more right to the bus lane than he did. Stewart sat on the horn and pointed the way back into the traffic jam that daddy had felt was meant for other people.

The 4X4 nudged half of itself back into the right-hand lane, enough for Stewart to mount the kerb and get by.

"Try it again."

Wilson dutifully pressed redial for the eighth time on the mobile number they had for Paul Mulchrone.

"Still voicemail."

The bus in front of them made to slow down as it approached a crowded stop. Stewart laid on the horn again. The bus driver picked up on the none-too-subtle hint and sped back up. As their car passed, several commuters expressed their displeasure through the medium of mime. Wilson resisted the urge to give an apologetic wave.

Five minutes and a good deal of industrial strength swearing later, Stewart pulled the car across traffic on the North Circular, around a corner and onto Richmond Gardens. It was a cramped looking cul-de-sac of terraced houses surrounded by a few streets of similar. Croke Park stadium loomed ominously in the background. Admittedly, it may only have appeared so to Wilson because he'd always hated GAA, and his dad had forced him to go along to matches anyway. Politics was politics.

Stewart killed the siren and turned off the engine. The cul-de-sac looked positively serene, like it was wondering what all the fuss was about.

"What number is he?"

"Sixteen," said Wilson, pointing at the house three doors from the corner.

"OK, follow my lead. Keep your eyes open and your mouth shut."

Wilson nodded and they exited the vehicle.

When they reached the door, Stewart rang the bell. There was no sound of movement from inside. Wilson tried to look through the frosted glass but couldn't see anything beyond blurred static shapes.

Stewart pressed the bell again and raised his voice.

"Mr Mulchrone, it's the Gardai. Can you…"

"Well it's about time!"

Wilson and Stewart turned around to look at the source of the voice. Behind them stood a woman who was in her seventies, a dressing gown and a very bad mood. She was glowering at them from a doorway across the street.

"I've been ringing you for months about that gobshite's car."

"Madam," said Stewart. "We're not here about a car. Can you go back inside please?"

"Don't you Madam me! This fecking monstrosity has been sitting here for months." To emphasise her point, she stepped down onto the pavement and walloped the blue Ford Cortina sitting in front of her house with a rolled-up copy of *The Herald*. The car had seen better days thought Wilson, but then so had that dressing gown.

"Like I told that lesbian from the council," she continued, "if it doesn't move, it's not a car, it's a fecking eyesore."

"Madam," Stewart said, "if that vehicle is someone else's property, then please refrain from attacking it and go back inside."

She scrunched her face up like it was in the midst of eating itself.

"Don't you talk to me like that, I know my rights. My name is Theresa Corrie and I pay my taxes. He'd one of his useless mates round here earlier on trying to fix it, for all the fecking good it did. It's still sitting here like a useless lump of… lump of…"

The old woman looked around her, as if she'd temporarily put down the appropriate insult and now couldn't find it.

"Wilson," Stewart whispered, "deal with this."

"Yes, boss."

Wilson started moving across the street, his hands outstretched, trying to remember his training on how to placate an irate member of the public. Behind him, he could hear Stewart repeatedly ringing Mulchrone's doorbell, more out of frustration than hope.

"Shite!!!" the old woman proudly proclaimed, having finally found the word she'd misplaced. The look of satisfaction on her face indicated she clearly felt her efforts to locate it had been worthwhile.

"Sitting here like a lump of shite, lump of shite!" she repeated. To emphasise her point, she walloped the car with her paper on every word.

"Please madam... ouch!" Wilson's attempt to politely guide the woman back towards her front door, had earned him a wallop across the earhole with *The Herald*.

Stewart turned, and met the old woman's glare with one of his own.

"Right, love, that's assault. We're here as part of an ongoing murder inquiry and you're in our way. Inside – right now, or I'm charging you with assaulting a police officer."

"Oh, oh – hark at him, Charlie big potatoes..."

She looked around theatrically, playing to an audience that wasn't there. Wilson looked between her and Stewart, unsure what to do.

"Threatening me!" she continued. "Ha! Sure – you wouldn't say boo to a black lad, but me – a kind-hearted pillar of the community, you'd throw me in jail for protecting myself from his sexual advances!"

She pointed the rolled up newspaper at Wilson, who stepped back and looked sheepishly around him. A man in full sexual retreat.

"Wait," said Stewart, "what did you say?"

"Sexual advances!" she hollered.

"No, not... One of his useless mates..."

Stewart dropped to his knees and peered under the car.

The old battleaxe went back to walloping the bonnet to add emphasis to her every word. "It's getting so honest decent people like me..."

"MADAM!"

She stopped, halted by Stewart's tone of voice and by the fact he was now holding his gun in his hand. Wilson could feel his own mouth drop open in shock. He couldn't remember all of his firearms training, but he was pretty sure this didn't qualify as a proportionate response. The old duffer had finally lost it. He had been making weird remarks about being too old for this shit all week, and then giving Wilson peculiar looks.

"Back away from the car now."

"Why should I?" She glowered at him defiantly.

"Because," Stewart spoke calmly and deliberately, "there's a bomb under it."

CHAPTER SIXTEEN

Brigit stopped to look in a shop window, checking she hadn't picked up a tail. She'd seen this on telly numerous times. You look in the reflection and see if anyone is following you. It was proving trickier than she'd imagined. In a movie, the extras would all walk by in straight lines and some over-muscled Eastern European guy would stutter-step, look around in confusion and give himself away. In reality, actual people were proving to be much messier than that. She'd never noticed before but on a cold winter's day, pretty much everyone was wearing a long black overcoat. It looked like a hitman convention back there.

She'd started doing the reflection trick after she'd realised the impracticalities of stopping at random to look subtly behind you. At one point, she thought she'd been quite clever, halting suddenly and taking out her phone as if looking at a map. This had given her the opportunity to take a good look at all the passers-by. She'd spent a couple of minutes checking out a tall Middle Eastern looking woman standing outside Bewley's Café. She had long legs and dyed blonde hair that ran to halfway down her back. Brigit had initially dismissed her as a threat but then admonished herself for falling prey to lazy sexism. Women could be hired thugs just as easily as men. In fact, they'd make a much less conspicuous tail, as she'd just proven.

Brigit had turned away when the blonde had noticed her looking. When she glanced back, the woman was once again looking in her direction. Brigit's pulse had raced but she'd tried to play it cool. After a couple of minutes it had dawned on her, from the blonde's perspective, she was acting suspiciously too. There was a good chance they were stuck in that awkward little game where two people are simultaneously trying to see if the other is looking at them, without being seen themselves. Brigit had been just about certain that was what was happening when the blonde's friend had turned up. She'd been pointed out and then both women had looked at her suspiciously. As Brigit had turned to make a hasty exit, she'd nearly floored one of those bloody moving statues. Instead she screamed, accidentally kicked his hat full of coins over and scampered off red-faced and mortified. Espionage was tougher than it looked.

That regrettable incident had occurred down the north end of Grafton Street. She'd since zigzagged up and back around the various side streets and was now on Clarendon Street, opposite the Westbury Hotel. This was her last attempt to 'check her six' before she headed up and across into St Stephen's Green.

She would have been embarrassed to admit to anyone what she was doing, although it did feel justified. First there'd been the revelation of who Brown really was. Maybe she should have played it cool to that nice DI Stewart, but who hadn't read *Hostage to Love*? Brigit was an obsessive fan of true crime. Most of her friends, if they read at all, generally went for tedious romance novels. The Rapunzel case was one of those rarities that combined the two. Usually, if the books she read featured any romance, it was over long before the dead bodies started showing up. Jackie 'Grinner' McNair reappearing was dramatic for several reasons; not least of which was that he supposedly died 30 years ago.

After wrestling with her conscience for a shamefully small amount of time, she'd decided to ring Paul to tell him what she'd found out. She had promised to keep it to herself but, despite him slamming a door in her face, she did feel she owed Paul the truth for dragging him into whatever this was. She didn't know what to make of his belief that someone was trying to kill him. On the one hand, he did seem a tad paranoid and secretive. On the other hand, last night someone had actually tried to kill him. She figured that she of all people had to cut the guy some slack on that front. That wasn't to say the weirdness with the cat wasn't a big red flag.

Then there'd been the voicemail she'd received after she'd finished her call to Paul. It had been DI Stewart, telling her to report back to his office at Garda HQ in the Phoenix Park immediately or, failing that, just to walk into the nearest police station and stay there until she heard from him. That'd put the wind right up her. She'd tried ringing Paul again but there'd been no answer. She pretended to herself that she had carefully considered her options, before deciding to go ahead with meeting him anyway.

Which all led back to the rather embarrassing truth of her situation; She didn't want to admit it to herself much less anyone else, but she was absolutely loving this!

Her Mam had often said that Brigit's problem was she thought she was too good for an ordinary life, but she didn't think that was fair. Brigit just felt that an ordinary life wasn't good enough for anybody. It felt like she'd been born in the safest and most boring time in human history. Everywhere in the world had been discovered. Even outer space, it seemed, was full of, well, just boring old space. There had to be more. There had to be some adventure, some magic, left in the world.

She'd desperately wanted to leave Ireland, to go out and see what life really had to offer. That was the reason behind nursing. Sure, it was no route to the high life, but there was probably an Irish nurse working in every damn country on the planet. She'd been all set to go a few years ago, an Australian contract lined up for as soon as she'd finished her training. Then Mam had got sick and, well, that was that.

She'd not resented having to do it, of course not. It was her mother. Taking care of her was the very least she could do. Maybe she resented having to be the responsible one. Her three brothers were big on 'whatever it takes' pronouncements but short on practical action. They'd each come and visit a different night of the week, and mam would insist on cooking them a dinner and making a fuss. Then they'd go back home, leaving a sink full of washing up. They'd given up an evening a week, Brigit had given up a whole new life. Then Mam had slipped away on an infuriatingly sunny Tuesday and, amidst the tears and cups of tea, she'd noticed her father sitting quietly in the corner, the loneliest man in the world. She'd brought it up with her brothers but they'd been stupid enough to think that him saying he was fine meant he was actually fine. She'd taken the job in Dublin and felt guilty as hell doing even that. Still, she went home every week, quietly making sure that he was eating right and was properly supplied with clean pants. And she didn't resent that either, how could she? What was it they said? Life is what happens when you're making other plans.

She must have been looking in the window of the clothes shop for a while, because she noticed one of the assistants looking back at her from behind the counter. She was one of those women who looked like she could have been a model, but she was an inch too short and a mile too unhappy about it. Brigit made a show of closely examining one of the coats in the window. It did look nice. Eggshell white with a fake fur lining that looked warm against a winter's chill. She had already bought a coat but she wasn't sure yet if she liked it. In her experience, the mirrors in shops lied and could not be trusted. Only the one in her flat told the truth, harsh as it often was. This meant for someone who honestly hated shopping, she spent a lot of time bringing things back. She caught sight of the price tag on the coat in the window. All those nights playing poker with her brothers for 2ps really paid off, as she was able to keep the shock from her face. Three grand!? Whoever could pay that kind of money for a coat never needed to stand outdoors.

The assistant advanced forward slightly, scenting the blood of commission in the water. Then Brigit saw her clocking the shopping bags she was carrying and the 'new best friend' smile tumbled from her lips. Nobody who'd been inside any of the stores Brigit had apparently visited had any business swimming in these waters. Brigit gave a massive smile back. Every time somebody wound her up, she liked to imagine the unhappy future life they'd have thanks to their crappy attitude. Enjoy your three marriages and your highly-strung nightmare children, ye stuck-up cow.

Brigit turned, and after one last scan of her surroundings, headed in the direction of the park. She didn't know what was going to happen next and she wasn't at all sure she was doing the right thing. She also felt more alive than she had in years.

CHAPTER SEVENTEEN

Paul sat forward on the bench, hugged himself and stamped his feet, doing the pointless things that people do when there's no real way to warm yourself up. He'd taken refuge in one of the two identical Swiss Shelters that sat on either side of the park's central circular green. The yellow 'I Beat Cancer' t-shirt was giving him precious little protection from the biting November wind. He cursed himself for wasting the few minutes he'd had before having to flee his home on sorting through DVDs, rather than doing practical stuff like putting on some more clothes. At times like this, it was hard for him to run from the suspicion that he might be an idiot.

He'd not really felt the chill on his walk down to St Stephen's Green. Constantly checking he wasn't being followed, coupled with the throbbing pain in his testicles from his earlier unhappy landing, had distracted him nicely. Now, the adrenalin rush had worn off, except for the tangy metallic taste it had left at the back of his throat. He was feeling cold, alone and testicularly sensitive.

Stephen's Green would have been rammed at this time on a summer's day with young lovers and old strollers, whiling away the hours amidst the carefully corralled nature. On a dank November afternoon, however, it was more of a pedestrian throughway than anything else. Amidst the manicured lawns and painstakingly maintained flowerbeds, primed to burst into glorious colour in the summer months, business suits hurried by under dark winter coats. Everyone was on their way somewhere else. Everyone except the man on the run, and the old lady who was so in love with Jesus she just had to dance about it.

She was in her seventies, well-dressed, and with one of those helmet-like hairdos that look like it could withstand nuclear Armageddon unruffled. She also appeared to be considerably happier with her lot in life than any of the passers-by, who were subtly altering their trajectories to avoid her. She didn't have any music, at least not that anyone else could hear. Still, there she was, dancing a one-woman conga line back and forth across the central path that traversed the park, seemingly oblivious to the world around her.

"Hello."

Paul jumped as Brigit sat down on the bench beside him.

"Jesus, you nearly scared the life out of me."

"For a man who thinks people are out to kill him, I'd have thought you'd be paying better attention."

"I don't *think* people are trying to kill me, I know they are." Paul pointed at his wounded shoulder to emphasise his point.

"How is your arm?"

"Fecking freezing, like the rest of me."

"How come?"

"I left the house in a hurry."

Brigit started rummaging through her shopping.

"Somebody's had a productive day I see," Paul said, referring to her bags.

"Well, when you've been suspended from work and ungrateful gits are slamming doors in your face, all that's left is to get the Christmas shopping done."

Paul looked down awkwardly.

"I'm sorry about the—"

"Shut up and put this on."

Brigit pushed a green jumper towards him. He spread it out on his knees to look at the design on the front. It featured the grinning face of a reindeer. Paul guessed the designer had been going for joyful for the creature's expression and just over-shot horribly. A 'here's Johnny' demented grin sat beneath wild eyes. It would have made a tremendous warning poster for the dangers of cocaine. This reindeer looked like he wanted to tell you about the incredible screenplay he was going to write and the amazing dude he'd just met in the toilets. Mind you, thought Paul – if on your one working day of the year you've to pull an all-nighter while travelling at supersonic speeds, dragging some fat drunken prick around the globe, you'd probably need a little pick-me-up too.

"What on earth is this?" said Paul.

Brigit looked embarrassed. "Last year, we had 'Christmas Jumper Day' at the hospice and I was criticised for apparently not 'getting into the spirit of things', so..."

"You're going to wear this, in front of fragile elderly patients? Why not go the whole hog and just throw some tinsel around a Grim Reaper costume?"

"Are you saying you'd rather freeze? Because I'm happy to let you."

"No, no," said Paul quickly, removing his sling and carefully sliding his wounded limb into the sleeve. Brigit watched him.

"I just realised," she said. "I've bought a stupid jumper for a job I no longer have."

"What?"

"They suspended me this morning for breaking the rules on visitors. I've got to go in front of a disciplinary committee."

Paul tried to look sympathetic as he popped his head out of the top of the jumper.

"Suspended isn't the same as fired. I'm sure it'll be fine."

Brigit made that throaty humming sound, the internationally recognised noise for 'I seriously doubt it.'

"How do I look?" asked Paul.

"Like an idiot who isn't going to die of hypothermia."

He gave her an exaggerated thumbs-up. "Result!"

They sat in silence for a moment, looking around the park. Brigit pointed over at the old woman.

"Is that the famous dancing lady?"

"No. That old dear used to get down up on O'Connell Street. Besides, I'm almost certain she died a few years ago. Her name was Mary Dunne I think."

She'd been a Dublin institution. An ordinary-looking old lady who year after year had danced about on a traffic island, waving a cross and name-checking Jesus with the frequency of a rapper at an awards show. You do anything for long enough and you become an institution. Paul had walked past her once while she'd been quietly waiting at a bus stop. It'd been weird. Like seeing a teacher out of school.

"So who is that then?"

"I dunno – some kind of weird tribute act."

"Hmmm," said Brigit. "Maybe it's reincarnation?"

"Wouldn't that really piss off a Catholic?"

"Speaking of people coming back from the dead, it turns out our Mr Brown was in fact one Jackie 'Grinner' McNair."

"So you said. Who is that exactly?"

"Have you ever heard of the Rapunzel case from the eighties?"

"Is that the one where the hostage ran off with the kidnapper?" said Paul. "Stockholm Syndrome and all that?"

"Well, you've taken a lot of the romance out of it there but yes, that, more or less. Basically, rich dude's young naïve trophy wife gets kidnapped, and falls in love with the kidnapper. They both give everything up to run away and be together."

"Hang on, was Brown or McNair or whatever... was he Romeo in this little fairy tale?"

"God, no."

"Good. He didn't strike me as the romantic leading-man type."

"He was the best mate-slash-accomplice."

"Are you telling me people are trying to kill me because of something that happened before I was born?"

"Possibly," said Brigit before diving back into her bags. "I got you a present."

"Oh no, really. The jumper was more than enough. I feel bad, I didn't get you anything."

"Don't worry about it. There's still plenty of shopping days left," said Brigit as she handed him the paperback she'd finally located in her bags.

"*Hostage to Love*," he read. "The shocking true story behind the Rapunzel case. Wow – that is a dreadful title."

"Appalling; but, despite that, it was a bestseller. They're supposed to be making it into a film. Colin Farrell is rumoured to be interested."

"Fuck a duck!"

Paul flicked through to the photographs section in the middle. The first photo was a rather staid family portrait of a young woman in her early twenties with long blonde hair, sitting in a chair, flanked by her rather severe looking parents.

"That's the Cranston family. Proper English toffs."

"They look it," said Paul. "All three of them look like they've got sticks up their arses."

Paul pointed at the pretty girl. "Our Juliet I assume?"

"Yeah. She was stunning," said Brigit.

"I suppose, if China doll Disney princess is your thing. I bet she was a hoot with a few cans of scrumpy in her though. Like the man said, it's the quiet ones you've got to watch."

"Certainly turned out to be the case with her. By all accounts, Daddy Cranston wasn't much fun to live with. The Rapunzel name for the case allegedly came from what the Cranstons' staff called the daughter in private. She was kept all but locked away through her teenage years. Up until she married..."

Brigit turned the page to reveal a picture of Daniel Kruger.

"Jesus!" said Paul. "He's like what's his name from Batman, Two-Face."

Kruger did have a facial disfigurement on the left side of his face.

The picture was taken outdoors, Kruger appearing to be scowling at the camera.

"Don't be mean," said Brigit. "His face got burnt in an accident when he was a kid if I remember correctly."

"Sorry, it's just a bit... shocking. So hang on, he married whats-her-face Cranston?"

"He did. Mind you, he only had her for just over a year. Which brings us to... the three amigos." Brigit pointed at the picture on the far side of the book. It showed three young men, suited and booted as if at a wedding. Judging by the glassy drunken grins, a pretty good one too. Paul read the caption beneath. On the left, stood the oldest of the three men, who was also the tallest. Gerry Fallon was powerfully built, with a boxer's nose. Even smiling, he seemed to carry an air of threat. He had the look of the classic alpha male. Everything about him said, 'I can handle myself, and you don't want to find out how well'. He had brown eyes and a cocky grin, like he was humouring you for now. You could see the family resemblance to the man he held in a playful headlock, but Fiachra Fallon made his older brother look like a very early rough sketch for what was to follow. Paul's flag didn't fly that way, but even a straight man could see Fiachra was a heartbreaker. He'd a Hollywood idol smile and that beautiful lost-boy look about him that would have had women wanting to mother him and a lot more besides. The final member of the trio was McNair. What struck Paul initially was the sheer ordinariness of the man. It was odd to think that this young man had become the cadaver that had launched itself at him yesterday. There was no similarity there. It was as if, by the time Paul had crossed his path, the cancer had already taken away everything that made McNair the man he once was.

He looked again at Fiachra Fallon.

"So that's Romeo then, is it?"

"Yep," said Brigit.

"Feck it, I'd have run away with him myself," said Paul.

Brigit pointed at Gerry. "And that is Gerry Fallon, who covered up the young lovers' escape, like all good big brothers should."

Paul shrugged. He'd have to take her word for it on that part. He closed the book.

"Here's the thing though," said Brigit, pointing at the book, "according to that, Grinner McNair died thirty years ago."

"My perforated shoulder would beg to differ."

"Indeedy. He and Fiachra Fallon were supposed to have had a falling out on the fishing boat that was taking them, and Fiachra's lady-love, out of the country. McNair, the story goes, wasn't wild about the idea of being one lover's tiff away from prison, not to mention losing all that money."

"Ah. Had he no sense of romance?"

"Apparently not. Following a dramatic bit of fisticuffs, Grinner fell into the North Atlantic."

"Shit the bed. There's nothing like a happy ending."

"He drowned and the young lovers headed off into the sunset, and a new life together in America or Canada or Australia or Carlow. There's been no end of sightings over the years."

"And they didn't care about the money because..."

"They had each other."

Paul mimed retching. Brigit ignored him.

"So a man who was supposed to be dead, wasn't – but he is now. Why is somebody trying to kill me over that?"

Brigit had been trying to find a way around to this subject. She was hoping to figure out exactly how irrationally paranoid Paul had become.

"Who do you think is trying to kill you?"

"I've no idea who or why. I just got a phone call telling me to run."

"That was very sporting of them."

"It wasn't from whoever is after me. It was a warning from somebody I know. Somebody who owed me a favour."

"Did McNair tell you anything before he...?"

"Tried to kill me?" Paul finished. "No. It was mostly demented rambling. He thought I was the son of an old friend of his. He talked about having a daughter who he hasn't seen for ages. I think he thought I was going to hurt her. Honest to God, he was off with the fairies. None of it made sense."

"He didn't mention any locations or anything like that? Like where the young lovers might've skedaddled off to?"

"Nothing I..." Paul racked his brain, trying to recall other fragments of the conversation he'd had with the dying old man. "He thought he knew my dad – and my uncle, that's it. Nothing that'd be worth killing me over."

"Is it possible..." Brigit paused, trying to think of the right way to put this. "Is it possible, somebody was trying to wind you up about this whole thing? Like that copper that was sitting on your doorstep this morning."

"No, that's not Bunny's style. He doesn't do jokes."

"Who is that guy?"

Paul gave a mirthless laugh. "Believe me, we don't have time for that story."

"OK well..."

They both looked off into the distance as a silence bloomed between them, neither knowing what to say next.

Brigit felt her phone vibrate in her pocket. She'd been ignoring it for the last 30 minutes but now looking at it at least filled an awkward gap in the conversation. The number that flashed up was the same mobile she'd been seeing repeatedly for the last hour. That meant it was DI Stewart.

"Hello?"

"Miss Conroy, where are you?"

"I'm... shopping."

"Did you not get my messages?"

"Sorry, I've been..."

"You need to head back to my office immediately."

"Right, well I'll drop in again later."

"*Now* Miss Conroy."

"Why?"

"There have been... developments."

"What kind of developments?"

There was a pause at the other end of the line. Brigit looked at Paul.

"Alright, if it'll make you take this seriously. In the last few hours, McNair's daughter has been killed and we've found a bomb under your friend Mr Mulchrone's car. I don't know what is going on, but your safety is my top priority. Please, come in."

"I'm on my way."

Brigit hung the phone up and then stared at it, trying to process what she'd just been told. Paul looked at her.

"What? What is it?" he asked.

"Well... the good news is you're not paranoid."

CHAPTER EIGHTEEN

Tyrion 4.12.AX4 – Secure server software
Initialising private peer-to-peer communication
Please wait ... Initialised.

RoyTheBoy07: Please give update.
CerburusAX: Target one has been successfully removed.
RoyTheBoy07: And?
CerburusAX: We had problem with target two. Not at location and backup failed.
RoyTheBoy07: By 'backup' do you mean the fucking big bomb you left under his car?
CerburusAX: Not our usual methods but U gave us little time.
RoyTheBoy07: And now you've got the attention of half the police in Dublin, thanks to your incompetence!
CerburusAX: I told U – too short a time frame. We got one of two.
RoyTheBoy07: You shot a housewife, well done.
CerburusAX: You gave bad information.
RoyTheBoy07: We don't want excuses, we want results.
CerburusAX: I want proof niece is OK.
RoyTheBoy07: And I want you to do your job.

CerburusAX: No proof, no job.

RoyTheBoy07: Very well. your niece is dead.

CerburusAX: Don't threaten us.

RoyTheBoy07: Then don't threaten me. Work to reacquire target. We will also attempt to establish whereabouts.

CerburusAX: We want proof of life.

RoyTheBoy07: I am told she keeps asking for tatu? What is that?

CerburusAX: Means daddy. You are scum.

RoyTheBoy07: Sticks and stones Draco. You are a hired killer, do your job.

CHAPTER NINETEEN

"Keep those people back behind the barriers."

Detective Wilson raised his voice so the uniformed guards manning the barricades could hear him clearly. It was important in this kind of stressful situation that people knew who was in charge, especially as it was him. At least it was until Stewart got back. The old duffer was currently off interviewing the residents of Richmond Gardens in an effort to get a description of the man who'd planted the bomb. The two uniformed guards looked at Wilson, then briefly at each other, before returning their gazes to the crowd that was already standing behind the barrier.

There was quite a crowd gathering. Every house within a two street radius of Richmond Gardens had been evacuated and most of those people were now standing about, waiting for something exciting to happen. Others had been steadily joining them since the barriers went up; quite a few of the crowd now had pints on the go. Dubs love nothing more than a bit of free entertainment. The Gardai had been forced to close part of the North Circular Road to the south and Summerhill Parade to the east, two of the main arteries out of the city. Wilson could hear traffic honking and growling in the distance, enraged by whatever was making Friday evening's gridlock even worse than usual. An enterprising ice cream van had pulled up just down the road and was doing a roaring trade. It was the wrong time of year but, judging by the queue, location appeared to be trumping seasonal trends. Wilson could hear snippets of conversation over the background hum of traffic noise and chatter.

"Is it Bono?"

"What're ye talking about?"

"It's somebody famous, yeah? It better not be some fecking politician, unless it's the Clintons or something."

"It's a bomb."

"Feck off. Who'd be planting a bomb around here? Sure if it went off, ye'd barely notice."

"I'm telling ye, it's a bomb. Do you think I'd have evacuated my gaff for an unexploded Bono?"

"It's probably the Muslims."

"What Muslims?"

"The terrorist Muslims. Your Isis and that."

"Isis me hole. It'll be the Protestants."

"Why would it be the Protestants? There's been a ceasefire for ages."

"And besides, the prods can't do bombs – everybody knows that."

The most serious risk of anyone breaking the cordon came from the photographers. The location of the barriers meant they couldn't quite manage to get the bomb disposal boys and Croke Park in the same shot and it was killing them. The army bomb squad had turned up about 20 minutes ago, closely followed by an RTE outside broadcast van. Wilson was secretly hoping it would be that redheaded one who does the news in Irish. He fancied the arse off her. Siobhan O'Sinard or something, wasn't it? Siobhan O'Sexy – that's what Gareth had called her. Gareth had been his flatmate since uni and, while he was a top man, it occurred to Wilson that he really should get his own place. He couldn't be bringing Siobhan back to the apartment he shared with Gar and his unacceptable foot odour.

In an ideal world, Wilson would give a statement on the situation – firm, masterful. Women went mental for that sort of thing. He just had to hope that Stewart stayed out of the way, and the chances of that weren't great. Who wouldn't want to be on the telly? The old duffer would probably want to wave to his wife. Luckily the bomb squad didn't give statements to the press. There was no way he could have competed with them. "I defuse bombs" – those three words had to make panties drop. Lucky sods.

Wilson was distracted from his thoughts by an insistently raised voice.

"Here, you. You. Guard!"

He turned to see a large man in his forties, with a receding hairline and an expanding gut, leaning over the crowd control barriers. His belly was so large, it was technically breaking the cordon. He wore a Dublin football jersey, two years out of date and two sizes too small. He pointed a chubby finger at Wilson.

"Yeah, you. Come 'ere."

Wilson stepped over towards him.

"Yes, sir?"

"Is this the Muslims or the prods?"

"The Garda Síochána cannot comment on an ongoing security situation."

"Do you not know, son?"

Out of the corner of his eye, Wilson caught one of the uniforms smirking.

"We are unable to comment at this time."

The large man glanced back around at the crowd surrounding him and raised his voice.

"He doesn't know."

"We aren't allowed to divulge."

"Yeah, yeah, yez don't know. I'll wait for one of the proper coppers to turn up."

"We cannot, at this time..."

The large man cut across, mimicking Wilson with an

effeminate high-pitched voice. "We, the Garda Síochána, cannot, at this present moment in time, find our arse with the application of both hands, but we are phoning for additional resources to assist in this matter. Please hold, your call is important to us."

Several people in the crowd laughed. Wilson gave a tight smile, trying to give the impression he was enjoying the banter.

He leaned towards the guard to his left.

"I'm going to liaise with the bomb squad. You know where I am if you need me."

The guard gave a perfect parade ground turn and snapped off a sharp salute, complete with heel click.

"Yes, sir!"

Wilson retreated and took out his phone, trying to pretend that the gales of laughter didn't bother him.

The bomb squad's three vans blocked off most of the view of Richmond Gardens. Stewart and Wilson's unmarked black Ford Mondeo sat about twenty feet behind them. It was a prime spot, right in the line of sight of the TV cameras that he could now see had finished setting up. Christ – was that Siobhan he could see deep in conversation with some guy in a high-vis jacket? How was her red hair so bright on a grim day? It was like there was a sun shining just on her. She was shorter than he expected, which was good. He was only five eight himself and he didn't like women towering over him in heels. He needed to text Gar to see if he could Sky+ the news. Ideally Wilson would've loved to be captured by the cameras in deep discussion with the bomb squad, but the head army guy had made it very clear early doors that his input was not required. The selfish prick was clearly after all the glory for himself. Unprofessional.

Wilson glanced in the direction of the bomb boys. They seemed to spend a lot of time talking. He supposed the job required a cautious approach, unless you wanted to be brought home in a KFC bargain bucket.

Wilson stopped suddenly and did a double-take. A large man in an ill-fitting sheepskin coat and a black suit was casually leaning against their unmarked car, watching the bomb squad work while calmly licking an ice-cream cone. There was supposed to be a strict cordon. Wilson would have somebody's arse for this. He hurried over.

As he got closer, Wilson could see the ice cream was a 99. The man had positioned the flake bang in the centre and he was systematically licking around it, like a dog avoiding medication.

"This is a restricted area. Who are you?"

The man turned his head slowly and gave Wilson a quizzical look, the kind you'd get off a woman in a bar who was trying to decide if she'd let you buy her a drink or not. Then he turned back to continue watching the show. He took an uncomfortably long lick of his ice cream, before responding in a strong Cork accent, "Who the feck are you?"

Wilson took his wallet from inside his coat and flipped it open in one practised motion, which he had in fact practised.

"Detective Wilson, National Bureau of Criminal Investigation."

The man's eyes stayed fixed on the entrance to Richmond Gardens.

"Well, I'll be the one-eyed son of a cock-eyed Suzie."

Wilson snapped his wallet closed again. He'd no idea what that meant but this man was starting to really irritate him.

"And you are?" asked Wilson.

"Detective Sergeant Bunny McGarry, Summerhill. I'd shake your hand but ..."

He indicated his ice cream, leaving Wilson in no doubt as to his relative importance in relation to it.

The man who was claiming to be Bunny McGarry turned his ice-cream cone through ninety degrees with careful precision, and continued his systematic licking.

"I need to see some ID."

"You could whip yours out and look at it again if you'd like?"

Wilson could feel his cheeks redden. "ID now!"

"What's the magic word?"

"What?"

"You heard me. I'm not enjoying your tone."

"This is a closed scene. Even if you are who you say you are, you're not supposed to be here without permission. Now ID or I'm going to place you under arrest, and we'll see how you like my tone then."

McGarry smiled. "Well, look at the big balls on the new lad. I'm not going to lie, your sheer fecking manliness has got me a teeny bit aroused."

"Less of the bullshit," said Wilson.

"I couldn't agree more," responded McGarry.

The bomb squad were now moving about the vans, as if preparing to do something.

"Do you reckon they have one of them robots?" continued Bunny. "I always wanted to see one of them in action."

Wilson knew what this was. For the last couple of weeks, he'd been putting up with Stewart's ribbing. This was the next stage in the process of testing the new guy. He couldn't back down.

He moved to stand in front of the man that was calling himself Bunny McGarry, blocking his view of proceedings. "Do I have your undivided attention now?"

The man carefully rotated his cone again. He spoke without taking his eyes off it.

"Sonny, trust me when I say – you don't want my undivided attention."

Then Bunny looked up and they locked eyes, or at least Wilson tried to. The man's left eye was lazy, which left Wilson unsure of exactly where to look.

Bunny waited for Wilson to look away before he spoke again. "I'm here to see Jimmy Stewart. I've a personal interest in proceedings."

"I don't give a shit if that's your car that's about to be blown up. Get back behind the barriers."

"Consider this your second and final warning on the tone."

As if acting under its own volition, Wilson's hand snapped out and slapped the ice-cream cone from Bunny's hands. Before it'd hit the ground, Bunny's left hand had grabbed Wilson's testicles in a vicelike grip. Wilson tried to react as the pain surged through his lower body but McGarry moved much faster than Wilson would ever have expected for a man his size. His body was spun around in one fluid motion that left him leaning up against the car. Bunny's left shoulder pushed against Wilson's to hold him upright, leaving his mouth only inches from Wilson's ear.

"Scream like a little girl and I'll fecking make you into one."

Bunny raised his left hand slightly, forcing the younger man to stand on his tippy-toes.

"You..." a subtle increase in the firmness of Bunny's grip caused the rest of the words to die in Wilson's throat.

"Hush now," whispered Bunny. "We've had enough talking from you I reckon. Let's not make a scene for the TV cameras. No sudden movements or you'll be singing soprano in the Garda choir."

Wilson looked at Bunny as he casually scanned the crowd behind them. It seemed the car had sufficiently blocked their view. Nobody appeared to have noticed anything unusual about the two policemen having a cosy little chat. The location of Bunny's left hand had gone entirely unnoticed, except by Wilson, who could think of little else.

"Now, ye little hairy-arsed goat humper. You and I are going to have a little talk about respect." Bunny glanced quickly at Wilson's face. "At some point, ye might want to start breathing again."

Wilson realised he had been holding his breath and slowly expelled the air in his lungs. He could barely see through the tears in his eyes.

Bunny looked down at the ice cream lying forlornly on the ground. "I was enjoying that. Do you not know children are starving in Africa?"

Wilson went to speak but was again stopped by another firm squeeze on his gonads.

"That was a test. You're done yapping, remember?"

"Hello, Bunny."

Both men looked up to see Jimmy Stewart, a Styrofoam cup in each hand, standing beside the bonnet of the car.

"Jimmy," said Bunny with a nod.

"I see you've met Wilson."

"Yes," said Bunny, returning to glaring at the side of Wilson's head. "He showed me his ID and everything."

Wilson shot Stewart a pleading look. Stewart shook his head slowly and turned his eyes to heaven.

"We're currently having an engaging conversation about the importance of manners," said Bunny. "Manners, and cooperation between departments."

"I can see that. I can also see you've got quite a firm grip on his bollocks there."

"I do."

"While I've no great desire to see him breeding in the future either, I'd still ask you to show a little restraint. His voice is irritating enough without going up two octaves."

"Well, a quick twist of the wrist and he'll have a permanent reminder of how to deal with a request from a fellow officer."

Stewart glanced between the two men.

"I think he's already learned that lesson. I'll be happy to help you with your enquiries. Can I ask your interest?"

Bunny looked directly at Stewart, ignoring the whimpering Wilson beside him.

"Paulie Mulchrone is one of my boys."

"Ah – I see."

"What's he got himself into?"

"I'm not sure. He might just have been in the wrong place at the wrong time." Stewart nodded towards Richmond Gardens. "He certainly seems to have pissed off somebody, best guess Gerry Fallon."

Bunny whistled. "Feck's sake. The little eejit must have a death wish. It's all this hipity hopity music the young fellas are listening to I reckon."

Bunny scowled at Wilson again, like this was somehow his fault.

"I've been trying to get hold of Mr Mulchrone," said Stewart, "assuming he's still alive of course. No luck so far. Maybe you could help me with that?"

Bunny shifted uneasily. It was hard to tell through the tears forming in his eyes, but Wilson thought for one second that he actually looked embarrassed.

"Can't help you there. Myself and himself aren't getting on the best these days. Bit of a sensitive situation."

"I see. Speaking of which..." Stewart inclined his head towards Wilson.

"He owes me one euro eighty," said Bunny.

"What?"

Wilson and Stewart both followed Bunny's eyes down to the 99 on the ground.

"Ah, I see," said Stewart. "Wilson – give the man one euro eighty."

Wilson looked at Stewart, who gave him an insistent nod. He reached into his right pocket very slowly and felt around his change. He pulled out a two-euro coin and held it out.

Bunny looked at it, then released his grip on the Wilson family jewels and took the coin from his hand. Wilson slid down the side of the car, gasping in ragged breaths of urgency, as if he'd just surfaced from an unforgiving sea.

Bunny took some change from his own pocket and looked at it. He picked out a twenty-cent coin and dropped it on the ground in front of Wilson.

"There's your change. Never let it be said Bunny McGarry isn't a fair man."

"Course not. May I have a moment with my associate please, Bunny?" asked Stewart. "How about you go grab your ice cream, and then you and I will have a chat?"

"Happy days."

Bunny ruffled Wilson's hair and then quickly stepped away, heading for the ice cream van, whistling tunelessly to himself.

Wilson looked up at Stewart, tears of outrage glistening in his eyes.

"I'm going to—"

118

"No." Stewart raised his voice to cut him off dead. "You'll do absolutely nothing."

He bent down slightly and handed Wilson the lukewarm cup of tea, which he took gingerly.

"Bunny McGarry," Stewart began, "is a legend. He's a tad... let's call it rough around the edges, but he's a good copper."

Wilson went to speak but a stern look from Stewart convinced him silence was the better option.

"He has his own unconventional brand of community policing. He runs the St Jude's hurling club. Every young fella around here goes through it at some point, whether he likes it or not. Bunny knows everybody, and everybody knows him. He clears more cases than damn near anybody on the force and this is his patch. You will show some respect for that. As the man says, if you want to get on, you've got to get along."

Wilson couldn't believe what he was hearing. "He assaulted me!"

"Do you have any witnesses to that fact?"

Wilson looked at Stewart as he casually drained the remains of his tea.

"Have you ever seen the film LA Confidential?" asked Stewart.

Wilson shook his head. Stewart sighed. "Course you haven't."

"What's your point?"

"Bunny is a bit like Bud, the hot-headed cop Russell Crowe plays. And you're like... thingy, the bloke who was in neighbours..."

"Jason Donovan?"

Stewart slapped the car, suddenly remembering. "Guy Pearce. He plays this strait-laced cop. They start off as bitter enemies but in the end they team up to take down the bad guys."

Wilson started to stand up slowly, using the side of the car for assistance.

"You think me and him are going to end up as friends?"

Stewart considered this as he looked at Bunny standing patiently in the queue for the ice cream van, yakking away to two old ones.

"No. Bunny doesn't have friends, and if he did, you'd not be one of them."

"So what's your point?"

Stewart looked up as if trying to remember.

"I'm not sure I had one."

Wilson glared at him.

Stewart sipped his tea and looked off into the distance.

"Is that yer one who does the news in Irish?"

CHAPTER TWENTY

"Just... calm down."

Brigit was wearing flat shoes but she was still finding it difficult to keep up with Paul, as he zigged and zagged his way out of the park. He was headed for the Leeson Street exit, through the busy Friday evening pedestrian traffic. He didn't even look back as he spoke.

"Calm down? Calm down she says!"

"There's no need to panic."

Paul stopped and turned abruptly, his sense of outrage at the inaccuracy of that statement momentarily outweighing his compunction to flee. His about-turn caused a mini pile-up. A lady with a pram had to veer into oncoming foot traffic to avoid hitting Brigit. Nobody said anything, but there was some definite tutting at the lower edges of the aural spectrum.

He glared at Brigit with such ferocity that she took a step backwards.

"No need to panic? People are planting bombs – *bombs* mind you, under my car. I've no clue why but gangsters, real life gangsters, are trying to kill me. I can't go home, I've no money, no... no anything, except this!" In the air in front of him, he waggled the shopping bag containing two framed photographs, a vinyl record, a pack of three itchy pants, and the recently acquired copy of the book *Hostage to Love*. It represented all of his worldly possessions not currently within the blast radius of unexploded ordnance.

"As far as I'm concerned, there is a need for panic. In fact, it was for situations exactly like this, that panic was invented!"

"You could go to the police?"

"Oh please!" said Paul. "I do that and Greevy will..." He stopped.

"Who is Greevy?"

"None of your business."

"Alright then, where are we going?"

"We? You can go wherever the hell you like."

"No," said Brigit. "Screw you. You can't keep blaming me and then not let me help."

"I can and will. What help could you possibly be?"

"I've got money, a car, I know a lot about... the case."

She'd actually been going to say crime in general, but chickened out when she realised how stupid citing an addiction to American detective shows and crime novels would sound. She decided to move on before he could respond. "I got you into this and I'll help get you out. I'm not letting you wander off like a clueless eejit to get yourself killed, leaving me to feel guilty about it for the rest of my life."

"What if I don't want you following me?"

"Tough. Just you try and outrun me. I'll tackle you to the ground. I played rugby for the county."

Paul raised his eyebrows and Brigit's eyes narrowed in response. Her voice lowered to one of those whispers that sound louder than ordinary speech.

"Go ahead, make a joke about that – I dare ye."

Paul took a deep breath. "Alright fine, come on then."

"Right, but enough of the power walking. We need to blend in."

Paul nodded and headed towards the exit at a more reasonable pace, Brigit walking alongside him.

They got lucky and hit the pedestrian lights on green, crossing over amidst the throng. They walked up Leeson Street in silence, both looking around them nervously to see if anybody was following.

Earlier, Brigit had found this fun – now it seemed all too real. It was only enjoyable checking for homicidal maniacs tailing you when you didn't really believe deep down that they'd be there.

Brigit jumped as the phone in her pocket vibrated. She took it out and looked at the screen.

"It's Stewart again."

Paul stopped walking. "Don't answer it – no, hang on – do, I want to know if my car and thing is OK but... but – Don't... no, screw it – Do."

Brigit stood there with her finger poised over the screen. She turned her eyes to heaven before looking back at Paul.

"Alright, do."

She hit the button and put the phone to her ear. As she did so, she stepped up onto the stone steps leading to one of the grand old Georgian terraced houses that lined both sides of the street. A shiny plaque indicated they were standing on the doorstep of the Embassy of the Republic of Cyprus. She briefly had the thought everybody else probably had when they first saw it. How many Irish people get drunk and do something silly on holidays to justify that?

Paul moved in beside her, leaving both of them out of the steady flow of passing commuters.

"Hello... ohh..." Brigit looked confused. "Yes, I mean no, I mean — hang on a sec."

She took the phone away from her ear and put her hand over it.

"It's for you."

"What? How'd he know I was with you?"

"I dunno. I never said I was meeting you. Besides, this isn't Stewart. I could tell them you're not here?"

"Right, and who have you been talking to for the last ten seconds? Give it here."

Brigit handed the phone over to Paul.

"Hello."

"Paulie boy, sounds like you're having quite the day."

The voice on the other end, while unexpected, was instantly recognisable.

"Bunny – how the hell did you know I was here?"

Paul and Brigit instinctively looked around them again, scanning the street for signs they were being watched.

"What can I tell ye Paulie boy, I'm a master fecking detective. Also – if you remember – yourself, meself and the Leitrim lovely had breakfast together this morning."

"Oh right well. It's been fun catching up but we're busy."

"Feck's sake Paulie, don't be a gobshite. Whatever you've done to piss off Fallon—"

"I didn't do anything." Paul interrupted. "There you go, instantly blaming me..."

"I'm not blaming you for feck... Look, just come in and we can sort it out. You have my word."

"Your word! Are you joking, Bunny? I learned long ago I can't trust you."

"This is... this is different, Paulie. Jesus boy – they've already killed some poor girl and they put enough C4 under your car to make you the first Mick in space. Cop yourself on."

At that moment, an itchy sensation at the back of Paul's brain, the certain something that'd been bothering him ever since Brigit and he had sat talking on that bench, made itself known. A couple of facts finally collided and formed into a coherent thought.

"Here's the thing, Bunny. Brown or McNair or whatever the hell you want to call him. He'd been a patient at St Kilda's for what, three weeks?"

Paul looked at Brigit as he spoke. She nodded to indicate he'd got that right.

"In that time he didn't have one single visitor, not one. At least not until last night when I dropped in to say hello."

"What's your point?" asked Bunny.

"My point," said Paul, "is that it doesn't sound like Gerry Fallon had any idea that McNair was there, does it?"

"Well..." Bunny was sounding less sure of himself now, "I guess that's a possibility."

"In fact, when you think about it. All of this chaos kicked off today when the police figured out who Brown really was."

"That's—"

Paul cut across him, determined to finish his point. "Your lot find out that one piece of information and, suddenly, I've got a big target on my back. Forgive the cliché, Bunny, but with friends like you, who needs enemies?"

Paul hung up the phone.

CHAPTER TWENTY-ONE

Jimmy Stewart hit redial on the phone and placed it to his ear. After a beat, he heard the cheerful tones of Brigit Conroy yet again telling him she was awful busy doing God knows what right now, but to leave a message and she'd get back to him. He stabbed at the disconnect button angrily and resisted the temptation to hurl the handset at the wall opposite.

Himself and detective sergeant Bunny McGarry stood huddled in the mouth of an alleyway away from the throng. More gawpers had turned out to watch the shenanigans on Richmond Gardens as the evening had progressed. It'd been three hours now and the crowd were getting restless. Stewart was only guessing, but he imagined this was the first time in their careers that the bomb squad had been slow handclapped.

Throughout DI Stewart's several attempts to ring Nurse Conroy's phone back, Bunny McGarry had remained absolutely still beside him, a far off look in his eyes.

"It's no good. They're not picking up," said Stewart.

"Here's the thing," said Bunny, "he's not wrong is he?"

"What do you mean?"

"We find out that your stiff is McNair, and all of a sudden the last eejit to speak to him and the corpse's only living relative are both dead, save for a hiccup in the plan." Bunny nodded his head towards the bomb squad.

"What're you saying?" Stewart asked.

"I'm saying something here stinks worse than a wino's arse on Sunday."

"Are you questioning my integrity, Bunny?"

"No, Jimmy," said Bunny. "We're not bosom buddies but I've known you long enough to understand that if you were dirty, you'd not be thick enough to put yourself front and centre like this."

Jimmy exhaled. "Thanks very much for that ringing endorsement."

"But there's a rat here and somebody needs to find the little cheese-bothering prick."

Stewart looked hard at Bunny's good eye.

"What's your interest here, Bunny?"

"I told ye, Paulie Mulchrone is one of my boys."

"Half a wing of Mountjoy Prison could say the same, Bunny. You trained hurlers, not altar boys."

"Ha. Do ye have any idea how many former altar boys I've locked up over the years?"

"My point is..." Stewart hesitated, then said the thing that had been bothering him since Bunny had shown up. "I've seen Mulchrone's arrest record. I've seen his role in the Madigan's job."

And there it was. Stewart watched the other man carefully. Bunny looked understandably embarrassed. Stewart would bet the farm that he was the first person to dare bring this subject up for a very long time.

Madigan's had been the biggest security van company in the country a few years ago. Their complex out in Swords had been dubbed 'the Irish Fort Knox'. Impenetrable, or so they'd have had you believe. That had been proven spectacularly wrong nine years ago when some boys had paid a visit and made off with the pre-Christmas cash take from half the pubs, clubs and restaurants in Dublin. Two million and change. They'd used state of the art technology, mixed with military-style precision timing, and a level of ingenuity far beyond your everyday gobshite with a gun.

It'd been the first big test for the freshly minted organised crime unit, and nearly killed it stone dead. Bunny McGarry had been one of the chosen Untouchables. His years of invaluable street-side know how were seen as a shrewd addition to the force within a force. Rumours flew and pretty soon it came down to Paddy Nellis. A former housebreaker who'd steadily moved up and up the criminal ladder, due to being considerably smarter than the average bear. Dublin was a small town and that level of talent had always marked him out as one to watch. Madigan's was seen as his graduation to the big leagues. The Gardaí had quickly been able to trace a couple of boys with an ex-British armed forces history who'd been in and out of the country at about the time of the job. Outside help made sense. Nellis was known to distrust the standard of talent available on the local market. Most jobs like this, somebody's big mouth more often than not got everybody a trip to the funhouse. Loose lips couldn't sink ships if they were several thousand miles away at the time.

That wasn't to say the police hadn't had leads to go on. One of the raiders had been required to show his face when he'd driven the stolen van containing his team into the compound. His hat had fallen off to reveal a head of bleach-blond hair. The CCTV tapes had been destroyed with an industrial magnet within 60 seconds of the breach, but two security guards had seen him. One of the crew had also slipped up; three members of staff all hearing him say 'C'mon, Paul, pull your finger out son.' It was the only thing any of the crew had said during the whole two minutes and fourteen seconds they were in there. The police had been in the midst of pulling together jackets on any and all known associates of Nellis, when the investigation had caught a break.

It had always amazed Stewart how otherwise smart criminals couldn't resist coming back to a crime scene for a gloat and a gander. The problem with being clever enough to get away with it is other people not knowing how clever you are. That's why it is standard procedure at most crime scenes to take pictures of the crowd of onlookers. The trawl of the crowd outside Madigan's had turned up Paul Mulchrone. There he was standing about, gawping away like a tourist. His recently dyed bleach-blond hair made him stand out. An 18-year-old kid, too impressed with himself to keep his distinctive head down.

Bunny was the one who spotted it. In hindsight, he'd almost certainly been meant to. Mulchrone was dragged in and placed in an identity parade. The security guards were 100% certain he was the man.

They grilled Mulchrone for 24 hours. He denied all knowledge, said he couldn't remember where he'd been that night. They figured charging him would make it real, burn away the misplaced confidence of youth. They would soon turn the strong silent type into the supergrass needed to bring everybody down. Senior sources in the investigation let it be known to the press, dominos were falling.

They waited until the morning after he'd been charged before the trap was sprung. Mulchrone had an alibi. Not just an alibi, the mother of all alibis.

At the time of the heist the Minister for Justice, no less, had been out in Tallaght watching the first production in a new community theatre, an am-dram panto of Snow White and the Seven Dwarfs. RTÉ had been there too, getting some footage for a piece about the new facility, and to buff up the Minister's 'man of the people' credentials. Amidst all the dropped lines and double entendres, there was Mulchrone, giving a fairly underwhelming performance as Dopey.

There was absolutely no way he could've been in Swords on the other side of Dublin holding a shotgun to a manager's head while his buddies cleared out a safe. The investigation team tried to suggest it was somebody else in the footage, but no dice. The cast all verified his identity. Out of desperation, they even checked whether Mulchrone, with his complicated family history, could have a previously unheard of twin brother. Again, nothing. Some made the case for trying to charge him with wasting police time but senior command knew a PR disaster when they saw it coming. Not only had they spent days on a humiliating dead end, but Paddy Nellis's lawyer was able to scream blue murder about police harassment.

That was how smart Nellis was. Stewart remembered being told about it a few years ago at the retirement do for one of the detectives involved. They had figured it out months later. Nellis must've noticed that the nephew of one of the ex-British Special forces boys looked quite like Mulchrone. He'd probably met the young fella when he'd travelled to Preston six months previously. That's what'd given him the idea. Some hair-dye and finding a convenient film crew and voila, he made the problem of a member of the gang having to show their face, into a booby-trap to destroy an investigation. It'd been clever, damn clever. Nellis had counted on Bunny, and he'd duly walked the whole investigation right where he'd wanted it to go.

Sure, they had kept going but now that they'd got two eyewitnesses who'd given unsound identifications, they had worse than nothing. Quietly it went away, and Bunny went back to Summerhill Garda station where he'd started, and where he'd stayed ever since.

Bunny took a small flask out of his coat pocket, unscrewed the cap and offered it to Stewart.

"Fancy a warmer?"

"No thanks."

"Suit yourself." Bunny took a quick nip, smacked his lips and gave Stewart a long hard look.

He screwed the lid back on and the flask disappeared back inside his vast coat. Bunny moved in close enough that Stewart could smell the harsh whiskey on his breath and feel the spittle as he spoke. "Mulchrone was a bit of a langer a few years ago and if it turns out he's back playing the gurrier, I'll boot his arse into jail and go get a cream bun. But if he isn't, then I'm not going to let shites like Fallon go gallivanting about shooting down one of my boys in the street. It sets a fecking precedent. D'ye get me?"

Stewart backed away slightly. "Point taken." He figured that was as much as he was likely to get. Bunny seemed angry. Bunny always seemed angry, but for whatever reason, his anger didn't seem to be directed at Mulchrone.

"It got pushed upstairs," said Stewart, his own anger making his decision for him.

"How so?"

"As soon as the name Rapunzel appeared, the top brass got involved. I was told to hold off doing anything. While I was sitting there with my thumb up my arse, somebody was killing poor Pauline McNair."

"Christ. Do you reckon they're going to hang your skid-marked panties out to dry?"

"That doesn't bother me, Bunny. I'm all but out the door. What bothers me is, I take pride in the job, I always have, and some arsehole somewhere is playing me for a fool. If this is my last go round, I'd like to leave without any more bodies in the ground."

"Fair enough. Who got themselves involved?"

"Who didn't? I met with O'Rourke, on herself's behalf."

"Jaysus, mammy and daddy."

"Yeah. Some PR woman from the Ministry of Justice too, Veronica Doyle."

"Which means every little politico in the fecking tree knows, one of which Fallon owns."

"At least," said Stewart. "They're putting a task force together. I've got a meeting as soon as I'm done here. Do you want me to see if they'll bring you in?"

"Feck no! I don't play well with others, just ask your soprano of a partner."

"You certainly do know how to make an impression."

"Tell you what, Jimmy, you do what you do. Work the case by the book and watch your back."

"What're you going to do?"

"I'm going to put my hobnailed shit-kicking boots on and have myself a wee rat hunt. Will you keep me in the loop?"

"As much as I can."

"Can't say fairer than that."

Bunny extended his hand and they shook.

"Don't be a stranger."

Bunny turned, belched loudly and departed, hugging his sheepskin coat to himself as he headed off into the chill November night. Stewart watched him go.

In the distance, he heard the percussive pop of a controlled explosion, followed by a cheer.

CHAPTER TWENTY-TWO

They walked in silence up Leeson Street before turning right to follow the Grand Canal. There was a feeling of impending rain in the air. The shock, the adrenalin, the sense of absurdity to the whole thing had worn off. All that was left now was the cold hard reality. The police could not be trusted and whatever unseen forces were after them were deadly serious. Brigit didn't know where they were going, but she didn't want to ask. They both needed to feel like they were heading somewhere. That somehow they still had control.

They passed a woman who was studiously ignoring the fact that her terrier was taking a dump by cooing 'C'mon sweetie, finish your wee wee.' A homeless bloke sitting on a bench looked on in disgust. He caught Brigit's eye as they passed and shook his head. "Some people!"

They crossed the road and passed by the Barge pub. Despite the winter chill in the air, the pavement was full of boisterous Friday evening drinkers, pints in hand, fags on the go, lively chatter bubbling around them. A sense of carefree abandon permeating through the air. The endless possibility offered by five o'clock on a Friday. It all just seemed to highlight how outside the ordinary world Brigit and Paul now were.

Brigit used the silence to run through what few facts they had over and over again in her head. Along with everything else, she felt embarrassed. Normally she figured out the murder by the first ad break. How had she missed what in hindsight seemed blindingly obvious? There was no denying it: the police identifying the deceased Mr Brown as being Grinner McNair had led to this. Paul was right. A woman was dead and it was only by sheer chance that he wasn't too. The police had a lot of questions to answer.

Brigit noticed Paul was staring at an old brick maintenance shed on the far bank of the canal. On its water-facing side someone had graffitied in large stylised block capitals the words 'Only The Rivers Run Free'.

Paul stopped suddenly, and put his hand on her arm.

"Look, I've been thinking. I appreciate your help but you don't need to be here. This is getting heavy. Somebody is trying to kill me just because I 'might' know something. It's not safe for you."

Brigit spoke softly. "And where am I going to go?"

"I dunno – just hand yourself into the cops. You'll be fine, it's not you they're after."

"No thanks," she said, trying to sound braver than she felt. "Don't get me wrong, I'd dump your annoying arse in a second if I could, but you've not thought it through. Like you said, somebody is trying to kill you just because you 'might' know something."

"So?"

"So I drove you home from the hospital, I'm with you now – both of those facts the Gardai know..."

"Oh crap," said Paul, "which means so does whoever is — "

"Exactly," said Brigit. "If you're a loose end, then I'm one too. They'll assume I know whatever you do."

Paul sighed. "I wouldn't mind so much if we actually did know something."

"Too right," said Brigit. "Might as well be hung for a sheep as a lamb. So, where are we heading?"

"We're going to see a man about a balloon."

"Right."

"Sure you don't want to make a run for it?"

"Nope. And besides, don't think you're making off with that sweet jumper."

"Ah shucks," he said, looking down. "The only upside to this cyclone of shite was all the free stuff."

"Speaking of which, Fingers McGraw, any chance I can get my phone back, please? Cheeky sod."

"Ah – I've been thinking about that. Thing is..."

Brigit glanced over at the doors of The Portobello pub as they passed it on their left hand side. Her eyes ran straight into those of a man who was exiting. They saw each other dead-on, in the kind of way that neither side could pretend they hadn't.

"You have got to be kidding me," said Brigit.

Paul turned around, subconsciously crouching, looking for the source of danger.

"What is it? Hitman? Cops?"

"Worse. Fiancé."

Paul's head snapped back around to gawp at her.

"Ex-fiancé," she corrected.

CHAPTER TWENTY-THREE

"Bridgie – hi!"

Paul turned to look at the source of the voice. It was a guy of about 5-foot-8 with the kind of grin that gave Cheshire cats a bad name.

"Duncan – hi!"

Brigit's voice took on the saccharine lilt of a sixteen-year-old preppy American teenager. It shouldn't be possible but Paul felt her left ear was glaring at him, daring him to mention it.

"Fancy meeting you here!" Duncan spoke in the kind of accent that came from a whole different Dublin to the one Paul had grown up in. His was a Dublin of leafy suburbs and private schools. The Dublin where drinking a bottle of vodka and then chundering in the back seat of a taxi made you a 'legend'. Paul came from the other Dublin. The same one as the poor bastard who had to clean the taxi.

"Small world!" said Brigit.

Paul gave Duncan an assessing look. On closer inspection, it appeared his blond quiff had been surgically implanted. It was a good job but that was exactly the point. You could always spot a plastic pitch by how smooth it was. This guy's head was pure artificial turf. Paul had always wanted to know where that hair came from. A donor? A dog? The patient's own arse? He figured now was probably not a good time to ask.

Duncan looked in his mid-thirties, a bit jowly around the face, with a smart suit that, like the hair, looked tailor made. He didn't seem Brigit's type at all. Mind you, thought Paul, how on earth did he think he knew her type? They'd hardly spoken until last night. With all that had happened since, it seemed like a lifetime ago.

Duncan and Brigit hugged quickly then stepped back. It was time for the introductions. Only now did Paul realise the woman standing beside Duncan was with him. If Duncan and Brigit seemed an odd combination, it had nothing on these two. She looked about twenty, and was attractive in that way that said, 'this took an awful long time, I hope you appreciate it.' Tall, blonde, skinny. Breasts that looked so impossibly pert, they reminded Paul of intensely interested meerkats.

Paul considered himself a feminist. Which meant, in practical terms, the voice in his head wasn't allowed even to think the word 'bimbo'. Not until a woman said it first. Judging people by their looks was wrong. He knew this.

"This is Keeley," said Duncan.

"Hiya!" she trilled.

Paul discovered in that moment that he was, however, totally fine with judging people by the sound of their voice.

"She works in the office," said Duncan. "I'm just giving her a lift home."

Funny how they are both holding shopping bags from the same stores thought Paul.

"And," said Brigit, "this is Paul."

Duncan looked him up and down.

"Nice jumper."

It took every ounce of restraint Paul possessed not to issue a hair-based response.

Duncan extended his hand. Paul had to shake with his left.

"Oops," said Duncan. "What'd you do to the arm?"

"Ahhh – windsurfing."

And why not? Paul had always fancied it. In fact, he'd read two-thirds of a book about it that he had got for 50 cents from a charity shop.

"So how do you two know each other?"

"Friends," said Brigit.

"Patient," said Paul at the same time.

Duncan smiled. "Ah Bridgie – taking your work home with you?"

Brigit smiled back. "You can talk."

Duncan winced slightly. Paul stored that one away to ask about later.

"Well," said Duncan, "supes to see you. We should get cracking. I'm dropping Keeley home. It's on my way."

Keeley, God love her, actually looked pleasantly surprised by this. Like she honestly believed there'd been a change of plans and she'd got out of doing something she didn't want to.

"Yes," said Paul. "We've to crack on too. We're being pursued by a deadly criminal conspiracy of indeterminate reach."

"Terrific, enjoy that."

And then they were gone, leaving behind a fond memory and the overly sweet cinnamon smell of Keeley's perfume hanging in the early evening air.

"Don't say a word," hissed Brigit.

She was now power walking in the direction they'd been going, keen to get as far away from the embarrassing scene as possible.

"She seemed nice," said Paul.

Brigit mumbled something under her breath that Paul didn't quite catch, but he was 95% sure it involved the word bimbo.

CHAPTER TWENTY-FOUR

DI Jimmy Stewart was annoyed.

Annoyed with damn near everyone and everything, not least himself. As he'd feared, the circumstances around the death of the artist formerly known as Martin Brown had gone from unusual, past awkward, through complicated and all the way to clusterfuck. Brown was Grinner McNair, McNair's daughter was now dead and the last two people to see him alive Brigit Conroy and Paul Mulchrone, were in the wind. If Stewart had been allowed to do his job without interference, Pauline McNair might still be alive. Instead, she had lived a life where the only thing she had got from her absent father was his unwitting role in her death.

Stewart had just come from the first meeting of the McNair task force, under the leadership of DI Kearns. Kearns was a political animal and the whole thing stank to high heaven as far as Stewart was concerned. He'd been debriefed beforehand and then Kearns had taken control of the situation, leaving Stewart and Wilson standing there like a couple of spare pricks. Kearns had then explained to the assembled posse how damn near nothing had been done all day. Never mind that he and Wilson had discovered a bomb that could've taken out half a street. The earlier unofficial chat with

Assistant Commissioner O'Rourke was of course not mentioned either, nor was it ever going to be. Stewart could feel himself being manoeuvred under the gunge tank for the inevitable internal inquiry. They were not yet officially linking the deaths of Pauline McNair with the bomb found under Mulchrone's car as 'all angles were to be examined'. A brief rundown of McNair's history was given, although it was more noteworthy for what was not said. DI Kearns had managed to give an account of the kidnapping of Sarah-Jane Cranston without ever mentioning the word Rapunzel. Even 30 years on, those eight letters were still toxic as far as the Garda Síochána were concerned.

Tasks had been assigned to everyone on the team bar himself and Wilson. They'd been told in patronising tones that they could head off home if they liked. Kearns had cracked on that Stewart must be tired, having been in since 7:30AM. Smart-arsed little so'n'so. As it happened, Stewart was a little tired, but he was a lot angry and that was more than enough to keep him going. He was also angry enough to change the habits of a lifetime and cut a few corners in the interests of justice. Who said you couldn't teach an old dog new tricks?

He turned the corner to the IT services area. He was in luck: it was 7:30PM and Freddie Quinn was still at his desk. He was a short, pudgy man who couldn't grow a beard but was trying anyway. He was undoubtedly going for rugged and manly, but he'd ended up with IT geek who'd been lost at sea. The beard looked even more out-of-place than normal; thanks to the smart suit Quinn was wearing. This was the first time Stewart had ever seen him in one. He looked about as natural as those monkeys in the old PG Tips adverts when they were carrying pianos up stairs.

"Freddie, how are you fella?" asked Stewart, leaning against the partition beside Quinn's desk.

"I'm not here," Quinn replied, not even looking up from his screen, as his fingers danced across the keyboard sitting on his lap.

"It looks like you are."

"Your eyesight has gone old man. I was out the door fifteen

minutes ago. I'm currently on my way to an anniversary dinner with my lovely wife."

"Ah, isn't that sweet. How's the wife's sister by the way? You remember, the one who got caught in possession of some wacky baccy a couple of years ago and you asked for my help in making the charge disappear."

Quinn stopped typing and glared up at him.

"I do remember that. I particularly remember how you not only refused to help, but also gave me a long speech about how Guards pulling stunts like that was what got us such a bad reputation."

"I did say that, didn't I? Anyway, you know the request that Kearns just put in to get a location trace on the mobile phones of Brigit Conroy and Paul Mulchrone?"

"It's gone in but it'll take a while."

"Yeah. I need it right now."

Quinn barked a laugh.

"Well, Jimmy, seeing as you love rules so much, I refer you to the 2011 Communication Act, section 6-1." Quinn grinned up at the ceiling as he recited it from memory. "A member of the Garda Síochána not below the rank of Chief Superintendent may request a service provider to disclose to that member data retained by the service provider in accordance with section 3 where that member is satisfied that the data is required for—

A – the prevention, detection, investigation or prosecution of a serious offence,

B – the safeguarding of the security of the State, or

C – the saving of human life." Finished with the memory section of the test, Quinn leaned forward and started typing again. "So, I'm afraid you're going to have to wait for sign off from up the chain, then wait for the phone company to get around to pinging their phones, and you could not pick a worse time to ask for that than a Friday night by the way, and then, maybe, you'll get what you need. Aren't rules fun?" Quinn beamed a smile full of sneer up at Stewart. He was disconcerted to see Stewart smiling calmly smiling back at him.

"Yes, rules are fun, and now, you're going to break every one of them."

"Am I fuck."

Stewart picked up a folder and used it to nudge aside some empty Coke cans and sandwich wrappers on Quinn's desk. He created just enough space to lean himself against it, to the younger man's clear irritation. Stewart casually took the keyboard off Quinn's lap and placed it on the desk, so he had his undivided attention.

"You try and come the heavy, Jimmy, and I'll have HR on your arse in a flash."

"Relax, Quinn, I'm not gonna touch you. We're just two work colleagues shooting the breeze," said Stewart, as Quinn glared up at him through bitter beady eyes. "Have I ever told you how, when you find yourself at my stage in life, what's the best way to put this, a trip to the loo can take a bit of time?"

Quinn wrinkled his nose in disgust. "Why the hell do I..."

Stewart ignored him and kept talking. "You know that expression for it – 'dropping the kids off at the pool?' Well, as you go on in life, a dump takes so long it feels like you've got to walk the little tykes there one at a time." Stewart gave a light-hearted chuckle.

"Does this have a point, Jimmy? I've somewhere I need to be."

"I was merely pointing out how I happened to be sitting quietly in a cubicle up in the fourth floor gents a couple of months ago, when you and Detective Sergeant Ryan were having a chat in there, in the mistaken assumption you were alone."

Quinn's face dropped like Wile E Coyote when he's just run out of cliff.

"I heard you telling him how you getting a location on his ex-wife's phone for him was a big no no and he said, and I think I'm quoting him accurately here, 'I sorted out your beeping sister-in-law's beeping drugs bust so you can beeping shut the beeping hell up and get me the beeping location'. He does have quite a mouth on him, doesn't he, that Detective Sergeant Ryan?"

"Now, Jimmy, let's not..."

Stewart picked up an action figure from Quinn's desk and

casually moved its arms about. "After a bit of back'n'forth," Stewart continued, "you said there was some other naughty ways you could use to find her location. At which point, Detective Sergeant Ryan assured you that he'd never mention you if it came back to haunt him. Fair play to Detective Sergeant Ryan: far as I know, he's never spoken your name to anybody. I suppose we can still call him Detective Sergeant Ryan, can we? Although, I know he is currently suspended, awaiting the results of that inquiry into his harassment of the former Mrs Ryan."

Quinn had turned so pale by this point, Stewart was worried he might be about to hurl on his shoes. "OK, look."

Stewart leaned forward suddenly, putting his hands on either arm of Quinn's chair and his face close enough to smell the Monster Munch on his breath. "There's only one thing I want to hear from you."

"I can't guarantee anything," said Quinn. "It depends on what type of phones, their security settings, which network they're on —"

"I don't want excuses Quinn, just results."

"OK, look – I'll do my best. I'll be back here straight after my dinner and —"

"Now."

"Ah, come on, Jimmy, be reasonable! What am I supposed to tell the wife?"

"Tell her it could be worse. Tell her she could be married to Detective Sergeant Ryan."

CHAPTER TWENTY-FIVE

Paul and Brigit rounded the corner onto Clanbrassil Street.

"Right, here we are."

"The Thai massage place?" asked Brigit.

"What? No, don't be daft."

Paul glanced at it as they walked by. In the window was a handwritten sign on a piece of cardboard that read 'seriously, <u>NOT</u> that kind of massage.' Clearly, somebody had had enough of people expecting a little bit more.

Paul stopped one door along. He looked at his watch and then at the opening times printed on the shop's door. 5:54PM, six minutes to spare.

"Hang on – this is it? This is where we were going?" said Brigit.

"Yeah," said Paul, pointing up at the rather worn and faded sign featuring the name *The Balloon Man,* alongside a grinning clown. Clowns struck Paul as creepy at the best of times, but the devil horns and goatee the local kids had added did nothing to help the situation.

"But... " said Brigit, "I thought when you said 'we're going to see a man about a balloon' you meant..."

"What?"

"Well, I dunno. I thought it was some kind of street slang."

"For what?"

Brigit rolled her eyes and puffed out her cheeks.

"How the hell would I know? I'm a nurse from Leitrim. I'm not au-fait with the patois of the Dublin criminal underground."

"And I am?"

Brigit blushed slightly at this.

"Well... you are from Dublin."

"And all Dubs are criminals?"

"That's not..." Brigit folded her arms. "You know that's not what I meant. Is now really the time for us to be having this conversation?"

"Fair point," said Paul. "I'm going in. You stay here or you'll make him nervous."

"Why would I make the balloon man nervous?"

"Well, he's a criminal."

Paul flashed Brigit a cheeky smile and then pushed the door open with his good hand.

The bell chimed as Paul entered the shop. The gangly six foot six frame of Phil Nellis turned to look at him, a half-deflated balloon held to his lips and a guilty expression on his face, like a dog who'd just been discovered chewing on his owner's favourite slippers. Then recognition flashed in his eyes and his expression changed to one of horror. Unfortunately, the helium in his lungs rather undercut the anger in his words, turning them into a plaintive high-pitched squeal. "What the fuck are you doing here?"

"Nice to see you too, Mickey Mouse."

Phil's face reddened and he took a quick slurp from the can of Red Bull on the counter, before coughing to further clear his throat. "What are you doing here?" he repeated, if not in his normal voice, at least one that was coming in for a landing.

"You rang me, Phil."

"No, I didn't."

"Yeah, you did. You told me I was in danger and I had to run."

"I've no idea what you're talking about."

"I recognised your voice." That wasn't technically a lie, Paul had recognised his voice. Once he'd mentally recalled the very short list of people he knew who would ring him to tell him his life was in danger, it had been depressingly easy to figure out.

"You couldn't have recognised my voice," said Phil triumphantly, "I disguised it."

Paul could see Phil mentally replaying what he'd just said, before his face reddened and he shook his head in silent self-admonishment. Whilst Phil was a criminal, he'd never been accused of being a particularly good one. Still, God loved a trier, as did the criminal justice system. Phil had done wonders for conviction statistics. He released the grip his fingers held on the mouth of the balloon and it flew to the floor with a resigned sounding raspberry. He collapsed into the chair behind the counter. It was an odd feature of the Phil Nellis physiology that, while he was very tall, it was all limbs. Once he sat down, he went from being the tallest fella in the room to the shortest. He'd been that way for as long as Paul had known him. It had gotten him the nickname daddy-long-legs. Other kids had shouted it as they regularly threw objects at his head. Children could be so cruel, although in Phil's case, thanks to his fundamentally flawed design, it was fair to say God had started it.

"Look," said Paul, "I really appreciate the warning, but I need some serious help here."

"You shouldn't even be here! I said run, not run here!"

"Well," said Paul, "I am here and..." He drew in a deep breath: "I'm calling in that favour."

Phil looked aghast. "What? No! The warning was the favour."

"Nope, that's not how it works. I'm owed a favour, I get to say what it is. That's how the favour system works. You can't have people arbitrarily deciding when favours are paid off, there'd be chaos."

"But... no, I... ah, come on, be fair!" Phil pleaded.

"Fair? People are trying to kill me, Phil!"

Phil looked around in alarm. "Keep your voice down for Christ's sake, somebody will..."

Phil stopped talking. Paul could actually see the impact as a thought suddenly struck him.

"Are you wearing a wire?" asked Phil.

"Why would I be wearing a wire?"

"Entrapment!" Phil said it with a gleeful look in his eyes. Like he'd finally got the upper hand on someone, for possibly the first time in his life.

"You have to tell me if you're wearing a wire, don't you?" said Phil.

"Do I?" said Paul.

"Yeah – if I ask, I think. Or that might be just in America."

"OK." Paul spoke loudly, "For the record, I am not wearing a wire."

"Record? What record? Who is keeping a record?!"

Paul sighed, exasperated. "For Christ's sake, it's an expression, Phil."

"Ah no, I'm not getting caught out again. People are always playing me for a gobshite. Like that time with that woman who said she was a stripper dressed as a guard, but she turned out to be a guard dressed as a guard."

"Focus, Phil!" said Paul. "Relax, OK – it's me. I promise you, I'm not wearing a wire."

Phil clicked his fingers.

"Take your clothes off!"

"I'm not going to—"

"Strip – now!" said Phil, slapping the counter with his hand to emphasise the point.

"By any chance, is that what you said to the guard who turned out to be a guard?"

Phil squeezed his lips tightly together and folded his arms.

Paul looked at him for a long moment.

"You're not seriously going to make me..."

Paul shook his head in disbelief but the one thing he knew with Phil, he had always been very loyal, both to people and ideas. Once one had taken hold, Phil wasn't dropping it without a fight. They'd been inseparable back in the day. They'd even played on the St Jude's team together. Phil hadn't been very good, but what he lacked in coordination, he made up for in a willingness to get hit. A lot. He figured it was going to happen anyway, might as well happen playing sports.

"Alright, fine," said Paul.

He removed his sling and then slowly slid the Christmas jumper over his injured arm.

"Nice jersey by the way."

"Shut up."

Paul dropped the jumper on the floor, revealing the 'I Beat Cancer' t-shirt beneath.

"Seriously, are you in fancy dress or something?"

Paul flicked the Vs at Phil with his good hand, before repeating the process to remove the yellow t-shirt. Once completed, he stood in the shop, semi-naked and feeling very exposed.

Phil motioned his hand in a circle.

"And the rest."

"Feck off. Before you ask, I'm not giving you a lap dance either."

"Have you got something to hide?"

"Nothing you didn't see in PE."

Paul stared into Phil's eyes for a very long moment, weighing things up. Like it or not, he desperately needed help. This lanky idiot was pretty close to being his last hope. He looked around to confirm that nobody could see in from outside. The last thing he wanted was Brigit witnessing this. He'd never live it down.

"Right, fine."

With one hand, Paul quickly untied his belt, released the button on his jeans and unzipped them. Then, with what little dignity he could muster, he shimmed the jeans down his legs. He pointed at his underpants.

"And before you ask, no way!"

Phil considered this.

"Alright, fair enough."

"Good," said Paul. "Now you."

"What?" said a suddenly nervous Phil.

"Yeah. How do I know you're not wearing a wire?"

Phil drummed the fingers of first his left hand, and then his right hand on the counter, a contemplative look on his face.

"No, fair point."

Phil started unbuttoning the front of his shirt.

Paul shook his head. "Oh don't be such a…"

Before Paul could finish admonishing Phil for his gullibility, the bell over the front door pinged.

Paul didn't look around. He just closed his eyes and waited for it to be over.

"Hi, I was wondering…" Paul heard the shock in the man's voice as he walked in on one man who was nearly naked, and another who appeared to be in the act of undressing.

"D'ye know what, it's fine. I'll…"

There was a quick shuffle of feet and the bell above the door pinged again.

Wordlessly, Phil moved across to lock it, while Paul started awkwardly re-dressing himself.

"Phil, I need to speak to your uncle."

"You'll be doing well, he's dead."

"Oh, sorry."

"It was last year. He'd a dodgy ticker for a while, conked out on the job."

Paul, just placing the sling back over his shoulder, stopped and looked at Phil. "Do you mean?"

Phil looked back at him as he again replayed what he'd just said in his head. "Ughhh – Lord no, not – 'on the job'." Phil threw in a couple of hip thrusts, to show he'd belatedly understood the mental image he'd created. "I mean, he was robbing a house out in Skerries. He liked to keep his hand in."

Legend had it that Paddy Nellis had been the finest housebreaker in Ireland, before he'd moved into other areas. He used to joke that he'd been in more houses than Phil and Kirsty combined.

"That's terrible," said Paul.

"Ah, it's probably how he'd have liked to go. Heart attack, right there on somebody else's kitchen floor, a rucksack full of their antiques on his back. Nice couple, they came to the funeral."

"Sorry for your loss," said Paul, "but... who is in charge now then?"

"That'd be my Auntie Lynn."

Paul turned and looked at Phil.

"Really?"

"Oh God yeah."

"What's that like?"

"To be honest," said Phil, "she's taken a lot of the fun out of crime."

Phil moved back behind the cash register and started locking various things.

"Seriously, Paulie, you can't be here. If Lynn finds out..."

"How did you know?"

"What?"

"That I was in trouble?"

Phil compulsively shoved his fingers in his mouth and started tearing at his nails with his teeth. It brought back so many memories of him doing that as a young fella.

"Phil?"

"Alright, look. It was Gerry Fallon's son, Gerry Junior. His da sent him over to talk to Auntie Lynn about you. People know you're linked to us, because of the thing."

Paul nodded.

"I... might've overheard something through the door. They wanted to know if you were with us now and all that."

"What did Lynn say?"

"What do you think? Of course not."

"Nice of her."

"Cop on, Paulie, these are the Fallons. They weren't asking permission, they were just checking facts."

"So then you..."

"Went and rang you, like an idiot."

Phil took a long brown leather jacket down from a hook behind the counter.

Paul softened his voice. "Thanks, Phil, I do appreciate it."

"Yeah, well," said Phil, as he started to put on his jacket, "you're welcome. Now, for the love of God, would you please go away?"

"I will. Just as soon as I've talked to your auntie."

Phil stopped, one arm into his jacket and glared at Paul.

"I'm cashing in my favour, Phil."

Phil angrily shoved his other arm into the jacket.

"I am going to be in all kinds of shit for this."

"So where is she?"

"She's water dancing."

Paul considered this. "Is that some kind of street slang?"

Phil furrowed his brow as he looked at him, drumming his fingers on the counter once again. "No. It's Friday. Water dancing."

CHAPTER TWENTY-SIX

DI Jimmy Stewart was out of breath.

He'd had to climb three flights of stairs, which was doing nothing for his mood. As he made it up the final few, he made an effort to look less winded than he was, but the sweat making his shirt cling to him told the tale. Back in the day, he'd have been sprinting up these stairs. That's what he liked to tell himself at least.

42 minutes after Stewart had made his 'request', Quinn had rung him back and asked to meet in the stairwell. It was all a bit OTT on the cloak and dagger front and showed that Quinn's instincts for subterfuge hadn't improved. Two people meeting for a casual chat in the stairwell? Quinn might as well have held up a neon sign saying 'Engaged in dodgy activity'. Stewart didn't care; he was five days from a gold watch. What he wanted was a result.

If Stewart was sweating, it was nothing compared to Quinn. He was pacing back and forth on the landing like an addict in the latter stages of withdrawal. With darting eyes, he watched the older man negotiate the final few steps. The lad seriously needed to cut down on the caffeine.

"When you said..." panted Stewart, "to meet in the stairwell, I assumed you meant on the bottom floor... not the top."

"Is this a set-up?" blurted Quinn.

"Set-up?" grinned Stewart. "I already told you I don't know anything about any fucking setup; you can torture me all you want." He looked into the younger man's expression of sweaty incomprehension and sighed. "Seriously, Reservoir Dogs?"

"What are you going on about?"

"Never mind," said Stewart, with a shake of his head. "Why the hell would I be setting you up?"

"For revenge."

"Don't flatter yourself, Quinn. We had a minor spat, big deal. Do you've any idea how many people have properly pissed me off in my 41 years on the force? If I was going out for revenge, you'd rank somewhere between the moron who never quite fixes the coffee machine, and whatever thieving so'n'so keeps taking my yoghurts out of the fridge."

"Maybe you're being used by the inquiry into Ryan, trying to get evidence."

"Because that's what I'd do in my final week on the force? After all those years of service, be remembered as the bloke who turned Judas on the way out the door? Cop yourself on, Quinn. Your buddy Ryan posted one of his own turds through his ex-wife's letterbox. They've got enough evidence on him already. Now – have you got something to tell me or am I going to boot you down these stairs?"

Quinn flinched away. He was five foot nothing and, although Stewart was knocking on the door of sixty, he reckoned he could comfortably take him. Not that he was going to try, but there was no harm in Quinn not realising that.

"Well, it's just that the whole thing smells dodgy. That fella Mulchrone's phone is off, but Conroy's showed up."

"And?"

"That's what's odd. It's here."

"Here?" asked Stewart. "Maybe she's come in."

"No, I mean – not 'here' here. It's down the other end of the park."

"Oh for... is that all? Jesus, Quinn, the Phoenix Park is like the

153

biggest city park in Europe or something. That's a coincidence, and not even that big a one. Christ, you're paranoid."

"Oh yeah?" said Quinn, sticking his chin out defiantly. "Then explain this. I went in using the locator app on her phone. The networks have an over-ride and I accidentally 'happened' upon the password."

"I understood none of that but go on?"

"So, how come somebody else accessed her location 13 minutes before I did?"

Stewart didn't say another word. He was too busy taking stairs two at a time.

CHAPTER TWENTY-SEVEN

Paul had once found a great book in the three for five euros bin about how the mind works. One of the chapters had been on something called the spotlight effect. Basically, we all believe other people are paying way more attention to us than they actually are. Paul knew that, in general, this was true. However, now that he was standing in a swimming pool, with his heavily bandaged right shoulder wrapped in a shopping bag, while his left hand hung onto his underpants for dear life, he knew it wasn't his imagination; he really was becoming the centre of attention.

'Water dancing', as Phil had described it, was in fact aqua-aerobics. Auntie Lynn apparently attended classes at the Saint Vincent's Baths on Tuesday mornings and Friday evenings. The class took over most of the shallow end of the pool, leaving two lanes for the dedicated swimmers on the left side, and an area of the deep end free for a few teenagers to engage in as much high jink and heavy petting as it was possible to get away with under the watchful eye of the lifeguard. Normally, that would not have been much, but the lifeguard's attention was currently firmly fixed on the weirdo with the bandaged shoulder who was walking across the pool. One fifteen-year-old kid in particular was using the situation to gain a life-alteringly significant feel of some side-boob.

The woman at reception had questioned how Paul was going to swim with his arm in a sling. He'd lied and said that he was there on the advice of a physio, to work on his leg muscles after 'the accident'. This had all seemed like a much better idea half an hour ago. He had figured at least here Lynn would be forced to speak to him, if for no other reason than to get rid of him. After class, it would have been all too easy for her to walk away. It also removed any possibility of her sharing the family obsession that he might be wearing a wire.

This was all assuming he didn't get thrown out first. The rapidly degrading structural integrity of the pair of bargain itchy underpants he was using in lieu of swimming trunks had effectively made this a race against time. Paul concentrated on achieving what he thought was the kind of underwater walk you'd do if you were doing it for physical therapy reasons.

The sharp tang of whatever chemicals they used to de-pee pools these days made his eyes and nose burn. As he slowly marched himself along the edge of the shallow end towards the aqua-aerobics class, he could hear the instructor's voice booming over the hubbub, exalting his class to 'lift those legs, ladies' and 'feel the stretch'. The class consisted of about a dozen women. Paul couldn't accurately gauge their ages from behind, but he reckoned most of them wouldn't see the other side of 40 again. They all wore swimming caps, making them even harder to differentiate. As he wandered into their collective eye-line, Lynn Nellis had become easy to spot. The other women just looked uncomfortable at Paul's presence, whereas she looked absolutely livid.

Paul stiffly waved his right hand and then followed with a 'should I come to you or...' point, doing all he could to convey the impression that they were old friends, meeting by happy coincidence. Lynn's face grew even darker and then she jerked her head towards the other side of the pool. As Paul started walking across, Lynn stepped out of line, mouthed a quick sorry to Mr Aqua-Muscles and headed across to meet him.

They stopped when their paths intersected. Lynn was wearing a purple swimming cap and a tight smile over gritted teeth.

"What the fuck are you doing here?" she hissed.

"Nice to see you too, Auntie Lynn," replied Paul, trying to keep it light and non-confrontational.

"I'm not your bloody auntie."

Which was correct. Truth be told, she was not Phil's auntie either. She was in fact his second cousin. Lynn and her husband Paddy had taken Phil in when he was eleven and raised him as their own. Before that, he and Paul had been in a couple of foster homes together. Phil had always behaved more awkwardly around Paul after he'd been adopted, like he was suffering from survivor's guilt. Paul hadn't minded. He had spent quite a lot of time around Lynn and Paddy's house, and they had always been welcoming. Paul guessed it was partly because they felt sorry for the odd little orphan boy, and partly because Phil hadn't exactly been blessed with an abundance of friends. Phil had come home from school with a lot more bruises than even his extreme level of clumsiness could explain away.

Lynn gave Paul an appraising look. Her facial expression made clear that the appraisal hadn't gone well. "Look at the state of you! And for Christ's sake, take your hand out of your pants. You'll have people calling the guards."

"I'd love to but I don't have swimming trunks with me and these pants aren't holding up too well. If I take my hand away, someone will definitely call the cops."

Lynn shook her head and mumbled curses under her breath.

"Well," said Paul, trying to steer the conversation into happier waters, "this aqua-aerobics stuff must be great, you're looking fabulous." He'd have said it regardless, but it happened to be true. Lynn was probably somewhere about fifty, but if he hadn't first met her seventeen years ago, he'd never have guessed it. She'd kept the same firm figure she'd always had. It was weird to think of her in these terms, as he'd been a kid when they'd first met, but in hindsight she'd always been a looker. Dark red hair framed a slender face, with the bright green eyes that hinted at the fiery temper she was rightly known for. No doubt a few hearts had broken when she'd married Paddy Nellis. Perhaps a few may have even offered her a chance to rethink that choice when, only a year later, her new husband had gone down for a three-year stretch for armed robbery. She'd stood by him, though, and when he'd got out, having served every day of his sentence for keeping his mouth shut, they'd adopted her cousin's orphaned son and raised him as their own. Those three years had been the only time Paddy Nellis had ever seen the inside of a prison cell. He'd not gone straight but he'd got smart.

"Look," said Lynn, "I don't know what the hell you think you're doing here but there's nothing I can do for you."

"People are trying to kill me, Lynn."

She looked around nervously but there was no way anyone could have heard them over the general noise of the pool.

"I know that. What I don't know is how you know that, and come to think of it how you knew where to find me."

In answer, Paul nodded his head towards the three rows of stacked benches that made up the viewing area at the side of the pool. There, amidst the pregnant lady with a pram, a teenage girl sulkily texting and a couple of tremendously bored looking husbands reading the paper, sat Brigit and Phil. Phil waved back nervously. Lynn rolled her eyes.

"Feck's sake, that boy will be the death of me," said Lynn. "D'ye know, when you two were kids, we had him tested. See if they could figure out why he was so... y'know. These days, he'd probably be ADHD or ADD or whatever else they call it. Back then, they couldn't get past thick." Her voice brightened up briefly. "Who's the girl he is with?"

Paul hesitated. "It's probably better if you don't know."

Lynn sighed. "If she's with you, you're probably right. I just thought he might finally have found a reason to get out of his room and stop playing that fecking orc and fairies game, whatever it's called." Lynn stopped, clearly feeling she'd allowed herself to rather wander off point. "Look, the both of you need to get out of here."

"I've got nowhere to go," said Paul.

"And that's my problem, is it? Just go anywhere and be happy if you're still alive when you get there."

Paul paused and looked her straight in the eye. "Lynn, your husband, God rest his soul, told me if I ever needed it, I had a favour. I'm calling it in now."

Lynn laughed a humourless laugh. "Jesus, Paul, cop yourself on. Paddy is dead – and so is any debt he had to you."

"But..."

"But nothing. You got paid for what you did for us, and paid well. Do you want to know the truth about my sainted husband? Love him as I did, he was the smartest eejit on God's green earth. Sure – he robbed a load of money and got lots of slaps on the back and winks from blokes down the pub. Thing is, after you'd taken all the expenses out of it, laundered it, factored in all the planning that went before, and the hassle that went after, it was a waste of time. The only reason this family has anything to its name is that I took what little was left and invested in the balloon shop, the taxi company, a couple of knocking shops and, yeah, I lent some people some money and I wasn't shy about hiring some lads to go get it back if they didn't pay. It ain't glamorous, but it's a life. Paddy, may he rest in peace, might be remembered as the Robin Hood of The Liberties but I'm the one who had to actually make the money. The man had brains to burn, he could have made ten times more in a suit than he ever did with a gun, but most men are just boys who're allowed to buy booze. So don't go telling me that I owe you anything."

"Could you not have a word?" asked Paul, hearing the note of pleading in his own voice.

"With Gerry Fallon? Are you kidding me? Do you know who he is?"

"Yeah, he's some big time gangster."

"No," she said, shaking her head vigorously, "you don't get it, do you? You know how all these other so-called 'criminal masterminds' have their nicknames? The General, the Penguin, the fecking Unicorn or whatever. Do you know what Gerry Fallon's nickname is?"

Paul's silence was his response.

"Exactly, because he doesn't have one. Early doors, he subtly let it be known to journalists and anybody else who mattered, that the first person to stick a name on him would regret it. He didn't get into this to get famous, he did it to get rich, and he's very good at it. He was discreet, he was methodical and, more than anything, he was brutal. Anyone that got in his way, they never found a body. It's hard to pin a murder on somebody when you've not got a corpse. Nowadays, he gets a percentage on everything, whether people realise it or not. Bookies, girls, every shipment of that filth…"

The Nellis family had always been strongly anti-drugs. It was the heroin boom of the late nineties that had left Phil in the foster home in the first place.

"Gerry Fallon is the invisible man, unless something or someone threatens that. God help you, it looks like you have."

"But… I honestly don't know anything. It's a big misunderstanding. Tell him I'm no threat to him, I swear."

"Jesus, Paul, grow up," she said, her tone more of sadness than anger, "if Gerry Fallon wants you dead, you're as good as. I'm sorry for your trouble but it isn't mine, and don't go bringing it to my door."

"But…" said Paul, as much to himself as Lynn, "you're my last hope."

"Then, you've not got one."

It was hard to tell amidst the moisture of the pool, but he thought he saw a tear in Lynn's eye.

"Does Phil know anything?" she asked. Paul shook his head. "Good. Then get gone and don't come looking for us again. I like you Paul; I've always liked you. You were a good kid and, Lord knows, you didn't get the easiest start in life. So here is what I'm going to do. I'm going to go back and finish my class. Then, I'm going to have a shower and get dressed. Then, and only then, I'm going to ring somebody and tell them you turned up. I'll say I tried to keep you here long enough for me to contact them without raising suspicion. I'll say I thought I had, but at the last minute you got cold feet and legged it. Phil is going to see you get into a taxi outside and he is going to tell them that too. I'm sorry, but a head-start is all I can give you."

"There's no other way you can help me?"

Paul was surprised as she put her hand on his face and stroked it softly. "Son, not even God can help you."

CHAPTER TWENTY-EIGHT

"So how long have you known Paul?" asked Brigit. She'd been sitting beside the gangly man she'd gleaned was called Phil on the uncomfortable wooden bench in virtual silence for ten minutes, and it was starting to get to her. Actually, what was really getting to her was Phil's left knee. It had been jangling up and down beside her constantly. She felt like she was sitting beside a washing machine on a never-ending spin cycle. Between that, the constant nail biting and the repetitive incantation of the phrase 'Lynn is gonna kill me', he was becoming incredibly annoying.

"What?" Phil replied.

"Paul, how long have you known him?"

"Ah, ages. We were in homes together as young fellas."

"Homes?" It was only after Brigit had said it, that she realised it may've been a spectacularly insensitive question. Phil didn't seem that bothered though.

"Foster homes. We were in one out in Blanch, then separate for a while, then back in one just off Parnell Square. The Blanch one had been really nice, but then Barry Dodds tried to burn it down and ruined it for everybody. Such a prick that Doddsy."

"He sounds it."

"Oh God, yeah," said Phil. "He put my hand in a bucket of warm water while I slept once, trying to make me pee the bed. It didn't work though. Paul stopped it. Then when Doddsy walked into the bathroom next morning, the same bucket only fell on his head. It was pure class. Paul is dead smart with stuff like that."

"So, did you two live together long?"

"Until Auntie Lynn and Uncle Paddy took me in. I was the lucky one there I suppose. Shit," said Phil, turning to her. "You don't think she'll boot me out of the house now, do you?"

Brigit gave him a quizzical look, trying to figure out if he was joking or not. "You still live with your auntie?"

Phil looked at her as if she'd slapped him in the face. "She's got Sky Movies – Sky... Movies!" He said it with an air of unmistakable reverence.

"So, what happened to Paul's family?" asked Brigit.

"Long story. His mam, God love her, she was never right. She was from up North, fell in love with a British soldier and they, whatcha-me-called-it, scalloped together."

"Do you mean eloped?"

Phil thought about it and then shook his head. "Nope, I'm pretty sure it's called scalloped. Anyway, they tried England for a while, Manchester, I think it was. That's where Paulie was born, but his ma couldn't settle over there. There was some trouble or other. Then they moved to Dublin, thinking that might be easier but no good. To be honest, his ma, she was..."

He twirled his finger beside his head and nodded knowingly, like this was some form of highly specialised medical opinion.

"Lynn said she was one of those maniac depressive types."

"Manic?" guessed Brigit.

"What?" asked Phil.

"Never mind."

"Anyway, she was always up and down. Your best buddy one minute, your worst enemy the next. Eventually, I suppose, Paul's da couldn't hack it anymore. He left. Never heard from again."

"And his mum?"

Phil shook his head. "In and out of care, so Paul went into fostering. She'd come see him and it'd all be 'we'll be living together in a house, we're going to America, your Dad is coming back...' then she'd be gone again. One time when she came to see him, she just started singing at the top of her lungs. Other lads were ripping the piss over it. Paulie got into a lot of fights. Eventually, she had her accident." Phil stopped to bless himself. "It was only me, Paddy, Lynn and Paul at her funeral. And Bunny of course."

"Bunny?" said Brigit.

"Yeah."

"Who is he exactly?"

Phil looked at her in shock, unable to comprehend anyone living in a world that didn't have Bunny McGarry in it.

"He's like the sheriff of Dublin, man. He's also the head honcho of St Jude's hurling team. He gets others to help out and that — couple of coppers and one of the teachers from Fintan's — but it is his gig, man. Everybody plays there. Worst junior hurling team in Dublin."

"Worst?"

"Generally, yeah. Dangerous, though. You've got to give them that. Most heavily penalised team in the league, so they say. Bunny is very good at shouting, but he wouldn't be the greatest on the finesse side of the game. The only good team they ever had under-12's was our one. In all the years before and since, we were the one that nearly won a trophy. Would've done but for Paulie."

"Did he mess up in a game or something?"

"No, he never messed up in a game. He was a natural so he was, you should've seen him. Even as a 12-year-old, he could drop a free over the bar from 40 no bother. We'd foul them, they'd retaliate, Paulie would score the points and win us the game. It was a simple game plan but it worked. "

"So?"

"So Paulie didn't play in the final. He and Bunny had a big falling out."

"Over what?"

"Ah, it was ugly so it was. They gave us these tests in school, right?

A few of us were pulled out for special attention after. Me, Doddsy, Horse and a few of the others, we got these extra classes from this nice lady, for y'know – being thick. At least until Doddsy tried to burn the classroom down. He is such a dick."

"And Paul was in these classes?"

"Jaysus, no. They gave him some more tests. I only found out by looking in his bag, because he was trying to keep it quiet, but they said he had one of them genius IQs and that."

Brigit looked down at the man who was now clambering carefully out of the pool, one shoulder heavily bandaged, the other arm desperately clinging onto a pair of pants that were barely maintaining his modesty.

"This nice couple, they were whatcha-me-call-its... lecturers! From Galway. They were talking about taking him in, like proper taking him. They were friends of the woman who did the tests. That's dead unusual. Normally after like 10, nobody is ever going to proper adopt you. It was all looking great and then..."

Phil paused for dramatic effect.

"Then?"

"Bunny got involved. It was happening, and then suddenly it wasn't. Paulie took it bad, man. Blamed Bunny for everything. He reckoned Bunny didn't want him moving 'cause of St Jude's. So he walked away from the team, wouldn't play in the final. We got absolutely hammered, man. It was a massacre, and Paulie never played again."

"Christ," said Brigit. "Bunny is bearing a grudge about a stupid hurling game?"

"Ehm." Phil looked sheepish. "Not exactly. Are you wearing a wire?"

"What? Why would I be..."

They turned at the sound of a fist being pounded on the thick glass between the pool and reception. There stood Paul, looking like a drowned rat. It appeared he'd gotten dressed without making much effort to dry himself first. It dawned on Brigit that as well as trunks, he didn't have a towel either. It would've been comical but the expression on his face was anything but.

He waved frantically at Brigit and mouthed something.

It didn't take a genius IQ to figure out what it was.

Run.

CHAPTER TWENTY-NINE

DI Jimmy Stewart was beyond annoyed.

Annoyed was nothing but a happy memory. Angry was sailing away in the rear-view mirror. He'd now reached incandescent fury. He held the phone to his ear as he listened to the slow rhythm of the ringing tone over the white noise of the torrential rain. His heart pounded in his chest. He was standing in ankle-high grass as a frenzied torrent of rain crashed down around him. There would be flash floods. It would make the news. He had left the office so fast that he'd forgotten his coat. His suit offered no protection having become a miserable sodden weight that clung to him. He pinched at his soaking shirt front to try and let his skin breathe. Underneath it, he could feel the medal of St Michael, the patron saint of Policemen, pressed against his chest. His teary-eyed mother had given it to him on his first day on the streets. She'd not spoken to her brother, Jimmy's uncle Tom, for five years after. She'd never forgiven him for not getting her youngest that job in Guinness's.

Wilson stood slightly ahead of him, half in the beam from Stewart's torch. He could sense his accusatory glare, like all of this was just the latest way of screwing with the new guy. Stewart had brought him, not so much because he was the only member of the recently assembled task force he could trust, but because he was the only one who didn't know enough to ask questions as to where they were going and why.

The location Quinn had sent to the map on his phone had been a yellow dot in the middle of a large green area of the Phoenix Park. Stewart had floored it; nearly giving the old lad tasked with raising the barrier on Garda HQ's main gate a heart attack, not to mention reducing a learner driver to a blubbering wreck. He could feel bad later. Right now, his head was full of two women.

The first was Pauline McNair. He'd never met her, didn't even know what she looked like, but he'd done nothing and she had died. In truth, he didn't need to know what she looked like. His mind did what it always did. Every victim was automatically replaced with someone close to him. His wife, parents, daughters, son - each had swapped places with the dead many times. He'd never told this to anyone, what would be the point? He knew what they'd say and he knew he couldn't change it if he tried. Deep down, he didn't want to. Somebody should care, somebody should always care. In his head, Pauline McNair was his eldest, lying in the hallway with two in the chest and one in the head, while his grandson Jack bawled in the next room. This was what made him good at the job and good for little else. It was also why he could never relax. Every time a loved one walked into the room, a retinue of ghosts crept behind them.

The other woman was Brigit Conroy. She'd been smart, lively and alive. He was damn sure going to keep her that way. According to the map, Stewart was now standing in exactly the spot where her phone should be. All around them lay open space containing a whole lot of fuck all. The only thing they'd found had been some deer shit, which Wilson had discovered with his no-doubt expensive left shoe. All of this was why Stewart was ringing Freddie Quinn, and why he could feel that blood vessel in his temple throb.

Just before it went to voicemail, Quinn answered and unknowingly saved his own life.

"Hello?"

"If this is your idea of a joke Quinn, then you have fatally misjudged my sense of humour."

"What do you mean?"

"What I mean is I'm standing in the middle of a wide open field and there is ab-so-lute-ly fucking nothing here. Nothing!"

"That's not my fault."

"Remember our little chat about grudges?" said Stewart. "Well, I lied. You are now numero uno on my shit list. I know a lot of people, I'm owed a lot of favours, and I'm going to use up every last one to fuck you for life if you are pissing me about now."

Quinn sounded suitably panicked. "Calm down, Jimmy. That's the location that came up for the number. Hang on, maybe they've moved – I'll check again."

"You do that."

"It'll take a minute to get logged back in. Are you OK to wait?"

"Of course I'll wait," snapped Stewart, "what the hell else am I going to do?"

Upon hearing this, Wilson threw his hands in the air, in a theatrical show of exasperation.

Stewart moved the phone away from his ear. "And you can shut up and all. Welcome to what being a detective really means. It's not all kicking in doors and driving through piles of cardboard boxes in a Gran Torino."

"What on earth are you on about?" said Wilson.

"Starsky and Hutch?"

Wilson gave him that blank look that Stewart was becoming all too familiar with.

"Seriously, were you raised by wolves or something?"

Wilson didn't respond, instead going back to wiping his soiled shoe on the grass. Deer may be the majestic royalty of the animal kingdom, but their shit still stank. Stewart could smell him from here.

"I'm sending you my dry cleaning bill," said Wilson.

"Just stick it in my farewell card," said Stewart, "it'll be something to remember you by."

Stewart put the phone back to his ear. "Quinn?"

"Nearly there."

Jimmy looked around again. They were a couple of hundred yards back from the road, where he could see the evening's steady flow of traffic meandering by. The bike and pedestrian paths that ran parallel were deserted. This was the kind of weather that put all but the most hardcore lunatic joggers off, and even if a dog-walker had been willing, the pooch would have had the sense to refuse. The rest of the park slouched around them in the diluted darkness as the light from the city bounced off the clouds.

"Nearly there and..." Quinn almost whispered it: "It's still showing the same location."

"What new bullshit is this?" shouted Stewart.

"Just hang on," said Quinn. "It's the park. They've got no mobile phone towers in there so the location is inexact."

"How inexact exactly?"

"I dunno," said Quinn, "within a couple of hundred metres maybe?"

"Oh for... stay by the phone."

"But I need to..."

"Don't care," said Stewart, before hanging up. He looked around him. 150 yards away at a 45-degree angle, lay an area of about a dozen trees. Not that big, but big enough to hide in, or hide a body in, thought Stewart. To the right, about 200 yards away, lay one of the ringed off ponds that were scattered intermittently around the park.

Stewart pointed at the trees. "You take there, I'll check out the pond."

Wilson looked too miserable to argue, and instead trudged off in the direction indicated. Stewart started heading towards the pond. As he walked, he made an attempt to slow his breathing. Being found dead of a heart attack on his last week on the job, face down in deer do-do, was not how he wanted to be remembered. He shone the torchlight on the ground in front of him, in an effort to preserve what was left of his shoes. He regularly had the piss taken out of him for the gleaming polish of their leather. He didn't care. He'd been the youngest of five boys, he'd been twenty before he owned a pair that didn't carry someone else's scuffs.

As he moved towards the pond, Stewart noticed something – a faint light. He turned off his torch to see it better. Yes – there! As he moved closer, and more of it came into view, he could see the dark outline of a car parked on the far side of the pond. It was parked with its back to Stewart but he could now make out that the light was coming from the front seat. He looked in Wilson's direction and gave a low whistle, before flashing his torch on and off. He could see the beam of Wilson's light stop and change direction to follow him. Stewart turned off his own torch and quickened his pace. He didn't want Conroy and Mulchrone to get spooked and bolt.

As he got closer, Stewart thought he could make out that it was a dark blue or black BMW. He also saw the rough unpaved dirt track – on which the car was parked – leading away from the pond to one of the side roads. It must have been there to give access to the park's groundskeeper. Along with the hammering of the rain and the dull distant rumble of the traffic on the main road, he could make out another noise now. An insistent high-pitched whine. Whatever it was, it was getting closer. He was about 80 feet from the BMW when through the trees he was able to see a single headlight beam bobbing along on the side road. A motorbike, travelling unusually slowly. As he watched it, the whine of its engine suddenly increased as it picked up speed, turned and started heading down the dirt track towards the BMW. Stewart broke into a run as he saw the motorbike kill its front light. He could see the motorcyclist outlined against the lights of the city now. He appeared to be pulling something out of his jacket.

"GUN!" shouted Stewart, and started to draw his own from the holster under his left arm. As his hand, slick with sweat and rain, fumbled at the clasp, his right foot made contact with something. The smooth sole of his left shoe betrayed him on the soft earth. He slammed down. Hard. Messy. Face first. Couldn't get hands out in time to break his fall. Winded. His gun spilled from his right hand, his left wrist jarred as the torch twisted. The medal of St Michael dug into his chest.

He spluttered and spat the mouth full of wet grass. Pushed himself onto his knees and scrabbled around for the gun. "No no no no no!"

As his hands flailed around him, he looked up at the BMW. In a film, this was when the world would go into slow motion. Instead it all seemed to be happening fast. Horribly, unstoppably fast. He saw the outline of the motorbike as it slowed to a steady pace, drawing level with the stationary vehicle. He could see the arm, the gun extended. Then from the darkness, the figure of Wilson rushed by him. He stopped, crouched and unleashed a shot, just as the motorcyclist fired his weapon. The two shots rang out in quick succession, as if one was an echo of the other. The motorcyclist flew backwards off his bike so perfectly that the bike kept moving forward without him, like a riderless horse in the Grand National, still intent on winning.

And then the screaming started.

CHAPTER THIRTY

"What do you mean you've not got it anymore?" said Brigit.

They were standing on the pavement outside of the kind of convenience store you could find anywhere, although it'd taken a frustratingly long and wet walk to find this one. This kind of shop didn't normally sell umbrellas, and it turned out this one had been no exception. The Asian guy behind the counter had however agreed to sell Brigit his own personal golf umbrella for her last remaining thirty euros in cash. He was reading a university book on economics but he seemed already intimately familiar with the core concepts of his subject. It had been a seller's market and the guy had known it. Herself and Paul were now stood huddled on the pavement under the umbrella, using this new shelter to have an argument.

Since leaving the swimming pool, they'd taken a taxi, then a bus, followed by a walk, and then another bus, then they'd walked some more. Now, they were somewhere out in the southside suburbs that Brigit didn't know. She'd a sneaking suspicion Paul didn't know it either. He'd assured her they were heading somewhere, he just wanted to make sure that they weren't followed. His paranoia had seemed justified right up until the point the heavens had opened. She'd not brought an umbrella with her when she'd left the house this morning, but then she did have a car. She'd tried to make the case for going back to get it, but the image of the bomb that might be sitting under it had rather taken the shine off that idea. It was in the St Stephen's Green car park, which was a worry. A couple of nights in there and the fees would be more than the car was worth. If she didn't get it back by Monday, it'd be cheaper to blow it up herself.

"They can trace mobile phones. I had to get rid of it," said Paul.

"But... it was my phone!"

"Exactly, if I'd told you I was getting rid of it, you'd have made a big fuss."

"And exactly what do you think I'm going to do now?"

"There's no point now. It has already gone."

"But that's because... Christ, you are infuriating! Could you not have just turned it off?"

"No, they can still find it if it is turned off," Paul said, before adding, "I think."

"You think? You think?! Well, we could check that fact by Googling it on my three-month old phone, but wait – we can't! You went and bloody threw it away!"

"I didn't throw it away. As such. I know where it is."

Brigit wasn't even listening anymore. "I'm on a two-year contract as well and ahhh..." She threw her head back like she'd just taken a jab to the face: "I turned down the bloody insurance too!"

"Relax, alright. Worst case scenario: I'll buy you a new one."

"You'll buy me a new one? Can I remind you, the only reason you finally admitted you'd not got my phone is because you want to spend my last eighty-five cents on a phone call. How in the hell are you going to buy me a new phone?"

"Shush," said Paul, glancing around nervously. "You're causing a scene."

"Trust me, I have not even begun to cause a scene. Wait until I shove this golf umbrella up your..."

"Need I remind you, people are trying to kill me?"

"I know, and I'm about to save them a whole lot of time and effort."

"You're being melodramatic now."

It was at this point she raised the umbrella with the sincere intent of walloping him, but she held off at the last minute as a thought occurred to her.

"Wait. What does 'as such' mean? You said you haven't thrown it away 'as such'?"

CHAPTER THIRTY-ONE

DI Jimmy Stewart felt numb.

He watched the flashing blue lights on the last of the ambulances, reflecting off the dulled metal of the fencing surrounding the pond. The siren whooped once and was silent. There wasn't any traffic to hurry out of its way in the Phoenix Park at this time of night, and nobody had what could be defined as life-threatening injuries. Well, apart from the dead guy.

Stewart had been standing there a while, waiting, although if you asked him what for, he couldn't have told you right then. People would have questions, lots of questions. Someone had given him an umbrella, which he duly held over himself, although he had long-since been soaked through. Behind him, the Technical Bureau guys battled to erect a tarpaulin in an utterly futile attempt to preserve the scene against the still torrential downpour.

He stared at the BMW in silence. With all that had happened, Stewart didn't feel like he had the brain capacity to process it all. The whole day had begun to feel like one of those unpleasant stress dreams. Maybe if he could just focus on some of the facts that clearly didn't make sense, it would force him to wake up. Where to start though?

Neither Brigit Conroy nor Paul Mulchrone had been in the BMW. About the only sense he'd been able to get out of the couple who had been was that their names were Duncan McLoughlin and Keeley Mills. He'd no idea what they were doing in the middle of all of this. That wasn't entirely true. He had a very good idea what they'd been doing. Two people in a parked car in a secluded area of the Phoenix Park after dark, his granny could figure that one out, and she'd been dead for 25 years. What he couldn't figure out was how this related to Brigit Conroy and Paul Mulchrone. It surely wasn't some kind of coincidence. What were the odds that he and Wilson had stumbled upon an unrelated ambush? This was Dublin: assassination wasn't that common a pastime.

Speaking of unreal odds, then there'd been Wilson's 'hero shot'. One shot, straight through the glass visor of the helmet belonging to a motorcyclist moving at speed, taken from about 70 feet away. The odds were surely astronomical. Stewart cringed as he remembered his own tumble. He prided himself on being capable and yet, when the rubber had met the road, he'd been on his knees in the dark, searching in the long grass for his gun like a sad old fool. And Wilson, Wilson of all people, had saved the lives of Mr McLoughlin, Miss Mills and, feck it, almost certainly his too.

He'd not even had a chance to thank Wilson for what he'd done. The younger man had sprinted over to his fallen foe and, upon seeing up-close the damage a bullet could do to the human head, especially after it ricochets around inside a motorbike helmet for a bit, Wilson had promptly lost his lunch and then fainted dead away, smacking his head on a rock on the way down for good measure. He'd be OK, having regained consciousness almost immediately. Stewart had cleaned him up as best he could before the first responders had arrived. It felt like the very least he could do. He'd walked him into the ambulance, once the civilians had been dealt with. Stewart would also have a word with the techs. Wilson had scored a spectacular winning goal, there was to be no mention of the unfortunate post-match incident.

Stewart realised he was staring at the bullet hole above the front left tyre of the BMW. It was the one shot the assassin had gotten off before Wilson had so spectacularly taken him out. It couldn't have been more than a foot from hitting the car's occupants. One of the techs had excitedly told him the assassin's recovered weapon had been a Glock 17 9mm with a 33-round clip. If Wilson hadn't been here, the couple would be dead now. So, thought Stewart, would he.

A thought struck him and he moved towards the BMW. He took a handkerchief from his back pocket and opened the passenger door. Then, he took his phone out and once again rang the phone of Nurse Brigit Conroy. Over the drum of thick raindrops on the roof, he heard a faint buzzing noise. He moved his head around and eventually determined it was coming from the back seat. He opened the back door and rang it again. A faint light at the bottom of one of the shopping bags revealed its location. It sat there beside what looked, to Stewart's inexpert eye, like some rather expensive lingerie. Well, that was one mystery partially solved. The next question was how had it come to be there?

Stewart jumped as his own phone, still held in his hand, began to vibrate. Unrecognised number. He considered letting it go to voicemail but then decided against it. "DI Stewart speaking."

"Hello, Inspector. This is Nora Stokes from Greevy and Co Solicitors. I need to speak to you urgently."

"This isn't a great time, Miss Stokes."

Stewart carefully closed the rear car door and started walking towards Phillips, the head tech. They'd need that phone processed fast.

"It is regarding my client Paul Mulchrone. He has asked me to act as a go-between for himself and the police."

Stewart stopped dead in his tracks. "When did you last speak to him?"

"I just got off the phone with him."

"Is he OK? Is Brigit Conroy with him?"

"Yes," she said, "they are both alive and well."

"Where?"

"I'm afraid he wouldn't tell me that."

"Have you got a number for them?"

"No. He rang me from a pay phone. He told me he has got rid of his mobile. To be honest with you, I think he's become rather paranoid."

Stewart glanced over at the corpse of the now extremely dead motorcyclist. "Oh, I wouldn't say that."

CHAPTER THIRTY-TWO

Brigit looked up the sloping driveway that led to a large detached house. Mansion was probably a more accurate word. She wasn't sure what the line was between house and mansion; it'd never come up before.

"Here? Really?" she asked.

"Here. Really," replied Paul.

This was not what she had been expecting. She wasn't sure what she had been expecting, but it definitely hadn't been this. A crack den maybe? Or a storage garage? A sleazy hotel? All Paul had said was that there was somewhere they'd be safe. He was right on that score. Nobody would believe they were here. Brigit was actually here and she didn't believe it.

She'd have guessed at least six bedrooms, possibly more. In a street full of big, expensive looking properties with the kind of security gates that gave the unspoken message 'visitors not welcome', this house was the biggest. It was a period property of such a size that the phrase 'servants' quarters' would've probably appeared in its description, back in the day when people still referred to having servants. Of course, in this area of Dublin, they undoubtedly did still have servants, but she'd bet they didn't call them that anymore. It was made of that old grey stone, the one that made the phrase 'a man's home is his castle' seem less of a metaphor and more a statement of fact. If Brigit had spent less time reading about crime and more time reading a certain kind of romance novel, she'd have been better able to describe it. This was the kind of home the heroine would either give up to be with the man she loved, or where she'd live after she nabbed the rich bloke whom she was definitely not interested in just for his money. In short, this was the kind of real estate that was a significant plot point.

As they walked up the drive, Paul held his hand out, palm up. "Typical. Now it stops raining!"

Brigit collapsed the golf umbrella and struggled with the tricky clasp to close it, all the time looking around her in awe. Once past the trees that blocked the view of the house from the road, she saw the fountain in the middle of the expansive lawn, a cherub shooting water out of its mouth. Stick a referee's jersey on him, and he was perfectly located to officiate the game of five-a-side the lawn could comfortably hold. There was the sweet smell of wet, cut grass in the air. As they reached the top of the drive, where the large glass sunporch stretched out before the house proper, a disturbing thought struck her. She put her hand on Paul's arm to stop him and leaned in to whisper, while trying to look casual.

"We're not going to," she pursed her lips and wobbled her head in a way she thought communicated a lot more than it did, "y'know."

Paul gave her a quizzical look. "No, I don't know."

Brigit leaned further in, glancing around as she did so. "Break in?"

Paul leaned in and spoke in an exaggeratedly loud whisper of his own. "Only if the doorbell doesn't work."

She leaned back, slightly embarrassed, as he shook his head in mock exasperation. "Honestly, what do you think of me?"

Brigit blushed. "I was just, well…"

Paul leaned forward and pressed the doorbell. Its sonorously deep tone felt appropriate for such a grandiose looking property. It was immediately met with a shouted response from somewhere in the depth of the house, in a haughty sounding female voice. "Oh mucking hell!"

Brigit glanced across at Paul, who gave her a reassuring smile.

"This is Dorothy's house. She's a lovely old dear who swears like a trooper, but sticks Ms in to be polite."

"OK."

And then he added as an afterthought, "Oh, she also thinks I'm her grandson."

"What?"

Before she could say anything else, the inner door opened to reveal a small woman in her eighties. Her hair was white, neatly tied back into a bun and she sported a floral housecoat over a jumper and slacks. She wore thick horn-rimmed glasses on a chain around her neck. Her frail appearance was belied by her piercing blue eyes. They had the kind of ferocious intensity that left anyone trapped in their gaze feeling like a small woodland creature who'd mistakenly wandered into open ground. She took one look at Paul and turned sharply around to shout back into the hallway behind her.

"Pang Lee, put the mucking bins out girl."

"Hello, Dorothy," said Paul, raising his voice to be heard through the glass door. "It's not bin day tomorrow. Today is Friday."

She turned and looked at him, more annoyed than confused.

"But you come on a Monday, Gregory."

"I do, normally."

"Hmmm, that does explain why she has left for the day already. Probably seeing that dreadful man. So why are you here?" asked Dorothy, not unkindly.

"Can't a grandson come around to visit his favourite grandmother?"

"You want to spend Friday night with your grandmother? I knew you were gay."

"I'm not gay."

"Liberace always said that too."

"As did a lot of people who weren't gay, Dorothy."

"I don't mind it myself. Lots of people are doing it these days. Good luck to 'em. Just don't be one of the dancing ones, they get to be annoying very quickly." Dorothy looked Paul up and down, as if seeing him for the first time. "Good God, boy, what've you done to yourself?"

Paul gingerly lifted his right arm in its sling. "Nothing serious, Grandma, I just pulled a muscle at the gym."

"Actually, I meant the jumper, but yes that too."

"Anyway," said Paul, "I wanted to introduce you to my friend..."

Paul was interrupted by the glass door opening outwards and Dorothy pushing by him, in a sprightlier manner than Brigit would've expected from her frail appearance. The older woman stopped in front of her, more than a little too close for comfort. Dorothy put her glasses on and looked up at her, the lenses magnifying the old lady's eyes to the size of accusatory saucepan lids. The stooped posture of old age took some of Dorothy's height away, leaving her as a five-foot question mark. The experience of being that close to those eyes reminded Brigit of the one time she'd tried to use a sunlamp.

"What's your name, young lady?"

"Ehm..." said Brigit, glancing at Paul, unsure of what to say.

"Speak up, girl, don't look at him. You know your own name, don't you?"

"Yes," said Brigit. "I'm Brigit Conroy. Nice to make your acquaintance, Mrs ehm..." Brigit stalled, realising she was short on quite a lot of details.

Paul attempted to interject: "Grandma, she..."

Dorothy stopped him with a raised hand, her eyes never leaving Brigit.

"Are you pregnant?"

"Certainly not."

"Hoping to marry into money?"

Brigit was on the back foot, but she was due a rally.

"Absolutely not, I have my own job. I'm not property to be bought and sold."

Dorothy stared up at her, then back at Paul before returning to Brigit.

"I like her," she announced. "She's got mollocks. Not enough of it about. So what's going on here?" Dorothy waggled a finger back and forth between them.

"We're just friends, Grandma," said Paul.

"Pah," dismissed Dorothy. "No such thing. Unless you really are gay?"

She looked at Paul.

"You caught me out, no flies on you," Paul chuckled.

"Don't patronise me, Gregory. Although, the young lady could be a lesbian?"

"She isn't," said Brigit.

"Nothing wrong with it," said Dorothy. "Jenny Clarke was one, mucking fine girl. Very practical people. In my experience, you cannot beat a lesbian in a crisis."

"Probably because they're never tempted to do stupid stuff to impress men," said Brigit.

"Hmmmm," said Dorothy, "not a bad theory that."

"Right then," said Paul, "maybe we can..."

Dorothy turned her head to the left at the sound of a car door slamming.

"Brimson, that you?"

Through a gap in the hedge, Brigit could see the next-door neighbour, all of 60 feet away, stopped dead on his driveway, like a rabbit in headlights. Dorothy must have only been going by sound but she clearly had the ears of a bat. The terrified expression on the man's face indicated she'd guessed his identity correctly.

"Yes, Mrs Graham. Hello."

"Don't you hello me. If that cat of yours mhits on my mucking lawn again, I'm shooting the little munt!"

Mr Brimson looked like he was about to form a diplomatically-worded response, but was discouraged from it when Dorothy took the gun out of the pocket of her housecoat and started waving it about. "I'll pop a cap in it, you see if I don't," said Dorothy, before leaning towards Brigit to add in a conspiratorial whisper, "I've been watching *The Wire*. Can't understand a bloody word they're saying but nevertheless marvellous!"

It looked like quite an old handgun but Brigit still shared Mr Brimson's alarm. After all, it being old didn't mean it didn't kill people. Not all the deaths in World War One had been from the cold. Brigit looked at Paul in alarm, but he raised his hands in a placating gesture. Brimson tried to get through his own front door so quickly that he bounced off it, his shaking hand unable to get the key in the lock first time.

"So, Grandma," said Paul, "aren't you going to invite us in?"

"Yes, alright, come on then." Dorothy turned and headed back inside.

Paul stepped through into the sunporch. Brigit followed him in, just far enough to grab his arm and spin him physically around.

"Easy!" said Paul.

"What the hell are you doing?" said Brigit. "Are you conning that sweet old lady?"

"Sweet?" Paul asked with a smile. "You saw the gun, right?"

"That doesn't — she thinks you're her grandson?"

"Yes, I've been visiting her every Monday for nearly two years now."

Brigit gave him a horrified expression. "But..."

"You do remember how we met?" said Paul.

"Well yeah but that's different, I mean... coming around to somebody's house."

"I visited her when she was in hospital and we got on so..."

"But —"

"And FYI – I'm pretty sure they've had all of her guns disabled, so don't worry. It's just for show."

"All?"

Dorothy's head appeared around the door.

"Are you two coming or not?" She glanced at them both and her eyes lit up. "Having a discussion about the state of the relationship, are we?"

"No," said everyone who wasn't Dorothy.

"Suit yourselves. Get inside, please. You're letting the heat out. I'm not made of money you know."

She waved the gun at them in the least threatening manner it was possible to wave a gun. It was just the thing in her hand at the time.

Paul entered quickly and Brigit followed, Dorothy slamming the door firmly behind them.

On instinct, Brigit ducked when she entered the hall. It had high ceilings but 'the wonderful sense of space' that presenters on TV property shows would have referred to was slightly ruined by the screeching eagle descending from above. On second glance, Brigit realised it was permanently frozen at the point of attack and suspended from wires. She looked around: dozens of sets of dead eyes stared balefully back at her. It was like someone had shot and stuffed an entire forest's worth of wildlife.

Dorothy stopped and turned to look at her, before waving her gun about absent-mindedly over her shoulder.

"Ah – sorry about all the death. Husband was a mucking lunatic, God rest him. Never met an animal he didn't want to shoot. I thought it would only be appropriate to have him stuffed and put in the hall too, but apparently there's rules. Tea?"

CHAPTER THIRTY-THREE

"Morning, sleepy head," said DI Jimmy Stewart.

Wilson looked gingerly around the private hospital room he was in, before focusing on Stewart's face and squinting at him for a couple of seconds.

"Who are you?" asked Wilson.

"I'm, ehm... You took a knock to the noggin... I mean the head and, ehm..."

Oh Christ! Stewart looked at the floor and tried to gather his thoughts. When he looked back up, Wilson was beaming at him.

"Ahhh, you little prick!"

Wilson laughed and then put his hand to the bandage at the back of his head.

"Ouch," he said, "only hurts when I laugh."

"Well, serves you right," said Stewart. "I brought you some grapes."

"Ah lovely."

"Then I ate them because you were asleep, and I was bored."

"Right. Still, it's the thought that counts."

"How are you feeling anyway?"

"Yeah, alright – you know. I made a bit of a fool of myself."

"Bollocks you did. You saved the lives of two innocent people, not to mention probably me as well. Nobody cares about the other stuff." That wasn't entirely true. He'd had the assistant Medical Examiner at the scene giving out about guards spewing their guts up over her corpses. Like it was something the poor lad had done for a bit of craic on a night out.

"Well…" said Wilson, turning a bit red around the jowls under the bandages wrapped around his head.

"Don't go getting modest," said Stewart, "it really doesn't suit you. By the way, have you ever had like special training in shooting? Because that was pretty bloody incredible."

"No. To be honest, I was average at best in the firearms class down in Templemore."

"Really?"

Wilson nodded. Somehow, the idea that the shot had been some kind of fluke was both comforting and unnerving. On the one hand Wilson wasn't Robocop, on the other Stewart was even luckier to be alive than he'd thought. Despite the St Michael medal, he'd not been to a Mass in 20 years; he might have to put in an appearance. It wasn't that he didn't like the idea of there being a God, he'd just never seen evidence, and he of all people needed that. The idea of there being a divine being was one thing, the concept of Wilson being his righteous angel of vengeance was quite something else.

"Are Conroy and Mulchrone alright?" asked Wilson.

"It wasn't them in the car."

"Who was it then?"

"A couple by the names of Duncan McLoughlin and Keeley Mills."

"Who the fuck are —"

"Exactly. All I know is they had Conroy's phone. They're both down the hall now."

Wilson looked concerned. "Were they?"

"Shot?" asked Stewart. "No, and all thanks to you on that score. She suffered shock and he…"

Wilson clearly wasn't listening. He was trying to put it all together. "Alright, hang on a sec. I know I took a wallop to the head, but how'd they have Conroy's phone?"

"I don't know and I can't ask them." Stewart hesitated, before deciding that the lad deserved the truth. "I've been suspended."

"What?"

"Didn't follow procedure when I got the phone's location. Violation of civil rights, so DI Kearns called it."

"But they'd have been dead if you hadn't."

"Yeah, I tried pointing that out too. First time I break the rules in 41 years and I get caught. At least now I know I'd never have made it as a dirty cop."

"Ah, this is crap. C'mon we're going to find out why they had that bloody phone."

Wilson tried to struggle his way out of the bed that he was now discovering he'd been rather aggressively tucked into.

Stewart stood up. "Whoa, whoa, Dirty Harry, easy there. You can't go questioning them either."

"What? They suspended me too?!"

"No, relax. You're on mandatory paid leave because of the whole 'shooting that assassin in the face' thing, not to mention getting injured in the line of duty. You'll be up for a medal by the way. I made it very clear you were only there following my orders. I acted entirely alone when I broke into the phone company's whatcha-me-call-it..."

"Database?"

"Yeah, one of them."

"Well that story stacks up. I'm impressed you've become a hacker. You couldn't figure out how to put paper in the printer yesterday."

"I read an article on one of those things."

"Websites?"

"That's the one."

"So after all we've been through, we can't talk to our only lead?"

"Don't worry," said Stewart, "I've got my best man on the case."

Stewart smiled at Wilson. An awkward silence descended onto the room.

"Look," said Stewart, trying to find words. He wasn't very good at apologies; he'd lived his life trying hard to ensure he didn't have to give them. "You kinda saved my…"

"Forget it," said Wilson.

"No," said Stewart. "Fair's fair. I was frankly, a bit of a prick to you and…"

The door opened and in strode Dr Sinha, much to the relief of both men.

"Ah, the good doctor," said Stewart, before indicating Wilson. "The patient woke up."

"So I see," said Sinha. "Detective Wilson, how are you feeling?"

"Fine."

"Super. Well, as I told you in ER, you only have a mild concussion and a couple of stitches in a minor head wound, nothing serious. We just need to keep you in overnight for observation."

"OK," said Wilson.

"Now, about Mr McLoughlin," said Dr Sinha.

"Excellent," said Stewart. "You asked him?"

"I did."

Wilson looked at Stewart.

Stewart shrugged. "What? I told you I'd my best man on the case."

"He said…" Sinha whipped a notepad out. "I took it down so I would get the quote exactly correct."

"Good thinking," said Stewart.

Sinha looked nervously between the two men. "And I definitely will not get into trouble for this?"

Both he and Wilson chorused how there was absolutely no possibility of that. Still, thought Stewart to himself, maybe best not to mention it.

"He said," Dr Sinha continued, "Brigit Conroy? What the…" Sinha looked embarrassed, "ehm, actually there is a lot of 'language' here, perhaps you…"

Sinha held the pad out towards Stewart, who took it from him.

"Right," said Stewart, scanning down the page, "I see what you mean."

"Ahem," said Wilson pointedly.

Stewart looked up. "Sorry. Well, to give you the PG version. Mr McLoughlin claims he met miss Conroy, his ex-fiancée apparently, and — some windsurfer bloke — which I assume is our boy Mulchrone, earlier today and - well lets just say, the next time they meet, it'll probably be a fair bit less friendly."

"And they gave him her phone?"

"Nah," said Stewart, "I'm guessing they dumped it in his shopping bag."

"Don't think too badly of Mr McLoughlin," said Dr Sinha. "He is in an understandably emotional state because of his... injury."

"What injury?" asked Wilson. "I thought he didn't get shot?"

Dr Sinha glanced at Stewart, who shrugged. "Don't look at me. You're the doctor."

"Well," said Dr Sinha, playing for time, "I don't suppose you're familiar with *The World According to Garp*?"

Stewart laughed. "Believe me, you're barking up the wrong tree trying to make film references to this one, Doc."

"Actually," said Wilson, "I read the book."

"Oh," said Stewart, who was embarrassed to admit that he'd not realised there was a book.

"Yes," said Dr Sinha. "Well, if the book is like the film..."

"Which starred Robin Williams, God rest his soul," said Stewart, and then felt embarrassed by his own transparent attempt to reclaim some sort of higher ground.

"Yes," said Dr Sinha. "A wonderful actor. I was a big fan of Patch Adams myself."

Stewart pulled a face. Dr Sinha may well have saved lives on a regular basis, but some things couldn't be forgiven.

"Hello?" said Wilson. "Can we get back to this guy McLoughlin, please?"

"Right, well..." said Dr Sinha, looking like he was in whatever Hindus have instead of hell. "You see... the thing is..."

"Oh for," said Stewart, through a mixture of pity for Dr Sinha and annoyance at how long it was taking. "This Mills woman was, ahem – performing a sexual act on Mr McLoughlin when the shooting started. And, well – turns out she is quite jumpy. Not to mention bitey. "

"You mean…" Wilson's look of horror made it abundantly clear that he knew exactly what Stewart meant, and that he wished with all his heart he'd not asked.

"Yes," said Dr Sinha, "although I am pleased to report, he will regain complete use of his… area, eventually."

"Right," said Stewart.

"Good," said Wilson.

"Yes," said Doctor Sinha.

Then all three men held an impromptu moment's silence as they each looked at a different piece of blank wall and had a private moment of reflection.

The silence was broken when the door opened and a rather harassed looking nurse poked her head in. "Sorry, Doctor, we need you immediately."

"I actually finished shift thirty minutes ago, Joanne, I'm just helping the detectives…"

There was the sound of something metallic hitting a wall and something made of glass smashing.

"It's Mr McLoughlin's girlfriend doctor…"

Dr Sinha looked confused, "But we sedated her. She should sleep through until…"

Some other things crashed into some other things, and several voices were raised. The nurse winced. "That was Miss Mills. Not the woman who just came into reception. She is fully awake and really fucking angry."

"Oh," said Dr Sinha in confusion, followed by "ohhhhh" in understanding.

The nurse looked at the two policemen. "We could really use some help?"

"Suspended."

"Me too."

Well, thought Stewart, it seems Mr McLaughlin's area might not be out of the danger zone yet.

CHAPTER THIRTY-FOUR

Brigit leaned back on the sofa, stretched her arms out and yawned. With everything that had happened in the last 24 hours, she'd grabbed maybe four hours of fitful sleep on a cot in the nurse's room back in St Kilda's, which now felt like a lifetime ago. Now that the adrenalin from the day's events was wearing off, her body was reminding her how tired she was. She'd have considered being this sleepy at 10:40PM on a Friday night to make her feel like an old woman, except she was in the company of an actual old woman, and she was showing no signs of slowing down.

The evening's second game of Risk continued in an air of good-natured squabbling behind her, as Brigit sat with Paul's copy of *Hostage to Love* on her knee. She had been a participant in both of the games of Risk, although not for that long. She'd not played since she was a kid and had needed to be reminded of the rules before they started. In the first game, she'd thought she'd been doing quite well, until Dorothy did that thing where she traded in cards to get extra armies and wiped her off the map in one turn of bloody rampage. Some people would've been inclined to go easy on the new girl; Dorothy was clearly not one of those people. She'd then gone on to destroy Paul, taking great delight in mocking him as she did so, for being just the latest fool to come undone trying to invade the East in winter. In the second game, Brigit had tried harder and, as a result, lost faster. She'd then excused herself to go read 'that book she had on the go' while the others battled it out to the bitter end.

Although she'd not discussed it with Paul, clearly nothing could be said about their situation in front of Dorothy. As far as she was concerned, Paul was her grandson and they were here on a social visit. Albeit a visit that'd turned into a sleepover, Paul having rolled out a weak sounding excuse about his apartment being redecorated. Dorothy had shrugged it off casually; it wasn't like she was short of bedrooms. Brigit would have felt worse about being party to this fraud, except it was rather difficult to identify anyone who looked like a victim.

Brigit had read *Hostage to Love* twice before but it was entirely different now. Suddenly the electricity of immediacy crackled from the pages. The people in those pictures were truly alive and part of her life now. Apparently, at least one of them was trying to kill her. She moved back and forth, refreshing her knowledge of certain parts of the story, but she kept coming back to the pictures. Sarah-Jane Cranston, the pretty young thing who'd gone from being trapped under the thumb of overbearing parents to being sold into a loveless marriage. Fiachra Fallon, he of the dancing eyes and the matinee-idol smile. Maybe he'd been as trapped in his own way. Doomed to follow his older-brother-cum-substitute-father into a life of crime, whether he'd wanted to or not. Two star-crossed lovers that'd recognised in each other a kindred spirit. They'd broken free of the chains that bound them and made for a better life. Brigit prided herself on being more cynical than most, but you'd have to be made of stone to remain entirely unaffected by that.

Then she looked yet again at the picture of the young Gerry Fallon. His eyes now seemed to be filled with a soul-piercing malice. Had he really ordered the slaughter of an innocent young woman earlier that day just because her father had been an old acquaintance? Had he then followed it up by asking for a man he'd never met to be blown to smithereens for reasons even the victim didn't know? There was so much of this that didn't make sense.

Her contemplation was interrupted by the sound of a lady in her eighties whooping with delight. Brigit turned to watch and couldn't help but laugh as Dorothy proceeded to do a less than dignified victory dance around the table. Paul's grumpy pout made it all the more hilarious. This was no social game. Brigit had seen 'The Pad', an article of damn near religious significance to the two of them. It listed everything they played on their games nights, and the current score in their battle without end. Dorothy had a significant lead in Scrabble and Risk, Paul was winning only Gin Rummy. There were other pages for Cluedo, Monopoly and draughts but clearly they had their favourites. Dorothy appeared to enjoy Risk most of all. She stopped dancing and leaned on the table opposite Paul.

"Never mind, Gregory," she panted happily, "or, as I believe your generation would say, 'suck it!'"

Tears streamed down Brigit's face as the mad old dear proceeded to do another victory lap back the way she had come. Even Paul had to crack at this, laughing despite himself.

Once the dancing had finished, Dorothy patted herself down and surveyed the room.

"Well, I must be to bed. Can't handle more than two world wars in an evening at my age. Gregory, I'll allow you to clear away the scene of my victory. Brigit, could you assist me with the plates, please dear?"

"Of course," said Brigit, instantly on her feet, ever keen to be the good guest. The table before her was strewn with the debris of their impromptu meal. It was only when she'd started eating that Brigit had realised how hungry she was. She'd not had anything all day bar a bruised banana in the nurses' room. Amidst all the chaos, basic sustenance had gone by the wayside. The food had mainly consisted of mince pies, macaroons, Jammie Dodgers and Jaffa Cakes. Paul, clearly intimate with Dorothy's fridge, had prepared both himself and Brigit a roast beef sandwich too. The whole thing had seemed oddly reminiscent to Brigit of the sort of feasts the Famous Five had enjoyed. Brigit had devoured all of those books in one summer. In hindsight, they were the beginning of her obsession with crime. All that had been missing from the evening's feast had been the lashings of ginger beer, whatever the hell a lashing was. It'd been replaced with a nice bottle of white wine, which also lay empty on the table.

Brigit gathered the plates and glasses onto a tray, and then carried them into the kitchen. Dorothy picked up the wine bottle and followed her.

"Just shove everything into the doo-daa, dear."

"Dishwasher?"

"That's the one."

"Right," said Brigit, looking around the large kitchen, deftly designed to comply with the house's period ambiance, while simultaneously being secretly crammed with every modern convenience no doubt. "Ehm, which one is it?"

Dorothy looked about at the cupboards arrayed around her, as if seeing them for the first time. "One of these I should imagine."

Brigit found it on the third attempt and began loading. "So, I see being a despot hell-bent on world domination comes naturally to you."

"It's in the blood," said Dorothy. "I believe there's a German skulking somewhere in the branches of the family tree."

Brigit laughed. "Paul certainly doesn't enjoy losing."

As soon as the words were out of her mouth, Brigit could almost hear them thunk to the floor. Stupid, stupid, stupid! She looked up and noticed Dorothy's eyes. They were as alert as ever, looking hawkishly back at her. Brigit had a sneaking suspicion this woman hadn't missed a thing in her entire life.

"Ehm, Gregory, I mean," she mumbled towards the ground as if praying for it to open up and swallow her.

Dorothy moved on silent feet across the room and closed the kitchen door behind them. Brigit looked up at her and was surprised by the calm smile that greeted her. Dorothy softened her normally strident delivery.

"It's alright, dear. You see, my grandson, not unlike my idiot son, has one defining characteristic. He's an arsehole. The gentleman currently putting the Risk away, is not."

"You didn't put an M on the front when you swore that time," said Brigit.

"I feel no need to be polite about my grandson. Ideally, I would like to give him as little thought in a day as he undoubtedly gives me."

"But…" said Brigit. "How long have you known?"

"Oh, quite a while. Probably since I first met him," said Dorothy.

"But," said Brigit, "if you knew, why don't you just tell…" She nodded her head towards the door into the front room containing Paul.

"Oh, it'd be awkward at this stage. Why upset a happy balance? And I won't deny, I do look forward to his visits."

"And it really doesn't bother you?"

"What, dear?"

"Having a stranger in the house?"

"Nonsense. You don't need to know who somebody is to know who they are. He's a kind-hearted soul who, outside of the one really big lie, is in his own way as honest as the day is long. Do you know why I win at Risk?"

Brigit shook her head, confused by the segue.

"Because he," she said, pointing at the door, "is obsessed to a fault with trying to control Australia. It is the easiest of the continents to defend. It's like there's a funny little voice inside him longing for his own little sanctuary, somewhere to call his own."

Dorothy took off her glasses, letting them dangle down onto her chest by the chain. She looked out the window, watching the distant light of an airplane as it peeked out briefly from a gap in the clouds. "I did have someone check into him for me. I… I know a little but I stopped. It felt oddly intrusive, to look into his life when he's not here. Does that sound strange?"

Brigit rubbed her hand along the back of her neck.

"No, I suppose not."

"Have you ever known what it's like to be truly alone? I mean, as a permanent state? To have an existence empty but for your presence in it?"

"I don't," said Brigit. "I'm... that must be really hard for you."

Dorothy turned and gave a sad smile that made her suddenly look much older. "Oh, my dear, you misunderstand. I wasn't talking about me."

Dorothy looked at the door briefly, before turning away and straightening some objects on the counter that didn't need straightening.

After a few long moments, she resumed speaking, the normal strident tone returning to her voice. "So," she said, "how much trouble is Gregory in?"

Despite all that had just been said, he was still Gregory. Brigit didn't know how to respond to her question. "Ehm, he's OK..."

Dorothy turned and put her glasses back on.

"Please, dear, don't you start mollycoddling me too or you shall be sleeping out in the dog kennel tonight. Gregory doesn't go to the gym and I've enough medical knowledge to know that whatever is under that hideous jumper is a wound and not a muscle strain. Not to mention the fact that he wouldn't just turn up here out of the blue. Not unless something somewhere has gone very wrong. So, I repeat, how much trouble is he in?"

"It's... it's not great."

"Can you help him?"

"I think so."

"Excellent. I shall not pry. I shall trust your good judgement to tell me what you need to as and when. Do let me know if I can be of any assistance. I really couldn't bear to have to join one of those tedious bridge clubs."

"Thank you," said Brigit.

"You'll find a first aid kit under the sink. There's a room up on the third floor that still has some of my dear departed Jacob's clothes in it, as I can actually hear that hideous jumper lowering the property value. And most importantly..." Dorothy reached across and pulled another bottle of wine from the rack on the counter, "there's this."

Dorothy handed her the bottle of wine with her left hand, and then for the slightest moment, she tenderly touched Brigit's face with her other hand. Then, she walked towards the kitchen's other door, the one leading into the hall.

"Thank you," said Brigit.

"You already said that, dear. Don't repeat yourself, it's the sign of a feeble mind. Gregory knows where the guest rooms are. Enjoy the monkeys."

Brigit watched the door close behind her.

"Wait, monkeys?"

CHAPTER THIRTY-FIVE

Paul carefully dropped the needle onto the record and closed his eyes briefly as the guitar intro of *You Told Me* softly swirled about the room. The banjo kicked in, followed by the shuffling drums. With a gentle reverence, he put the cover down on Dorothy's old but beautifully-maintained record player. He gave the fire a quick poke, threw on another log and then returned to his seat on the oversized sofa. His shoulder ached and he was tired to his very bones. Still, the fire was soothing and the music held him like the comforting arms of a lover.

Before him, on the coffee table, sat the album's cover. While the other three Monkees gurned for the camera, Mike Nesmith's stoic expression almost pleaded to be taken seriously. Through an extensive trawling of second-hand record stores over the last three years, Paul had managed to find vinyl copies of ten of the eleven studio albums the Monkees had recorded, the one exception being the 1970 release *Changes*. It was hard to get hold of second-hand, mainly because nobody had bought it first-hand. It had peaked, which is almost certainly the wrong word, at 152 in the US charts and it hadn't even registered anywhere else. When push had come to shove, though, *Headquarters* had been the album he'd chosen to save.

Forget *Desert Island Discs*, death knocking on your door will quickly triage your music collection down to the bare essentials. Along with the itchy underpants and two framed pictures, the album that'd spent eleven weeks of the Summer of Love at number 2 in the Billboard charts behind *Sgt Pepper's Lonely Hearts Club Band* had been his luxury item.

Brigit entered and sat down on the sofa beside him, a bottle of wine in one hand and a large lunchbox in the other.

"Get your kit off," she said.

"Whoa, whoa there, missy. I don't know how things work in Leitrim, but up here in the Big Smoke, you have the bottle of wine <u>before</u> you start making those kind of demands."

Brigit looked down at the album cover on the table. "Ah, the Monkees. Now I get it."

"Get what?"

"Nothing."

"You and Dorothy were in the kitchen for quite a while. What were you talking about?"

"Oh, y'know, girly stuff, Risk tactics, that kind of thing. Now, come on, off with the jumper. I need to take a look at that shoulder."

Paul started slowly pulling off the jumper.

"Are you sure you're qualified to do this?"

"I'm checking your stitches, not performing open heart surgery."

Paul threw the jumper down on the armchair beside him and then carefully pulled the yellow t-shirt over his wounded right shoulder.

Brigit gave him an assessing look.

"There's a tiny bit of blood showing on the bandage," she said.

Paul pointedly didn't look down. "I'm sure it'll be fine." He went to put the t-shirt back on. Brigit slapped his hand away.

"Don't be daft, I need to check it. Make sure you've not ripped your stitches."

Paul's stomach did a somersault at the mention of ripping.

"Are you OK?"

"Yeah I'm just... not a big fan of blood and all that."

"Right. Tell you what. How about you just sit back and close your eyes, and I'll just have a quick peek?"

"I'd rather not."

"Or, I could tell you in detail about some of the operations I sat in on during my training? I once saw a gallbladder being removed."

Paul stared daggers at Brigit, who smiled sweetly back at him. "Just let me take a look. It'll be over before you know it."

Paul sighed, sat back and closed his eyes. Brigit began to remove the bandages slowly.

"So," she said, "big fan of the Monkees then?"

"Kinda."

"I've seen them on telly. Is 'Hey hey we're the Monkees' on this one?"

"No."

"'Daydream Believer'?"

"Nope. None of the catchy well known ones are on this album."

"Oh, God, you're not one of *them* are you?"

Paul opened his left eye and looked at her.

"Them?"

"Y'know, music snobs," she said, before dropping her voice down an octave, into a passable hipster impression. "Yah, I was like totally into their early demos before they sold out and went all commercial. They'd one track that was just the bass player pooping on a tambourine, it was amazeballs."

"No, I'm not one of them," said Paul, trying to ignore the feeling of fresh air on his shoulder, and the feeling of Brigit's fingers on his naked skin. "For a start, this album was after the two albums with all the catchy tunes."

"Yah, I'm actually a big fan of their post-commercial phase, when they did some really innovative things with bagpipes," continued Brigit.

"Are you going to keep being sarcastic?"

"I'd imagine there is a very high probability of that, yes. This might sting a bit."

"I think you're over-estimating the devastating effect of your – OUCH!"

The ouch was for whatever Brigit had wiped across his wound. "Ah right, you meant that. Not much of a warning."

"Relax, ye big wuss," she said, "or I'll tell you about infections you can get from—"

"OK, OK, OK," said Paul, leaning back and closing his eyes again.

"So, why this album then?" Brigit continued.

"Well, you know how journalists are always talking about the great moments in music history. Dylan going electric, The Beatles performing on the roof at Abbey Road—"

"Janet Jackson's boob going solo at the Superbowl."

"Exactly. Well you probably heard how The Monkees were the world's first manufactured band?"

"Were they?"

"Yeah, yeah – they were actually put together for the TV show. It worked brilliantly too. In 1967, they out-sold the Beatles and the Rolling Stones combined. Combined, mind you!"

"Fancy," said Brigit, without a great deal of sincerity.

"Then," continued Paul, "Mike Nesmith, that's the one in the hat."

"I always preferred the drummer."

"Everybody preferred the drummer," said Paul. "But – Nesmith did something truly amazing. He convinced the other three to fire the session musicians and the songwriters. Then they went into the studio and, for their third album, for the first time, they tried to do it themselves. They basically formed a real band out of the fake one they were already in."

"And it worked?" said Brigit.

"Well, kinda," said Paul. "I mean, there's nothing on the album as good as *Daydream Believer* or *Last Train to Clarksville* but..."

"But?"

"Don't you get it? They took the lie of what they were and they made it real."

"I get it," said Brigit. "They became proper artists. They reclaimed their souls and went on to critical acclaim..."

"No, not really. In fact, in the long run – it was a bit of a disaster. The critics still hated them and they weren't producing the catchy tunes that radio wanted anymore. They even tried to resell their souls pretty soon after, when they realised they'd killed the golden calf."

"Goose," said Brigit, as she began re-bandaging Paul's shoulder.

"What?"

"You can't kill the golden calf, it was a statue. The golden goose was the one who laid the golden eggs, that's the one you can kill. Mind you, when you think about it, surely laying golden eggs was doing awful things to that goose's digestive system."

"Whatever," said Paul. "The point is – this album captures a moment. It's four guys doing what they can to make what they are really mean something. I guess, I dunno – I just like the idea of that. Does that make sense?"

Paul opened his eyes and looked at Brigit.

"Yeah, yeah it does."

They held each other's gaze just a moment too long before both looking away in embarrassment.

Paul glanced down at the book that was still in his lap.

"Here's what I don't understand…"

"The continuing popularity of Simply Red?"

"No, although also, yes," said Paul. "What I was referring to is – why is somebody trying to kill us?"

"Ah, the two hundred million Euro question," said Brigit, as she ripped some tape off a roll, and stuck down the end of the fresh bandage she had just applied. "And you are done. For God's sake put some clothes on, your creepy nipples are freaking me out."

Paul looked down. "What's wrong with my nipples?"

"They're like the Mona Lisa's eyes, they follow you across the room."

Brigit sat back on the sofa and began applying the corkscrew to the bottle of red wine as Paul re-dressed himself.

"I know what you mean though," said Brigit. "We've been so busy running, we've not really thought about why. What could McNair have told you that's so scared this Gerry Fallon fella?"

Paul left the jumper to one side. In the warmth coming from the fireplace, he didn't need it. "I keep going over it in my head. He talked a lot about dying."

"Hardly surprising," said Brigit, as she pulled the cork out of the bottle.

"Phil told me that Gerry Fallon has a son," continued Paul, as Brigit filled both their wine glasses without asking. "McNair said how I looked a bit like my father and my uncle. I assume he thought I was this Gerry Fallon Junior then."

"Who," said Brigit, "he was clearly not happy to see."

"I bet he thought they'd kill him if they found him."

"Judging by what has happened since, he may've got that bang on. Cheers," said Brigit, raising her glass in an unanswered toast before putting it to her lips.

"He kept telling me how he wouldn't say anything. Pleaded really."

"So the question is what did McNair know that he was promising not to say?"

"That's the annoying thing," said Paul, "he never said. Getting killed for something you don't know seems like a really shitty way to die."

"What could it have been though?" asked Brigit, as she folded her legs underneath herself on the sofa and looked into the dancing flames of the fire.

"Well," said Paul, "he'd have been able to implicate Fallon in the kidnapping."

"Yeah," replied Brigit. "Exactly. *He* would. Legally, though, it doesn't matter if he told you everything and who shot JFK to boot. Anything you know is 'hearsay'. It'd never stand up in court. I get why he'd want McNair dead but that doesn't explain you, and by extension me. Dead men tell no tales."

Brigit reached down and handed Paul the glass of wine he'd left untouched on the table. Clearly, Nurse Conroy did not like drinking alone.

"Maybe he wants revenge on me because he thinks I killed McNair for somebody else?" said Paul.

"Nah," said Brigit, "that wouldn't explain why McNair's poor daughter, God rest her soul, got done in too."

Paul stopped to think about this. In the rush, it hadn't really registered with him. A woman he'd never met was dead because of what had happened in a hospital room just over 24 hours ago, between him and her father. He had to add that to the ever-growing pile of things he didn't know how to feel about.

"McNair," said Brigit, "didn't die when the book says. If he escaped with old Romeo and Juliet, maybe he knows where they are?"

"Maybe," said Paul. "Is that worth killing to protect though?"

Brigit put her glass down on the table in front of her and picked up the bottle for a refill. She shot a meaningful look at the still virtually-full glass in Paul's hand. He dutifully took a large gulp in an effort to keep up his end of the unspoken bargain.

Brigit pointed the bottle at him.

"It could be worth killing for," she said. "Think about it. You're Gerry Fallon. You've not exactly got a healthy respect for the value of human life. It's 30 years later. Your brother and his missus have a whole new life somewhere, a family. Nobody would want to up sticks and run at this stage."

"I guess," said Paul. "I know I'm not looking forward to it."

"Looking forward to what?" said Brigit, tilting the bottle to her glass.

"Running."

Brigit stopped pouring and looked at him. "What are you talking about? You can't just run away."

"What do you think we're doing now?"

"Well, hiding – temporarily, while we figure out a plan of action."

"I'm running," said Paul. "That is my plan of action."

"But you can't just leave!" said Brigit, a hint of outrage in her voice.

"You watch me," said Paul. "I am getting the hell out of here, ASAP."

"And go where? Do what?"

"I've no idea," said Paul. "I haven't planned beyond staying alive."

Since his talk with auntie Lynn, that one thought had dominated his mind. Run, get away, live to fight another day. The only downside of that plan, was that some donkeys would achieve a considerably higher standard of living. Bastards!

"But..." said Brigit, looking around, searching for her counter-argument. "It's not exactly heroic, is it?"

"Whoever said I was a hero?" said Paul. "Fallon wants me gone. I have a very limited range of choices."

"There is another one," said Brigit. "We could find the secret Fallon is keeping and reveal it to the world. Then, there'd be no reason to run."

Paul took another sip of wine. "So let me get this straight Nurse Conroy. Your plan is that we solve a thirty-year-old case that nobody has got close to cracking? The one where the last and best witness died last night?"

"Well... yes, basically," she responded. "I've not worked out the finer details yet."

"No shit, Sherlock," said Paul, raising his glass in mock toast. "Good luck with that. I'll be in somebody's car boot on the ferry to Calais."

"Fluent in French, are you? And what'll you do for money when you get there?" asked Brigit. "Your plan is about as crap as mine."

"Fair point," said Paul. "To be honest with you, I am way too tired to think about it now. Let's talk about something else."

Brigit drained the last of her wine.

"Like what?"

"Well," said Paul, "there's the other big mystery."

"Which is?"

"Your ex-fiancé, Harry Hairplugs."

"Absolutely not."

Paul grabbed the bottle of wine up from the table. "C'mon, fair is fair. I let you operate on me..."

"Oh, please."

"I think I deserve an explanation of what happened there."

Brigit rolled her eyes and then held her glass out.

"Alright, but this will take a lot more booze."

Paul gave Brigit a generous refill, before topping his own glass up with the last remaining drops. He placed the empty bottle back down on the table and then nodded at her.

"Fire away."

"God, where to start?" mumbled Brigit.

"Well, how did you let that hunk of burning love get away?"

She cringed. "Oh stop. For a start, he didn't always have..." Brigit waved her hand around the top of her head.

Paul pulled a face of mock surprise. "Wait, you are kidding – that ain't natural?"

"Well, only in the sense that it must've grown somewhere at some point."

"Actually," said Paul, "I've always wondered about that, and you'd be in a position to know. Does that hair look like it could've been transplanted from his arse?"

Brigit whacked him on the arm. Not hard but, it being the right arm, the contact caused a stab of pain in his shoulder. He winced.

"Oh God, sorry," said Brigit.

"No, totally my fault," replied Paul.

"Actually, you're right, it was. In fact, if you're going to make any more gobshite remarks like that, you should probably swap sides, so that your wounded shoulder is out of walloping range."

Paul made a show of considering this, then stood up and walked around the coffee table to the far side of the sofa. Brigit rolled her eyes and shifted over into the space he'd just vacated. He wiped some imaginary dust off the sofa cushion with his good hand, before showily sitting down in a prim and proper manner.

"You may continue."

Brigit walloped him on the good arm.

"What was that for?"

"I'm sure we'll find out in a minute," she said. "So, I met him at a Christmas do about four years ago. He's an architect. My friend Elaine worked in their office for a bit as a temp. She got invited back to their crimbo party. I was required to provide moral support and witness testimony for the inevitable autopsy she would be holding the next day. She was there to show Dave from Logistics how fabulous she was, and how she didn't need him. The plan was to ignore him, and whatever happened, I was to stop her either getting into a fight with or shagging Dave."

"So what happened?"

"She both shagged and got into a fight with him, I am still not sure on the order. There was a free bar, things got a little blurry."

"You're an awful wingman."

"In my defence, I was a bridesmaid at their wedding two months ago, so it turned out alright in the end."

"Ah, romance."

Brigit walloped Paul on the arm.

"That's a down payment on the next one. Anyway," she continued, "at the end of the night, a nice guy helped me get her into a taxi."

"Duncan?"

"Duncan. He texted me a couple of days later. I'd apparently given him my number and... next thing you know we were a couple."

"Aren't you leaving out a load of romantic detail there?" asked Paul.

"Not as much as you'd think. To be honest, I wasn't in a great place at the time. I was supposed to be off seeing the world but then my mum got sick and suddenly even Dublin felt like it was too far away. I was going backwards and forwards to Leitrim the whole time. He was supportive in his way. Didn't mind me being away most weekends. It sounds stupid but it was nice to feel I had someone."

Paul nodded. "That's not stupid," he said, before taking a sip of his wine.

"After a couple of years, he proposed, and I said yes. I was stuck. The world was off-limits and it felt like life was leaving me behind. I figured maybe I should try wanting what everybody else wants, d'ye know what I mean?"

Paul nodded.

"But deep down," Brigit continued, "I knew it was a terrible idea. It didn't feel like I should, but I had convinced myself that all the romantic stuff was nonsense anyway. He was a nice guy and blah blah blah. Plus, to be honest, my Ma was so happy when I told her. More than anything, she wanted to see me walk down the aisle before..."

Brigit looked away. She produced a tissue from somewhere and dabbed at the corner of her eye. Paul suddenly felt bad, like maybe he'd pushed too far. He reached over and touched her softly on the shoulder. She turned around and punched him on the arm.

"What was that for?"

"For making me get all teary-eyed, ye prick," she said, smiling as she said the words, to show there was nothing behind them. The tissue disappeared back to wherever it had appeared from and she continued. "We tried to rush it, y'know, for mum, but cancer won the race. We'd booked the wedding in for a Wednesday in December, so we could get the church. She only made it to October."

"I'm sorry," said Paul.

Brigit waved away his condolences.

"Then I found myself with a fiancé and, for the first time really, we started seeing a lot of each other."

"And?"

"I realised I was marrying a complete cock."

Paul laughed despite himself. He clamped his hand over his mouth as quickly as he could. Then, before Brigit could move, he said, "I got this one," and punched himself gently in the face.

"Thank you," she said. "So, staring down the barrel of unhappy ever after, I did what needed to be done. Only, I did it three weeks before the big day."

"Ouch."

"Embarrassing for everybody, humiliating for him. We lost the deposit on the hotel. I'd had to tell all the guests. That was a fun series of phone calls."

"I bet."

"I felt awful, really awful, for two months. Then I found out that the bald arsehole had been so terribly supportive all the time I'd been away because he'd been fucking around behind my back the whole time."

"What a prick!"

"Amen," agreed Brigit. "I couldn't even get the satisfaction of breaking up with him because I'd already broken up with him."

"So was it…" asked Paul, "yer one we saw today? Keeley?"

"The affair? No. From what I've heard since, he was humping everything that'd stand still long enough. But the 'main affair' – that was a woman called Linda. I'd even met her a couple of times. Lovely lady, if you don't mind trout-faced whingers."

"They are my type," said Paul.

"Well you're out of luck. Last I heard, her and Duncan are living together now. No, Keeley is no doubt 'the new Linda'. Can't say I have much sympathy for the old Linda. She helped Duncan establish a system where his pernicious penis makes the decisions. She can't be overly surprised when she doesn't like the results."

"Sounds like a lucky escape."

Brigit took a sip of wine. "I suppose," she said. "Still, depressing as hell though. Any idea what it feels like to settle for somebody, only to find out that they didn't settle for you?"

"Ah boo hoo," said Paul.

Brigit gave him a look over the top of her glass. "Clearly the punching in the arm is having a limited effect. I may have to move onto other, more sensitive, areas."

"No," said Paul, "I'm serious. OK, Astroturf head was a disaster but at least you avoided it and, you do have people asking you to marry them. That's not nothing."

"Are you seriously telling me your love life is in a worse state than mine?" said Brigit, a note of challenge in her voice.

"Absolutely. Hands down!"

"Ha," she responded, "not a chance."

"OK," he said, "let's make it interesting. Person with the least depressing love life gets the next bottle of wine."

"You are on, Monkee Boy, fire away."

"Alright," Paul said, "I've not had a relationship that's lasted longer than a month in my entire life."

"Pah," said Brigit, "nowhere close. I'd to put a wedding dress on eBay, my friend."

"Alright," said Paul, and then he stopped. He looked at his life and he couldn't begin to figure out how to explain it. How could he? He'd locked himself into a staring match with a dead woman and he'd been unwilling to blink first. He'd let his anger consume him for seven years until it had burned everything else away. The world had moved on and he'd stayed still, not living, just surviving. He'd known all of this of course, for a long time. It had all been there, lurking in the background. You could say this for having multiple attempts made on your life in 24 hours, it did wonders for your internal clarity.

Brigit waved her hand in front of his face. "Hello in there, Mr Grumpy Pants. You do realise you've completely stopped talking don't you?"

"Sorry it's just... It's complicated."

"Oh bollocks."

"Excuse me?" said Paul, taken aback.

"I mean, sorry, I probably shouldn't say this, but it isn't. It's one of the big lies that we tell ourselves, 'It's complicated.'" Brigit put her glass down on the coffee table, warming to her subject. "I spend my days mostly surrounded by people who are, to put it in terms you'd understand, waiting for the very last train to Clarksville. Do you know what I've never heard any of them say ever? 'It's complicated.' That's because, when you look back at it, it almost never is. Nuclear physics is complicated. The middle east is complicated. Our lives? They're actually pretty damn simple, we just somehow make them difficult for ourselves. Of course, I nearly married one of the world's all-time greatest arseholes so I'm probably not the best person to give advice."

Paul was as surprised as anyone, when he leaned across and kissed her.

Then, she kissed him back.

Then, they kissed each other.

There was no thought to it. Paul's body took control away from his mind and the two of them locked together. Paul's wounded shoulder got squeezed slightly in the press, but he didn't care. Brigit shifted her body position around as they kissed until she was straddling him. Then — the things that happen in these situations — began to happen. Sitting as she was, there was no way he could have hidden that from her even if he had wanted to.

He kissed her neck. God, she smelt amazing. As he did so, she leaned in and nuzzled his ear. She whispered:

"Simple."

And then his brain kicked back in, and started asking questions, awkward questions. 'What do you feel about her? Could she be the one? What does any of this mean?' Even as she slid across him and laid herself down on the sofa, the questions kept buzzing annoyingly around his head. He tried to tell them, 'shut up, I don't care,' but that was the thing, he did. He really did. Even as his fingers started working their way down the buttons of her blouse, her helping him out due to his one handed clumsiness, the unhelpful thoughts just buzzed louder and louder. 'Don't mess this up, don't mess this up, don't mess this up.'

Then, in the corner of his eye, he noticed the bandages she'd removed earlier, hidden under the coffee table where he'd not have seen them from a sitting position. He saw the bloodstain, and a whole other unhelpful part of his brain kicked in. Suddenly he was woozy.

He tried to look away, to refocus. Unfortunately, he could feel the things that happen in these situations, beginning to un-happen. He started to panic, which didn't help at all.

"Is everything OK?"

"Yep, yep, yep," he could hear his own voice, high-pitched and hollow sounding even to his own ear. He leaned back on his haunches and tried to think.

"It's just…" he stammered, "my shoulder is giving me gyp."

"Right," she said, "absolutely."

"And it is really late."

"Yeah," she agreed, "I am totally wasted."

"So maybe we should…"

"Yeah."

As he lay in bed later, glowering his self-loathing up to the ceiling, he replayed it all over and over and over again in his mind. It had all gone really well, right up until the point it hadn't. As he remembered the last part, he turned his head and slammed it repeatedly into the pillow. That was the bit where he'd wished her goodnight and patted her on the head.

It all felt very… complicated.

CHAPTER THIRTY-SIX

Gerry Fallon looked down and swore under his breath. He hated a lot of things in this life: Thai food, the Germans, country music, tweed, the colour purple — both the actual colour and the film the wife had made him sit through — Leeds United, cricket, knee length shorts, salads, politicians, ballroom dancing, the fucking English and whatever dickhead had come up with the prostate exam. He hated all of these things but, right there and then, in that one moment, the thing he hated most in the world was the small white ball sitting in the grass before him.

The golf had been his solicitor Michael Ryan's idea. The smug little rodent was standing over in the middle of the fairway, that encouraging smile no doubt plastered across his pudgy little face. He was useful, no question, and morally flexible, even for a lawyer, but that didn't stop Fallon wanting to boot the patronising weasel in the knackers every now and then. Ryan may've had the idea, but it was Mrs Fallon that had really pushed the whole golf thing. She wanted to be a pillar of the community, get invited to charity balls and sit on committees. He'd taken the girl out of Ballymun, and now she was keen to take the Ballymun out of the girl.

He couldn't blame her too much, he supposed. He'd been doing something similar himself, even if in his case, it was more for protection than appearances. He'd carefully built up the legit side of things for the last 15 years, making sure his name never made the papers and that the Gardaí never came within an arse's roar of him. He didn't do anything directly these days. He was never in the same room as merchandise. He couldn't remember the last time he'd held a gun or wrapped his hands around some little scroat's throat. He was too smart to micromanage himself into jail like so many before him had. Still, there was a little part of him that missed it. There was a lot to be said for being able to fix a problem by walloping somebody. The harder he'd walloped the ball today, the further it'd travelled in the wrong direction. In the last two years, he'd gone through four coaches and three sets of clubs, all to no noticeable improvement in his game. His scores had been so bad, Ryan had wisely stopped saying them out loud after the sixth hole.

They were part of a four-ball, in what was supposedly a celebrity scramble event. That meant he'd spent a grand for the privilege of a 7:30AM tee time in the dank drizzly rain. The celebs were supposedly drawn at random. Fallon had been at four of these things in the last two years though, and he'd noticed that the same attendees kept 'randomly' drawing the A-listers. Some arsehole banker had got Brian O'Driscoll again and the fit redhead who did the news in Irish. Fallon's team consisted of his lawyer, who was undoubtedly charging him in some way for his presence, a bloke who apparently did the traffic reports on the fecking radio and some floppy-haired posh kid who played a North Dublin drug dealer on a TV drama. Ryan had nervously insisted that them drawing him had been a total coincidence, and that somebody somewhere wasn't having a dig. Still, Fallon had had to seethe quietly while the radio muppet quizzed the ponce about the gritty realism of the show. Ryan had tried to make an in-joke of it, but that had just wound Fallon up more. The pudgy little prick wasn't a gangster, no matter how many times he'd watched the *Godfather*. On another day, Fallon might've played along, but this was not the week for it. He wasn't in the mood to humour anybody.

No, golf didn't relax Fallon at all. Given all that was going on, he'd tried to pull out the night before, but the wife had hit the roof at the mere suggestion. She wanted him to 'network'. Fuck knows what that meant. Besides, as Ryan had pointed out, it was important that he be seen to be going about his life as normal. Keep his distance while things played out. Everything was in hand. That was what they kept telling him. So, here he was – going against every instinct in his being, standing in the rough off the 14th fairway, waiting for a politician, two fund managers and one of the shit ones from Boyzone to get the fuck off the green, so he could almost certainly get nowhere near it with his third shot.

As the four-ball in front finally began to move off, Fallon took his 7 Iron out of the bag and tried to run through the ever-growing list of things he'd been given to remember. He settled into his stance, placed the club head in front and then behind the ball. He waggled the club head. He waggled his hips. He stuck his chin out. He straightened and then relaxed his legs. Then he looked up at the target, to see a suddenly tiny green that was somehow much further away now. Just as he was about to look back down to stare at the arse of the ball, a golf buggy swerved out into the middle of the fairway, blocking his shot.

Fallon swore and threw his club down. He looked over at Ryan, who gave him a nervous shrug. The cart headed towards them, its ruddy-faced driver looking back and forth at the various golfers before turning and heading towards Fallon. Fuck's sake! He'd been at one of these things before where they had sent around some 'comedian' to entertain the punters. It'd been tedious. Some nobody in a Hawaiian shirt banging on about Pandas and not being able to get his end away. Fallon briefly toyed with the idea of beating a comic to death with his 7 Iron. It'd be the best use he'd have gotten out of the club since he'd bought it.

As the cart pulled close, Fallon dismissed the notion. He didn't know who the driver was, but he'd a fair idea what he was. A heavyset bloke of about fifty in a long black sheepskin coat sat in the driver's seat. He was munching his way through a large bag of popcorn, while seemingly driving the cart with his knees. He pulled up beside Fallon and stopped abruptly.

"Well, shit the bed, if it isn't little Gerry Fallon himself," he said. The accent was unmistakable. Cork – that was another thing Fallon needed to add to his list.

The man tossed the bag of popcorn onto the cart's tiny dashboard and unfolded his considerable bulk from inside it. As he stood, Fallon noticed he was holding a hurley in his left hand. The newcomer extended his right for a handshake. Fallon glanced around him and then took it, playing along for the moment.

"Nice to meet you, Mr...."

"The name's Bunny McGarry. You're going to want to remember it."

"Oh, don't worry, I won't be forgetting it in a hurry."

Fallon smiled as both men tried to impose their will via the medium of handshake. Chuck in a bit of coal and you could probably make a diamond in there.

The man calling himself Bunny glanced down casually at Fallon's ball and then up at the green.

"Dear oh dear Gerry, looks like you're in a spot of bother."

"Nothing I can't handle – officer."

The man's eyes lit up on that last word. It'd been a guess but an educated one.

"Ah, does my fame precede me?"

"No, I just know your type."

"Is that so?"

"Yeah. I've always been good at smelling bacon."

The man calling himself Bunny laughed. "That's funny, I could always spot scum."

Fallon laughed in turn, as if they were old friends who were meeting by happy coincidence. The pressure in the handshake went up another notch.

"And how did you know where to find me officer?"

"Ah," said Bunny, glancing about him nonchalantly, "I know some people, who know some people, who hit some people."

"Ha, very good," said Fallon, the smile on his lips not extending to his eyes. The handshake was becoming painful and sweaty now but he wasn't going to be the one to blink first. "So, is there something I could help you with, Guard?"

"Paulie Mulchrone."

"Who's that?" said Fallon, before looking around him. "Is he playing in one of the other four-balls?"

Bunny laughed again. "No, no, he isn't. He's currently missing presumed scared shitless. Somebody is trying to kill him, ye see."

"Is that so? These young people today, I dunno. I blame the video games. Well, if I see him, I'll let you know. Now if you don't mind..."

Fallon had to resist the urge to pull away as the man leered forward suddenly, close enough that Fallon could smell the popcorn and stale whiskey on his breath.

"He's one of my boys, do ye understand me? One of *my boys*. I'm not gonna let him get gunned down in the street like a fecking dog. This is your one and only warning. Anything happens to him and I'll know where to come looking, and rest assured, Gerry boy, I will never stop."

"Are you threatening me, guard?"

"Let's call it some helpful advice."

"My high-priced lawyer is over there and I'm pretty sure he'd call it harassment."

"So it's true. Big bad Gerry Fallon has gone soft."

Anger flashed across Fallon's face. He squeezed yet tighter on the handshake and pulled Bunny closer, putting his mouth to the other man's ear.

"Do'ye want your fucking go, ye wonky-eyed Cork prick?"

"I'll give you the first shot free," replied Bunny, offering his chin.

Fallon moved back a step, gave the other man an appraising look, then tossed his head back and laughed.

"I bet you'd love that."

Bunny smiled back. "D'ye know, I really would."

"Do you like jaffa cakes?" asked Fallon.

"Not especially."

"I do. Bloody love them. I am a devil for the biccies, so the wife is always saying. Every man has his weakness, I suppose. What's yours I wonder?"

"Kryptonite."

"Ha. Funny man. Got a wife? Girlfriend? Boyfriend?" He said the last with a wiggle of the eyebrows.

"None of the above, I'm afraid. I'm not as lovable as I first appear."

"Well isn't that tragic. Who'll be at your funeral?"

"A lot of scumbags, I'd imagine. Just to make sure I'm really dead. They'd be too scared to dance on the grave though, afraid I'd reach up and take them down one last time."

"Ha," said Fallon. "I'm sure you're just being modest. I bet you've got lots of friends who'd miss you, and vice versa."

"Oh Gerry, you are humping up the wrong pant leg now, fella. Nobody likes me, not even me. That's why I'm your worst nightmare. Ye see, I'm in danger of having just two things in my life, you and the booze, and I'm supposed to be cutting down on the booze."

Ryan appeared beside them, his pudgy face looking up at them nervously as he tried to figure out what this was. Two large men, well over six foot, all but banging together like rutting stags.

"Is everything OK, Gerry?"

Bunny McGarry looked down at him and flashed a tight smile.

"This your pet, Gerry? Well isn't he adorable."

"Yes, Michael, all fine. Officer McGarry was just giving me some advice on my swing."

The two men finally disengaged from the handshake.

"That's right, yeah," said Bunny, "all part of the service. Remember what I said Gerry, keep your eye on the ball..."

Before Fallon could react, Bunny hopped the golf ball up onto the hurley and bounced it once. Ryan squealed and dived to the ground to avoid the swinging stick's flightpath as it sent the ball hurtling off into the distance.

"...and follow through!"

Bunny turned and nimbly hopped back into the golf cart, with a grace that belied his size.

He looked up at Gerry, a twinkle in his eye. "Oh, and by the way, a jaffa cake is a cake and not a biscuit."

And with that, he was gone, throwing a wave behind him as he headed down the fairway in the opposite direction he'd come from.

Fallon watched him go, his teeth grinding.

"That is... outrageous!" said Ryan, still sprawled on the ground. "I will be lodging a complaint as soon as..."

"Shut up," said Fallon. "Add him to the thing."

"But Gerry, he's a Guard. I must advise against..."

Fallon turned sharply and glared at Ryan, so much so that the smaller man flinched.

"I couldn't give a shit what you advise. We're in my area of expertise now. He goes on the list."

Ryan shook his head dumbly and slowly started getting back up.

Fallon looked up at the green, one hundred and twenty yards away, where his ball was sitting front right, 6 feet from the hole.

First green he'd hit all day.

CHAPTER THIRTY-SEVEN

"How'd you sleep?"

"Fine. You?"

"Fine. How's the shoulder?"

"Fine."

"Good."

"Yep."

"Excellent."

Dorothy sat at the breakfast table, her head turning back and forth, as if watching a tremendously dull game of tennis. "Good God," she said, "if it'll help break the tension, I could shoot one of you?"

She patted the old revolver that lay on the kitchen table beside her.

"There isn't..." started Paul.

"There's no..." continued Brigit.

Dorothy barked a sharp laugh of dismissal. "Yes, yes, I'm old, not dead, remember? Although if this breakfast is an indication of the scintillating level of conversation I can now expect, someone book me a one way flight to Switzerland."

Paul looked across at Brigit, who blushed and proceeded to move the remains of her scrambled egg around her plate some more.

Neither of them had said anything about what had happened, or rather hadn't happened, the night before. The problem was they were struggling to find anything else to talk about. It was like last night's events were a vast ravenous black hole, intent on sucking in all conversation around it. Paul had endured a fitful night's sleep, the pain in his shoulder and the mortifying embarrassment in his soul taking turns to disturb him. He'd considered numerous possible approaches to broaching the subject of what had happened, dismissing each in turn. He'd then gone onto considering time travel and why those lazy scientists hadn't invented it yet.

"Pang Lee?" said Dorothy in a raised voice, tapping her knife against her plate. She then looked around her, with a look of confusion on her face. "Oh, of course – Saturday. She has her day off today."

Dorothy stood, placed her plate on the counter and then shuffled towards the patio doors leading into the large back garden. "I'll leave you to it. I'm off to swear at some plants." With that, she opened the patio door and walked out into the cold winter sun.

Brigit watched her go and then reached under the table and produced a notepad and pen.

"Right," said Brigit, "while you were asleep, I did some research."

"Wait, where? How?" said Paul.

"On Dorothy's computer of course."

Paul looked out into the garden, at the woman currently having an animated if one-sided conversation with some roses. "Dorothy has a computer?"

"Yes," said Brigit. "In her computer room."

"Oh," said Paul, slightly ashamed of his own assumptions, "fair enough."

"FYI," said Brigit, "she doesn't know how to delete her search history. She has Googled some very specific terms regarding the actor Tom Conti."

"Ugh."

"I know! Still, if you want to get her a birthday present, a shirtless picture of him would be a big hit."

Brigit smiled, then caught herself doing it and looked away nervously. The concept of sex existing, much less people having any urges whatsoever in that area, was clearly off the table.

Paul ran his finger between his shirt collar and neck. While by no means the biggest reason, it was another cause of his discomfort. He wasn't used to shirts, especially not ones with starched collars. He was also uncomfortable sitting there in a dead man's clothes. When he'd woken this morning, the light blue shirt and red sweater had been lying at the end of the bed, presumably put there by Dorothy. She'd also laid out a pair of slacks, ironed with a crease so sharp they could probably cut glass. He declined to wear those, his own jeans thankfully passing the sniff test. Between the shirt that was a little too tight and his own, fresh on, extra itchy underpants, he felt like his skin was alive, and not in the good way they're always talking about in those ads for shower gel.

"So anyway," said Brigit, "I checked all the news websites. A picture of the bomb squad blowing up your car made the front of the *Irish Times*."

"Oh, right. I don't suppose any of the reports mentioned whether or not that would be covered by third-party fire and theft insurance?"

"Funnily enough, no. Seems like the cops are calling it a 'non-terrorism related gangland incident.' There's a whole opinion piece in the Indo about the shocking rise of drug-related crime in Dublin."

"Oh brilliant, now I'm a suspected drug dealer too. That'll look good on the CV." Paul would have a hell of a time explaining that to Greevy, assuming he lived that long.

"The point is, they've not publicly linked the bomb with McNair or Rapunzel. The death of Pauline McNair is mentioned in separate reports but they've not released her name or anything. There is also no mention of her father being alive and then dead."

"Is this good news or bad news for us?" asked Paul.

"I have no idea," replied Brigit. "Either the press don't know or the cops are somehow keeping a lid on it for the minute."

"Can they do that?"

Brigit shrugged. She'd read about that kind of thing happening in books, but had no idea about how it would work in real life.

"So," said Paul, "the Gardaí aren't talking to the press but they're talking to Gerry Fallon. I'm glad I don't pay taxes."

"Which brings me to this," said Brigit, holding up her pad. "As I see it, we have four possible sources of clues as to what is happening."

"Hang on a sec, are you Nancy Drewing this?"

"Look," she said, throwing the pad down onto the counter. "We can either try and get a grip on our situation or sit here with our thumbs up our arses, waiting for whatever is going to happen..." Brigit paused, "to happen. Personally, I'm sick of the feeling that someone is trying to screw me."

Brigit winced slightly at her own unfortunate choice of words, but maintained a defiant eye contact with Paul. "I'm just saying, hear me out and let's see if we can do something better than hiding and praying."

Paul looked at her for a long moment. He had wanted to run, he still wanted to run, but he'd not come up with any ideas on how to do that.

"To be honest," he said, "I'd not even thought of the praying thing. OK. What've you got?"

"Right," she said, "like I was saying, I reckon we've got four possible sources of info. Number one – the Gardaí."

"No way, don't trust 'em."

Brigit nodded. "I agree, although let's not write them off entirely. We should stay in contact with that Detective Inspector Stewart via your lawyer lady."

"Agreed."

"Number two," said Brigit, "Gerry Fallon."

"What the?"

"I'm not saying we go to him, I'm just saying – he clearly knows what is going on."

"Yeah, he's doing it!"

"But I was thinking, maybe your friend and his auntie could help us out if..."

Paul raised his hand. "Not going to happen. They've already got themselves in enough crap. Lynn was very clear on that. As far as they're concerned, we are now toxic."

"OK. Number 3 – Daniel Kruger."

Paul raised his eyebrows in surprise. "Yer man, the horrible hubby fella?"

Brigit nodded.

"And how're we going to do that? Isn't he away off in South Africa?"

Brigit shook her head. "Nope. He disappeared from view but he's still living in Ireland. Not even that far away, up in the Wicklow Mountains."

"How'd you find that out?"

"He's well into his seventies now, remember. I'm in a group on Facebook. It's a load of nurses I trained with. I asked them, they asked about, somebody had worked for him…"

Brigit grinned sheepishly. Paul could tell she was delighted with herself for this bit of investigating, although she was trying not to show it.

"Holy crap, finally a use for Facebook," said Paul. He had tried it briefly but Number 11 had changed their WIFI password and that had been that.

"Which brings me to number 4."

She held up the copy of *Hostage to Love* with a flourish.

"The book?" asked Paul, not trying to hide his disappointment. "You think that trashy fairy tale, which we already know is at least partially bollocks, is going to tell us something useful?" Paul shook his head. "If I were you, I'd have put the Kruger thing fourth, as that was your big ta-dah moment."

Brigit stuck out her tongue and flipped to the back of the book.

"Not the book smart arse, the guy who wrote it, Mark Brophy." She held up the page showing the picture of the author. A bright-eyed young go-getter of a reporter. At least he had been back in the eighties. "I was reading through it again and it hit me. It even says it in the introduction; names have been changed to protect people's identities and for legal reasons. The book isn't all he knows, it was all he could print."

She tossed it down onto the table with a flourish.

"So how do we get hold of him?" asked Paul.

"His website just has contact details for his publisher."

"Dear Fairytale Press," said Paul in a sing-song voice, "we're being hunted by psychos, any chance of a chat with what's-his-face?"

"Or…"

"Or?"

"Or…"

Brigit let it hang in the air. Paul smiled, raised his eyebrows expectantly and waited.

"We head to Brogan's pub tonight where the man himself is quote 'Mad keen for a feed of pints after watching Ireland v the All Blacks.'"

"How did…?"

"Twitter."

"You're yanking my chain."

"Nope." Brigit extended her arms and took a bow. "Ta-fecking-dah."

"So, Sherlock, your entire investigation is being conducted using social media?"

"Yep. And imagine how much easier that would be if some gobshite hadn't thrown away my phone?"

CHAPTER THIRTY-EIGHT

"This is a terrible idea," said Paul, not for the first time.

"So you keep saying," Brigit replied, "and yet here we are, doing it anyway."

Paul spread his legs and leaned back against the rough stone of the wall.

Brigit looked at Paul, then up at the wall, all twelve feet of it.

"This is totally doable."

"My arse."

Brigit put her hands on her hips and glared at him. "If you've not got anything positive to say, don't say anything at all."

"A day and a half ago, you asked me to do you a quick favour in exchange for a lift home. Since then, I've been stabbed, had my car blown up and I'm on the run from some kind of criminal Godfather who has the Gardaí in his pocket. I'm now assisting you in breaking and entering. If I restricted myself to only talking when I'd something positive to say, I'd be a fecking mime by now."

"Breaking? What're we breaking? We're hopping a wall!"

Before Paul could reply, Brigit took three steps back and started rocking back and forth on her heels.

"Whoa, whoa, whoa, what're you doing now?"

"I'm taking a run up."

"And now we know what you're breaking. Me."

"You'll live. You've got one perfectly good arm, don't you?"

"At the moment, but it's not even noon yet. I'm sure you can change that."

Brigit mimed a yawn.

Paul hunkered down a little more and braced himself against the wall.

"Terrible idea."

"Now, where have I heard that before?" asked Brigit.

In his own defence, Paul considered the entire day so far to have been a rapid-fire succession of terrible ideas. While he'd agreed in principle with the idea of going to see Daniel Kruger, he'd not considered the practical considerations. For a start, they would need a car. It turned out Dorothy had one, and not just any old car. Oh no, a classic Bentley, no less, which had been sitting in her garage since her husband died. Its dark green paint had gleamed under the garage lights with a shimmer of regal elegance. Paul had tried to subtly point out to Brigit that it didn't exactly fit the inconspicuous 'on the run' look they were going for, but she dismissed his objection. He'd also tried to point out the vehicle lacked any form of tax or insurance, and the guards were traditionally mad keen on that kind of thing. They'd cameras and databases and all sorts these days. This had also been summarily dismissed. As Brigit said at the time, "Yes, and I personally love the bit in the movie where Jason Bourne rings up a call centre to update his insurance prior to engaging in a high speed chase."

Which brought him to his real objection. Paul was extremely keen to avoid ever being in a car driven by Brigit Conroy again. The idea of the car in question being worth more than a decent-sized house just made it all the more horrific. Putting Brigit behind the wheel of a classic automobile was like leaving your baby to play in the middle of the motorway. It didn't tempt fate, so much as seal it. The problem he had was he couldn't find any way of pointing this out without, well, pointing this out – and he didn't want to do that either.

In Brigit's defence, she was clearly trying to drive more carefully than usual. She'd barely clipped that lion on the way out of the driveway. In the lion's defence, it was made entirely out of stone and could only bear a minimum of responsibility for the collision. She mumbled something about the car having a much bigger turning circle than she was used to. Paul thought of the winding narrow roads awaiting them in the Wicklow Mountains and shut his eyes. Then he kept them shut. He'd not intended it but, right there and then, the idea of pretending to fall asleep had struck him as one of sheer genius. He knew what he didn't see could still hurt him, but at least this way the last thing to pass his lips before death wouldn't be an embarrassingly girlish scream. From what sneaky peeks he'd taken, the view out the passenger window would've no doubt been spectacular, but it was very hard to enjoy the scenery while simultaneously being terrified of colliding with it.

Brigit, for her part, let him sleep and only swore softly when the world got in the way of her driving. After they'd been going a while, she went around the radio dial a couple of times before finding a station she found agreeable. With the music and the hypnotic rhythm of the road, Paul felt his bad night's sleep catching up on him. He drifted off, a smile on his face as Brigit hummed along to some raggle-taggle rock song about drinking all day.

The next thing Paul knew, he was awoken by being poked in the head.

"Gah – what'd we hit?"

"Nothing, thank you very much."

"And why're you poking me in the head?"

"Would you prefer I shook your injured shoulder?"

"Ah right, fair enough. So are we there?"

"Kind of. I've followed Martha's directions but I can't see any big house. She said it was a big stately home kind of thing. I've seen nothing that looks like that."

Paul looked around him. They were in the countryside. It all looked alarmingly green. He was not in his element.

They drove around for a while but Paul couldn't spot a country mansion Brigit had somehow missed. Eventually, they'd stopped and asked for directions from a lady out walking four dogs. Once they'd convinced her that they really weren't in the market to buy one, she'd set them right. Turned out, the reason they couldn't find the Kruger place was that it was so big. The roads they'd been driving along were long and featureless because they served as boundaries to the Kruger estate, which took up half the side of the particularly nice mountain they were on. After some further doubling back, some arguments and a regrettable meeting with a holly bush, they'd eventually found the gates to the estate.

The gates had clearly been made hard to find by design. Immense slabs of thick oak reinforced with steel bars criss-crossing them. These were the kind of gates that tank drivers would have had to take a long hard look at. Brigit pressed the button on the intercom and, after a short delay, was greeted by a cold, unaccented female voice.

"Can I help you?"

"Hi," said Brigit, in her best cheerful business voice. "We're here to speak to Mr Kruger, please."

"What is it regarding?"

"It's ah..." Brigit looked at Paul, who shrugged. "It's a personal matter."

"Mr Kruger does not speak to strangers about personal matters."

"Alright. We have vital information regarding the disappearance of his wife."

"And Mr Kruger definitely does not speak to strangers about that. Good day."

The intercom had made an unpleasant buzzing noise and then went dead. Brigit had tried it three more times, with no response. On the fourth attempt the female voice returned, no longer even trying for politeness.

"You are standing on private property. Fail to comply with this final request to leave and the Gardaí will be called."

"Please wait," said Brigit. "Just listen. We really do have information that will be of..."

The voice at the other end flared anger. "Do you have any idea how many fraudsters and worse attempt to contact Mr Kruger about this every year? You people should be ashamed of yourselves. The police have been called. Go away!"

The intercom went dead and gave no response when Brigit pressed the button again. Paul pulled her to one side.

"Look, it was a good idea, but we can't hang about here, getting into a fight with some arsey receptionist. If she has called the guards, then we need to get gone, and pronto!"

Begrudgingly, Brigit had eventually complied and driven them away.

At least for about half a mile down the road before pulling over. Paul had initially assumed she was doing that getting out and stomping off in a huff thing that he'd seen people do in movies. Mind you, seeing as she took the keys with her, it wasn't like he could drive off and leave her. After a couple of minutes, Paul begrudgingly got out of the car and followed her into the forest. He found her twenty yards in, staring up at a 12-foot wall.

And here they were.

Brigit ran at him and Paul cupped his hands, being careful to let the left one take the majority of the weight, the right being there primarily for moral support. He heaved her up until she was standing with her right foot on his left shoulder.

"I've got the top of the wall!"

"Super," he groaned.

"And you said this would be hard!"

"You're not the one being stood on."

"I just need a tiny bit more height."

Paul got a brief taste of Brigit's sneaker as it made its way onto top of his head.

"Feck's sake."

"Nearly there..."

And then Brigit's weight was off him. He turned to see her heaving herself onto the top of the wall. He debated trying to reach up and give her a further shove, but seeing as the only thing within reach was her arse, he decided against it. She threw one leg up onto the wall and then stayed in that position, dangling precariously.

"Ehm, Paul?" said Brigit.

"Yes?"

"There's a gentleman on the other side of the wall who is pointing a shotgun at my head."

Paul heard a twig snap behind him. He turned around to look.

"Ah. I wonder if he knows the gentleman on this side of the wall, who is also pointing a shotgun at my head?"

Brigit sighed. "I'd imagine he probably does alright, yeah."

CHAPTER THIRTY-NINE

Miss Choi, the owner of the cold and emotionless voice from the intercom stood before them looking, well, cold and emotionless. Cathy, a Filipino nurse that Brigit had worked with, had once spent a lunch-break enlightening her on how to distinguish the various nationalities from that part of the world. She couldn't remember it all now, but judging by Miss Choi's skin tone and facial features, she'd have guessed Japanese, although experience had shown you were always best not to guess. What was not in doubt was that she was very beautiful, scarily beautiful in fact, and not just because she was in command of the big lads with guns. Her smart business suit subtly accentuated an athletic physique and, even glaring as she was, her skin had the flawlessly creamy look that plastic surgeons had been trying and failing to achieve for decades. Her long flowing black hair framed a face that featured large soulful brown eyes. It was only when she looked into those eyes that Brigit pushed her estimate of Choi's age from mid-thirties to somewhere over fifty. Something in them hinted at the kind of tired that never went away.

Back at the wall, Brigit had been instructed to climb down and rejoin Paul. The man she thought of as Paul's big lad casually kept his shotgun trained on them both, until her big lad from the other side of the wall turned up a few minutes later in a Land Rover. They weren't the chattiest; all queries being met with an instruction to be quiet. Both of their captors had dark brown hair and could possibly have been brothers, although Brigit guessed cousins was more likely. It was only when she saw them side-by-side that she realised just how big they were. The big one was 6-foot-3 with a chest as wide as a door. The bigger one was 6-foot-6 at least and, while not quite as wide in the shoulders, he had the kind of physique that loomed whether it wanted to or not. Neither of them were 'gym bunny big' as Brigit thought of it. This wasn't muscle for the sake of muscle; this was the kind of bulk only nature and constant physical activity combined to produce. Their clothing and shotguns indicated they were groundskeepers. Brigit felt sorry for any pheasants that kicked off.

They bound first Paul's hands, and then Brigit's, with masking tape, before placing them into the back of the jeep. Big shoved Paul in, Bigger politely assisted Brigit. Ah, good Irish lads who'd been taught by their mammies to respect women. Bigger had at least picked Paul's sling up off the ground and shoved it into his back pocket.

The drive through the estate was uncomfortable, both for the bumpy ride and the silence. She could tell Paul was in one of his moods. The instruction to remain quiet was robbing him of the chance to make this a purposefully awkward silence as opposed to an officially mandated one. The mud splattered back window didn't offer much of a view of the estate as they passed, and Big and Bigger remained silent throughout. The lads were no great loss to the tourism industry.

After a bumpy five-minutes they were bundled out of the Landrover and into what looked like the large back kitchen in a grand stately home. In Downton Abbey, this'd be where the staff hung out. With its stone floors and a grand aga, you could be mistaken for thinking it'd stayed the same for a hundred years but Brigit spied a microwave tucked away in a partially closed cupboard. Brigit and Paul were deposited onto a bench, while Big and Bigger leaned against the counters, shotguns held casually over their shoulders.

"So lads," said Paul. "How long have youse been in the henchman game?"

Bigger grinned, Big scowled.

When the door swung open, both men instantly sprang to attention as Miss Choi entered.

"Congratulations on both your perseverance and ineptitude," she said, looking at Brigit and Paul in turn. "We have security footage of your attempt at trespass, which we shall be passing onto the authorities. Rest assured, we will be pressing charges. Have you anything to say for yourselves before I make the call?"

"I don't suppose sorry would cut it?" asked Paul.

"No."

"Really, really sorry?"

Bigger chuckled and then stopped immediately at a glance from Choi.

"One thing," said Brigit. "Could you just let your boss know that Grinner McNair is dead."

"Hardly breaking news. That gentleman..." Choi stopped and corrected herself. "That man died thirty years ago, which is before your companion was born."

Oh, cheeky cow.

"Right so," said Brigit. "I guess the man who died two nights ago in St Kilda's Hospice is an entirely different Jackie 'Grinner' McNair. If I was you, though, I'd still nip out early and get tomorrow's papers."

Choi tried to appear disinterested, but Brigit could tell that somewhere behind that perfect façade, wheels were turning, questions were being asked.

"We look forward to reading it. And how, pray tell, is this of relevance to you?"

"Oh, we're the last two people to see him alive."

"He stabbed me," added Paul, pointing at his shoulder. "I had a sling but the little fella took it off me."

Brigit noticed Bigger's eyes light up. She was pretty sure 'the little fella' could expect some slagging over that one. When she looked back at Choi, she found those big brown eyes staring down at her.

Brigit stared back defiantly. The other woman looked away first and whispered something to Big, who nodded. She then turned and wordlessly walked out of the room.

Brigit turned to look at Paul. "I told you this would work."

"Really? *This* – is your idea of a plan working?"

"We're here, aren't we?"

"Will you two shut up?" said Big.

"Tell ye what," replied Paul, "could one of you two do me a massive favour and shoot her?"

"Don't mind him, lads," said Brigit. "He's just your typical whinging Dub."

Big glanced at Bigger and this time they both shared a smirk.

"Ah that's how it is, is it?" said Paul. "All culchies together. Isn't that bloody typical. Here's an idea, how about you shoot me now? It'll save her the trouble of making it happen, because I guarantee you it's only a matter of time."

"I told you to shut up," growled Big.

"Or what?" responded Paul. "No offence but I've been threatened by that many people in the last two days, it's starting to lose all of its impact. Did you see that car being blown up on the news last night? That was mine. All you've got is that peashooter."

Big opened his mouth to respond but Bigger waved him off as he stood to attention. A moment later, the door opened and Choi returned.

"Take off your shoes."

"Excuse me?"

To be fair, thought Brigit, these were really nice carpets. If it'd been her house, she'd have insisted everybody took off their shoes too. That didn't mean that herself, Paul and their two armed guards didn't look ridiculous as they all stood there in their socks. She guessed this was what a drawing room looked like. Big and Bigger looked surprisingly nervous, seeing as they were the ones holding the guns. The revelation that Bigger was wearing socks featuring Fozzie Bear from the Muppets did nothing to enhance the air of menace they were trying to maintain. At least his were in good nick; Big's red and white striped affairs were notable for his big toes sticking out of the top of each one. She guessed he'd be taking scissors to those nails tonight too. What would his mammy say, showing her up like that?

The door in the far right corner of the room opened with a soft automated whoosh sound. An old man in an electric wheelchair entered, followed by Choi. The hair had greyed to a salt and pepper mix, but he was unmistakable a much older, frailer version of the Daniel Kruger whose picture she'd stared at in the book over breakfast. The wheelchair had come as a surprise. She guessed maybe it was that which made him seem so much smaller than she'd expected. As he turned to reveal the right side of his face, with its angry red skin curling around his eye and snaking down beneath the neck of his shirt, Brigit found herself trapped in that most human of reactions; not wanting to look but not wanting not to look either, both choices feeling rude. Kruger was wearing a tie under a stuffy tweed outfit. Only the rich dressed that way at home on a Saturday morning.

"Ms Conroy and Mr Mulchrone, please take a seat." His accent was the kind of pure Afrikaans that normally made everything sound like an order, but its edge was undercut by a slight gasping frailty. Brigit had no idea what was wrong with him but she'd guess the wheelchair was not a temporary feature.

Brigit and Paul sat down on the sofa that lay perpendicular to the fireplace. Despite the early hour, a fire burned in it, making the room feel unpleasantly warm, or maybe that was the effect of the guns.

Kruger briefly looked at Big and Bigger in turn.

"Thank you, Declan, Connor. You may untie our guests and then go about your business."

The two men hesitated and looked from Kruger to Choi, who in turn hesitated. All of them caught between not wanting to follow the command given, but not wanting to disobey it either. Kruger, for his part, looked into the fire as the wordless negotiation went on over his head, aware but patiently and confidently awaiting its inevitable resolution. Choi begrudgingly nodded and then added, "Please wait in the kitchen, gentlemen." Big and Bigger removed the tape from Paul and Brigit's wrists and then departed as instructed.

As the door closed, Kruger turned his gaze back to the sofa.

"So, Margaret tells me you have some information you'd like to share?"

He then sat there in impassive silence as Paul laid out, more or less, what had happened over the last two days. McNair's attack on Paul, his death, the car-bomb and the death of McNair's daughter, and then finally the confirmation from Lynn Nellis that Gerry Fallon was indeed the one behind it all. Despite owing her nothing, Paul still withheld Lynn's name. He also skated over where they were staying, for obvious reasons.

Kruger looked up at Choi after Paul had finished. She said nothing but Brigit noticed her hand was now resting gently on Kruger's shoulder.

"This is all... very interesting," said Kruger. "May I ask, what is your motive behind bringing it to my attention?"

Paul glanced at Brigit before answering. "We're caught up in whatever the hell this thing is and we thought if anyone might know what's going on, it'd be you."

"I'm afraid I may not be of as much assistance as you hope. After the... incident, I had numerous investigators searching the globe for Sarah-Jane but they never found anything beyond rumours and speculation. Similarly, while we did find issues with the official version of events, we found no trail as to where my wife may be."

"What issues?"

"The Gardaí," he was unable to keep the bitterness from his voice as he said the words, "were, at best, incompetent. Does it not strike you as odd that such a supposedly massive search for a missing person turned up nothing? That even after the fact, they never found where she had been held?"

Brigit and Paul let the questions hang in the air.

"I can tell you that I believe her not to have been held in the Kerry area, as postulated. That was one of many red herrings. I am convinced she was taken somewhere in the west of Ireland."

"But," said Brigit, "the witnesses saw them getting on a boat near Dingle."

"Ah yes, the witnesses. One of whom was not who he said he was, and the other who we know received an inexplicably large sum of money soon after. I would suggest you talk to them, but they are now both conveniently dead."

"Oh," said Paul.

"Convenient for Mr Fallon that is, who, as you have already seen, clearly does not like loose ends."

"But if you knew that there were these mistakes in the investigation, why did you not say something?"

Kruger shifted in his chair.

"Oh I did, Mr Mulchrone. I also wanted to sue the publishers of that damnable book. If I had my way, I would have spent every penny available to me, in the pursuit of my wife."

"So why didn't you?" asked Brigit.

Kruger shifted in his wheelchair and again looked up at Choi, whose eyes filled with sadness as she looked down at him.

"My family, Ms Conroy, were..."

For what felt like a long time, the room fell silent except for the crackle of logs in the fire. When he eventually spoke, Kruger stared down at the floor, avoiding making eye contact with anyone. "A family can just about bear the embarrassment of its eldest son being deformed, but a cuckold too? That, it would seem, is too much. They very much wanted the whole shameful affair to go away."

Brigit could not help but feel for the man as he looked up again, a mix of bitterness and terrible sadness in his eyes.

"They didn't want the embarrassment thirty years ago and, from what little communication there has been since, I doubt their opinion has changed."

Ms Choi cleared her throat. "I think all that needs to be said has been."

Kruger raised his hand to stop her. "I wish I could be of more

240

assistance to you. Having said that, if you do discover whatever secret Mr Fallon is hiding, rest assured, I will see that you are handsomely rewarded for helping finally put this matter to rest."

Choi pointed towards the door and began to move towards it. Beside her, Brigit felt Paul's weight shift as he started to stand. She remained seated and looked Kruger directly in the eye. She knew she should not say what she was about to. As her mam had once said to her, it wasn't that she spoke without thinking, it was that she thought about it and then always said it anyway.

"You should know... I... If we find out where they are, we will not be sharing that information."

Brigit felt her face redden as the other three people in the room stared at her. She glanced to her right to see Paul looking at her open-mouthed.

"I'm sorry but it wouldn't be right," Brigit continued, "to take money to destroy two people's lives, if they really are innocent of any wrongdoing."

Choi moved towards her. For one brief second Brigit thought she was about to be slapped.

"Margaret," said Kruger, softly but firmly. Miss Choi stopped, looked about her, momentarily unsure, as if waking from a dream, and then returned to stand behind her employer.

"Would you like to know how I met my wife, Ms Conroy?"

The question took Brigit by surprise. She nodded nervously.

"It was at a party," he said, before adding with a slight chuckle, "actually, no, it was avoiding a party. There was a big bash for something... there is always something. I was in a room, quietly reading a book. Sarah-Jane came in, ostensibly looking at the paintings but really, as I, simply avoiding all those people. She was..." Kruger returned to looking into the fire, lost in his own memory, "spectacular."

Brigit shifted nervously. "She was very beautiful," she said.

Kruger looked up, as if startled. "Oh no." Then he smiled. "I mean, yes, of course, she was stunning but that is not what I meant. Beneath that shyness, she was so intelligent, articulate, charming.

The sound of her laugh could make…" Kruger trailed off, an embarrassed look on his face. He cleared his throat before continuing. "I am not, as I believe you would put it, 'good with people'. I have had this disfigurement," he waved his hand at the angry red skin on his face, "since childhood. It has made socialising difficult. I have but a few close friends. With Sarah-Jane though… when she looked at me, it was not as others look at me."

Brigit found herself looking at him intently, at the side of his face that was not disfigured. He would undoubtedly have been a handsome man, no, he was a handsome man – once your eyes looked past the obvious.

"I may be the fool the world sees me as. The man whose wife ran off with her kidnapper. I may be all of that. However, I know how I feel. I love my wife and I will do so to my dying day. I also believe she loved me." His voice started to rise with anger. "Someone constructed a fairy tale for the world. My wife was the trapped princess and I… well, I make a good monster, do I not?"

He extended his arms, Brigit looked away, feeling ashamed.

"You read this story in a book from the pages of which, as you yourself have told me, a man supposedly 30 years dead came alive and stabbed your companion. Another man is now trying to have you killed for what he thinks you might know, and yet you still believe it. You still believe that I am the monster."

Kruger reached his hand up to touch Choi's as it rested on his shoulder. He lowered his voice again. "I am still married to my wife. I could have had our marriage annulled long ago, but I did not. Until I know for a fact that the love I felt we shared was a lie, I cannot and will not 'move on.'"

Brigit could not help herself. She looked up at Choi, who turned her head to look away.

"I don't seek vengeance, I just have to know. Connor and Declan will take you back to your car. Good day."

And with that, he turned and left the room, as Brigit and Paul sat there in silence.

CHAPTER FORTY

Nora Stokes could smell trouble. Actually, thanks to the cream she'd been told to liberally smear all over herself to protect her skin through the strains of pregnancy, she could really only smell the sickly sweet stench of coconut. The stuff was strong, but it was too cold outside to open a window. Greevy, despite repeated assurances, had not got the boiler fixed before he had buggered off to Italy to save his sham of a marriage. That meant the heating had two settings, blazing inferno or off. It wasn't much of a choice but she'd gone for inferno. At least that way, between the heat and the smell of coconuts, she could occasionally close her eyes and relax into the blissful fantasy of being on a warm tropical beach somewhere. Then the baby would kick and she'd remember her current state and how, if she really were on a beach, Greenpeace would soon show up and try and roll her back into the sea. Then she'd feel bad for thinking that and apologise to the baby. Currently, her days seemed to consist of wildly fluctuating emotions, bizarre cravings, and an exciting array of physical discomforts and indignities. Oh – and smelling like a deep-fried Bounty bar.

All of that she could more-or-less cope with. It was the bloke sitting outside the door that worried her. 'The reception area', as

Greevy grandly called it, was really just three chairs at the top of the stairs. You could see whoever was waiting through the glass door between it and the office proper. Unfortunately, this meant they could also see you. The man currently staring in at her looked like he was sent from central casting for the role of thug number 2 in a gangster movie. He was sporting the shaven head, the tattooed knuckles and even the scar running down the side of his face.

For the last 20 minutes she'd been stalling, pretending to do paperwork, taking imaginary phone calls, sending important imaginary e-mails. There was a loud cough that clearly wasn't a cough from outside. This fella obviously wasn't going to take the hint. She hadn't intended to even bother opening the office today, but it was the only number Paul Mulchrone had for her, and she'd had that message from DI Stewart to deliver.

Thug number 2 stood up and pointedly looked into the office. Nora held up her finger to indicate just one minute, and did one final rearrange of the articles on her desk. She had thought that if she bought enough time, something would come to her. It seems she had thought wrong.

Nora looked up and smiled. "C'mon in. Sorry for keeping you waiting."

The man lumbered into what was already a small room and made it feel a whole lot smaller. He sat down and looked around.

"Bleedin' hot in here."

"Yes, sorry about that. The heating is a bit temperamental. Feel free to take off your coat if you'd like." Or just leave. Please leave.

The man placed his hands on the leather jacket he was wearing and then changed his mind. "S'alright."

Nora extended her hand. "I'm Nora Stokes, and you are?"

The man gave Nora's hand the look people normally reserve for unrequested genitalia. "You don't need my name."

Nora took her hand back. "I'm afraid I do – for our records. I can't go giving out legal advice without knowing the client's name, now can I?"

"It's Mick, Mick... Keane."

The gap between the first and second names was so long, Nora could actually see him trying to be clever. She duly noted down the man's false name on her pad, and resisted the urge to ask to see some ID.

"And how can we help you today, Mick?" 'We' because, remember, there's lots of people working here.

"I'm looking for someone. He's a client of yours – Paul Mulchrone."

Nora shifted in her seat, trying to disguise any form of reaction. Trying to hide that this was now exactly what she'd been afraid it was.

"Right, I'm afraid we can't help you." Why had she not just phoned the police? Because she'd been so determined to not be the over-reacting silly pregnant woman, that was why. Now that the worse case scenario was coming to pass, it was too damn late. She glanced longingly at the phone before looking back at the man who definitely wasn't called Mick Keane.

"But you're his lawyer, right?"

"Due to client-lawyer confidentiality, I'm afraid I can't even confirm or deny that. You understand."

She'd spoken to Mulchrone an hour ago when he'd rung the office. She'd passed on the message DI Jimmy Stewart had left. It had been an odd sensation, having a policeman ask her to tell somebody else that they couldn't trust the police. To tell them that a hitman had been killed trying to assassinate two other people that they'd mistaken for you. Mulchrone had gone very quiet. Then he'd said he'd ring back later. He'd hung up the phone so quickly, she'd forgotten to give him her mobile number. If Greevy, the cheap bastard, had spent a few more quid a month, they could have had a phone line that diverted to a mobile. She'd be sitting on her sofa right now, getting overly emotional at fabric softener adverts. She'd debated going home anyway, and then she'd had the unhelpful thought about what kind of mother would she be if she didn't help two people who were in danger. These days, her bloody stupid internal monologue kept asking awkward questions like that. She was trying to ignore the future and forget the past. Trying so hard to focus on getting through one day at a time. That pissy little voice that wouldn't shut up had got her here.

The man who wasn't Mick Keane laid his hands on the desk. Now they were close up, Nora realised he had HATE tattooed across both sets of knuckles. Where was the love?

"Look darling, it's a simple question. Are you his lawyer or what?"

"No solicitor is going to answer that kind of question for you, Mr Keane. Now if there isn't anything else I can help you with…" Please leave, please leave, oh God, please leave.

He slammed his fist down on the desk, making her jump. She instantly pulled back, placing her hands across her belly defensively.

"Stop pissing me about," he said.

She looked around the room. "My boss is going to be back any minute."

"From Italy?" he said, grinning wide enough to show an unhappy collection of teeth. "It's really simple. Just tell me where Mulchrone is and I'll be out of your hair."

"Are you really the kind of man who is going to threaten a pregnant woman?"

"I just assumed you were fat," he said, sneering in a way that suggested this new information changed absolutely nothing.

Nora felt as if she might cry, but dragged in a deep breath, determined not to give this prick the satisfaction.

"Now, are you going to tell me where he is or do I have to make you?"

"I don't suppose you'd believe that I really don't know?"

He laughed. "No."

Then he stood up and leaned over the desk, his fists propping him up, a twisted grin playing across his lips.

"Your mother must be so proud of you," said Nora.

"She was a stupid bitch and all."

Nora smiled. "So that's where you get it from!"

He had only the briefest of moments to look confused, before he got maced, right in his great big stupid face.

He pulled back and rubbed his hands into his burning eyes, stumbling briefly, before careening messily over the chair behind him. Spitting and swearing profusely, he rolled about on the ground for a few moments, before staggering back to his feet. He shoved his right hand into the pocket of his coat and withdrew a gun. "Right you fucking b…"

He was interrupted by the unhappy sensation of his entire body going into spasm. His right hand involuntarily tossed the gun away into the corner, as 240 volts surged through him. A scream escaped his lips, just as the large fried breakfast he'd eaten, enjoyed and almost digested made a hasty escape out of his other end.

Nora had, in truth, never really liked her Uncle Graham. When she'd met him in childhood, both she and her siblings had found him a little odd. An expert in agricultural sciences, Graham had spent most of his life being sent around the world by the Irish government as a form of economic aid. As her mum had explained it to Nora, he was off teaching Africans how to grow things. In hindsight, he'd never really known how to deal with kids. He'd also been completely useless with teenagers, and he was clearly at a loss as to what an appropriate present for a girl was. Her brother had got a shield from an African tribe once; it had been the talk of the whole school for weeks. She, on the other hand, had got a rug. What 13-year-old girl didn't want a rug?

And so, it was with a heavy heart that Nora had let her mother guilt her into going to dinner with Uncle Graham, when he was back in Dublin for a conference last year. The man had lived in Kenya for three years, but apparently he couldn't last a night in Dublin on his own. He'd been really rather charming to be fair. As an adult, Nora could see that he was a nice man, albeit one that was a little socially awkward, and a little too into crop rotation. Uncle Graham for his part had been worried about Nora. Her mother had shared with him her oft-expressed fears for her daughter's safety up on the mean streets of Dublin, hanging about with all those criminals. So at the end of the night, he'd insisted a gift upon his niece. It was what he called a Taser. In fact, it was a glorified cattle prod. She'd explained to him that such devices were illegal in Ireland. He'd explained to her that if she ever needed to use it, she could worry about that bit after. He'd smiled and guessed she probably knew a good lawyer.

As Nora Stokes stood over the groaning form of the man who wasn't called Mick Keane, the air a heady mix of coconut, burnt flesh and excrement, she decided to name her unborn child Graham, if it was a boy. Hell – even if it was a girl. They could stick a couple of fancy accents in there and pretend it was French or something.

She reached for the phone and was about to ring 999, when she thought better of it, and dialled another number instead.

"Fucking bitch."

This time he screamed even louder.

"And just so you know," said Nora, "this thing goes up to ten. That was a four, fancy a five 'bitch'?"

CHAPTER FORTY-ONE

They looked like a couple that weren't talking, which was exactly what they were. Brigit and Paul were sat beside the window, looking at anything that wasn't each other. They were in the kind of moulded plastic seating that was deliberately designed to be uncomfortable if you sat on it for more than fifteen minutes. They'd been there for over an hour. Paul was fairly sure his arse had fallen asleep. He envied it.

After they'd been dropped back to the Bentley by Big and Bigger, the first part of the drive back to Dublin had been relatively subdued. Seeing Kruger's pain laid out like that had been unsettling for them both, and it'd done nothing to uncomplicate their situation.

"Do you believe him?" Paul had asked.

"That he loved her? Probably. It doesn't mean she felt the same though. He wouldn't be the first person in the world to misjudge that."

Then they'd fell into silent reflection until Paul had spotted the phonebox.

The call to Nora Stokes had done nothing to lighten the mood. Paul's stomach had turned when he heard the details of the foiled assassination attempt on Brigit's ex and his latest mistake. When he'd dropped Brigit's mobile into their shopping bag, he hadn't thought that... Well, wasn't that it? He hadn't thought. He'd been so obsessed with dumping a phone he suspected could lead trouble to their door, he'd got rid of it any way he could. Why had he not just dumped it into the canal, like he had his own? Or, as Brigit had pointed out, he could've just taken the SIM card out. He could have done a hundred different things, if he'd just stopped to think. Instead, he'd thought he was being clever, leading the police on a wild goose chase, having them follow a phone that was no longer in Brigit's possession. He'd never been great at thinking ahead, and now that had almost got two innocent people killed.

When he'd told Brigit, she'd hit the roof. Many people wish their ex dead, but there's a big difference between the idle threat and almost making it happen. She'd shouted at him, and he'd shouted back. She'd not been wrong, but at the same time, she of all people couldn't give him a bollocking. Who'd dragged who into this situation? Everything that'd happened in the last two days was brought back up, everything except what'd not happened the night before.

Then, they'd driven into the centre of Dublin in silence. Not total silence, there'd been quite a lot of honking, wincing and hand gestures. Now here they were, eating fast food slowly while they watched Brogan's pub on the opposite side of the street.

"And you're sure he wasn't in there?" asked Brigit, without looking up from contemplating her three remaining fries.

"Yes," said Paul, for the third time. He'd been sent in on a sweep of Brogan's as soon as they'd got there. He'd gone around every little nook and cubbyhole, carefully checking there was no sign of Mark Brophy in any of them. He'd even spent a ridiculously long time at a urinal in the gents, making sure that he wasn't in any of the three stalls. The most recent picture they'd been able to find of Brophy when they'd searched on Dorothy's computer had been from the dust jacket of a book he'd released last year. He was a fairly stocky man, with a head of long blond hair that was thinning slightly above a forced looking grin. If you took the photos off all of his previous nine books, you could've made a compelling flipbook of a man looking less and less smug about his lot in life. Since the publication of *Hostage to Love* nearly thirty years ago, it appeared he'd tried his hand at pretty much every genre that wasn't true crime, with less and less success. The reviews for *Bloody Lovely*, a vampire love story set in rural Ireland had been particularly brutal. Paul had quite liked the one that'd started 'Oh just suck off'.

"So, if he's definitely not in there," said Brigit, "then who is that smoking a cigarette outside?"

Paul looked over and scanned the front of Brogan's. It wasn't that big a pub, being closer to the 'proper old lad's boozer' than the 'modern super pub' end of the market. The tables inside had that kind of finish you only get by spilling beer on varnished wood a thousand times, and the carpets showed damage that pre-dated the smoking ban, if not the Easter rising. In the laneway to one side of the front door, out of the flow of early Saturday evening revellers, stood three men smoking and chatting. One of them was tall with a head of bushy hair and glasses, looking like a low-rent knock-off of Where's Wally. The second one was about the right height, size and age – but unless Brophy had recently become black, it wasn't him either. Paul was about to ask Brigit what on earth she was talking about, when the third man turned around. Paul had discounted him from the get-go due to his build. The Brophy in the picture they'd seen earlier was a stocky guy, this man was about eight stone heavier, none of it muscle.

"But," stammered Paul, "that guy doesn't look like Mark Brophy, he looks like he ate Mark Brophy."

"Really, you're going to use this as an opportunity to do fat jokes?" responded Brigit. "OK, so he's put on a few pounds."

"A few?!" Paul said while pointing at Brophy.

"Could you do me a favour and not point at the guy we're trying to surreptitiously locate?"

"Right. Sorry." Paul withdrew his finger.

He looked at Brigit as she stood up. He'd been so distracted with feeling guilty, angry and embarrassed over their fight in the car, it suddenly dawned on him that they'd not discussed any plan of action once they'd actually found Brophy. Just walking up to him and blurting out that his only successful book was bullshit seemed like a tricky conversation starter.

"What're we going to do?" said Paul.

"You, are going to stay here and try and keep out of trouble," said Brigit. "I am going to handle this."

"Fair enough," said Paul, trying not to look hurt.

Brigit brushed herself down, put on her jacket and then, after a moment's thought, opened the top button of her blouse.

Paul raised an eyebrow and she gave him a sarcastic smile in response.

"What can I tell you? Men are idiots."

And then she left. Paul watched her negotiate her way across the street.

"Yeah," he mumbled to himself, "we are. We really are."

CHAPTER FORTY-TWO

DI Jimmy Stewart (suspended) was repulsed.

If there was one part of the job he wouldn't miss, it was definitely the smell. Normally, when he'd been called to a dead body, he'd have brought the tin of Vick's from his desk drawer. A little on the top lip usually took the edge off the worst of it. The ripe ones were the foulest. The ones long enough dead for decomposition to have really kicked in. Those bodies were the hardest to get a result on too. You could often smell how bad a week you were going to have before you ever saw the body. Stewart had heard others ascribe a hint of sweetness to the smell, but he'd never understood that. It was just rotten, putrid death to him. The stench clung to clothing too, like a nagging ghost, demanding to be avenged. When he'd given up the fags, the long-suffering Mrs Stewart would occasionally comment on the new and unpleasant whiff she detected now and then from his clothes. He'd not had the heart to tell her. He'd made up stories about having to go dumpster diving for evidence instead.

So this was not the worst smelling scene Stewart had been called to, not by a long shot, but it hands down won that award in the sub-category of scene that didn't feature a dead body. He'd taken the stairs two at a time and heaved open the door to the inner office of Greevy and Co. Solicitors, only to reflexively reel back at the olfactory assault. Detective Donnacha Wilson (inactive through mandated medical leave) ran into the back of him.

"What the fuck?" said Wilson. "It smells like someone baked a shite!" It may've been lacking in bedside manner, but it was an accurate description.

If the smell was arresting, the sight that greeted them was doubly so.

A pregnant woman was standing bent over in the centre of the room. In one hand she held what looked to be a particularly nasty cattle prod. It was hovering 3 inches above the back of a prone figure that lay spread-eagle on the ground. In the other hand, she was holding a can of mace that was pointing directly at DI Jimmy Stewart's face. The woman was caked in sweat, and her eyes were puffy from crying. "Stewart?"

"Yes," said Stewart, "that's me. Nora Stokes, I assume?"

"ID," she said.

"I don't have any. I've been suspended. Wilson?"

He looked around at the younger man, whose head was currently wrapped in a large white bandage. "Shit, it's in the car."

Stewart took a step back. "OK, Miss Stokes, just relax. I am DI Jimmy Stewart. We spoke last night on the phone. You might recognise my voice?"

She looked at him, her eyes screwing up with concentration.

"Say something else?"

"You look like you could use a cup of tea."

She dropped both weapons and staggered back to lean on the desk, placing her hands on her lower back.

"Right answer. Christ, my back is killing me!"

"Are you OK?"

She nodded through heavy breaths.

"Did he lay a finger on you?"

She shook her head. "He tried."

The threat of vengeance from above having been removed, the

prone figure on the floor piped up. "I've been assaulted! I want to press charges!"

Stewart leaned down to take a good look at the man's face.

"Mick Sherry, as I live and breathe. Long time no see. You appear to have shat yourself, Michael."

He lifted his head up. "It's her fault."

"Really? I look forward to hearing you explain that in court."

"Boss."

Stewart looked up to see Wilson pointing at something in the corner.

"Ah. By any chance, have you lost a gun, Michael?"

"I've never seen that before in my life."

"Of course you haven't, and I'm sure the fingerprint evidence will back you up entirely on that."

"I demand a lawyer!"

"You're in luck, there's one here, but she doesn't appear to be a massive fan of yours."

The man Stewart had correctly identified as Mick Sherry made to stand up. Stewart moved his foot to rest on Sherry's fingers.

"Stay right where you are, Michael."

"This is police brutality."

"I sent your Uncle Terry down twice and your brother down once," said Stewart. "They're both irredeemable criminals, but not bad lads as those sorts go."

"What the fu…"

Stewart put just enough weight on his foot for Sherry to realise that silence was his best course of action. "My point is, you just pulled a gun on a pregnant woman. I'm pretty sure not even your own family would object to me kicking seven shades of shit out of you right now."

"Six," said Nora Stokes.

Jimmy Stewart gave her a quizzical look.

"Six," she repeated. "He's already expelled one shade himself."

"Fair point," said Stewart, before turning to Wilson. "Cuffs?"

The younger man shook his head.

"Alright, Mick, I'm going to take Miss Stokes outside to freshen up, but detective Wilson is going to stay with you. He, if anything, takes an even dimmer view than I do of scum who assault women."

"I didn't... agh!"

Stewart pressed down a little further on his fingers. "The fact that you were unsuccessful in the attempt, Michael, does not help your case one iota."

Stewart moved his foot away and turned to Wilson.

"We'll be just outside. If he moves, shoot him somewhere memorable."

Wilson nodded. Both he and Stewart knew that Wilson hadn't got a gun, but he was confident Sherry wouldn't test that. Today was not proving to be the scumbag's lucky day.

Stewart picked up the mace and the cattle prod from the floor, and then he guided Stokes out past her former assailant. While she freshened up in the loo, he put the kettle on. By the time she emerged, he'd have two teas ready. He'd also have had time to think about the thing he hadn't wanted to. The thing that'd been nagging at him since Nora Stokes had called him. The thing he now had no choice but to deal with.

As luck would have it, when he'd received the call, he'd just driven Wilson home from St Katherine's Hospital. Stewart had insisted on doing so over Wilson's protestations. It was the kind of thing you did for your wounded partner. Besides, now that he was suspended, there wasn't much else for him to do. They'd been parked outside Wilson's flat like a courting couple at the end of a second date, except Stewart had been in the middle of another awkward attempt at thanking Wilson for saving his life.

When he'd finally got home last night, Stewart had found sleep hard to come by. He'd kept running through what happened in the park over and over again in his mind. He couldn't let go of the image of the long suffering Mrs Stewart standing in the lobby of Garda HQ, tearful and proud, as they unveiled her departed husband's name on the marble plaque. Shot in the line of duty. Only on the plaque instead of that, it just said – too proud, too slow, too old. Despite the extra time he'd had to think about it, his second attempt at both apologising to and thanking Wilson had been going even worse than his first. Nora Stoke's call had been well timed. Stewart had just accidentally quoted a Celine Dion lyric, and he'd started rambling in a desperate attempt to cover.

As Nora emerged from the toilet, Stewart held out the mug of strong builder's tea.

"Better?"

"Better."

"Are you absolutely sure you don't need a doctor?"

"I'm fine." She gave him a tired smile. "Just knackered and pregnant."

"How long until?"

"Two weeks. I'm working as late as possible to save up the maternity leave."

"Right enough. Should I phone the dad?"

Nora Stokes blushed. "Let's leave that one alone, shall we?"

"Ah right, fair play." It was Stewart's turn to look embarrassed.

They both sat down in the waiting room. Through the closed door they could see Wilson standing guard over his prisoner.

"For what it's worth," said Stewart, "this story will make you a hero to every copper on the force."

Stokes gave a tired laugh. "And how many criminal defence lawyers can say that?"

Stewart slurped his tea and then turned to look at her. "So what do you want to do?"

"Well, as my own lawyer, it is my job to tell me that possession of a Taser-like device is a ten grand fine, up to five years in prison and I'm pretty sure disbarment."

"He had a gun."

"And I doubt I'll see prison, but I'll still be out of a job. You'd be amazed how big on ethics the legal profession gets when the public are watching."

"Taser? What Taser? I didn't see any Taser?"

Nora Stokes looked at him and smiled. "Having the police cover something up for you, that's the kind of thing that could compromise a defence lawyer's integrity."

"At the risk of sounding like a misogynistic fuddy-duddy, a copper isn't helping you out, the father of three daughters is helping you out. I'm just sorry we can't charge this gobshite, excuse my language."

"I was going to say massive dickhead, so you're excused."

"I can guarantee he won't press charges."

Nora Stokes gave him a worried look.

"Oh no, not like that. More than one way to skin a cat."

As he guided him down the stairs, Jimmy Stewart kept a firm grip on the power cord from the kettle that was binding Sherry's hands. He'd never in his 41 years of service pushed a suspect down the stairs. He'd also never been more tempted. The smell wasn't even in the top three things that repulsed him about his captive. The fact that he had no choice but to release him boiled his blood.

Once off the bottom step, Stewart pushed him forward and out the door, into the small tarmac-covered car park outside. It was currently empty save for Stewart's Rover and Stokes's Opel. Wilson fell into place beside him. Miss Stokes had remained upstairs, opening windows and whatever else she could do to battle the smell issue.

"Right, Michael, remember what we discussed. This is your lucky day."

Sherry mumbled something unintelligible, which was probably just as well. Stewart was itching to do something he knew he'd regret. He spoke into Sherry's ear as he untied the cord.

"She ever sees or hears from you again, Michael, and I will make it my life's work to destroy you. I'm retiring next week and I've got absolutely no hobbies. You do not want to make yourself my only interest, believe me."

Stewart gave the cord a sharp tug down, to emphasise his point.

"And you even think about pressing charges, I will rain down all manner of shit on you, pun intended. You'll be inside so fast your head will spin..."

Sherry tried to pull away, but Stewart grabbed his shoulder and pulled him back. "And when you get inside, I will personally tell every hard-nosed psycho I've ever sent down how you molested a pregnant woman."

"It wasn't like that."

"And I'm sure that fact will come out at the coroner's inquest."

Stewart pulled the power cord off and pushed Sherry out into the carpark. He and Wilson stood there for several minutes, watching his slow waddling walk of shame. When Sherry looked back, both men smiled and waved.

"What a scumbag," said Wilson.

"Lowest of the low. On the upside, I'm pretty sure you could tell he's shat himself from space."

They watched as two teenaged girls stopped and gave Sherry a look of undisguised horror as he walked past. Their laughter could be heard clear across the carpark. Wilson turned to go back inside, Stewart put his hand out to stop him.

"Here's the thing," said Stewart. "How did they know?"

"What?"

Stewart gave the younger man a searching look. He saw a flicker of guilt that removed the last shred of hopeful uncertainty that he'd been clinging to. "After Miss Stokes rang me last night, I didn't tell anybody on the task force. Sure, I should've done, but it was a busy night what with the bomb, and the assassination attempt, and my hero partner saving me from death and all that. Plus, I'm old and forgetful."

"Fuck's sake, Jimmy."

Wilson tried to move away, Stewart grabbed his arm and pulled him close.

"Look at me when I'm talking to you, Donnacha." He'd never used his first name before, Wilson probably didn't even realise he knew it. "I didn't say anything because we've got a rat, and the last thing I wanted was someone trying to get to Mulchrone through his lawyer. So I only told you, while you were lying there in your hospital bed."

Wilson pulled away, not in anger. He just looked like he might throw up. Stewart guessed he'd not fully realised until that very moment. At least there was that.

"I…"

"Do I need to take a look at your mobile, Wilson? Let me guess. Is Gerry Fallon an old family friend?"

Wilson stood bolt upright, a look of genuine outrage on his face, even as tears filled his eyes.

"Ah now hang on, Jimmy, you're way off. Here."

Stewart was surprised when Wilson thrust his mobile towards him.

"She rang me, while you were away upstairs with that IT guy. She just said they wanted to be kept informed, because of the sensitivity…"

Stewart scrolled down through the outgoing calls. There it was 11:27PM last night – Veronica Doyle. Wilson must have rang her as soon as Stewart had left him. "The fucking PR woman?"

"Honest, Jimmy, I thought it was just, y'know – helping them control the bad press over the Rapunzel thing. She said she just wanted to be in the loop, manage the media, that kind of thing."

Stewart sighed and tossed the phone back to him. "So you're not a rat, you're a politician. I suppose it's in the blood. Doesn't change anything." Stewart pointed up the stairs. "What happened up there, is on you."

Wilson just stared at the ground. "I know."

"This is how they get you," said Stewart. "Favours for favours. Next thing you know, somebody owns you."

"What should I do?"

Stewart stood and watched the traffic as the lights turned from red to green at the crossroads. Two young lads raced across, taking the chance and getting lucky this time. Young. Invulnerable. "What you do is, you learn the lesson. Last night you were the hero, today you're… not. Remember how both felt."

Wilson nodded.

"I'm going to stay here in case Mulchrone and Conroy call again."

"I'll do that."

"Oh no," said Stewart, a hint of a smile crossing his lips, "I've got a better gig for you. You're going to provide a pregnant woman with 24/7 protection until this thing is done."

Stewart turned and headed back towards the stairs. "And if I was you, I'd not piss her off. You saw what happened to the last guy."

CHAPTER FORTY-THREE

"What do you mean he wouldn't help?" said Paul, staring across at Brigit.

"Exactly that." Her eyes slid away from his and fixed on the girl mopping the floor instead. "I'm sorry, I... it was a stupid idea. I thought I could explain to him how we were in trouble and appeal to his better angels." She shook her head. "He must've eaten them, the fat prick!"

Clearly the ban on fat jokes had now been relaxed.

Paul looked at her and felt even worse than he already did. He'd watched her cross the road and then cadge a cigarette off Brophy. She'd then started a conversation with him and his friends. Paul could swear he'd seen the moment where she'd pretended to recognise Brophy and then excitedly explain how she was a big fan. The large man's face had been readable from across the street as it lit up like a kid's at Christmas. She must've said she was a big fan of *Bloody Lovely*. He was guessing Brophy had never heard that before, from anyone, even family members. His mates had left them to it, nudging and winking at each other as they stumbled back into the bar. Paul didn't know what disturbed him more, that they thought that Brophy might be 'in' there, or that the man himself might be thinking the same thing.

Watching Brigit work, Paul couldn't help but be impressed. She'd hooked and isolated the target in record time; those were some nice spy moves. He'd liked it less when other smokers had come out and Brigit had subtly guided Brophy further down the alley, away from the crowd. Alright, it wasn't exactly a dark alley on the wrong side of town. Paul knew for a fact it led to the stage door of the Olympia theatre. She'd more chance of getting discovered down there than of meeting any real danger, but still. He'd considered leaving Maccy D's to either join her or at least keep them in view, but he decided against it. He couldn't risk fucking up again.

Sitting there, slurping on the melted ice from his large Diet Coke, he had time to think. Brigit was right. He had spent a lot of time moaning and feeling sorry for himself. Alright, she'd got him into this, but she was also the only one trying to get him out of it too. The Gardai didn't care. The Nellis family were his oldest friends and they'd turned their backs on him. Yet Nurse Brigit Conroy, whom he barely knew, was out there trying to make it right. Putting herself in danger to fix something that had only really come about because she'd tried to give some comfort to a dying old man. She'd defied police instructions to tell him who McNair really was, she'd come up with the idea of going to see Kruger and she was over there right now, trying to get information out of Brophy. All Paul had done in that time was whinge, moan and almost get her ex-fiancé killed. Alright, her ex was a massive tool but that, in itself, was not worthy of the death penalty. He owed her an apology. Actually, he owed her more than that. It was time he stopped being the hurler on the ditch. It was time he got in the damn game.

Paul reached across the table and grabbed her hand.

"It's alright, you tried your best. How did he react when you mentioned Fallon?"

Brigit looked at Paul suspiciously, like she was expecting a punchline. "He nearly shat himself as soon as I said the name. He's terrified of him, but then everybody else seems to be too."

"Excellent." Paul stood up, took his sling off and threw it on the table.

"Where the hell are you going?"

"Do you remember what happened between McNair and me in that hospital room?"

Brigit rolled her eyes. "Oh, for God's sake! For the hundredth time, I'm sorry about…"

"No, no, no," interrupted Paul, "I meant before the stabby bit."

Brigit looked at him blankly.

"He thought I looked the spit of my da, one Gerry Fallon. Let's see if anybody else sees the family resemblance."

Paul entered Brogan's and looked around. He spotted Brophy almost immediately, sitting at the table at the corner, holding court. From the excited expressions on the faces of his companions, he'd lay good money the gobshite was telling them some cock'n'bull story about where he'd been for the last fifteen minutes. Paul manoeuvred himself into the queue for the bar behind a woman who was rocking a truly impressive pink Mohawk. He glanced over at the group in the corner and noticed Where's Wally doing the internationally recognised mime for a blowjob. Paul took a step towards them and realised that his adrenalin might be getting the better of him. Luckily, Mohawk moved at just that moment, so it looked like he was just making room for her to relay her tricky triangle of three drinks back to her table. She nodded her thanks and Paul slipped into the gap she left at the bar.

He waited patiently for the barmaid to finish serving three other people, and then he ordered a pint of Guinness. As it was settling under the tap, he saw Brophy out of the corner of his eye dragging himself out of his seat. Paul tried not to watch too closely as his target began moving his considerable bulk across the bar, excusing and thanking his way through the crowd. He was heading for the stairs down to the basement, where the loos were. Paul waved desperately to catch the barmaid's eye and then nodded at the nearly settled pint.

"Close enough," he said, trying to sound relaxed.

She gave him a disapproving look but topped it up as requested.

"Four ninety five, please."

Christ, thought Paul. He could get a whole six-pack of the normal paint stripper he drank for that. It had been a while since he'd bought an actual pint in an actual pub. Paul handed her a five-euro note and grabbed the glass.

"Keep the change," he said.

"Last of the big spenders! Looks like I'll be buying that yacht after all."

Paul didn't respond. He was moving towards the stairs Brophy had disappeared down about a minute before. He walked with as much speed as he could manage, through the crowded bar, without it looking suspicious. He made it down the stairs and turned right. He had to stop at the door to the gents to allow a large shaven-headed guy to exit. He gave Paul a funny look. In his eagerness, Paul realised he'd not stopped to put his pint down anywhere.

"I don't want to get spiked," he said.

The other guy raised his eyebrows and nodded, like that was a thing he'd have to worry about.

Paul pushed through the door and glanced around. His luck was in.

The urinals were free, as were two of the three stalls. Paul moved across to the sinks and looked in the long horizontal mirror. He could see in the reflection that it was indeed Brophy standing in the middle cubicle, and from the sound of it, he was right in the middle of a prodigious pee. Paul hadn't exactly planned this bit out in detail. He noticed that Brophy still had the toilet seat down, the dirty animal. That made him feel a lot better about what he was about to do. As far as Paul was concerned, peeing on a toilet seat should be a capital offence.

He took a gulp of his pint, placed it down on the ledge behind the sinks, and then moved into the middle stall right behind Brophy.

He shoved the big man forward.

"What the fuck..." exclaimed Brophy. Paul grabbed the neck of his blazer before he could turn around. Ideally, he'd have liked to close the cubicle door behind him, but there was barely enough room for Brophy in there, never mind the both of them.

"Well if it isn't acclaimed author Mark Brophy."

"Who the fuck are you?" Brophy sounded scared, which is exactly how Paul needed him.

"Now is that any way to speak to the son of an old friend?"

Brophy turned his head as much as he could in the confined space. Paul leaned forward to prevent him getting a good look back, and whispered in his ear. "My Da, AKA Gerry Fallon Senior, asked me to pass on his warm regards."

Brophy twisted a bit more, trying to get a better look at his assailant. Can't give him time to think. Got to keep him off balance.

"We hear you've been running your mouth."

"About what?"

Paul punched him in the kidney with his right hand. He got a stab of pain through his wounded shoulder for his trouble. It probably hurt him more than it did Brophy, but it was more for effect.

"Don't piss me about," said Paul.

"Sh... she came to me, I told her where to go. Honestly!"

"Took you long enough. About twenty minutes by my reckoning."

"I didn't..."

Paul shoved him forward again.

"You've got a big fucking mouth. Did you tell her that the boat didn't leave from Kerry?"

Paul took a stab in the dark, hoping that whatever investigators Kruger had employed had at least got that right.

"I told her nothing, I swear."

"Don't lie to me! We know they know that."

"They didn't get it from me. Fuck's sake."

Brophy sounded like he was about to cry. Now was as good a chance as he was going to get.

"Do they know the location?"

"What?" Brophy tried to move, but Paul shoved his body against him, keeping him trapped facing the toilet.

"The truth, ye fat prick!"

"I wouldn't tell them that. I swear."

C'mon, c'mon – give me something.

"You know the word you can't say. Tell me the word you can't say?"

"What the fuck?"

Paul's mind was racing, there had to be some way to get information out of him but this was the best he could come up with. He needed something. It was only a matter of time before…

A flash of pain shot through Paul's skull. His vision blurred and then his eyes closed. He felt himself bounce off Brophy's fat arse and then fall messily onto the damp tiles. Then hands were upon him, dragging him up to his feet as voices chattered excitedly through the fog around him.

"Who the fuck is this guy?"

"Never you mind. Just grab him."

"Did you see me, Doug? I twatted him with this bottle, right on the head. Boom! One shot. Down."

"Shut up and help him, Clive. Hold the cunt."

That last voice had been Brophy's, not sounding scared anymore. He sounded angry now. Paul could feel something oozing down the back of his head.

Then next thing he felt was his almost full pint of Guinness being hurled into his face. He could taste it on his lips.

He opened his eyes. Brophy was standing before him. He slapped Paul across the face. Paul tried to raise his hands in defence, but arms held him back. Where's Wally and the black guy, thought Paul.

Brophy leaned into him. "How fucking dare you. Coming around here, trying to intimidate me. I'm sick of this bullshit."

"Yeah," said a voice from behind.

"Shut up, Clive," said another.

Brophy grabbed Paul's chin and held it up. "You tell your dad that I have never broken our agreement and I never will. I've as much to lose as you do. Don't you dare pull this crap again."

Brophy shot a worried look over Paul's head at the two men holding him up, then he leaned in close to Paul's ear and whispered.

"And yeah, I know the word I can't say." He said it in almost a hiss. "Bandon!"

Brophy pulled back to look directly into Paul's eyes. "You tell him — that word, and a lot more besides, is with several different people around the globe. Anything happens to me, anything! And everything I know gets released. Now why don't —"

Brophy stopped talking as the door flew open.

"What in the hell is going on here?"

Brophy stepped back as the hands holding Paul released him, and then grabbed him again to stop him falling to the floor. Paul could see a man in his thirties, in a white shirt and black pants, standing in the doorway. A member of staff, had to be.

"He fell and cracked his head," explained Brophy, trying and failing not to sound guilty. "He's gee-eyed drunk, Dessie. Fecking senseless."

"I saw him walk in twenty minutes ago," said the man. "He looked fine to me."

"Drugs maybe," said a voice from behind Paul, which he guessed belonged to the black guy.

"Yeah right. Pull the other one, it's got my bollocks in it."

Paul saw the suspicion in Dessie's eyes as he came forward and looked at him. He moved Paul's head around and leaned over to look at the back of his skull. He could smell Dessie's aftershave. Whatever it was, it was wonderful.

"Fecking hell," said Paul's new favourite barman. "Right, give him to me." He threw Paul's left arm over his shoulder and took his weight. "Can you walk?"

Paul nodded, the movement of his head causing a wave of nausea to wash over him.

"C'mon so."

Dessie walked him out of the Gents and then stopped in the hallway. He leaned Paul against the wall and spoke in a low voice. "Do you want me to call the guards?"

"No, no, I'm grand," said Paul.

"Are ye sure? Slipped, my arse. That looked like three on one to me."

"I'm fine."

"We'll get you an ambulance then."

"No, no, no. No need..."

At the top of the stairs, Paul fended off Dessie's further attempts to help him. The whole pub looked on as he lurched towards the front door, testifying to his own glorious health all the way.

Paul clambered messily through the double doors, nearly knocking a woman over on her way in. The evening air came as a blessed relief. He leant against the wall, gasping. He began to feel queasy so he closed his eyes, hoping for the world to stop spinning. He could hear people tutting as they moved around him on the pavement. "Pisshead," said a voice.

Then he felt arms around him.

"Jesus! Are you OK?"

Brigit. Christ, she smelt even nicer than Dessie.

Paul opened his eyes and, after a couple of dizzy moments, he was able to focus on her. He gave her a wide grin. "Bandon."

Then he passed out.

CHAPTER FORTY-FOUR

Assistant Commissioner Fintan O'Rourke slammed the door of his car and looked up at his own top floor window. He'd seen the lights from a distance as he'd driven in. The house sat up on a hill, away from the main coastal road. After sitting through a long and tedious Chamber of Commerce dinner, he'd been looking forward to having the place to himself. It'd been a long week, and filling in for herself at functions like that was one of his least favourite parts of the job. Still, he'd turned up and smiled at the same old faces, and laughed at the same old jokes. Got to get along in order to get along.

Light spilled out from the windows of the converted attic, which could mean only one thing. His son Jason must have had a change of heart and come home for the weekend after all. He was in university down in Waterford, having crashed and burned out of his languages degree in DCU. While he'd never admitted as much, O'Rourke Senior had always had the strong impression his son had only signed up for it in the first place because of the high percentage of females on the course. He'd subsequently found Japanese so utterly impossible that he'd abandoned all hope of proceeding in alarmingly quick time, not even making it to the first year exams. O'Rourke had been inclined to teach the boy some hard life lessons by having him go out and get a job, but the wife had turned on the waterworks at the prospect of Jason being 'unqualified'. He'd subsequently suggested the Gardaí, his wife's derisive response to that option having led to a couple of weeks of domestic cold war tension. Business Administration in Waterford was seen as much more low-hanging and manageable fruit, surely not even Jason could drink his way out of that?

The wife was away in Durham for the weekend, visiting Jason's younger sister. O'Rourke didn't mind spending the money on Jenny's education, her results indicating not only that she regularly opened books, but that she refrained from using them as raw materials for rolling joints.

O'Rourke let himself into the hallway, tossed his keys into the bowl on the side-table and shouted up. "Jason?"

No response. The converted attic was Senior's sanctuary, a little treat to himself. Technically part office, it was really the snooker table and big screen TV that were its most enticing features. He could also stand out on the private rear balcony and have a cheeky cigar without drawing the wife's wrath. Jason knew all too well he shouldn't be up there. He was banned, ever since Senior had come home unexpectedly to discover his son on top of his beloved snooker table, buried up to the hips in some bit of skirt. He'd stopped short of hitting the lad, only because he didn't know who the girl was. The papers would love a bit of scandal to go along with their current obsession of tearing down the Garda Síochána. If he was at it again, though, O'Rourke didn't care about the headlines or the grief he'd get from the wife, he was finally going to give the boy the hiding he'd repeatedly asked for throughout the previous twenty years of his over-privileged life. It'd cost him the best part of 400 euros to get the table re-felted last time. It hadn't been technically necessary, there having been no actual damage, but it'd felt horribly defiled.

"Jason?" O'Rourke could feel his anger rising as he reached the first floor landing. In work, his every word was gospel and his every command was carried out to the letter. While at home, his gormless son rode roughshod over every rule, grinning like an idiot as he did it.

O'Rourke girded himself for the worst and pushed open the door. He scanned the room right to left. The table was blissfully unoccupied. Jason was, in fact, nowhere to be seen.

"Fuck's sake!!" said O'Rourke, leaping back in surprise.

Bunny McGarry, sitting in the leather easy chair in front of the TV, raised a tumbler of O'Rourke's obscenely expensive 12-year-old Milton whiskey in toast. "Commissioner, up your arse."

He had made himself very much at home, his large sheepskin overcoat slung over the arm of the chair, his hurley sitting across his knees.

"Jesus, Bunny, what the fuck are you doing in my house?"

"I wanted to have a chat."

"Then ring my office and make an appointment like everybody else."

O'Rourke looked around the room nervously and then closed the door behind him.

"I'm not really the appointment sort."

O'Rourke strode across the room and picked up the bottle of whiskey from the carpet beside Bunny. "You're not one for half-measures either I see. Do you've any idea how much this stuff costs?"

"Ah, put it on my tab."

O'Rourke walked across to the drinks cabinet and grabbed another glass. He half filled it and then pointedly left the bottle there. "How did you even get in? This house has a very sophisticated alarm."

"And I've got a very sophisticated stick," said Bunny, giving his hurley an affectionate stroke.

The alarm company were in for the mother of all bollockings on Monday morning. Twelve grand for something a muck-savage with a stick could apparently beat his way around.

"Tis a lovely place you've got here. I'm surprised you've not invited me around before."

"I would do, Bunny, but you've no fucking clue how to behave in polite company."

"What the feck bullshit is that?" said Bunny, the words spilling out in a torrent. "I'm a fecking delight at dinner parties."

Even now, after knowing the man for a quarter century, O'Rourke could never tell when Bunny was really angry, and when he was just pretending. He was getting an unpleasant sensation of déjà vu. That old sickly feeling that every conversation with Bunny McGarry was a game of Russian roulette. "Do you not remember my wife, Bunny? She certainly remembers you, and your performance at our wedding."

"Ah for..." Spittle flew from Bunny's lips as he gesticulated with his hands. "That swan could've broken some poor child's fecking arm."

"Not after you broke its neck it couldn't. Do you have any idea how much trouble I had over that?"

Bunny gave a smirk and raised his glass, draining the last of it.

O'Rourke used the brief gap in conversation to look at his old friend. His face had become a hodge-podge of unhappy reds, a sure sign that his drinking hadn't slowed down. He was long past the point where the body easily rebounded from ill treatment. He'd also put on a fair bit of weight, although he'd never been what could be traditionally considered athletic.

"So," said O'Rourke. "Enough of the flannel. Why're you here?"

"Paulie Mulchrone."

"That's Jimmy Stewart's case. Talk to him."

"Oh, I have, although he's suspended now."

O'Rourke was taken off-guard by this. "What the hell for?"

"Being a good copper. There's not a lot of it about these days."

"I'll make some calls in the morning. What do you care anyway?" O'Rourke looked at McGarry, his glass poised at his lips. "Since when've you and he been bosom buddies? I'd have thought he was a bit too 'by the book' for your tastes."

"Maybe I'm mellowing in my old age."

"Says the man who just broke into my house. This case has nothing to do with you, Bunny. A word to the wise, leave it go."

Bunny leaned forward, the mercurial intensity returning, and spoke in a low growl. "Mulchrone is one of my boys."

O'Rourke turned his eyes to heaven. "Oh, for feck's sake, you and your precious hurling team. Aren't you forgetting, he's also the lad who made you look like an incompetent idiot back with the Nellis thing?"

"I wouldn't put it quite like that."

"Well, speaking as the fool who pulled all kinds of strings to get you on that team in the first place, I would."

"You owed me that," said Bunny. "I might still be there if you'd stood by me."

"Bollocks, Bunny. Get off the cross, we need the wood."

The two men locked eyes. "Don't bother with your wonky-eyed staring bullshit either. We go back way too far for that nonsense to work on me."

Bunny stood up unsteadily and started looking at the trophy cabinet in the corner. He opened it before O'Rourke could think of a reason to stop him.

"That's right," said Bunny, a slight slur in his voice, "we go back a long way. I remember when you were a snivel-nosed little runt, fresh off the bus from Templemore. Like a lost child in the big city. Taught you everything you know, didn't I?"

"Ahh, you did alright. Some of those tricks took a long time to unlearn."

Bunny held up the statue O'Rourke had won in that trout fishing tournament two years ago, examining it like it was a fine work of art. "I took care of you though."

"And I've always taken care of you. Don't forget, it's thanks to me you have your cushy number. You're the only Guard in the country who can go weeks without answering to anybody."

"I get results."

"Yeah, and let's not forget the hassles some of those results cause."

Bunny put the statue down. "Speaking of results, Pauline McNair was an innocent civilian and now she's dead."

"What's your point, Bunny?"

"Some gobshite went around today and tried to put the squeeze on Mulchrone's lawyer, a pregnant woman."

"I repeat, what's your point?"

"Not forgetting the bomb, a fucking BOMB mind you, on the street where kiddies play."

"Again, what is your fucking point, Bunny?"

"You've a leak."

"A *possible* leak. I've got people looking into it."

"I bet you do. Jimmy Stewart reckons it's your PR woman. Veronica Doyle, is it?"

"That's a very serious allegation. Do you or DI Stewart have anything to back it up?"

"You'd have to ask Jimmy that. She's not the horse I'm backing."

"No?"

"No," said Bunny. He flicked the rim of a Waterford Crystal vase with his finger, the clear tone ringing out around the room. "That'd be you."

O'Rourke laughed. "Thanks for that, Bunny. I needed cheering up."

Bunny didn't look up from his examination of the trophy cabinet. "She reports to you, I'm sure."

"Feck off home and sober up, Bunny. If you're lucky, I'll pretend this conversation never happened."

"I spent the day catching up on my reading. I went through all your old case files, Fintan. The O'Rourke greatest hits in your meteoric rise to power." Bunny breathed onto the top of a golden golfer's head and then gave it a polish with the sleeve of his jacket.

"Do you like golf, Fintan? I recently took it up myself."

"Keep going the way you are, Bunny, and you'll have a lot more time to practice."

Bunny put the trophy carefully back where he'd found it. "All those intelligence-led big collars. Your career got a few big bumps taking down Gerry Fallon's rivals, did it not?"

"We landed the odd blow on him too."

"Oh yeah, just enough to be smart, no doubt. You've got to land a few punches, if you're going to throw the fight."

"I can't believe I'm standing here listening to this paranoid conspiracy theory bollocks, from you of all people."

"So I'm wrong then?"

"Dead wrong." O'Rourke moved across, grabbed Bunny by the shoulder and swung him around, before shoving his finger into his face. "Whatever you were, you're not that anymore. You've lost it, Bunny. I've been too soft on you for old times' sake. That report from two years ago, saying you weren't fit to serve? I was a bloody fool to get rid of it. I just count myself lucky that I realised that in time. Before you did something I can't fix. You've two choices. Get yourself off the booze, or in two weeks' time you're off the force. Is that clear?"

"You wouldn't."

"Try me."

Bunny said nothing, but O'Rourke could see the shake in his hand as he rubbed it across his face. There was a hint of wetness in his eyes.

"Have you got much else in your sad little life, bar the job, Bunny?"

A silence stretched out between them. O'Rourke stepped back and stared at the drink-sodden husk of a man. Bunny McGarry had been something back in his day, but that day was long gone. His old friend was dead. Only this remained.

Bunny looked down at the wooden varnished floor and glowered at it, as if offended by its presence.

"Well?" said O'Rourke.

After a long moment, the other man nodded. He seemed smaller now somehow. Beneath the drunken bravado and the reputation he'd so carefully cultivated lay a broken man. Pickled in bitterness and booze.

O'Rourke exhaled loudly and walked over to his desk. He lifted the cigar box's intricately carved wooden lid and withdrew one of the Cubans he'd got on last year's trip to America. He clipped the end, picked up the lighter, and only then did he look back at Bunny.

"I'm going out for a smoke. When I get back, you won't be here. I'll also never see you again. And if your name passes across my desk once – for any reason – that report that got lost will be found again. Clear?"

Bunny nodded and turned towards the door. He opened it and, without looking back, left.

O'Rourke opened the double doors to his balcony and stepped outside. There was a slight tremor in his hands as he lit the cigar. He could feel a tension headache building behind his right temple. Always when playing this game, there were trade-offs. This had been the week from hell. Fallon had him by the balls every which way. What'd he called it? Mutually assured destruction. This thing had been a disaster from the get go, but there was still a route out of it. He'd covered his tracks well, he'd thought. He certainly didn't need Bunny, of all people, pulling the high and mighty routine. On the upside, the drunken sot didn't have many friends left on the force. Back in his day, Bunny had been a sheer force of nature. But that was the old Bunny. He'd been dirty in his way but he'd had a code. He'd been the one who'd first taught O'Rourke that the ends justified the means. Wasn't that all he had done? Just on a bigger scale. Bunny's problem was he couldn't see the bigger picture. He'd never been able to see the bigger picture.

O'Rourke took a deep drag on his cigar and looked out over the hills, down onto Dublin Bay below. He could see lights out at sea, a late night ferry coming in no doubt. A thought occurred to him. He'd left the hurley behind...

Then the world turned upside down.

For a big man, Bunny could still move deceptively quietly. The first thing O'Rourke had felt was one hand on his back as the other grabbed his belt and heaved him over the side. He hung there in a terrible moment, looking down at the flowerbeds, three storeys below, nothing more than vague outlines in the darkness. He watched his cigar tumble, sparks flying as it bounced off the wall, before disappearing into the darkness below. His hands scrabbled at the cornices, desperately trying to find something to grip onto. And he screamed. Good Christ did he scream. Not words, just terror. Full-throated terror. He wasn't screaming to be heard, the house was too far away from the neighbours to raise any form of alarm. He was screaming out of sheer physical need.

He managed to wrap his arms around one of the white marble balustrade columns and held on for dear life. A pair of strong arms were wrapped around his legs, dangling him over the side.

A voice came from above, suddenly sounding a lot clearer than it had. "What's wrong, Fintan? Suddenly at a loss for words?"

"Fuck's sake, Bunny, pull me up, now!!" O'Rourke had clamped his eyes shut, concentrating all his energies on hanging on.

"Not until you tell me what I want to know."

"YOU'RE FUCKING MENTAL!"

O'Rourke's stomach lurched, as the arms above him adjusted their grip.

"Sure, don't we already know that? You've got your little report that says so. What was it again? Unstable, wasn't it?"

"Let me up and it's gone. I swear."

"D'ye know, I didn't want to believe it. I mean, I knew it was you from early doors, but I kept hoping. It was only when you threatened me that I knew for sure. What's Fallon got on ye?"

"Just – pull me up and we can talk."

"Ah but sure," said Bunny, the sound of strain in his voice, "aren't we talking now? And you're much less of a condescending prick upside down. Now what's Fallon hiding?"

"Jesus, Bunny, cop yourself on. You've no idea what you're dealing with."

"I know what you're dealing with Fintan – Gravity. And she's a mean auld whore. Now, Paulie Mulchrone?"

"Why do you fucking care?"

O'Rourke gave an involuntary yelp of terror as Bunny deliberately loosened his grip for a moment. He could feel his three-course meal from earlier rushing to leave him.

"Because he... IS ONE OF MY BOYS!"

"Alright, Bunny, you've made your point. I've seen this movie too.

We both know you're not really going to drop me, so drag me up while you still can, and we'll talk this out."

"Is that so?"

"It's a good bluff but the joke's over."

"Fair point," said Bunny.

And then he dropped him.

Assistant Commissioner Fintan O'Rourke's world was pain. If he moved any which way, agony surged through his whole body. He was vaguely aware of the damp soil that surrounded him, the fingers of his right hand were buried in it. There was the unmistakable smell of the horseshit that his wife put on the roses in the winter. She was mad keen to win some kind of award. He was surprised he could still smell. His nose was broken. The blood streaming down his face was making it hard to breathe. He couldn't move his left hand at all; he could feel bone sticking out of the skin of his forearm. His left knee also felt shot to hell and his right shoulder kept sending wave upon wave of sickening pain through him. He guessed a couple of ribs were gone as well. He could feel himself fading into sleep, his brain keen to remove itself from the body's agony.

A hand slapped him across the face.

"Fintan!"

His eyes flew open and the world spun around him, with the figure of Bunny McGarry looming over him at its centre.

"You fucking lunatic," rasped O'Rourke. "You're a dead man."

"Of the two of us, you're the one who looks in more immediate danger of that."

"You dropped me."

"I did. The secret to bluffing, I find, is not to do it. What're ye whinging for? You're still in a much better state than Pauline McNair."

"Fucking..."

O'Rourke trailed off, feeling the world go out of focus again, tasting the blood and soil in his mouth. He got slapped in the face again.

"Stay with me now. You've got to tell me what Fallon is hiding."

O'Rourke tried to laugh but the blood in his mouth only made it into a gurgle. "You already dropped me. Why the fuck would I tell you anything now?"

"Ah," said Bunny, "an excellent question."

Bunny stooped and picked something off the ground. It was O'Rourke's cigar, still lit. He took a couple of deep puffs to reignite it fully before taking it from his lips and smiling down at him.

"I dropped you once to prove I would. Now, you're going to tell me everything I want to know. Otherwise... I'll do it again, and I'd imagine the second time will *really* hurt."

CHAPTER FORTY-FIVE

"Ouch!"

"Stop squirming," said Brigit.

"I am squirming because you are basically rubbing acid into my head wound." Paul winced and pulled his head forward so fast, he very nearly head-butted Dorothy's kitchen table. "Seriously, is this necessary?"

"What? That we disinfect your wound? That depends. Normally, how clean is the floor of a gents' toilet?"

Paul grumbled under his breath but straightened up to allow Brigit to finish killing him with kindness. He looked at his own reflection in the glass door leading out into the garden, and then at the intense look of concentration on Brigit's face as she stared at the back of his head. She blew out of the side of her mouth to move a strand of her brown hair out of her field of vision. Then she looked up and noticed his reflection watching her. "What?"

"Nothing," said Paul, his cheeks reddening as he looked away. The kitchen wasn't a mess but it certainly wasn't clean. The plates from breakfast were soaking in the sink, and the couple of frying pans were still sitting on the stove. Dorothy didn't keep a tidy home, she kept staff who did that for her and they apparently didn't work Saturdays.

"This should really have a couple of stitches in it, not to mention the concussion you've almost certainly got. You should be in hospital now."

"Because my last visit went so well. Besides, we didn't go to all that trouble to finally getting a lead, a bona fida *lead* mind you, only to give ourselves up."

Paul was still buzzing from his stroke of genius/luck getting information out of Brophy like that. Alright, getting whacked on the back of the skull and a bit of a going over was not exactly part of the plan, but still, it'd worked. He'd done something, and something had worked. He was starting to get into this investigating lark. "So where is Bandon?"

He could feel Brigit rummaging around in his hair, still unhappy with what she was seeing. He felt a little bit like a monkey being groomed.

"It's a town outside Cork, isn't it? Although, are you sure he said Bandon?"

"What do you mean?"

"You had got a knock on the head. Maybe he said Brendan?"

"Brendan? Who the hell is Brendan?"

"Well, exactly. Or maybe he said Brandon?"

"What'd that be?"

"It could be Fiachra Fallon's new name in America. It's a very Yank name."

"Or maybe he said Branston," said Paul. "Y'know, because we're in a pickle?"

"I'm just saying —"

Before Brigit could finish just saying, the kitchen door swung open and Dorothy walked in, wearing another of her fetching housecoats. Today's featured an entire foxhunt, complete with horses and a pack of dogs. They'd been hoping to avoid seeing her until Paul's latest injury had been dealt with. Her rheumy eyes behind her jam-jar glasses grew even larger with inquiry.

"So, finally clocked him one, did you, dear?"

"Gregory just had a bit of a fall," said Brigit.

"Of course he did, and I'm a monkey's grandma." Dorothy placed her plate of biscuit crumbs down on the counter. "Physical violence is not the answer."

"Quite right," said Brigit.

"Yes," replied Dorothy, drawing her antique handgun from the pocket of her housecoat. "All you need to do is shove one of these in their face and say, 'give it up, mothermucker'."

"Dorothy!"

"Oh, do lighten up, dear. I've been watching that Sons of Anarchy. Tremendous! So who is up for a game of Monopoly?" Her eyes danced with excitement as she spoke: "And a takeaway! We could order from that nice Chinese place that…"

A thought struck Paul, milliseconds before his scalp experienced a searing pain. "CHRIST!"

Paul placed his hands on the table and tried to steady himself.

"Sorry, sorry, sorry," Brigit said. "Honestly, that's it – fully cleaned and ready for bandaging now."

Paul glanced up to see Dorothy looking at him with large wet eyes of worry. "Honestly, I'm fine."

"He is," assured Brigit. "Let me just finish this and then board games, grub and booze for all."

"Right ho." Dorothy shuffled out of the door that led towards the front room.

"Actually," whispered Brigit, "No booze for you. Doctor's orders."

Paul listened to the reassuring sound of the soft shush of Dorothy's slippers on the thick carpeting in the next room.

"She does worry about you, y'know."

"I worry about me too," said Paul. "I'm averaging an injury every other day. There was something important I was going to say…"

"Was it about Bandon?"

"I can't remember." Paul stared down at the table. It was bugging him. There had been something on the tip of his tongue and then it had slipped away. Brigit, for her part, started looking through Dorothy's first aid kit at her bandaging options.

"So you reckon he definitely said Bandon?" asked Brigit.

"I did, but you keep saying stuff like that, and now you're making me doubt myself."

"Sorry."

Paul drummed his hands on the table. "Bandon, yeah – Bandon. I say we run with that, otherwise I'm just some idiot who keeps getting walloped for no reason. Let's drive down there tomorrow."

"And do what?"

"Investigate, of course," said Paul, "assuming you can't solve the whole thing by having a quick rummage around in their twitter feed."

"You're very gung ho all of a sudden."

"OK, brace yourself but… you were right. It does feel good not to be just running away, to finally be in control of the situation."

Then the glass door to the garden slid open and a man in a balaclava calmly stepped into the room. He was pointing a gun at them.

Paul sighed. "Well, it was nice while it lasted."

The man held a finger to his lips, before speaking in a surprisingly soft and depressingly calm voice. "Are you alone?"

They both nodded. Paul detected a trace of an eastern European accent. The man cocked his ear and listened, before nodding as if satisfied. Then he slid the door closed behind him, leaving the gun trained on them the whole time.

"Would you put your hands in the air, please?"

The polite way in which he asked the question was in stark contrast to the gun that was rudely pointed at them. With no other option available, they both meekly complied.

"I have been asked to ask you: who have you told?"

Brigit and Paul looked at each other, before Brigit answered. "Told what?"

There was a long moment of awkward silence. Paul didn't mind it personally. He could take a lot of social awkwardness before death became the preferred option.

"I do not know," said the man. "I have not been told that, for obvious reasons."

"I swear," said Paul, "we can't tell anybody anything because we don't know anything. They just think we do. It's all a big misunderstanding."

The balaclava-clad man leaned his head to one side as if considering this, and then nodded to himself. "OK." Then he stepped towards Paul and pointed the gun at his head.

"Whoa, whoa. I just told you we don't know anything."

"Yes. Thank you. Now I am able to kill you and this unfortunate business can be over."

"Wait," said Brigit. "We've actually told loads of people."

"She's put it on Twitter."

He shook his head. "No, you did not. For what it is worth, I am sorry to do this. We have a code. We don't normally do civilians or women. "

"So why now?"

"They have my niece. Her father is already dead."

"Sorry to hear that," responded Brigit. Paul looked at her and she shrugged. "Well, I am."

"Why not just pretend we are dead?"

"That will not work. They will know. I have no choice."

"No, honestly I..."

"Reach for the sky!"

The heads of everyone in the room turned to face the door into the living room, where Dorothy stood with her gun extended in a shaky hand. The man in the balaclava swivelled his weapon towards her.

"Wait," screamed Paul, leaping to his feet and throwing himself in front of Dorothy. "It's not real it's not real it's not real!"

His entire body tensed for a shot that didn't come.

"It's an antique, it's been disabled," continued Paul. "Please, Dorothy, go back inside."

"There's some munt in a balaclava in my house."

"She's got dementia," said Paul. "The gun is just a harmless antique, honestly. Please, she has nothing to do with this."

"What is going on, Gregory?"

Paul extended his hands. "See! She doesn't even know my name. I'm the one you want; neither of the women know anything. Please, Dorothy, put the gun away." He started moving towards the man in the balaclava. Then he clicked his fingers.

"I remember now. It was Mickey, wasn't it?"

"What?" said Brigit.

Paul answered her without turning his eyes from the gunman.

"He's the delivery guy from the takeaway I always use. It occurred to me earlier. He delivered here a couple of times."

"Oh yes," said Dorothy. "They really are tremendous and very good value."

The balaclava-clad man looked at Brigit. "Your friend put them as his next of kin on his hospital form."

"What? Who does that?" asked Brigit.

"I'd nobody else alright?" said Paul, sounded hurt. "My last moments on earth and you're going to make me feel bad about my shitty life?"

"I was just..."

"No, keep going," interrupted Paul. "That's just terrific. That's one hell of a bedside manner you've got there. It's almost hard to believe you got me stabbed."

"Oh for... You're going to bring that up *again*?"

"Silence." The man spoke in a calm voice as he extended his gun towards Paul, who had been subtly inching towards him. "Stop moving, please. The trick where you distract me by having an argument has only ever worked in movies."

"Oh well, fair enough," said Paul.

"Wait, what were we doing?" asked Brigit.

The man's brown eyes looked into Paul's. "If it is any consolation, I offered your delivery man a lot of money and he would not take it."

"So how..."

"I offered him a lot of pain instead."

"Ah."

"Is he?"

"He is OK. There was no need for him to die. He really did put up a surprising amount of effort to protect you. You should be proud."

"I am a very good customer." A thought struck Paul. "I don't suppose he mentioned what his second name was?"

"It did not come up."

"Never mind. I'll ask him now. Hi Mickey!"

Paul waved behind the gunman, who turned slightly, before reacting with depressing speed when he realised it was a bluff. By which time, Paul had hardly begun launching himself at him. The man stepped back and expertly landed a left hook into Paul's jaw as he lunged. He went down, hard. The pain reverberated around his head. His left shoulder thumped against the polished metal of the cooker door as he crumpled to the ground, adding to the cacophony of pain. He rolled onto his back and felt the man's foot being placed firmly in the centre of his chest. Paul was dimly aware of both Brigit and Dorothy gasping and swearing in shock. He watched as the man quickly pointed the gun at each of them in turn, to stop any other ill-judged attempts at heroics.

"That was brave, predictable and stupid."

"Yeah," said Paul, struggling to draw air back into his lungs, "well you're going to shoot me either way, right?"

"True."

Paul watched with fascination as the barrel of the gun was turned downwards, to all of two feet from his head. He should have felt fear but he didn't have the energy.

He clamped his eyes shut and a shot rang out, followed by the sound of the glass in the patio door behind him shattering. Paul opened his eyes again when he realised that against all odds he could still do so. It hadn't been he who had screamed out in pain but the gunman, who was now awkwardly dancing about, his hand clutching the right side of his ribcage, where it appeared the bullet had grazed him. Paul grabbed the foot on his chest and twisted it, trying to send the man further off balance. He glanced at Dorothy, who looked shocked as she clutched her right wrist to her chest, her gun on the ground before her, knocked from her frail hand by the recoil. The gunman span back around. He held his left hand to his wounded side as he raised his gun towards Dorothy. Then, like a whirling dervish of fury, Brigit Conroy rugby tackled him through the patio door. Glass rained down around them as they fell out into the garden.

Paul grabbed the handle of the stove's door and dragged himself to a standing position. The room span around him as he clutched onto the counter in an effort to remain upright. He shook his head clear and looked into the garden. There was Brigit sprawled out on the paved area. Beside her, the man in the balaclava was on his knees, crawling through the broken glass to where his gun lay, five feet away.

Paul grabbed the nearest thing to him and rushed out through the smashed door, tripping on the frame as he did so. Shattered glass crunched beneath his feet as he stumbled forward. The man had picked up his gun and was turning towards him. With a wildly desperate lunge, before gravity and his own feeble body caught up with him, Paul delivered a forearm smash into the side of the man's head with the frying pan. He slumped down unconscious, before Paul tripped over his own feet and collapsed onto the grass behind him.

He lay there spread-eagled in the darkness, staring into the night sky. The clouds had cleared, leaving a rather nice view of some stars. The last thing he saw before he passed out was the Great Bear. He'd got a book on astronomy in the 'three-for-two euros' bin.

CHAPTER FORTY-SIX

"Hello?"

Paul was taken aback. He hadn't been expecting a male voice at the other end of the phone. He shifted the bag of frozen peas he was holding awkwardly against his left jaw in an attempt to lessen the inevitable swelling. He'd decided to abandon the sling on his right arm. Stitches be damned. If people were going to keep punching him, whacking him in the back of the head with bottles and attempting to shoot him, he wanted both hands free to fend off at least some of the blows.

"Hi, can I speak to Nora Stokes, please?"

"Is this Mr Mulchrone?"

"That depends. Who's asking?"

"It's DI Jimmy Stewart."

"I don't want to talk to the police." Paul looked at the unfamiliar handset of Dorothy's phone, looking for the button to hang-up.

"Wait!" said Stewart. "I don't blame you but you need to listen to me. There's been an incident. Nora had a visit from one of Gerry Fallon's thugs."

Christ, thought Paul, he kept dragging more and more innocent people into this. "Is she OK?"

"Absolutely. In fact, between you and me, she handled it bloody brilliantly. The woman is a badass. She left her mobile number for you if you need to reach her. My partner is staying with her to make sure she's OK. Look, I understand why you'd be sceptical, but I want to help you. In fact, I've been suspended for trying to help you. You can believe me or not, but I don't think you're in a situation where you've got too many friends."

Paul considered this. He'd never met Stewart but every time he'd come up in conversation, Brigit had said how she felt they could trust him. He looked out the shattered door onto the back lawn, where said nurse was currently checking on the physical well-being of the unconscious man that had been sent to kill them, having hogtied him first. It turned out she was an expert in knots as, in the least surprising revelation ever, she'd been a Girl Guide. Paul wasn't that worried about their assailant's health. His gunshot wound was minor and it hadn't been that big a frying pan. Besides, it wasn't like they'd met under the most favourable of circumstances. Dorothy, on the other hand, he felt terrible about. He glanced at her, sitting at the kitchen table, cupping her badly sprained wrist to her chest. Suddenly she looked so much frailer than she'd ever done before. He felt horribly guilty for bringing this to her door.

"Alright, take down this address. 17 Waverley Gardens, Blackrock. You need to wait 30 minutes and then send police and two ambulances. You'll find a sweet lady called Dorothy Graham. She's 83 and has a badly sprained wrist."

"Oh dear God," interrupted Dorothy. "Why is it that when a lady reaches a certain point in life, all of a sudden people are fine openly discussing her mucking age?"

"Hang on a sec," said Paul into the phone before holding it to his chest.

"Settle down there, 'Quickdraw'. By the way, Pang Lee told me all your guns had been disabled?"

"Yes, took me ages to fix it. Honestly, what use would a gun be that didn't shoot?"

Paul considered this. "You've got a point," was what he said, but all he could think about was the number of times she'd casually waved that gun at him over a game of Risk. He uncovered the receiver.

"Along with Miss Graham, age unknown, you'll find an unconscious man, with a non-critical gunshot wound, hog-tied on the lawn."

"Holy crap," said Stewart. "Who shot him?"

"That would be the sweet old lady. By the way, we've already called her lawyers, they will be here when the police arrive. Nurse Conroy and I will be long gone by then, but you have our assurances that she acted entirely in self-defence."

"Hence the lawyers," said Stewart.

"It's complicated. Her lawyer is Louie Dockery by the way."

Stewart sighed deeply. Even Paul had known that name. Turns out Dorothy had serious legal firepower at her command, as well as actual firepower.

"And where," asked Stewart, "will yourself and Nurse Conroy be?"

"Ah now, that'd be telling." Where they would be was on the way to Bandon, trying to figure out what on earth they were caught in the middle of. Now that they had no choice but to lose their only safe hiding place, their options were very limited.

"Fair enough," said Stewart. "I do have a message for you though, from Bunny McGarry."

Paul's pulse quickened at the name. "I've no interest in hearing anything he's got to say."

"Look, I know you and he have some very complicated personal history."

Paul laughed derisively. If that wasn't the mother of all understatements.

"But I also know he's been trying to help you, and he swears he has vital information."

"So why'd he not just give it to you?"

"It turns out, he trusts the Gardaí even less than you do. He said something about having a falling out with somebody during the course of his inquiries."

"I bet. That prick falls out with everybody eventually."

"Still, if I were you, I'd want to hear him out. As discussed, how many friends have you got?"

"Bunny doesn't have friends."

Stewart sighed again. He sounded almost as tired as Paul felt. "True enough but I'd meet him anyway."

"Well this doesn't sound like a trap at all. And where is this meeting supposed to take place?"

"He said you'd know where."

"What's that supposed to..." and then Paul stopped because he realised he did know exactly where. Typically bloody Bunny McGarry.

CHAPTER FORTY-SEVEN

A soft drizzle fell around them in the darkness. Brigit pulled the Bentley into the curb, turned off the engine and looked over at Paul. He was slouched in the passenger seat, the packet of frozen peas still pressed to his swollen jaw. They'd hardly spoken since they'd left Dorothy's house.

"Are you sure about this?" she asked softly.

He stared out the window. "No, I'm not sure about any of this. I'm not sure about trusting this lunatic old bastard. I'm not sure if I even want to see him, and I've no idea why he's trying to help me now. If he really is."

"Right," said Brigit. "I was actually only asking about parking here but —" Brigit shifted awkwardly around in the driver's seat to face Paul. "Do you want to talk this through?"

"Oh God, no. I'm having a bad enough night as it is, please don't make me talk about my feelings now too." Paul opened the door and awkwardly hauled himself out of the Bentley's plush leather seats. He understood why Brigit was concerned about the car. They were on Phillpot Street. This was not a place he'd have wanted to park his clapped out Ford Cortina, back before it'd been blown up by the bomb squad. That's why he knew that in the perverse logic of these streets, this car was as safe as it could ever be. They didn't even need to lock the doors. For someone to park this kind of car here, they were one of two things: epically stupid or 'somebody'. The local gurriers, assuming they'd any sense, wouldn't want to take the risk of guessing wrongly. There was more chance of them coming back to find somebody had washed it than done it any damage.

The wave of gentrification that'd swept over Dublin in the Celtic Tiger years of the nineties and early noughties had parted to avoid the whole Phillpot Street area. Its flats, and they were flats, no 'apartments' here, had remained almost untouched since they'd been built a hundred years ago. It may've been a fairly short walk from there to the centre of town, but you'd want to be walking pretty damn quickly, and carrying a big stick to boot. The most surprising thing about the area was how little it had changed since Paul had last stood on this street 15 years ago. The same down-in-the-mouth blocks of flats stood around them, picked out in places by the few working streetlights. The only thing that struck Paul as odd was the strangely sweet smell of burning tar and rubber that hung in the air.

Paul turned and walked towards the rusted old gates of St Jude's GAA club. 'Club' was a rather grand title for what was, in effect, one pitch and three portakabins which served as changing rooms. It didn't have a proper clubhouse and it was almost unique in Dublin GAA circles for being a club that played strictly hurling, no football allowed. The tall forbidding outer walls were topped with battered netting and were noticeably graffiti free. The netting looked even more careworn and ragged than Paul remembered. Theoretically it was there to stop sliotars leaving the field, but in reality every one of the surrounding flats probably had a ball through the window at some point. Nobody minded much, or, if they did, not much was said. There was an understanding. If anybody had any trouble from the criminal element, Bunny would be on the case. Every summer, he would also bring a bunch of his young fellas around; they'd repaint a few walls and generally take more care of the place than the council ever did. In exchange for that, the occasional leather covered ball travelling at high speed through your kitchen window was a small price to pay.

Paul stopped in front of the gates. They looked so small now. Back in his youth, they'd seemed massive – a portal to another world. In a way, they had been. Being part of that team was the only time in his whole life he'd felt like he'd belonged anywhere. The big chain with the padlock was lying on the ground beside the gate. He pushed through and Brigit followed him. The old gates squealed to announce their arrival.

Paul turned to his left and realised what the unusual smell was. The three portacabins were now burnt out shells of their former selves, wisps of dead smoke still rising in places. Amidst the carnage, on a deckchair, sat Bunny McGarry, a half-full bottle of whiskey in hand. He raised it in salute. "Ah, Paulie and Nurse Conroy, welcome to the barbeque."

Paul walked towards the burnt-out structures, looking around him in horror. "What the hell happened?"

"Gerry bastard Fallon is what happened, the fat-arsed son of a skinny-arsed whore that he is."

"I don't understand," said Brigit.

"Me and him had a little chat earlier, about how all men have their weaknesses. The bastard found mine in record time."

Bunny took a slug straight from the bottle; Paul noticed an already empty one lying discarded nearby. He moved forward and looked at what was lying on the ground beside Bunny. It was the remnants of a large sack, containing a load of half burned yellow and blue jerseys. Bunny looked down at them forlornly.

"They'd been new at the start of the season. Spent fecking weeks traipsing around finding a sponsor for those."

"Were you insured?" asked Brigit.

"Hah! Oh God, yeah. We have been ever since we got the fecking chandeliers installed."

Paul looked down at Bunny, squeezed into the deckchair that was far too small to contain him, his ever-present black sheepskin coat hugged tightly to him, closed against the elements.

"You're drunk."

"Not nearly as much as I intend to be."

"Is this why you dragged us over here, Bunny? So we can watch you wallow?"

Bunny glared up at Paul, his lips moving as if starting and abandoning several different responses, before he turned to look at Brigit instead.

"You should have seen yer man here, back in the day. He was the finest pure striker of the ball this field has ever seen. Could've played for the county, if he hadn't quit."

Paul could feel all the old anger rise in him. "Yeah, that's what happened. I quit. You're full of shit, Bunny."

"Punish me all you want, but why'd you have to go punish yourself? And the rest of the lads? We had a championship final!" There was a note of pleading in his voice, like this decision could be revisited. "D'ye know how many times we've got past the second round in the 17 years since then? Once! And we got that on a forfeit."

"Yeah, well, maybe I was sick of playing your stupid game."

"Fecking bullshit," he spat the words out, saliva speckling his lips as he spoke. "Call me a shite all you want, but don't disrespect the game. You fecking loved it. I know you did."

"I'd have loved a home more!" Paul nearly screamed the words at him, before he turned away. He hated this. He hated that Bunny could still get to him. That all these emotions could come rushing back to the surface. He hated how his hands were shaking, and how he could feel hot tears forming in his eyes. Now was not the time.

"I'm sorry." The words had been spoken so quietly that it took a few moments for Paul to realise that they'd not just been in his head.

He turned to look back at Bunny.

"What?"

"I'm sorry," Bunny repeated, staring down at the ground. "I'm sorry for everything."

"Christ, the great Bunny McGarry apologising. You must be drunk."

Bunny's deckchair creaked under his weight as he leaned forward.

"Ah for feck's sake, just take the apology and don't be a prick about it."

"Shove your apology up your arse, ye miserable old bastard!"

Paul could sense Brigit looking at him but he didn't want to make eye contact with her. He didn't want her trying to take his anger away. He had every right to it. He'd never had much, but this he owned.

"I messed up, alright?" said Bunny. "I messed up so many things in my useless fecking life, but messing up your life too is my biggest regret amongst the many. Y'know, since this thing started, people keep bringing up the Madigan's job to me. How you and Paddy Nellis made me look like a fecking eejit. They keep expecting me to be angry. Do you want the truth? I'm not. I had it coming and you gave it to me but good. Jaysus, truth be told, I was proud of ye."

"Yeah, so proud that you've been hassling me non-stop ever since."

Paul was taken aback by the look of shock in Bunny's eyes.

"Hassling ye? Hassling ye? I've been watching out for you. That was my worry. That you'd end up wasting yourself on becoming just another two-bit gurrier, running around doing little jobs for grifters like Nellis or worse, scumbags like Fallon. I didn't want your one big success in the world of crime to become the start of a shitting career in it."

"So what? You're expecting me just to forgive and forget now?"

Bunny shook his head and gave a sad little laugh. "Fuck no. I can't forgive me, and I can't think of one good reason why you should either. In fact..."

Bunny went to heave himself out of the deckchair. His right hand slipped on the armrest, sending him sprawling messily onto the ground, atop the scorched remains of the jerseys.

"Oh for fuck's sake," said Paul.

Brigit looked at Paul but he remained firmly rooted to the spot. Instead, she moved over to try and help Bunny up.

"I'm alright, I'm alright," he slurred, dragging himself

unceremoniously back onto his feet. "Standing eight count, I'm fine." He bobbed and weaved a bit to prove his point. "All I was going to say was..." he extended his chin out in Paul's direction, "hit me."

"What?"

"Hit me. C'mon, you'll feel better for it."

"Yeah, I've seen you fight before, Bunny. I'm not stupid enough to believe you."

Bunny crossed his heart and then held up three fingers. "Hit me, as hard and as many times as you like. I've got it coming. I promise I won't fight back, dib dib – scout's honour."

Paul's hands clenched into fists. "Don't tempt me."

"Tempt you? I'm fecking begging you."

"This is typical. You'd only offer this when you know my shoulder is screwed. I'd hurt myself more than you by trying."

Bunny's face became a mask of drunken concentration, as he pouted his lips in thought. Then he raised a finger and smiled broadly. "One sec."

He bent down, almost stumbling as he did so, and retrieved a hurley from the ground. He extended it out, handle-first, towards Paul. "Here ye go, use this – s' perfect. You get to wallop the bollocks off me, and I get to see you swing a hurl again. There's something in it for both of us."

Paul angrily snatched it out of his hands.

"Paul!" The outrage was there for all of them to hear in Brigit's voice.

"What? I'm just giving the man what he wants."

"Absolutely," grinned Bunny. "This is natural justice at its finest."

Paul adjusted his grip and pulled the hurl back.

"Paul, put that down this instant."

"Feck off back to Leitrim, love, this doesn't concern you."

"Don't talk to her like that," said Paul.

"C'mon ye pissy wee fecker, show me why not."

Brigit moved and stood in front of Bunny. "Enough!"

"Get out of the way, Brigit."

"No, I won't. I'm not going to stand by and watch you two idiots do whatever the hell this is. Need I remind you, WE are in trouble and WE are here because this fool is supposed to have information that can help us."

Their eyes locked. Paul looked at her for what felt like a very long time, before he slowly lowered the hurley. Brigit turned on her heels and faced Bunny.

"And as for you, you are supposed to be helping us. So either start doing that, or else we are out of here."

"Well you can fuck off."

Paul wasn't sure which one of them looked more surprised by the slap, Brigit or Bunny. She'd not put that much power behind it, but in his drunken state, it'd still been enough to cause him to stumble a couple of feet to his right.

"Stop making this all about you," she said. "Either help us, or get the hell out of the way." There was a pause when nobody spoke, before Brigit added in a much calmer voice. "I'm very sorry for hitting you. I'm not normally a violent person."

"You did rugby tackle a man through a plate glass door earlier," added Paul.

"Today is not a normal day."

"You've also hit me quite a few times."

Brigit glared at Paul, who sensed that now was a good time to stop talking.

"Bandon." Bunny spat the word out.

Paul gave a bitter little laugh.

"We know about Bandon," said Brigit. "We're heading down there now."

"Then you know feck all," said Bunny.

"Meaning?"

"Down? You've got the wrong Bandon. There's another one across in Mayo, a tiny village. That's the one you want."

"How're you so sure?" said Brigit.

"I got an old friend to tell me by dropping him out a window."

"And how do you know he wasn't lying?"

"Because he really didn't want me to do it again."

"What's supposed to be there?" said Paul.

"I've not got a fecking clue. All I know is Gerry Fallon seems awful keen for people to not have a look there. Good enough for me."

Paul and Brigit looked at each other.

"Well," said Brigit, "Kruger did say that he thought she was held somewhere in the West. Mayo does fit."

Paul turned back to Bunny, "anything else?"

"Yeah, I know who Fallon's boy in the Guards is."

"And?"

"The worst person imaginable. You can't trust anybody."

"Tell me something I don't know," said Paul, before adding. "Is that everything?"

Bunny nodded.

"Right, have fun cleaning this lot up."

Paul turned and started walking back towards the gate. Brigit caught up with him after a few steps and put her hand on his left arm to stop him walking.

"Wait a sec."

Paul stopped and looked at her pointedly.

"I think we should take him with us."

"What?! No way."

"C'mon, look at him, for Christ's sake."

"Exactly."

"He'd be very useful," she said.

"Are you high?"

Brigit started counting reasons off on her fingers. "Firstly, he's a policeman, it'd be nice to have one of those on our side."

"Bunny is only ever on Bunny's side."

"Secondly," she continued, "he does seem to have a flair for getting information out of people."

"Through violence!"

"Well, seeing how things have gone over the last couple of days, the chances are, there might be more of that."

"And?"

"And thirdly, if anything, he probably hates Gerry Fallon more than we do now. From everything you've told me, a pissed off Bunny McGarry might be the best weapon we've got."

Paul looked back and forth between Brigit and Bunny a few times. "Damn it. Alright."

Brigit patted Paul on the arm.

"Excellent decision." It was nice of her to say, but neither of them believed he'd actually been the one to make it. She started walking back towards Bunny.

Paul turned on his heels and raised his voice. "But I am sitting in the front seat!"

Brigit turned and gave him a humouring nod and smile.

"And... I'm in charge of the radio too!"

Brigit again nodded. Paul noticed Bunny looking at him in confusion. He could feel his cheeks redden. He turned and headed back towards the car as fast as he could. He needed to figure out how the radio worked as apparently, he felt strongly about it.

CHAPTER FORTY-EIGHT

Brigit awoke with a start and looked around her, her face flush with the embarrassment of waking up suddenly, anywhere, that isn't your own bed. She yelped involuntarily when she saw the stern pudgy face of a woman in her fifties glaring in the window at her, squinting eyes over lips puckered with disapproval. Brigit gave an apologetic smile and rolled down the Bentley's window. The woman reflexively pulled back in disgust and waved her hand in front of her nose, adding another layer to Brigit's embarrassment.

When they'd pulled over, it had been a stark choice: either leave the windows open and freeze to death in the bitter November night, or shut them and trap yourself in an enclosed space with the human rights violation that was Bunny McGarry's arse.

In what was probably for the best, Bunny had passed out on the back seat almost as soon as they'd started driving, once he'd delivered a brief but impassioned monologue on the injustice of Brigit taking his bottle of whiskey away. The first time he'd farted, it had been novel. It had broken the tension between herself and Paul. The entertainment value had however lasted nowhere near as long as the smell. The man's arse reeked like something had crawled up there and died a slow and painful death by cabbage. In the space of the few hours that they'd been pulled over in the pub's carpark, Brigit must have in some way become accustomed to it as, judging by the other woman's facial expression, the smell clearly had not improved.

"We're not open," said the woman in a surprisingly plummy accent.

"Excuse me?"

She pointed at the pub. "We're not open for several hours, and this is not a halting site. It is a private carpark."

"Yes, sorry, we just pulled over to rest."

The woman looked at Brigit's two unconscious companions, before pulling another in her seemingly endless array of disapproving faces. Clearly, something untoward was going on here, and she was not having it. Not in her carpark. Not on a Sunday morning.

"Good day to you." The way she said it made it very clear that she didn't really care what kind of a day Brigit had, just so long as she didn't have any more of it here.

Paul awoke at the sound of the Bentley's engine roaring into life and looked around him.

"Jesus, the country really does stink."

Brigit put the car in gear and pulled back out onto the N60. "That's not the country."

She'd pulled over for a few hours just outside Castlebar once she'd realised that reaching Bandon at 4AM was going to be of no use to them. There'd be very limited investigative opportunities when everybody was tucked up in their beds. Besides, if everybody else in the car was going to get some kip, she'd be damned if she was going to be the only one missing out. It had also been a good way of forestalling the inevitable, the moment when they'd have to face up to the fact that they'd absolutely no idea what they were looking for when they got to Bandon. Could it really be possible that Fiachra Fallon and Sarah-Jane Cranston had been living all this time in a small town in Mayo? Nowhere was that out of the way, was it? If not that, what were they hoping for?

They reached Bandon at 8:27AM, and the other end of it about seven seconds later. Even by the standard of country towns, it was small. Really nothing more than a crossroads, a pub, a church, a shop and about 20 houses. They'd passed a small primary school and a couple of playing fields on the way in.

"Where the hell is the rest of it?" asked Paul.

"Well," said Brigit, "there'll be surrounding farms as well, but it's a small town alright. What should we do?"

And there it was. The question she didn't have an answer to and, judging by Paul's facial expression, one he'd no more of a clue on than she did.

"We could say we're thinking of moving to the area?" he suggested. "Knock on a few doors?"

"Or we could go into the pub," added Brigit, "ask around?"

"Bollocks."

Brigit was surprised; she'd thought Bunny was still asleep.

"Moving to the area? To where exactly? D'ye think there's a house around here for sale that every local person wouldn't know about? And the pub? Yeah, the three strangers who turned up in the fecking Bentley asking questions, that won't arouse suspicion either."

"Alright then, what should we do?"

"Take the next turn then circle back around. We'll park this car at the school. That's as out of the way as you'll get around here. And then…" He left it hanging, waiting to be asked. Paul looked at Brigit: clearly he wasn't going to oblige. She rolled her eyes.

"And then?"

"We're going to Mass."

"That's your big plan?" asked Paul sarcastically. "The power of prayer?"

Bunny sighed theatrically as he sat up. "Small towns are made up of two things, people and buildings. Whatever we're looking for, our best chance of finding it is by looking for what's not supposed to be here. The best way of seeing the most amount of the people in one building at one time is…"

"Mass," finished Brigit.

"Mass," repeated Bunny.

"You're not just a pretty face, Bunny."

In response, Bunny farted loudly.

They parked the car and made their way back to the church on foot, timing it to arrive fifteen minutes before 10 o'clock Mass. They tried to keep a low profile as they walked in, although that was easier said than done. Paul was now sporting an impressive collection of injuries and Bunny looked like he'd lost a fight with a dumpster. Brigit was undoubtedly not looking too hot herself but it was best not to dwell on it.

Once inside, the trio grabbed a pew near the back and did their best to be unobtrusive. By the time the priest appeared, the church was relatively full, with a congregation of about a hundred Brigit reckoned. Not too shabby attendance-wise. It'd been a waste for their purposes though. She'd compared every man and woman who passed her to the mental pictures she held in her mind of what Sarah-Jane Cranston and Fiachra Fallon might look like now. Even allowing for hard lives or extensive plastic surgery, there was nobody who came close. Maybe they'd have more luck at the midday Mass.

Bunny sat on Brigit's right, his head buried in his hands as he knelt. She guessed the mother of all hangovers had finally kicked in.

"Are you OK?"

He spoke without raising his head. "Three rows up on the far side, brown wax jacket."

Brigit looked at the man indicated. She'd seen him walk in alone. He was mid-thirties at most, with a rat-tail hairdo, and a squirrely way about him. He was also way too young to have had anything to do with Rapunzel. He'd not have been old enough for a paper round at the time.

"Who is that?"

"That," whispered Bunny, "is the thing that is not supposed to be here. As soon as Communion starts, you," he pointed to Brigit, "back to the car with me pronto, and you," pointing at Paul, "follow him. Get car make, model, license plate."

"Who put him in charge?" asked Paul, a little too loudly.

The man in the pew in front of them turned and gave them a look. Paul waved his hand apologetically. He then turned to see Brigit giving him a look too. He nodded begrudgingly and kept quiet.

Brigit nipped out with Bunny as soon as Communion started, offering up a silent apology to her mother as she did so. She remembered all-too-well being spotted sneaking out of Mass early when she was a teenager. Her mother had been clever about it. Instead of grounding her daughter, she'd grounded herself. She didn't go into the village for two weeks, mortified for people to see her, after her raising such a wayward hellion of a daughter. This was long before Brigit had even heard the term passive-aggressive. It'd worked though. She'd stayed so long at the end of Mass after that, priests would regularly come up and ask if everything was OK.

"So who was that?" asked Brigit, as they walked back towards the school as quickly as they could without drawing attention.

"A creepy little shite called Jonny Carroll."

"You're sure?"

"I never forget a face, especially one I put behind bars about twelve years ago."

"Oh, what for?"

"Let's just say, you'd have to be really stuck to use him as a babysitter."

They had made it back to the school's small carpark in under ten minutes. Two young boys, their BMXs strewn carelessly on the ground, were staring at the Bentley like it'd just landed from another planet. The taller one looked at Brigit and Bunny with unreserved disappointment, and then walloped his snotty-nosed compatriot across the back of the head. "I knew it wasn't Kanye, ye lying ball-bag."

Paul staggered in ten minutes later, sweating from the exertion of speed walking. He leaned against the car, regaining his breath.

"Ford Mondeo, red, 04-G-17435... no 14735."

"Which way'd he go?" asked Bunny.

"I dunno," said Paul, before adding nervously, "I didn't actually see him get into the car."

"What?! How da feck do you know it was his car then?"

"He was... sorta standing near it with – you could tell by his body language and..." Paul looked fazed, "this old fella started chatting to me for some reason."

"For some reason?!" exclaimed Bunny. "You're in the country city slicker, where people are polite! Mammy Mary and all the saints, I give you one job to do! Do I've to do everything myself?"

"Well why didn't you then?" said Paul.

"Because Jonny Carroll might not be the sharpest tool in the box, but even he's going to notice if the man who sent him down is following him about. I was lucky to get out of the fecking church without being spotted."

"Ahhh, blow it out your foul arse, Bunny."

A huffy silence descended on the carpark as the two men leaned against the car and stared off into two different bits of distance. Brigit sighed heavily; this was going to be a very long trip. Maybe they should get back on the road? Do another sweep of the town before the midday Mass or...

Brigit opened the driver's door and hopped in.

"If anybody is interested, a red Mondeo just drove by."

By the time they'd got on the road, the Mondeo was out of sight around a bend. Brigit put her foot to the floor and, after two nervous miles, she got the Mondeo back in her sights just in time to see it take a left at a crossroads.

"Don't get too close."

"But don't leave too much room."

"Hang back..."

"But don't drive like you're deliberately hanging back."

"Everybody shut up!" she snapped. "This isn't the first time I've followed somebody."

It was. What she'd meant to say was she'd seen it loads on telly, but then had remembered how that would sound. To be fair, she'd rarely seen somebody cope with the unique problem of following somebody when there was no other traffic on the road, as was now the case. The constant advice had been ruining the moment somewhat though; James Bond never had to put up with that crap.

Brigit pushed the Bentley up to sixty when the Mondeo disappeared around a blind bend in the road. As they rounded the corner, she had to slam on the brake to prevent ramming right into the back of it. The Mondeo having become trapped behind a tractor that'd just pulled out of a gate, oblivious to the possibility of other traffic existing.

"Jesus!"

Brigit's heart pounded as the car skidded on wet leaves before coming to a stop, all of two feet behind it.

She was dimly aware of Bunny diving for cover in the back seat. As she looked up, she could see the man from the church looking back at her over his shoulder.

Bunny's hand pushed forward from between the two seats and slapped the horn, its loud honk ringing out.

"What the?" exclaimed Brigit.

"Don't look back at me," barked Bunny. "Quick, give him the fingers."

"What?"

"Do it!"

Paul obediently threw up his fingers and was greeted with an enthusiastic wanker gesture in response from the man in front. They could see him shaking his head as he drove off behind the tractor.

"Off you go," said Bunny.

"What was the point of that?"

"No eejit who is trying to follow somebody is going to almost ram them up the arse and then flick them the Vs. He's now thinking you're a pair of clueless gobshites from Dublin who don't know how to drive. What he's not thinking is – those people are following me. If the two of you could have a row now, that'd be fabulous."

"Your driving is bloody appalling," said Paul, with way more sincerity than necessary.

"How dare you! I was trying to keep up with the bloke that you almost lost."

"Perfect," said Bunny, "just like that."

Half a mile down the road, the Mondeo pulled out around the tractor and accelerated away. Brigit tried to follow suit but sod's law meant two cars were now coming the other way, blocking her path. They then reached a stretch of winding road where over-taking was impossible.

"We're losing him!"

Brigit laid on the horn in pointless frustration. All this got her was a relaxed wave from the man on the tractor. When they finally reached a straight bit of road, Brigit fired the Bentley out and around, getting way too close for comfort to a van in the oncoming lane. They came to a crossroads and looked each way. There was no sign of the Mondeo.

"Shit!"

In the absence of any other information, they went left for a couple of miles but there was no sign of their quarry. When they reached another crossroads, Brigit pulled a U-turn and zoomed back to the original crossroads they'd lost the Mondeo at, heading the other way. By this point, ten minutes had passed since they'd last seen it. With the headstart, it could be half way out of the county by now.

As they passed a couple of small side-roads Paul suddenly walloped the dashboard. "STOP THE CAR!!!"

Brigit slammed the brakes on, almost sending Bunny hurtling into the front seat as she did so. "Shitting Nora woman!"

Paul turned in his seat, his face flush with excitement.

"In the hospital, before McNair attacked me, he was rambling about death and all that. I thought it was random nonsense. At one point he asked me about believing in heaven or something, then he said he knew he wasn't going there."

"She keeps driving like this, we'll all be fecking joining him!"

Brigit aggressively shushed Bunny, she could see the fire in Paul's eyes.

"The point is, he said he wasn't going to heaven, he'd be going to the other place, six feet under. Only, he didn't say 'under ground' like people say, he said 'under the rock'... and..."

"And?" said Brigit.

Paul pointed behind them and they all turned to look. There, by the side of the road was a battered and worn wooden postbox. In the cracked and faded paint on the side were written the words 'The Rock.'

CHAPTER FORTY-NINE

'The Rock', as it turned out, was a fairly ordinary-looking farmhouse built on the top of a large rocky outcrop, surrounded by fields. Half a mile from the main road and with no other buildings in sight, save for a couple of disused sheds at the bottom of the hill behind it, it was the definition of remote. If 'The Rock' itself was something of an anti-climax, the fact that the Red Mondeo was parked outside thrilled Paul. He had been right.

Since Thursday night, he'd become entangled in some complicated web he didn't understand. Whatever it all meant, the best chance for answers lay inside that farmhouse.

When they'd turned onto the road, they quickly realised that the only thing on it was The Rock. The boreen was only wide enough to fit one car and, even then, overgrown briars clawed at the Bentley's flanks as it drove slowly through. Brigit stopped the car at the bottom of the gravel drive leading up to the house. "We need to get out of here before he sees us."

"What're we going to do?" asked Paul.

"I reckon we put the place under surveillance, try and figure out what's going on," said Brigit.

"Right."

"Yeah," chimed in Bunny, "I'll go get a fecking panto cow outfit and you two can stand in that field all day and try and peek in the windows."

Before anyone could respond, Bunny opened the back door and stepped out.

"What's he doing?" said Brigit. "Why's he opening the boot? Why's he got his hurley out? Where does he think he's going?"

Paul looked at her. "You're asking me like I have any more information than you do."

Bunny sauntered by, casually swinging his hurley by his side as he headed up the gravel driveway.

"Well, I guess that answers all of your questions."

"We should discuss this!"

"Don't look at me, you're the one who wanted to bring him."

Paul got out of the car and quickly strode up the driveway to catch up with Bunny, Brigit joining them a second later.

"What's the plan here?" she panted.

"Plan?" said Bunny. "There's no plan. I'm just saying hello to an old friend."

"And there is no need for violence."

Bunny turned and regarded her with surprise. "Moi? How dare you – I'm Mahatma fecking Gandhi, only, y'know, without the whole nappy thing."

"Asshole," spat Paul. Bunny and Brigit turned to look at him in surprise.

"That's a bit of a controversial opinion to have on Gandhi."

"I wasn't..." Embarrassed, Paul nodded his head towards the adjoining field. In it, regarding them with a look of belligerent boredom, stood a donkey.

"I'm not a big fan," said Paul.

Bunny was about to ring the doorbell when they heard singing from the back of the house. A nasally male voice was murdering some song about how he fought the law. The trio walked around the house to see the man in the brown wax jacket they'd seen earlier, hanging out his washing. His back was to them, and he was humming along to whatever music was in his headphones, bobbing his head and gyrating his legs spasmodically as he worked. He threw in a sharp 360-heel turn that went totally out of control at the midway point. That was when he saw Bunny McGarry beaming at him.

"Howerya, Jonny?"

In his haste to turn his spin into a sprint in the opposite direction, Jonny Carroll went flying over his half-full basket of washing and planted his face messily into the ground.

Bunny turned to look at Brigit. "I never touched him."

As Carroll tried to scramble away, Bunny calmly grabbed him by the scruff of the neck and heaved him to his feet. His iPod landed softly on the wet grass.

"Jaysus, Jonny, is this anyway to greet an old friend? If I didn't know better, I'd say you weren't pleased to see me."

Paul had heard people described as having eyes like a trapped animal, but he'd never known what it really meant until that moment. Carroll's eyes bulged and darted about frantically, looking at anything that wasn't Bunny. Looking for anything that could help him escape from Bunny.

Bunny shoved him up against the back wall of the house. "Last time I heard about you, Jonny, was all of eight years ago now. You were out on parole and the girl's family were mad keen to meet you. Rumour was they had, hence your unlamented disappearance. I'm so happy to see you alive and well."

"I... how did... I didn't... who are... why... it's not... don't... where did..."

"All excellent questions. Calm down, Jonny, you'll do yourself a mischief."

"I thought she was sixteen!"

Bunny casually lifted his hurl to leave it resting on the other man's shoulder.

"Now, now, Jonny, let's not go over old ground. You know how it upsets Mabel here. You remember her?"

Bunny moved the top of his hurley to rest under Carroll's chin, who nodded as briskly as he could in the circumstance. Bunny named his hurleys. Of course he did. Paul had forgotten that little tradition. It was Samantha way back when he was on the St Jude's team. He'd always warned his boys, anyone who was caught robbing would have a date with the lovely Samantha. It was a joke, a joke nobody wanted to test.

"I am impressed to see you're going to Mass though, Jonny, asking forgiveness for your many sins."

"I'm trying to be good, honest, Bunny. I'm on the side of the angels."

"Well isn't that marvellous? If only you'd shown the same dedication to the parole process."

"It's not my fault," pleaded Carroll.

"Of course it isn't," said Bunny, in that mocking Cork lilt of his, "Gerry Fallon made you an offer you couldn't refuse."

Carroll's eyes bulged so much, Paul thought his head was about to explode. "You know?!"

Bunny smiled calmly back at him. "Look where I'm standing Jonny. I know everything. Did you think this was a social call?"

"But Fallon said…"

Bunny pushed the hurl up until it applied pressure to Carroll's throat.

"You need to ask yourself a question, Jonny. Who're you more afraid of – Gerry Fallon in the future, or me, right here, right now?"

Bunny leaned in to put his face a couple of inches from Carroll's, so that the patented McGarry wonky-eyed stare filled his entire field of vision. "Well?"

"Yeah, yeah, yeah, Bunny, anything you want. He made me come here when the last guy died and… I'm as much a prisoner here as anyone."

"Of course you are. I'm sure the parole office will take that into account."

"Oh God, please, no. I can't go back. They'll kill me." He licked his lips nervously before continuing. "Do you… do you want to see him?"

Bunny looked back at Brigit and Paul, before turning to face Carroll.

"Sure, isn't that why we're here?"

CHAPTER FIFTY

Carroll led them down a set of rough stairs to the two sheds at the bottom of the hill, chattering away as he did so. Bunny seemed happy just to let him keep talking, and neither Paul nor Brigit wanted to interrupt. For better or for worse, Bunny was in charge now.

From what Paul could pick up, Carroll had been living there for a long time, about five years. He wasn't allowed leave for more than a few hours. Gerry Fallon came to visit from time to time. He made a reference to the odd special visit which Paul didn't understand. Carroll kept claiming that Fallon had threatened to do something to his dear old ma, and that was the only reason he'd agreed to do this. Paul still didn't understand exactly what 'this' was, but it did occur to him that for a man so allegedly worried about his poor old ma, Carroll at no point checked to see if Bunny could protect her.

He led them into the shed that was built up against the rock and turned on the single bare light bulb that dangled from the ceiling. Paul didn't know what he'd expected, but a dusty old shed full of broken furniture and ancient looking farm machinery was an anti-climax.

Bunny's voice was a low warning growl. "This better not be a wild goose chase, Jonny."

316

Their host looked around at them nervously. "It's not, I swear it. Hang on a second." He moved down the path that led to the back of the shed, where an extremely large wooden wardrobe rested against the back wall of rock. He opened it wide and then pulled across the curtain that hung at the back, to reveal a large and clearly thick metal door that was built into the rock-face. There was an electronic keypad on the metal frame beside it and underneath the small porthole-style window, in faded yellow paint was the word SHELTER.

Paul looked at Brigit and Bunny in turn, the same stunned expression on each of their faces.

"Holy crap," said Brigit.

Carroll bobbed nervously from one foot to the other. "Yeah, no, y'see yeah – apparently the old fella who owned this place back in the sixties was a bit of a fruit loop. Was convinced that the Yanks and the Russians were gonna blow the whole planet up or some shit, so he built a shelter out of the caves under the family farm. I don't know how Fallon found out about it, but he bought it way back in the day." Carroll looked around their faces and suddenly he looked very concerned. "You already knew that though, right?"

"Ah yeah, course we did," said Bunny, "we're just impressed by the door."

Carroll nodded, "Ah right, yeah." He quickly punched a code into the keypad. There was a loud hiss, followed by a click and then the thick door automatically swung itself open, to reveal a long dark cave descending into the rock. Now it was fully opened, Paul could see that the door was six inches thick. That farmer back in the sixties might have been a few cattle short of a herd, but he'd not skimped on the fixtures and fittings.

Carroll stood to the side and extended his arm. "After you."

Bunny pointed down the tunnel with Mabel. "Oh no, dear boy, after you. And Jonny," Bunny patted the hurley in his hand, "no funny business now, alright?"

"Yeah, yeah, yeah," said Carroll, turning to head down the tunnel like a petulant teenager being sent to his room. He clicked on a button on the wall and a string of small halogen lamps threw orange light into the darkness, illuminating the cave walls covered in a wet slimy residue.

Bunny leaned forward quickly and grabbed the end of Carroll's ponytail.

"What's the story?!" said Carroll huffily.

"I just don't want to lose you again, Jonny. Not so soon after finding ye."

Carroll muttered under his breath before he started walking slowly down the tunnel, Bunny in tow.

Paul looked at Brigit. "There better not be a lion and a witch down there."

"Couldn't get much weirder if there was."

Carroll's voice echoed up the tunnel to them. "Hurry up or else..."

With a soft squeak, the thick steel door began to swing slowly shut.

Brigit and Paul nipped in around it and then watched as it closed behind them.

"It does that," said Carroll. "Security feature. Y'know, in case of zombies and that."

Paul nodded. That made perfect sense.

They walked down the thirty-foot long cave, the walls drawing closer as they went, forcing them into single file. Green moss grew near the bulbs and shards of quartz in the stone reflected speckles of light. The cave descended at about a thirty-degree angle. Paul reckoned they must be about sixty feet below the farmhouse by now. As they walked deeper, strange noises could be heard coming from the tunnel in front of them. They echoed around them, mingling with the sound of their footsteps, making it difficult to make out what they were at first. Then, as they came nearer, Paul decided his ears must be playing tricks on him. It couldn't be, but it sounded a lot like a televised football match. They turned a corner and walked through another steel door, this one propped open and leading into a cavern that was about 20-foot by 20-foot. The only source of light was the big screen TV mounted on the far wall. It was indeed showing football highlights.

Paul wasn't a big footie fan, but it looked like a classic Manchester derby to him. He looked around in the flickering illumination the TV provided. A bed lay in the corner, with a basin and a large bucket beside it. Shelves holding hundreds of videotapes lined the walls. A worn and faded poster of a blonde woman with her sizeable breasts on full display stared down from the wall. Paul had seen her on one of those *I remember the Eighties* shows. He was fairly sure her name was Samantha Fox. In front of Miss Fox and her eye-catching assets sat a cross-training machine. In the far right corner of the room, Paul could just about make out another steel door in the rock, this one closed. There was an aroma of a strong air-freshener, but it couldn't mask the undertones of damp and a more insistent stench, which Paul guessed was coming from the bucket in the corner. In the centre of the room sat a worn sofa, it's back to them, facing the TV. While it didn't have much of a view and it was nowhere near local amenities, Paul had still seen worse flats than this.

Carroll reached over and flicked a switch on the wall. A similar string of halogen lamps to the ones used in the entrance tunnel blinked into life around them. A man with long ragged brown hair sat up on the sofa and happily waved his hand in the air without looking around.

"Hey, hey, big bad Jon."

"Hey dude," said Carroll, "you've got some visitors."

The man let out a whoop and span around. He leapt into a standing position on the sofa and gawped at them open-mouthed. If he looked shocked to see them, it was nothing compared to how stunned they must have looked to be faced with him. Whoever this poor creature was, he was a compelling advert for the importance of sunlight and access to dentistry. Take away the long ragged beard and thirty years of wear and tear, Paul reckoned they were looking at Fiachra Fallon. He was pretty sure he had that right, but the fact that the man was bouncing up and down excitedly on the sofa, quite literally bollock naked, was making it hard to concentrate.

"Fiachra!" said Carroll, "what've we talked about? Put on your pants!"

The man scrabbled over to his bed and quickly began pulling on some tracksuit bottoms, clapping his hands as he went. "Yes, yes, yessy, Jonny, Jon boy, Jonny-be-good!"

As he did so, Paul noticed the chain around his wrist, the other end of which was very firmly attached to the wall. He'd be able to walk around the room but not much further.

Fiachra stopped clapping his hands long enough to look excitedly to Carroll. "Are they... special visitors?"

"Yeah," said Carroll distractedly, "if you're good."

He started dancing about in a circle, the happiest person Paul had ever seen in his life, heedless of the chain wrapping itself around him. He kept looking over at them and then giggled away to himself with a demented glee, clapping his hands excitedly all the while. "Oh thank you, Gerry, big brother Gerry, best friend Gerry!!" Then he stopped, and for the first time the grin fell from his face. "Where's Gerry?"

"It's OK," said Brigit in a soft voice. "He's not here."

They all leapt back when he screamed. It was the wretched sound of a wounded animal. He scurried into the corner behind the cross-trainer and cowered there.

"No-n-n-n-nno. Can't have visitors when Gerry not here. Very bad, very bad, very bad, bad, bad!!"

Carroll glared at Brigit, who looked shell-shocked. He moved slowly towards Fiachra, holding his hands out and talking in a soft calming voice. "It's OK, Fiachra, he's coming. Gerry is on his way. You're OK. He's not going to be mad."

"No Gerry, no visitors!"

"I know, I know."

Carroll moved closer to him, making calming noises as the poor creature hugged the side of the fitness machine.

Bunny, Brigit and Paul huddled together.

"What in the flaming fucknuggets is this?" said Bunny. "Why would Fallon keep his own brother prisoner?"

They all looked at each other.

"I've no idea," answered Brigit. "The poor thing. He's obviously lost his mind completely."

Paul found himself trying to look at anything that wasn't Fiachra. "Maybe they had a falling out or something?"

"For thirty fecking years?" said Bunny. "Jaysus, Paulie, and there was me thinking you were good at bearing a grudge."

"Shit!" exclaimed Brigit, "Carroll!"

Paul looked up in time to see the steel door in the far wall close. They ran over, Paul trying the handle to find it locked. Bunny pushed him aside and slammed his shoulder uselessly into it. Then he pushed his face up to the round window.

"C'mon now, Jonny, don't play silly buggers."

The light came on, illuminating Bunny's face in its glow.

"It's some kind of storeroom," said Bunny, before raising his voice. "You can't get out of there, Jonny. Don't be daft." Bunny started banging his fist repeatedly against the steel. It didn't even make a satisfying noise, the steel being way too thick. "You come out of there right now, or so help me God, I'll rip your bollocks out through your fecking throat!"

"For Christ's sake, Bunny," said Brigit, "Are threats your answer to everything? He probably can't even hear you through that door."

"Good point." Bunny then proceeded to act out an elaborate series of threats through the medium of mime. The only effect this had was to start Fiachra howling again.

"Gerry gonna be mad, Gerry gonna be mad, Gerry gonna be mad!!"

Paul moved over towards him, pressing his hands out in a shushing motion.

"It's OK. Everything is fine. We're just playing a game."

"Ah bollocks!" exclaimed Bunny. "Carroll just won the game."

Paul turned to look at them. Brigit pointed glumly at the window in the storeroom door. "He opened a hatch in the roof and climbed up a ladder."

"Shit."

"Shit."

"Double shite with a cherry on top."

Fiachra slowly crawled out from behind the cross-trainer. He scurried to the sofa and grabbed the TV's remote control, before scurrying back. They all looked at him. He smiled up at them with a wide grin that contained ten teeth at most.

"I get to pick what we watch."

CHAPTER FIFTY-ONE

"Jesus, it fecking stinks in here," said Bunny, as he paced back and forth across the floor of the cave, waving his now useless mobile in the air.

"Smell the irony!"

Bunny stopped and glowered down at Paul. He and Brigit had decided to sit on the floor with their backs to the wall. Fiachra had already reclaimed his place on the sofa, and the bed didn't look the most sanitary of locations.

"What'd you say?"

"Ah, work it out for yourself, Colombo, and for Christ's sake, stop waving that phone around. Under this much rock, you've got zero chance at a signal."

Brigit looked up towards the roof and expelled a heavy sigh. "Will the two of you give it a rest, please? We could be here quite a while."

"Bit of an understatement," said Paul. "I believe the previous record might be thirty years."

Brigit looked over at Fiachra, who had resumed happily watching the football, having decided to apparently ignore their presence.

"Shush," said Brigit, "or you'll set him off again."

She looked around her at the cavern they'd been trapped in for nearly an hour now. It hadn't taken long to confirm what they'd expected, there was no other way out and both the main door and the door to the storeroom were locked. There was a keypad on the inside of the main entrance but Brigit's testing had determined that it locked itself out after you'd unsuccessfully tried a 6-digit code three times in a row. She'd started trying to work out how long it would take three people working in shifts to input every possible combination, then she realised that somebody could probably just change the code from the other side.

She lowered her voice. "Do you think this is where they held Sarah-Jane Cranston?"

"I guess," answered Paul. "You couldn't ask for a better hiding place. Even if police came to the house, what odds they find this place? I don't get what's going on though, do you?"

Brigit shook her head. "Brophy's book is clearly bullshit."

"Yeah. Next thing you know, we'll find out there aren't really sexy vampires living in Offaly either."

Brigit gave him a weak smile. None of them had dared to speak the unpalatable truth of their situation. Nobody in the outside world knew where they were, and Fiachra was all the evidence they needed that The Rock was an excellent place for someone to disappear completely. They'd inadvertently delivered themselves into Gerry Fallon's favourite cage.

Brigit stood up and then dusted her hands off.

"What're you doing?"

"I'm going to try and get some sense out of..." She nodded towards the sofa.

Paul pulled a face. "Good luck with that."

Brigit turned and slowly walked over to the sofa, being careful to walk into Fiachra's eye-line so as not to startle him. He shot her a suspicious glance and then went back to watching the TV. As she approached, she got a better look at him now that he was sitting more or less still. His skin had a sickly pale quality and there were dark rings around his eyes. His fingernails looked bloodied and chewed, as his hands absent-mindedly clawed at each other in his lap. She knew he was what 54, 55 years of age now, but he looked older. Actually, he looked as if he'd stepped outside the normal ageing process entirely. His skin lacked the creases you'd expect but looked flaky and patchy in places. He was thin but not to the point of being underfed.

"Hey, Fiachra," she said softly.

"I'm not allowed to talk to strangers," he responded, never taking his eyes off the screen.

"OK. Well my name is Brigit Conroy and I'm a nurse. There, now we're not strangers."

"Not allowed visitors without Gerry Gerry, ever ever."

"It's fine. Gerry is a good friend of mine."

Fiachra looked up at her warily but said nothing.

She decided on a change of tack. "So, are you a big football fan?"

He nodded his head repeatedly and started swaying back and forth giddily, pointing at the screen. "Yeah, yeah, yeah, United are my team. Best team in the world." Then he started singing, "Champione, champione, ole, ole, ole!" before descending into a fit of giggles.

Brigit moved slightly closer, her hand now resting on the arm of the sofa. "Who is your favourite player?"

"Rooney, Rooney, Rooney! I know all his stats, ask me anything!" His face now beamed up at her excitedly.

"Ehm... how many goals has he scored?"

"This season or ever?"

"Ever."

"Altogether or in the Premiership, FA Cup, League Cup, Champions League or internationals?"

"The... League Cup."

"Seven in twenty-two appearances, five for United and two for Everton."

"Wow, you really know your stuff. Do you mind if I sit down?"

He looked at her and then at the space on the sofa beside him. "It's a free country." Then he giggled. Brigit couldn't tell if he actually saw any irony in the statement.

She sat down slowly and then looked around the room. "This is a nice place you've got here."

"Yeah, it's mine, all mine. Not room enough for all of us though. You'll have to sleep in the bed with me!" Then he giggled again. Brigit tried to smile back at him. "How long have you been here?"

"Looooong time, only – I'm not really here."

"No?"

"No. I'm in America with Sarah-Jane Cranston." He said her name in a put-on posh tone of voice. "We're like Romeo and Juliet. They're gonna make a film of us!" He leaned towards her conspiratorially and she could smell the sour milk tang of his breath. "Colin Farrell is rumoured to be interested." He tapped the side of his nose with his finger and then returned to looking at the TV.

"Do you get lonely down here?"

"Not any more, I've got Sky Sports now. I like Jonny, he gives me the sports. He was an electrician, so he was, ha, ha, so he was."

"Oh, that's good."

"Yeah. He was much better than mean old Bob. He died."

Fiachra looked away and down at the floor. Brigit had no idea what was going through his mind, or whether his thoughts were so scrambled through the years of isolation that nothing really was anymore. He suddenly looked up at her, with big soulful eyes. Somewhere in there, buried under thirty years of unimaginable cruelty, she could see a flicker of those movie star looks, warped as they were.

He spoke softly, in a voice suddenly removed from the high pitched squeal in which he rambled. "Are you... going to be my special guest?"

Brigit patted his knee gently. "Sure"

And then he was on her. His chains jangled as his bony hands clasped around her throat. His long thin fingers stretching around her neck as his face became a mask of demented fury. She was pinned down on the sofa in an instant, her hands scrabbling uselessly at his forearms, which were thin but full of firm muscle. The pressure on her windpipe, the stench of his breath, the sight of his demented eyes – filled with bloodlust as they glared down at her. Small amoebas of light swam across her vision...

The hurley smashed into Fiachra's face. He was off her as quick as he'd pounced. She could hear him scrabbling away, yowling like a wounded animal. Brigit fell onto the worn rug in front of the TV and gasped for breath, the sound of blood rushing in her ears.

Paul fell to his knees beside her, his hands cupping her face. "Are you alright?"

She nodded, her hands rubbing at her throat. She could feel her own fingers tremble as they rubbed at her neck.

"Right, ye little scuttering whelp…"

Brigit turned to see Bunny, Mabel in hand, towering over Fiachra as he cowered once more behind the cross-trainer.

"Don't!" she croaked.

Bunny looked over at her and then back down at Fiachra, indecision etched on his face. Every fibre of his being clearly wanted to go against Brigit's wish.

"Don't," she said, more firmly.

Bunny raised the hurl above his head.

There was a metal clicking noise behind them. "Don't."

They all turned to see Gerry Fallon standing in the doorway, holding a gun in his hand.

"Don't."

CHAPTER FIFTY-TWO

For the second time in 24 hours, Paul looked down the barrel of a gun. His growing familiarity with the sensation wasn't breeding contempt just yet. It wasn't the gun that was the truly scary part. It was the face behind it. The eyes. One look into the eyes of Gerry Fallon and you saw it. Not fear, not excitement, not doubt – just a cold brutal certainty. He'd do whatever he considered needed to be done and not think twice about it.

Behind Fallon stood a face Paul knew all too well. No, not a face, an expression. The sneering jackal grin Jonny Carroll wore was all too familiar. He'd seen it on dozens of kids, the little weasel ones just standing to the side of every big kid who'd ever loomed above him. The memory brought back the taste of blood to his mouth. Most people say they hate bullies. Paul realised in that moment that who he truly hated was the person standing behind them, glowing with the joy of not being you.

The fact that Carroll had a gun in his hand too didn't seem important. Fallon was more than enough to kill them.

Fallon's eyes were fixed on Bunny, who still held the hurley over Fiachra's head, poised to strike.

"Drop the hurl."

"Why?" asked Bunny.

"Did you not notice the gun?"

"I did. And am I supposed to believe there's a version of what happens next that doesn't involve you killing me?"

Fallon shrugged. "No."

"Then if it's all the same, I'd rather batter some manners into this whelp on my way out."

Fiachra whimpered and threw his hands up around his head.

"Let me put it another way," said Fallon, turning the gun so it pointed at Brigit instead. "Lay a finger on him, and I'll shoot her in the gut, so you can watch her die. Slowly."

Bunny looked from Fallon to Fiachra to Brigit, then he dropped the hurley on the ground. "Well, if you're going to take all the fun out of it."

Fallon pointed at the door to the storeroom. "If you could all stand over there please."

As they shuffled across, Fiachra darted from his hidey-hole and went to cower behind his brother, his chain jangling as he scurried across the room. Blood was oozing from his nose, which looked bent out of shape following its meeting with Mabel. He rubbed his forearm across it, succeeding only in smearing the blood across his beard. Paul's stomach lurched at the sight of it, and he felt light-headed. Don't look at him. Focus on something else. Stay in the game.

Fiachra crouched low to the ground and tugged upon his sibling's trouser leg. "Gerry, Gerry, I said no visitors without Gerry, I said, I said, didn't I say? I said."

Paul concentrated on looking at Gerry Fallon instead, so he noticed the grimace of revulsion on the older brother's face as he pulled his leg away. "I know, Fiachra, I know."

"I said, I said."

"It's OK."

"Are they..." Paul saw Fiachra's face light up as he beamed across the room at them, "special guests, Gerry?"

Fallon looked down at his brother for a long moment, an unreadable expression on his face. "Sure."

Fiachra clapped his hands and whooped with glee.

"Shush," barked Fallon. Fiachra obediently put a finger to his lips and fell silent, his eyes still wide with a childish delight.

Fallon turned to Carroll. "Turn that off," he said, nodding his head towards the TV. "Then go and get his things."

Carroll nodded, obediently walking over to turn off the TV before heading back up the tunnel towards the entrance. Fallon looked down at his brother again, "And you go clean yourself up."

Fiachra scampered over to his bed and wiped his face on a towel beside the basin, much to Paul's relief.

"So, you two must be Mulchrone and Conroy? I've heard so much about you."

"Yeah," said Paul, "Grinner McNair sends his regards."

"So, he did talk?"

Paul laughed bitterly. "You paranoid arsehole. He didn't say a word, at least none that made any sense."

"So how'd you end up here?"

"By necessity," said Paul. "If you were going to kill us no-matter-what to protect your little secret, the only way out was to find it before you found us."

"Ah well," said Fallon shrugging, "no use crying over spilt milk. I had to protect my brother's location, couldn't take the chance."

Paul jumped with surprise as Bunny burst out laughing. Fallon's eyes narrowed in annoyance. "Is something funny?"

Bunny wiped tears from his eyes. "Ah yeah, tis fecking hilarious in fact. I just figured it out. It really is a fairy tale."

"Care to enlighten us?"

"Gollum there never left the country, because Sarah-Jane Cranston never left this room." Bunny turned to Brigit and Paul. "Have yous ever actually read the brothers Grimm? There are no Prince Charmings. What they do have, though, is lots and lots of monsters."

A silence hung in the cavern for a moment.

Fallon looked across at his brother, who was placidly sitting on his bed now, staring over at the blank TV screen, as if unaware of his surroundings. "It wasn't his fault," said Fallon. "I mean, we knew what he was from an early age, me and my mam. We didn't have the easiest of childhoods but... Animals, at first. He did some nasty things. Ma tried talking to him. I tried beating sense into him. Nothing worked. The badness was in him. You know what mothers are like though; she could never accept what he was. We thought he might grow out of it, especially when he got older and the women started falling all over him, but it was still there, just different. There was an... incident, I sent him away to Glasgow. Even looked at getting him help but..."

"He fucked up over there and they sent your psycho brother right back to you," finished Bunny.

"Yeah," nodded Fallon. "Eastern European hooker. Luckily, nobody was that bothered."

"Yeah," agreed Bunny, bitterness lacing his voice, "big stroke of luck that alright."

Fallon kept talking, entirely ignoring Bunny's interjection. "Grinner and I had been off sorting stuff for the ransom drop. We thought he'd be alright on his own. He'd been good for a couple of years at that stage, hadn't done anything..." Fallon looked over at his brother, a look of revulsion on his face. "Grinner came back here first and found her. What was left I mean. He ran."

"Smart fella," said Bunny. "You'd have killed him in a heartbeat to hide your little monster here."

"Well, you know what they say," said Fallon, "family is family. Him being what he is doesn't change that. Growing up, there was just us and our ma. I'd promised her I'd always look after him. I couldn't y'know... but he'd gone too far, he was dangerous. I couldn't let him go off out into the world. He'd do it again and then it'd all come out. I'd go down with him and it'd kill my ma."

Christ, thought Paul, what is it with all these psycho gangsters loving their dear old mammies?

"So," said Bunny, "you locked the little freak up here and invented a story to cover the whole thing up."

"And *Hostage to Love*," chimed in Brigit, "was the resulting pile of crap."

It was Fallon's turn to laugh. "Yeah. I told Brophy the basics, and he did the rest. He'd found out a little, you see, so I gave him the exclusive story, in exchange for his cooperation. I also put the fear of God into the little weasel. Our little fairy tale really caught the public's imagination, didn't it?"

Fiachra joined in without looking up from his fingers, "Colin Farrell is rumoured to be interested."

Paul glanced at Brigit, to see her looking back at him. They were both thinking the same thing. In a big house in the Wicklow Mountains, an old man would die wondering.

"And fair play to you," said Bunny, "you recovered from that early setback to have a glittering career in the field of criminal scumbaggery. There's not a heroin overdose that happens in this country which you've not got a hand in."

"Oh, save me the petty moralising. Wasn't it you who dropped your boss out a three story window last night?"

Paul looked over at Bunny. "Wait, that wasn't a joke? You really threw somebody out of a window?"

Bunny glowered back at him. "No. I pushed him off a balcony, he was already outside."

"Oh, well, that's alright then."

"In my defence, it was the prick who was giving this scumbag everything the police knew about you. The same prick who'd been protecting him for 30 years."

Fallon smirked. "Well, more like 25. The great Fintan O'Rourke. Real stroke of luck that. We found each other earlier and our little team worked out for all concerned."

"Yeah, he even helped keep an eye out to make sure nobody got near whatever little secret you were hiding out here."

"I told him it was a 'distribution centre'. He was smart enough not to want details. I trusted him, or rather, I trusted him to save his own arse, and he knew I'd more than enough to nail it to the wall." Fallon shook his head and grinned, as if sharing a fond memory. "He wasn't as smart at being dirty in the early days as he thought he was. Nobody is as thick as the cocky clever ones."

"And all this time," added Paul, "you've been hiding the family's dirty secret under a rock. Wondering when it'd come back to haunt you."

"I wasn't that bothered to be honest, not after the first few years. The one thing I hadn't expected was Grinner not having the sense to stay dead."

"Well sure, ye know what it is like near the end," said Bunny, "people get fierce sentimental."

Carroll appeared in the doorway, holding a sports bag in one hand and his gun in the other. Fiachra grinned excitedly at the sight of it.

"You'd be in the perfect position to know," said Fallon.

"I just figured something else out," said Bunny, looking at Carroll. "Big part of the Gerry Fallon legend. People he didn't see eye-to-eye with were always disappearing."

Fallon actually looked bashful. "Well, if I couldn't fix Fiachra's little problem, figured we might as well use it. He has had quite a few special guests over the years, as treats. There's an awful lot of bodies buried in these fields."

And there it was. It wasn't like it was a surprise. Paul knew it was coming, but he'd been avoiding thinking about it. They were all going to die here, and it probably wasn't going to be quick. They were to be the playthings of the monster buried under the rock. It didn't sound like a fun way to go.

He didn't know if your life was really supposed to flash before your eyes just before you died, but the moment did come with a great dollop of stark clarity.

"Before whatever is about to happen… happens, can we have a brief private word?" he asked, pointing at Brigit.

"I'm on a bit of a schedule here," responded Fallon. "Whatever you've got to say, say it now. No whispering."

Paul looked at her. She smiled back at him nervously. The terror that was rising in him, he could see in her too. He could also see her fighting it. Her determination to control the situation, rather than letting it control her.

"That…" he looked around at the four other men watching them, "that game of Risk from a couple of nights ago."

Brigit looked confused.

"The one we didn't finish."

She looked even more confused, then blushed as realisation hit.

"I want you to know, I really did want to play…"

"It's alright. You were tired."

"No, that's – that's not it. I just, I freaked out because I wanted to win so much you see…"

She nodded.

The room was silent for a long moment.

"Are they talking about shagging?" asked Bunny.

Paul blushed and looked at the ground. "Jesus Bunny!"

"What kind of a freak calls it Risk?" asked Carroll.

"Shut the fuck up," growled Bunny, pointing at him. "You've got a record that indicates romance isn't exactly your forte."

Fiachra giggled. Bunny pointed at him. "And as for you…" Fiachra flinched back. Bunny looked around the room, lost for words until his eyes came to rest on the poster of Samantha Fox. "She's a lesbian now." Fiachra gawped at the poster in shock, his big eyes pools of innocence once more, "so she'd have no interest in your little psycho pecker."

"Actually," said Brigit, "that isn't even in the top five reasons that women would not be interested in him now."

Bunny nodded. "Fair point."

"Enough," said Fallon firmly.

"Yeah," said Paul, "you're on a schedule. About that… you got here awful fast, didn't you?"

"Shut up."

Paul kept talking but he didn't look at Fallon, he looked at Carroll standing behind him. "You locked your brother up for 30 years to

334

protect yourself. You'd McNair's daughter killed, to protect yourself. You tried to have us killed, several times in fact, to protect yourself. And, even if Jonny here rang you straight away after he captured us, you must've been most of the way here from Dublin already."

Fallon pointed his gun at Paul. "You three love the sounds of your own voices. If you're so clever, how come you're here?"

"Because," said Brigit, looking at Paul, "we're loose ends, and more than anything, you hate loose ends."

"That's right," added Bunny. "These two have been running about blabbing their mouths. You don't know who knows what now. The genie is out of the fecking bottle."

Paul, Brigit and Bunny were now all looking at Carroll, whose rodent eyes were dancing around wildly, the gun jittering nervously in his hand. Paul figured Carroll wasn't the brightest but he really didn't need to be.

Fallon turned to look at him too. "Don't mind these idiots, this is all desperate nonsense. You'll have your money and be on a flight to Australia tonight."

Carroll nodded nervously. Fallon looked at him, sighed as he made a decision – and then shot him twice in the stomach. Fiachra howled as Carroll, a look of shock in his eyes, fell backwards out into the tunnel, his gun falling from his limp hand.

Paul and Brigit stepped back in fright. Bunny moved forward but was quickly stopped by Fallon's gun pointing directly at him.

"Great," said Fallon, "now I've got to dig the holes myself."

Fallon moved across and picked up Carroll's fallen weapon, before looking down at his presumably ex-employee. Carroll looked up with the pathetic expression of a dog that was getting a beating he felt he didn't deserve. Blood was seeping through the hands he held to his belly.

Paul felt the room spin. He placed his hands back against the wall and closed his eyes.

"What the feck is up with him?" he heard Bunny say.

"Shut up," snapped Brigit.

Fiachra sobbed. "Jonny, Jonny, Jonny. My friend Jonny…"

"Quiet!" said Fallon, tucking the spare weapon into his trousers, "I don't have time for your bullshit now."

"Yeah," said Paul, taking a deep breath and opening his eyes, "he's got loose ends to tie up. Like he tied you up for all these years."

"He'd never harm you though, Fiachra," continued Brigit, "he promised your ma."

"Your ma, who died last year," said Bunny.

Fiacra's turned to look up at his brother, his face a grotesque mask of disbelief.

"Oh," said Paul, "had he not told you that?"

Fallon stepped forward and pointed the gun at Bunny's head, a snarl on his lips. Bunny lowered his voice to a whisper that somehow echoed around the room. "Every man has his weakness."

Fallon lurched backwards as the chain attached to his brother's wrist wrapped around his neck. His left hand flew out defensively, grabbing at his throat, as the right hand holding the gun weaved a haphazard pattern in the air.

Bunny rushed towards them and screamed out as a bullet tore into his right leg, sending him tumbling to the floor. The two brothers then fell messily to the ground. Gerry's choking gurgles mixed with his brother's snarls as they rolled about. Paul and Brigit both held back, unsure what to do. Fallon walloped the handle of the gun into his brother's head a couple of times, which was greeted with animalistic howls of fury, but no slackening of the chain. Fiachra's legs were now tightly wrapped around his brother's waist, clinging on for dear life. Two more shots rang out, bullets ricocheting off the metal and dense stone. Paul ducked as one whistled by his ear.

Brigit spotted a gap and darted out the door to the prone figure of Carroll lying in the tunnel. Paul's eyes followed her and then quickly looked away at the sight of her knelt beside him, putting her hands on his bloodied mid-section. He didn't understand why she was helping the enemy at that moment. Bunny had been shot too and he was, well, less of an enemy. Paul glanced across at Bunny. Blood from the mad old bastard's wounded leg was smearing the worn carpet in front of the sofa, as he dragged himself towards his fallen hurley.

Paul ducked as three more shots rang out and then something bit him in the arse. He staggered forward, his hand reflexively reaching back to the source of the pain. He felt wetness and looked back to see his hand covered in his own blood. The world swam around him. He stumbled backwards as Gerry Fallon, his face blue and bulging, reared up before him, giving his little brother a piggy-back. The younger was using what teeth he had left to rip into his sibling's ear. The brothers Fallon hurtled backwards, slamming hard into the wall, once, twice, three times. A sickening thud echoed around the room each time. Then Fiachra fell away, slumping to the ground. A long smear of dark red blood ran down the wall to his crumpled form. His head didn't look good, there wasn't enough of it for a start.

Gerry pulled the chain away from his neck and then bent forward, gasping for air.

Paul heard a clunking noise.

Then there was a moment of perfect silence, a sliver of perfect peace amidst the fury and the thunder.

Paul looked down woozily and saw Gerry's gun sitting beside his left foot. Then he looked up, and his eyes met Gerry Fallon's.

Fallon started to reach for the gun in his belt that he'd taken off Carroll. Paul knew, there and then, if he went for the gun on the floor, he'd never make it. He was too unsteady, too dazed, too damn tired.

"PAULIE!"

He turned towards the sound of Bunny's voice to see Mabel arching her way through the air towards him. He reached out on pure instinct and caught the handle in both hands. Then – he turned and swung away.

It felt good.

The finest pure striker of a ball this field has ever seen.

The last thing he saw was Mabel's perfect kiss with Gerry Fallon's face, sending him careening backwards.

And then darkness.

CHAPTER FIFTY-THREE

St Katherine's Hospital, 4th floor, neonatal unit.

DI Jimmy Stewart was impressed.

"Yeah, it got pretty hairy for a while there boss."

"I can imagine."

"She'd planned for a home birth, you see."

Stewart nodded. He had rather strong opinions on the advisability of such things but he'd learned from bitter experience to keep said opinions to himself. He doubted that Wilson would've noticed if he spelt them out in 12 foot tall fireworks at that moment anyway. His eyes were firmly glued on the little battler on the other side of the glass. "Congratulations, though, you did well."

"The mother talked me through it to be honest. Her birthing partner wasn't picking up, and she wouldn't let me take her to the hospital. The ambulance crew said it must've come early because of the stress."

"The doctor told me they're both doing great."

"Yeah, she's just getting some kip – Nora – I mean, Miss Stokes."

"You pulled a baby out of the lady, Wilson, you're allowed to be on first name terms now, I think." Wilson tapped the glass lightly and waved. Stewart knew the baby couldn't see much at this stage in his young life, but he didn't have the heart to point it out.

"And, when I think..." Stewart noticed with alarm that Wilson's eyes were starting to well up. "When I think what I almost let happen. Telling that bloody Doyle woman and that thug going to Nora's office and..."

Stewart cut him off. "But it didn't happen. You made it right and you learned your lesson."

Wilson nodded his head firmly.

"No harm done, thank God. In fact, you've done well. You helped bring that little belter into the world, didn't ye?"

Wilson nodded and turned to beam at Stewart, who gave him a wary look.

"Don't go confusing this for a hugging moment, Wilson."

"Yes, Guv."

St Katherine's Hospital, 3rd floor, secure unit.

Assistant Commissioner Fintan O'Rourke glowered at the picture of the Virgin Mary on the wall. His wife was sitting in the chair on the other side of the bed but they weren't talking. She'd kept asking questions that he'd not wanted to answer. For a man with two broken legs, a fractured collarbone, a broken arm, three broken ribs and a punctured lung, he'd been forced to answer a lot of questions. There were probably a lot more coming too. As the wife sat there reading one of the stack of magazines she'd bought herself down in the hospital's shop, an unhappy thought dawned on him. His gobshite of a son was home on his own, doing God-knows-what on his snooker table.

The door swung open and Commissioner Jane Horsham strode in, followed by that pencil-pushing assistant that constantly followed her around. The fool that'd never lived down that one picture in the paper when he'd been carrying her handbag. She nodded at his wife. "Clare."

"Oh, hello, Jane," she said, standing like royalty had just entered or something.

"I'll keep this brief. Fintan, you're suspended pending investigation into numerous allegations of serious misconduct."

"You'll be hearing from my lawyer."

"Lawyer – singular? Christ, if even half of this shit is real Fintan, you'll be needing a lot more than one."

St Katherine's Hospital, 2nd floor.

"I think he's coming round... yes, he's trying to say something."

Dr Sinha leaned closer to try and make out what Paul was saying. He then straightened up and looked at Brigit in confusion.

"What was it?" she said.

"Ehm..."

"Well?"

"He said 'I knew she'd get me shot.'"

"Oh for Christ's sake!" Brigit threw her hands up in exasperation. "Like this is my fault too! I didn't shoot him, tempting though it is." Brigit stood on the other side of the bed. "Open your eyes, ye moany gobshite."

"Nurse Conroy," said Dr Sinha, shifting nervously, "that is not recommended bedside technique."

"Trust me, it's the best way forward in this situation."

Paul spoke in a croaky voice. "Watch her, doctor, she's got a history of violence."

As he opened his eyes, Brigit tried hard to look irritated but she couldn't really put her heart into it.

"Mr Mulchrone, welcome back. You just had a minor operation to remove a bullet from your..."

"Arse," assisted Brigit.

"Yes."

"Well," said Paul groggily, "I'm reliably informed that the gluteus maximus is absolutely positively the only place to get shot." He smiled weakly at Dr Sinha.

"By the way," said Dr Sinha, "I have also redone the stitches in your shoulder, which I believe you ripped playing hurling?"

"Close enough."

"And I've re-bandaged your minor head wound. We've taken an X-ray of your jaw. Just swollen, no permanent damage."

"Great."

"You will have to spend quite some time sitting on a rubber ring, and the bathroom may be a little tricky for a while as…"

"Doc," interrupted Paul, "could we perhaps list the indignities I've got to look forward to a little later?" He looked pointedly at Brigit. Doctor Sinha blushed.

"Absolutely, I will let you, leave you to, I will…"

"Fantastic."

"Yes."

He left, slamming the door slightly too loudly in his haste.

Brigit looked down at Paul and smiled.

"You got a ride in a helicopter."

"I know, how cool is that? Of all the injuries I've suffered, I think that part makes this one my favourite. How is everything?"

"Christ only knows," said Brigit. She shifted nervously. "The police have apparently started digging up the fields surrounding The Rock. One of the boys outside said they reckoned it'll be the biggest crime scene in Irish history. Lord knows how many bodies they'll find."

"Well, at least we're involved in a record."

"That's true."

Brigit and Paul looked at each other, then they looked away in embarrassment. Then they looked at each other again.

Paul started. "I don't want you to feel weird about…"

"What?"

"Y'know," said Paul.

"No," said Brigit, shaking her head. "I've no idea what you're talking about."

"The whole – me – taking down Fallon, saving your life thing. I don't want it to be all – life debt you can never repay. You being my servant for the rest of my days. Not necessary."

Brigit nodded solemnly, "That is very kind of you."

"It's OK. It was no big deal. I just—"

He was interrupted by Brigit breaking down into fits of laughter.

"What the...?"

"You eejit! You didn't save my life. I saved yours."

"Well now you're just being silly."

"Where were we?"

"You know where we were."

"Yes, but I don't think you do. We were trapped, in a locked bunker that nobody knew we were in. While you lot were so busy whacking and shooting each other, like a shower of gobshites, I..."

Paul rolled his eyes as realisation hit. "Ah shite. You went to Carroll..."

"And got the code for the door before the only person who knew it lost consciousness."

"Crap."

Brigit beamed happily. "Hence saving everybody's lives. You are most welcome."

Paul strained to sit up suddenly.

"Whoa, easy there, fella. You're not going anywhere."

"Bunny, where is he? Is he...?"

"He's OK. Well... he's... Actually, one of the nurses was just in here. It appears the hospital have lost him."

"LOST HIM?!"

Brigit put her hands out in a placating gesture as soon as she saw the horror on Paul's face.

"Not like that. He's fine. Well, other than a gunshot wound in the leg. What I mean is, they've actually lost him."

The Old Triangle, Public House

Eddie Jacobs turned the page of *The Sunday World* and looked around the pub. This place was deader than Jimmy Savile, and about as popular. On the upside, it wasn't his pub anymore, thanks to a bad run of cards and a couple of horses that had turned out to be dog food on legs. Skinner had been reasonable about it, all told. He'd taken the pub but Eddie had kept all of his limbs, even been allowed to stay on as bar manager. He didn't get paid much but, on the upside, he could drink himself into an early grave for free.

The place had gone downhill ever since Skinner had started using it as a base for his 'other ventures'. According to its accounts, it was rammed seven nights a week. Freshly laundered money was flowing out of it like water. He also had to put up with JJ, Skinner's boy – sitting there in the corner booth every day, waiting for people to come see him. Eddie had tried not to pay much attention, but he'd have to be blind not to see that the muscle-bound toerag was using the bogs to move more pharmaceuticals than a mid-sized chemist.

The door opened and a man limped in wearing nothing but a hospital gown and slippers. The pub got the occasional drinker from the hospital across the road but that was staff or visitors, and they typically never came back for a second visit. Patients were a new one though.

"Should you be in here?" said Eddie.

"Do I not look old enough?" said the man in a distinctive Cork accent, as he staggered over to a stool beside the bar.

"Do you know your arse is hanging out the back of that thing?"

"No shit. I just walked over here in a high wind. A couple of old ones on their way back from bingo just found out how unimpressive their husbands are. Pint of Arthur's finest, please," he said, clambering awkwardly onto the stool.

"Seriously, am I going to get in trouble for serving you?"

"Not near as much as you will if you don't. DS Bunny McGarry, at your service. Just looking for a quiet scoop to take the edge off." The man gave Eddie what he probably thought of as a winning smile. He had a wonky eye that turned it into more of a leer.

"You heard him. Go on, sling your hook."

Eddie's heart sank. He turned his head in the direction of JJ, who'd made that last statement. The bloke in the hospital gown didn't even look up. The last thing Eddie wanted was JJ making a scene. It'd be bad for business on every level.

"Your money is no good here, copper," continued JJ.

"That's handy. I've not got any."

Eddie tried to wave JJ away, but the big man just sneered and started making his way across to where the man sat. Eddie noticed JJ's acne was getting steadily worse, an angry red line of it now stretched from his neck up the side of his face. Fecking steroid-headed idiot. Eddie wasn't going to take the blame for this. It wasn't his fault this moron was always looking for a scrap. If this loon really was a copper, nothing good could come from this.

JJ stopped behind the man and loomed over him.

"Ah for fuck's sake, ye can see his crinkly old arse out the back of this thing."

"I'll tell you what," said the man, still addressing himself only to Eddie, "the feeling of air blowing around your bollocks is fierce liberating. I can see why the Jocks are so keen on those kilts."

JJ growled, unhappy about being ignored. He leaned in to speak into the man's left ear. "Are you going to leave or am I going to make you?" JJ placed his big meaty right hand on the man's shoulder to emphasise his point.

"C'mon, JJ..." Eddie said, before stopping as JJ shot an angry look at him across the bar.

"You wouldn't hit a man wearing glasses, would ye?"

JJ looked momentarily confused. "You're not wearing glasses."

Three things then happened so fast Eddie had to reconstruct it in his head afterwards to be sure of the order. Firstly, the man's elbow shot up and back, making a crunching contact with JJ's nose. Blood spurted from it as JJ reared back with a look of shock in his eyes. Then, the man's slipper-clad foot shot out and collided with JJ's right kneecap, bending him over as he howled in pain. Finally, the man's left hand came around, grabbed the back of JJ's head, and rammed it down into the counter hard, the impact leaving a dent in the woodwork. JJ fell to the floor.

The man, still sat on his stool, looked down at his opponent, lying in a crumpled whimpering heap on the floor. "Sorry, didn't see you there."

He then turned and beamed a smile at Eddie.

"Now, about that pint?"

EPILOGUE 1

The gates had been hard to find but she had mentioned they would be. He'd promised the long-suffering Mrs Stewart that they'd take a break as soon as his retirement had come through. Lord knows, she had been patient enough. She'd even agreed to a driving holiday around Ireland. All of this meant that he could fulfil two promises at the same time.

He looked back at the car. His wife didn't notice. She was too busy waving her phone about in exasperation. She was trying to Google a nice place to have lunch. A signal wasn't easy to acquire in the Wicklow Mountains.

Jimmy Stewart pressed the button on the intercom and, after a short delay, was greeted by a cold unaccented female voice.

"Can I help you?"

"Yes, my name is — " He stopped himself. He'd have to get used to it eventually. "I'm former Detective Inspector Jimmy Stewart from the National Criminal Bureau of Investigation. Brigit Conroy asked me to drop around and speak to Mr Kruger..."

EPILOGUE 2

Tyrion 4.12.AX4 – Secure server software
Initialising private peer-to-peer communication
Please wait.............. Initialised.

CERBURUSAX: Hello.
RoyTheBoy07: This account is now closed.
CERBURUSAX: Hello, Mr Ryan, we've been waiting for you. We thought you would come on here to move some money.
RoyTheBoy07: You have the wrong person.
CERBURUSAX: Michael Ryan SC, lawyer to Gerry Fallon. You engaged the services of the former owners of this account on behalf of your employer.
RoyTheBoy07: Job was not completed. Contract is void.
CERBURUSAX: You misunderstand, we do not seek money. We seek vengeance. You broke the rules. You took our friend's daughter.
RoyTheBoy07: She will be released.
CERBURUSAX: That is not required. As of two hours ago, she is on a plane to a distant location. Your men holding her are however dead.
RoyTheBoy07: That is not possible.

CERBURUSAX: Ha! Please check but be quick. Your flight to Bahrain leaves in three hours does it not?

RoyTheBoy07: I have money.

CERBURUSAX: Good, keep it. You will need it. We don't want it. We will give you a 24 hour start.

RoyTheBoy07: What do you want?

CERBURUSAX: You. But please, run. We want this to be fun. There are six of us you see. We have a bet. The one to avenge our fallen brothers gets a moose's head.

RoyTheBoy07: I don't understand.

CERBURUSAX: It is a very nice moose. You are wasting time you do not have.

RoyTheBoy07: Please, I am sorry.

CERBURUSAX: No but you will be. Now run little piggy, run.

EPILOGUE 3

Janine looked down at the man's empty face, then at all the machinery beeping and wheezing around him. "Isn't it an awful waste of money all the same?"

Carol looked up from her mopping. "What?"

Janine waved her hand about. "All this, just to keep this useless piece of shite alive."

Carol looked at her in horror. "Janine! That is a shocking thing to say. Every life is sacred!"

Janine stretched her aching back out. "My hole it is! We spend hours cleaning this place top to bottom on minimum wage. Meanwhile, they spend a fortune keeping this scumbag alive. Have ye not read the papers Carol? This is Gerry feckin Fallon, death is too good for him!"

Janine placed her mop against the wall. "Just because he's in a coma, it doesn't mean he can't hear you."

"Good!" said Janine, leaning in close to his face. "Murdering drug-dealing scumbag that ye are! Your son is in prison by the way. They say if you ever wake up, you'll be joining him for the rest of your crappy life."

Carol moved over and lay a hand on Janine's arm, her voice now an urgent whisper. "Janine – remember what Matron Burke said. You're to stay away from the patients!"

"Ara, I don't think she meant him. We should all get a turn whacking him with a stick." With that Janine turned and left the room, closing the door firmly behind her.

Carol looked at the door and then moved closer to the bed. The scent of her medicated shampoo mingled with her Lily of the Valley perfume and the stench of bleach as she leant over him. "I don't care what they say, I'm sure you're a very lovely man." She pulled her rubber glove off and ran her callused fingers through his hair. She glanced at the door again before placing a sticky wet nicotine-stained kiss on his lips.

She giggled. "Oh, bit of lipstick." She wiped his mouth with her polishing rag. "They don't understand what we have. I know you're lonely in there."

She took out her transistor radio and placed it on the bedside cabinet, twirling the dial to turn it on.

"Bit of company for ye. I'll be back to see you later."

As she wheeled her bucket out and closed the door, the song on the radio came to an end.

"And you're listening 94FM, keeping it country 24 hours a day..."

EPILOGUE 4

From *The Irish Times*, May 14th

Despite the lacklustre sales of his new book *Hostage to Fear*, his autobiographical account of being forced to support the fictitious version of events surrounding the infamous Rapunzel affair, author Mark Brophy claims he has been fielding calls from Hollywood.

Colin Farrell is rumoured to be interested.

FREE STUFF

Hi there reader-person,

I hope you enjoyed the book, thanks for taking the time to read it. If you liked it, you're in luck as there are six more in the series! (One of them is a prequel, the other is the sequel to the prequel, and then there's the sequel to that, and so on – so it is still technically a trilogy, just a really value-packed one).

Once you've finished those you might want also want to check out the McGarry Stateside series for more Bunny-shaped fun and games or MCM Investigations to follow the Dublin gang. Also, if you sign up to my monthly newsletter, you'll get the e-book of *How to Send a Message* – my short story collection FOR FREE. Several of the stories even feature Bunny McGarry at his belligerent best. The paperback is $10.99/£7.99 in the shops but you can go to my website WhiteHairedIrishman.com to sign up and get your free copy of the E-book.

Cheers muchly,

Caimh

ALSO BY CAIMH MCDONNELL

THE INCREASINGLY INACCURATELY TITLED DUBLIN TRILOGY

A Man With One of Those Faces (Book 1)

The Day That Never Comes (Book 2)

Angels in the Moonlight (Book 3/prequel)

Last Orders (Book 4)

Dead Man's Sins (Book 5)

Firewater Blues (Book 6)

McGARRY STATESIDE (FEATURING BUNNY McGARRY)

Disaster Inc (Book 1)

I Have Sinned (Book 2)

The Quiet Man (Book 3)

MCM INVESTIGATIONS (FEATURING BRIGIT & PAUL)

The Final Game (MCM Investigations)

Deccie Must Die (MCM Investigations)

STATESIDE STANDALONE

Welcome to Nowhere (Smithy and Diller)

WRITING AS C.K. McDONNELL

The Stranger Times (The Stranger Times 1)

This Charming Man (The Stranger Times 2)

Visit www.WhiteHairedIrishman.com to find out more.

THE STRANGER TIMES: C.K. MCDONNELL

There are dark forces at work in our world so thank God *The Stranger Times* is on hand to report them. A weekly newspaper dedicated to the weird and the wonderful (but mostly the weird), it is the go-to publication for the unexplained and inexplicable . . .

At least that's their pitch. The reality is rather less auspicious. Their editor is a drunken, foul-tempered and foul-mouthed husk of a man who thinks little of the publication he edits. His staff are a ragtag group of misfits. And as for the assistant editor . . . well, that job is a revolving door – and it has just revolved to reveal Hannah Willis, who's got problems of her own.

When tragedy strikes in her first week on the job *The Stranger Times* is forced to do some serious investigating. What they discover leads to a shocking realisation: some of the stories they'd previously dismissed as nonsense are in fact terrifyingly real. Soon they come face-to-face with darker forces than they could ever have imagined.

The Stranger Times is the first book from C.K. McDonnell, the pen name of Caimh McDonnell. It combines his distinctive dark wit with his love of the weird and wonderful to deliver a joyous celebration of how truth really can be stranger than fiction.

Made in the USA
Middletown, DE
26 May 2023

31493005R00215